Just Another
Woman

Just Another Woman

LEAH DUNCAN

authorHOUSE®

AuthorHouse™ UK
1663 Liberty Drive
Bloomington, IN 47403 USA
www.authorhouse.co.uk
Phone: 0800.197.4150

Published by AuthorHouse   05/28/2015

ISBN: 978-1-4969-8253-7 (sc)
ISBN: 978-1-4969-8252-0 (hc)
ISBN: 978-1-4969-8254-4 (e)

Print information available on the last page.

www.LeahDuncan.co.uk

My thanks to all the staff at Authorhouse who have helped me transform a very old manuscript into print. Thank you to all of you for putting up with my technical limitations and limited time availability. My particular thanks to Barry Lee and Nathan Draluck for their unfailing patience and endless encouragement and to Kathy Lorenzo for trying her best to keep me to a timetable. My thanks to my mother Mary, my sisters Margaret and Barbara for their unfailing support and for all the friends who have reviewed and offered suggestions to improve the story. Lastly, but by no means least thanks to my son Duncan who has tried to show me the mysteries of SEO, internet marketing, Facebook and Twitter. Thank you to all of you, I could not have made this happen without you.

Just Another Woman is dedicated to all the wonderful people, past and present, who I have been privileged to call my family.

Chapter One

"Poor education is the excuse we wave in defence of society's plight."

Our mistakes haunt us best in the middle of the night. The woman under the blanket was well aware of that. She was shaking uncontrollably because of hers. In the pitch black of this warm, clammy night she was shivering because of sheer terror and it was that terror that was feeding the grim possibility that she might die out here - all alone. And the blanket? It provided the only shred of comfort from the stark reality that her own stupidity had brought her here. A silent plea mouthed to some being she wasn't really sure existed, received her full attention, and hopefully His, because all expectation of other forms of help had long since evaporated. What her plea lacked in form, it more than made up for in emotional content, and even though nothing happened immediately — she was still marooned in the middle of nowhere, in a strange country with a storm on its way and unknown terrors prowling around outside - little by little she did regain control, stilled her quaking body and subdued the frantic images in her head. Those images had been fuelled by snatches of conversations from events long since gone, but never forgotten, and tonight, freshly endowed with the wisdom of hindsight, they had been able to torment her with their now obvious, but irrevocable, chain of cause and effect, all stretching back to that one day and its folly —the one that had really led her to this place.

"Stuff your happy endings! Stuff Shakespeare! He`s sh.." The lad stopped mid-word, reconsidered, then substituted… "an idiot!" It was hardly better.

Such an opinion was always going to create a stir in any A-Level English class and Jonathan Spicer had lobbed his like a fully primed grenade into the middle of this one. Such things did not happen in any of Sarah Chadwick's classes, even on the last day of term. A few of Jonathan's peers managed to suppress sniggers of disbelief, but the rest laughed out loud; this little bit of seasonal madness was going to make it a far more entertaining lesson than any of them had been expecting. All eventually

1

settled down into the sort of dutiful silence reminiscent of the crowd around the guillotine – like them anticipating the inevitable.

An early Christmas hangover seemed to be the most likely explanation for Jonathan's controversial contribution, but no one was about to chance checking it out. Someone with a nervous disposition broke into a giggle, and that momentarily distracted the teacher's attention from the culprit who was anxious to reclaim his newfound notoriety so spat out the rest of the anger that was consuming him, oblivious to the fact he sounded more like a small child trying to exonerate himself for pinching rather than any heroic unfortunate.

"Life isn't full of happy endings," he explained baldly. "It's the exact opposite! And if you don't think so, well, that makes you an idiot too. And guess what? I don't give a—"

A couple of his friends succeeded in knocking over an innocent chair and another scraped a second chair along the floor in a brave attempt to smother such uncensored language. Jonathan had thrown out a playground word – one they used when they were talking adult – not one ever breathed in class where they were forced to remain children. He knew that. He also knew as well as any of them that language was of some strange importance to the woman who stood in front of them. Today, he didn't give a toss about either.

Sarah Chadwick was in her mid-thirties but looked older. A poll among her students would have established some thought she was at least fifty. A few of them would have been serious. It did not help her cause that she was always dressed in a nondescript jumper over a white blouse and a well-worn, middle-aged-lady skirt. The only variety in her appearance was the colour of this uniform: she possessed it in grey, black, navy, and brown, and she rotated these without favour. Whichever colour she wore, her hair was always scraped back into some sort of containment at the back of her head in nothing remotely like what anyone would dare call a hairstyle, but then, nothing about her could be identified by the word fashionable, and the spectacles perched on the end of her nose did nothing to dispel the image of the middle-aged spinster school ma'am.

Ms Chadwick glared at the deliberately clumsy offenders from over the top of these glasses before returning her attention to Jonathan. She had not scheduled this little drama into her lesson plan, but then, nothing today had happened the way she had planned it, so her star pupil acting like the class black sheep should not have thrown her, but it had.

No one else knew it, but so far today Ms. Chadwick had risen above burnt toast, squabbles, arguments, headaches and disturbing personal revelations – and all of them before nine o'clock. It was now two o'clock and the day had not improved any since breakfast time, so she was weary. She'd had enough! And Jonathan's disturbance was the equivalent of that famous last straw. If she could, she would have sat down and wept, but something reminded her in time that teachers do not cry in front of classes of teenagers if they ever want to teach again. She knew she had lost the plot today; she simply had to live in hope that no one in this class had spotted it yet.

Her students had every confidence that this confrontation would turn out to be the equivalent of watching Juliet thump Romeo, or Hamlet stab his father -if not the aristocrat beheading the peasant, and it was that immortal line "Shakespeare is …an idiot," that had given it that power and raised it above the ordinary. Confrontations happened a dozen times a day in this school, but even the dullest and most rebellious had a clearer understanding of the meaning of the word irony now, because there he stood, their newest champion, like Ariel facing the wrath of Prospero - the only difference being this underling had no disappearing tricks to fall back on.

This class usually split into three fairly predictable and evenly-sized groups: the seriously studious, to which Jonathan normally belonged; the half-interested depending on the subject; and the plainly rebellious, 'why am I wasting my time on this drivel,' brigade. Right now they were all united in the same expectation: retribution. Even so, it was still easy to guess who were most delighted with this little drama because the rebels' main mission in life had always been to make every lesson as difficult as possible for the teacher without invoking any serious repercussions for themselves. They were the ones who would have liked to have said something similar; the fact none of them ever had was because they had all learned pretty quickly that Ms Chadwick was the very knowledgeable, single-minded, self-appointed defender of the Shakespeare faith in these parts, and that meant any negative stuff aimed at *him* earned *them* one of *her* lengthy lectures. It had taken the rebels less than a week to work that out, and in order to avoid these lectures, they had to avoid making controversial statements about Mr S! It was that simple. If they were clever enough, they could still get away with a little general trouble making to relieve the tediousness of serious scholarship; then they had only to risk incurring

Ms Chadwick's second-worst habit, quoting the man from Stratford ad nauseam! Lectures and quotes were both detested, the first because she went on and on, never knowing when to stop; the second because she was a know-it-all who regularly exposed their lack of knowledge about stuff they were supposed to have mastered. All the same, in any popularity poll the quotes would have come out way ahead of the lectures because they were the equivalent of a nasty but quick injection, whereas the lectures were more like serious surgery without anaesthetic! So far only the seriously studious had realised they would be unlikely to escape with a few quotes today; though every infidel should have realised it as much as the truly converted, because Jonathan Spicer's opinion had to have amounted to full-blown heresy in her ears.

Silence was gradually replaced by the solemn buzz of speculation although the only person who could do anything about returning the lesson to normal remained motionless. It was not a wise choice – the buzz grew louder. They would recognise her difficulty soon if she didn't do something.

"Yes, well," she said, clearing her throat. It was hardly an inspiring start; Prospero would have been appalled. "Never show fear in front of a class" had been an elementary lesson in training, and until now she hadn't. But this was not fear exactly. More like trauma. Every working day for the last eight years or so, she had dealt effectively with the awkward, the unruly, and even the plainly disaffected, but this rebellion from within the ranks of the favoured few had exposed a gaping hole in her experience, and the shock of it had robbed her of all her considerable capacity. Losing control of a class for any reason would have the same outcome -disaster, and wondering why she had not understood that until right this minute seemed to be either the result of the most appalling naiveté, or the product of unmitigated arrogance. Neither reason was flattering.

Increasing chatter persuaded her that now was not the time to be conducting inquests either, so she gathered together what little there remained of her wits, closed her copy of *Twelfth Night* and confined her panic to its pages, then she let the most disapproving eyebrow in all of north London front her recovery. She could do this much without effort; it was the result of years of practice. She tried her best to sound as confident as the eyebrow indicated as she responded, "That's an interesting observation, Jonathan. Would you care to elaborate?" It had about as much impact as someone on a tumbrel inquiring whether there was a problem, but at least it broke the spell, and as the class shifted in their seats and awaited that which was about to be delivered, she continued to try and salvage something of her lesson – a double disappointment for the bloodthirsty crowd who were breathless for that retribution scene, or at least for some of the famous Chadwick wit that had chopped down hundreds of other troublemakers. The possibility that the Chadwick legend was about to be sunk by one act of favouritism was unthinkable. Ms Chadwick did not realise that her reputation was in such jeopardy so she offered no more than a barely audible sigh as the rebel at the back of the class stood down and resumed his seat.

She was lucky to have escaped so lightly. The remaining tension in the class evaporated as quickly as it had built up: she had won. She hadn't exactly set out to win anything; she had simply wanted to keep order, teach a lesson, get the day over, go home … have a life. She dismissed the urge to analyse why Jonathan might have chosen today for his bombshell and concentrated all her efforts on her mop-up strategy. Okay, she thought, I can deal with this.

"Well, as you all seem to have so much to say, would anyone else like to contribute to this debate, then?" Her voice was firm again, no nonsense. It communicated her intentions perfectly, and she regained control without raising it any further so she consolidated her advantage by following up swiftly with, "No one with anything to add? Not even a witty comment?" She walked slowly around the desks and looked into each face as she passed. "All that noise, yet no one with anything to say? How odd! No one with anything funny to say – yet there *did* seem to be a lot of laughter. How very odd. *'What says Quinapalas'*, or you, Josh, *'better a witty fool or a foolish wit'?"*

Some recognised the quote, but most didn't. Some finally thought she had lost it. Rebellion over, she thought, inordinately pleased with herself. It could only be two minutes of a job to sort the rest out.

It was self-congratulation a mite too soon. "Act one. That clown?" The response had come from a student on the opposite the side of the room to Jonathan. The girl did not wait for any acknowledgement or acceptance before continuing. "'*Out of my lean and low ability, I'll lend you something.'* Act three, I think? Maybe Jono has a point." The fight had just been joined by Marcie Hadley, founder member of the real rebels.

Ms Chadwick smiled wryly, debating whether to applaud the girl's knowledge or condemn her audacity. In the end she did neither. "Okay,

Marcie," she said, trying to disguise the weariness in her voice, "would you like to explain to us what you mean?"

"Yeah, I would!"

"Then be my guest." This was sufferance, nothing more.

Marcie Hadley ignored it. "Well, I mean, if you think of all the stuff we've read just this year, with the exception of Hamlet, they all had happy endings, and even that came out sort of right in the end. Sad but right, d'ya know what I mean? Life just isn't like that, is it?" She held up her copy of the play. "Maybe Jono's right. Maybe people don't get happy ever after anymore … if they ever did."

"Right on one thing: this is fiction, not fact," Ms Chadwick said with more kindness than venom. She looked at both of them and controlled the temptation to smile; they made such an unlikely alliance, the sinner and the saint. She frowned instead, so the class awaited further developments. "How we have arrived at this point may be a little unorthodox," she said, passing over the point quickly, "but the pair of you have raised at least two rather interesting questions." The rebels looked stupefied, even the studious were puzzled because her meaning eluded all of them, though the studious did guess it had to be the cue for the lecture. "But now that they have been brought to our attention, we should perhaps take some time to examine them. It's not exactly what I had planned to do, but when my mental state is clearly in so much doubt, I can't see how we can possibly do otherwise." The ripple of laughter pleased her; she had carefully crafted her response in order to get it, but she carried on quickly, not wanting to lose her tenuous grasp on their compliance. "Jonathan," she looked directly at him and though he kept his head down, the rest of the class fixed their eyes on him quite sure this must be that retribution scene. "When you said that Shakespeare had it all wrong and that life wasn't full of happy endings, what did you mean exactly? Were you referring to the ending of this play in particular? Did you really expect a romantic comedy to have a tragic ending? Isn't that rather unlikely – naive, even? Or were you referring to literature in general? Did you mean that you are taking exception to all happy endings? Are you saying that this thing we call love, this thing that transforms life and turns drab reality to fairy tale, doesn't exist at all? Are you saying it only exists in novels and plays, not in real life? Is that what you are saying?"

It was difficult to say whether Jonathan, or anyone else for that matter, had meant that, or had even kept up with the gist of her argument at the

6

speed at which she had just delivered it. Jonathan simply shrugged his shoulders and remained silent: he looked ill. By now she reckoned she had worked out the reason for his outburst but there was little she could do about it without drawing more attention to his problem, or losing control again, and she didn't want to do either of those things. She had to keep control, and though she did want to help, this was the best she could manage right now, so he was just going to have to take it.

Thinking on your feet after a day like she had endured was no easy task. He had no answer to her questions, so she changed tack quickly. "Well, is that what you meant, Marcie?"

"Yeah, I think it is!" Even rebels can be heroes; even torments can be saviours and at that moment a silent prayer of thankfulness was offered up for Marcie Hadley; heroine of the hour and Jonathan's saviour – for this lesson, at least. For the first time ever, this girl's guaranteed awkwardness was welcomed, even encouraged; it passed as strategy, or at least made up for the lack of it.

"So maybe you think fiction is irrelevant?"

"Well, it does seem a bit daft when you think about it, doesn't it? Three times a week we all sit here pulling books to pieces. What's the point of it? I mean, we all know why we study geography and maths and science, because they're useful-like, but novels and plays? What is the point?"

"I am wondering why you chose to do A-level English Literature, then," came the dry observation as her teacher warmed to the challenge that had just been so cleverly delivered. "Do you agree with them Kevin?" she asked swooping down on an unsuspecting pupil.

"Don't know, Miss."

"And you never will if you spend all your time passing notes to Penny. Give it to me, please." She confiscated the offending note and the culprit had the grace to blush as his persecutor scanned its colourful contents before folding it and putting it into her skirt pocket. The class laughter subsided as she turned back to face them. This had to be an opening for one of her more acerbic comments at least -but she didn't comply this time, either. She was surprising them in more ways than one today. "Now, can we please get back to the lesson? Where was I? Oh yes. Do we believe that fiction is complete make-believe and an irrelevancy? Marcie asked you to think about the books we have read, and I am going to ask you to do the same. We have already mentioned *Twelfth Night* and *Hamlet,* so think about the others. Think about Dorothea's heartache when she realises that

Edward Casaubon is not the man she thought he was – and remember that realisation did not happen until *after* she had married him. Do you think her pain was simply make-believe, or can we find a parallel in real life? And later when she meets Will, are her feelings for him unreal as well? Do people not face such dilemmas? Do real lives not change like this?"

No one ventured their thoughts. "Okay, what did you read at O–level, Shah?" The boy muttered the name of the book, and she asked the same question of several others before announcing, "Great! These should be heavy enough even for the pain and suffering brigade! Anyone read anything else? No? Well, these two books will do fine. Think about Bathsheba Everdene, torn apart by her feelings for Sergeant Troy, and then think about Cathy's feelings for Heathcliffe. If you are going to dismiss fiction as just make-believe emotion, be very sure that you have looked at a range of it, not just the happy endings that don't suit you. There should be enough in these two books alone to convince you that fiction is not all irrelevant happy endings. The stories might be make-believe, but the people in good fiction need to be real, display real emotions, feel real love, experience real success, suffer real pain, and yes, sometimes have happy endings because the law of averages dictates that there must be some. So if you find that you can't agree with Jonathan and Marcie, then maybe you can agree with me that there must be some real happy endings. Therefore it must be as okay to write about them as it is to write about tragedy." She paused briefly to consider if she was making sense. No one would have dared tell her if she wasn't. Then she added her single concession. "Maybe not all of us will get the opportunity to be a Jane Eyre, or a Viola …"

"That's a relief!" one of the boys at the back whispered loud enough for everyone to hear. This class hardly ever missed a cue, and it erupted once more into laughter and cheering.

"I am so glad that you feel that way, David," she said sarcastically.

"Don't know, Daz. I think you'd make a nifty Viola!" Everyone laughed, and a few whistled and jeered.

"That is enough! What is wrong with this class today?" Ms Chadwick demanded.

A lone voice ventured from behind the cover of its text book. "It's Christmas."

"Thank you, Neil. I am also aware of that fact." It did not calm the excited pupils, so she replaced her chalk on the ledge beneath the blackboard, wiped her hands carefully, and sat down at her table. She appeared to be studying the chalk dust on her fingers, but she was really searching for what came next. Thinking on one's feet and keeping control was a tougher act than ever on the last day of term. When she looked up, order had been restored because they had all misread her actions, but she was not one to look a gift horse in the mouth so she stood up and continued to observe them silently for another minute or so. She had a pretty authoritative presence and her silences were at least as effective as some of the more vocal staff members' best screaming. When everyone was sufficiently intimidated by this silent scrutiny, she broke it with perfect timing.

"Surprising as it may seem, I am aware that it is Christmas. To be precise, I know that next Wednesday is Christmas Day, and please correct me if I am wrong here, but according to my understanding it is still officially only one day, is it not?" No one chanced a witticism, and so she continued over the low hum of disapproval. "You see, I also know that four weeks from now *is* mock exams, and five months from now *is* the real thing. And right now, forgive me for saying this, but you are all acting like third years because it is the last day of term." It was a perfect line, a perfect reprimand, and it hit their carefully nourished images spot-on. No self-respecting, almost-adult sixth former liked to be mentioned in the same breath as the naughty children so far beneath them. "And as none of you are writing so fluently about plot or characterisation I cannot detect sufficient passion or knowledge of the text, so I remain convinced that you do not know your material well enough. My opinion may not matter to you, but the fact that examiners may think the same should. And as this digression gives us an opportunity to discuss some passions and knowledge, it seems too good an opportunity to miss, does it not?" Fortunately she did not conduct a survey, but those who had been hailing Jonathan as their champion only minutes before now recognised him as the cause of all this suffering, and while she paused for breath, they turned and scowled at him.

The lecture wore on and on. It seemed set to last the whole lesson if not more. The only light relief was when Marcie Hadley managed to throw in one of her uninvited contributions, but apart from that the class listened, doodled, or snoozed according to type while Ms Chadwick wore out the passion in her soul.

"So, we all agree that literature is something that entertains us in some way but that can, and should, include making us happy as well as making us sad? Looking at our list makes me think that most of us would agree that fiction is concerned with stories of bravado and courage, of heroism and valour, or of tales of cowardice and shame. Tales of sacrifice and greed, love and hatred, sagas of fame and fortune, knights on white chargers, or maybe knights come in white sports cars these days." It was her single concession to levity. "But either way, they probably still come to rescue damsels in distress. Sometimes they lose, and sometimes they win." she emphasised.

"I'll have one that wins, then, Miss," Marcie chipped in spontaneously. The rest whistled and clapped noisily.

Ms Chadwick ignored them all and smiled at the miscreant benignly. "I hope you do, Marcie," she said sincerely; reviewing possibilities that the girl could not possibly comprehend. "All of this should help us to put together a simple definition of fiction. We could say something like, 'Fiction is an illustration, a means of recording and illuminating one person's view of the exquisite or the eccentric, the tragic or the humorous.' Anyone disagree?"

If they did, this time they were keeping quiet, so she was able to progress to her final point, which involved an experiment – a brave gesture considering the history of today's lesson. But never one to avoid a difficult assignment, she challenged the class to write down how they saw themselves in ten years' time. "Hey, let's be very daring about this! I want you all to take a minute to imagine yourself at thirty. Yes, I know it seems impossible to think that you will ever be thirty, but believe me, you will, and sooner than you think. I want you to write down who you will be and what you want to have achieved by then. Take a couple of minutes! I don't want an essay, just brief points."

"You mean actually imagine when we are old?" a brave soul dared. Everyone laughed.

"Is thirty old?" she queried, so clearly shocked it prompted someone to ask how old she was. "There's no need to speculate; I am not going to tell you."

The girls giggled, and there were a few "Aw, Miss" pleas, but she ignored them all. Within thirty seconds there was silence apart from an occasional sigh or whisper and the rustling of paper. The time passed quickly so there were cries of "I've not finished" when she asked them to stop.

"Okay. Did anyone find that impossible to do?" No one answered, so she nodded at the boy nearest to her, intending him to read out his list. He argued against that, and rather than get involved in another long debate she asked for a volunteer and picked up her chalk to write as the girl started her list.

"I put I would like to be married or be in a serious relationship."

Ms Chadwick wrote, 'marriage/partner,' on the board without debating the issue. "I'd like to have a well-paid job," the girl continued, and Ms Chadwick wrote 'career/good job,' underneath her first point. "I'd like to own my own home and drive my own car. Have enough money to pay the bills and go on holiday. Oh, and have some saved in the bank."

"Slow down – I can't write that quickly. What came after own home?" The girl repeated the items, and Ms Chadwick wrote 'own car' and 'financial security' before asking, "Is that all?" The girl nodded. "So, how many of you included marriage or a partner as one of the things you wanted?" A few hands went up tentatively, and then a few more, encouraged by the fact they were not alone. Eventually nearly all the class had joined in. She counted the number of hands and wrote it down before proceeding to do the same with each item on the board. After the final item she asked, "Okay, has anyone got anything different? Yes, Jason?" His hand had shot up almost before she had finished speaking.

"I'm going to be a famous lawyer."

The class laughed as she turned back to the board. "Excuse me! No one is allowed to laugh or pass judgement on what anyone else wants. '*I have spread my dreams under your feet, Tread softly because you tread on my dreams.*' Do I make myself plain? Jason, we already have career up there." The lad protested that fame had not been mentioned, so she added it to her list. "How many of you wanted fame?" There were no other hands, so she wrote one against the item. "Anyone recognise the quote?" she asked hopefully. No one did, and so she tutted in a way that made it clear that they should have, but she said nothing more about it. "Has anyone got anything else to add?"

"I want a Lamborghini Comtache."

"I'm sorry?"

"A Lam-bor-ghini Com-tache," Jason repeated slowly.

"Yes, I heard what you said. Just tell me what it is, and I will write it down."

The boys in the class jeered, and its future owner looked horrified as he asked, "You really don't know?"

"Would I ask if I did?"

"I bet Marcie can tell you what it is. Can't you, Max?" another boy shouted.

Without waiting to be invited, today's heroine responded, "Sure. It's a car, Miss."

"We already have car," Ms Chadwick pointed out naively.

"But it's not just *any* car," Jason protested, "although I suppose 'dream car' might do."

To save further argument, she added dream car to her list, and immediately every male hand in the class shot up. A few girls followed suit.

"Okay, so how many of you have *actually written down* you want a dream car?" The groans and complaints were in direct proportion to the number of raised hands. "Yes, it has to be written down. So how many do I have?" The number of hands diminished rapidly until there were only two left.

"I want to be a millionaire." There was a hum of approval, but only one other person had written that down: Jason.

"Okay, anything else? Is that it?"

"I want a family." There were more groans, mostly from the boys.

"Do I need to remind you of the ground rules? How many of you wanted a family?" The count for those having written family down eventually produced a sizeable number, and it included many boys; they had only been reluctant to be the first one to mention it. A couple more items were added and then she rubbed the chalk dust from her hands and asked, "Has anyone got anything left on their list that isn't covered by these items on the board?" She waited a moment then said, "Okay, why did we do this?" There was silence. "Well, does anyone have a comment to make?"

This was Marcie's cue, and never one to miss an opportunity she rose from her seat and waved her hand demurely. "I am going to marry Jason," she said whimsically, seizing the moment for maximum impact. Everyone cheered except her bemused teacher.

"Why is that?" She had been hooked by the theatricality of Marcie's announcement and had swallowed the bait.

"*Because* ... he is the only one who is going to be rich and famous, drive a Lamborghini, and not have kids," Marcie explained ingenuously. "And I can share that. In fact, I'll queue for that!"

The cheering and banging of feet and desks was deafening as Jason stood up to respond, "See me later, Max. I'll show you how to jump the queue!"

Ms Chadwick had to retire content with being cross with herself for ending up as the straight guy feeding lines to a comedienne. It was too late to recall her words and too dangerous to be angry so she had to let the class settle down naturally by appearing not to be bothered.

"Most of us wanted the same things," a girl at the front suggested as the class quietened down.

"Only two of us wanted to be millionaires," someone else added.

"All of your comments are correct," their teacher observed fiercely. "If we look at what you *did* want, there are some common themes. First is a partner." She underlined it. "Second is a career or good job, third is family, and tied for fourth are a home of your own and financial security. Compared to these things, very few of you wanted to be famous or wealthy. Is that a surprise?" Some people nodded. "I know some of you wanted to add things, but can you see why I couldn't allow that. I asked you to list your real priorities, and adding afterwards would have ruined the whole point of the exercise."

"Yeah I can see that," Marcie said impatiently. "But what has all this got to do with what we were talking about?"

"Patience!" Ms Chadwick smiled sweetly, because now it was her turn to deliver the punchline. "I think we were talking about why it is there are so many happy endings in literature. Yes? Well, here's another question for you. How many of you wanted misery, deprivation, pain, and unhappy endings?" For the second time that lesson everyone looked around: no one had raised their hand. "Exactly. No one. No one mentioned divorce, illness, or death. No one said pain. Yet all of us will get some." She checked Jonathan's pallid face before adding more seriously, "Pain comes in many forms, not just illness. It will visit each of our lives at some time. I cannot tell you otherwise without being a liar. Pain is never pleasant or easy, and I am sure all of us would prefer to be without it, but life is not like that. In a strange way there is a price to be paid for each of these things." she gestured at the items on the board. "The risk of pain is part of it: love someone, and you risk losing them, and you will feel pain at their loss. But should that stop you from loving in the first place?" Her words had a sobering effect as everyone silently contemplated where their lives might cross this unrequited boundary.

"So," she added more cheerfully, "maybe the real reason we write and read things with happy endings is because this is what matters most to us. These are the things that mirror our own aspirations, our own hopes, and literature – even though it is make-believe and one person's point of view – needs to reflect that. It can certainly challenge us and make us think

13

more deeply about our own experiences, dare us to see things a different way, to see how others deal with pain and overcome it, or give into it and are destroyed by it. But I don't think we could cope with literature where everything was pain and misery, because it would be the opposite of everything we are seeking, the opposite of everything to which we aspire. You see, I think that we all want to be happy. We all want happy endings." For the first time in the entire lesson she had everyone's undivided attention, and she did not waste it. "The playwright and the novelist know this," she continued. "They know that they cannot make everything doom, gloom, and unhappiness – one, because we wouldn't believe it, and two, because we couldn't cope with it. They can warn us by showing us misery and the darker side of life, but they generally provide resolution to enable us to look at difficult topics with some degree of safety. We all need hope to nourish us." There were sufficient signs of agreement that she had finally made a statement most of them could accept, that she asked, "Does that satisfy the first part of Jonathan's and Marcie's problem?" with certainty. It was a question that clearly did not require an answer. "Now to the second part. Shakespeare is an idiot?" she asked incredulously. The class relaxed and laughed with her and because of the last fifteen minutes she was confident enough to extend a new challenge to her opposition. "So who is going to start us off? Jonathan? Marcie?"

Neither of them answered.

"Do you really want to know?" a boy at the back of the class asked.

"Of course. Why else would I ask?"

"Well, you are sort of like a fan of his, aren't you?" the boy queried nervously, anxious to avoid yet another lecture.

"I suppose you could say that," she mused. "But I hope my being a fan does not mean I am not open-minded enough to discuss your opinions?"

"Without prejudice?" another boy interjected.

"Without prejudice." she repeated humorously. "I am glad to see that you are taking this lawyer business seriously, Jason. Yes, Marcie, do you want to say something?"

"Yeah! For starters, my mum thinks Shakespeare is a pain in the—"

"Neck!" Ms Chadwick interrupted smartly, not waiting to find out to which particular body part Marcie's parent had referred.

"And she's not the only one to think that, either," Marcie finished.

"No, she's not," Ms Chadwick agreed, much to her adversary's surprise. "In fact, no less a person than Charles Darwin wrote in his autobiography,

'*I have tried lately to read Shakespeare and found it so intolerably dull that it nauseated me.*'"

The ripple of clapping and laughter made Ms Chadwick realise that Mrs Hadley and Charles Darwin had more than one ally in this class. This was serious stuff.

Marcie waved her hand and was invited to speak. "My mum always says, 'I don't know what you have to be reading that rubbish for!' And she means it. I don't know what to say to her."

Ms Chadwick's response was deliberately unapologetic. "That rather depends upon whether you agree with her or not, does it not?"

"Suppose so, but what I mean is, if Shakespeare is such a genius as you keep telling us, shouldn't his genius be recognised by everyone?"

"Why?"

"Because that's what genius is, isn't it?"

"That is an interesting point. What do the rest of you think?" A heated debate on the nature of genius followed. It focused on whether that designation must warrant universal recognition. Marcie conceded that Shakespeare might have been accepted as a genius back in the sixteenth century but that needn't mean people saw him as one today. "Because it's 1985, not 1585!" That excited sympathy from some of her classmates but provoked denial from others. Ms Chadwick managed to restrain herself from providing accurate historical details of Shakespeare's genesis as a writer in favour of allowing the class to debate - a miracle in itself. Marcie's argument split the class into its predictable camps, Jonathan stayed silent, but the rest bandied names like da Vinci, Mozart, and Beethoven in defence of their theories. Even people like Mrs Hadley would have been pleased to have heard Elvis Presley, the Beatles, and Laurence Olivier getting a mention, though she may not have been as keen as some about Adam and the Ants, Madonna, and some current Hollywood movie stars achieving such recognition. But at least Shakespeare, who had started the debate, seemed to have as many in favour of him being accepted into this august body as did any of the above, which must have meant something.

Ms Chadwick brought the discussion to a close when she realised the lesson time was almost at an end and as she had finally decided where this could lead, she was anxious to get there before the bell. "Thank you for all your comments. Some things I have noted from our discussion lead me to believe that one, genius is not constrained by time, two, it is not necessarily ever appreciated by everyone; no one you have mentioned has received total approval. Three, whether or not you like him, Shakespeare is generally accepted as a genius, not an idiot. Four, as with everyone else who has been mentioned, whether you appreciate him as a genius has a lot to do with knowledge and understanding – in other words, plain familiarity."

"So Shakespeare is just an educated con!" Marcie persisted.

"No, I don't think so."

"But you've just said—"

Ms Chadwick was a bit flustered. "I know what I have just said, and I don't think your phraseology is either accurate or flattering. Charles Darwin was educated."

"So how come he didn't rate Shakespeare?"

"He was a scientist!" She had said it before she could stop herself, so she laughed in an attempt to hide her embarrassment. "And if you tell anyone I said that, I shall deny it categorically." She was alert enough to notice the knowing looks that passed between several of her students. It meant they knew about the gossip. She fought back the embarrassment and cleared her throat hoping that she was not blushing too noticeably as she tried to continue in a light-hearted manner by emphasising, "Seriously, many well-educated people do not love, or even like, Shakespeare, but I am glad that you find that as difficult as me to believe, so he is not an intellectual conspiracy to condemn you to hours of suffering."

"With respect," Jason the Lawyer intervened, "that's not what she meant. How come we have to have him thrown at us for years before we can see it?"

She nodded slowly. "Have you ever thought that you might make a good barrister, Jason?" Everyone laughed, and he smiled, pleased that she had thought his question sufficiently testing. It was a smile that was soon to be wiped from his face. "Perhaps we should set ourselves a question to discuss this. We have just over five minutes of class time left, and as it is obviously something that inspires a great deal of passion on both sides ..." She turned to the board to write slowly as she formulated her question. "Can we identify the qualities in Shakespeare's writing which substantiate this label of genius?" This was where she had been heading for the last ten minutes or so, and she was already congratulating herself for steering the discussion so successfully that she felt sufficiently confident to add, "And why, if he *is* a genius, do we need to be educated to appreciate him? Who wants to start us off?"

She was interrupted again. "Your question is loaded and doesn't allow for us who don't think he is a genius."

She looked more than a little flustered by this assertiveness, but she joked, "I am beginning to think you might make the famous bit as well, Jason." After some thought she offered, "Will, 'Discuss critically the statement that Shakespeare is a genius' meet with your approval?"

He thought for a moment before agreeing, and then she erased the question and wrote up the new one. "Please keep your points brief, and I will list them."

Another heated debate followed, which she chose to end before the class descended into total anarchy. Today was proving to be hard work all round, and she had long since begun to regret the vain impulse that had suggested it would be easy to defuse Jonathan's allegations, but it was too late for regrets. She had followed her vanity and there was no turning back now – she had to keep plodding on. She glanced at her watch: three minutes to the end of class. Three more minutes to hold it all together.

"Okay, that is enough. Quiet!" She knew she was losing it when she had to raise her voice. All the class looked at her; they knew it, too. She ignored them, cleared her throat, and continued primly. "All of the things you have listed are excellent points to consider." She went back over their list. "Is there anything missing?" No one said anything, so she pointed to the items on the board and repeated them one by one. More silence. There were less than two minutes to the end of class now, and most people had already decided this lesson was over, so the sound of bags being dragged from under desks was getting louder by the second.

"Well, if I might add my opinion to your list *before* you put your things away, I would say that one of the most fundamental evidences of Shakespeare's genius lies in his ability with words." Her appeal was largely ignored because they knew that they were within minutes of freedom, but in a final attempt to register her say, she continued to raise her voice over the increasing clatter. "Words. Language. Something so simple but powerful, Shakespeare's use of the English language is perhaps the most telling evidence of his genius. His ability with words is without equal. He captures human aspirations, fears, and joys so vividly that the replay situation – that is, when we read him or act him – is as emotive an experience as the recording must have been for him. In other words, we can live in it. You may not agree, but please read a few selections before you decide. I would suggest Richard's and Hamlet's soliloquies, and maybe

Cleopatra's dying scene. Then go laugh with Bottom or Andrew Aguecheek. They all speak like real people with real pains and real concerns, and their words are exactly that: they are their words. Bottom speaks as Bottom, and so on. Do you follow me?" The people that nodded did so in an attempt to avoid any further explanation, but they got it anyway. "Shakespeare's genius with words does not end with him painting real people. He takes language and composes something very different. In the best bits the meaning is interwoven and reinforced by the rhythm of the words. The result is genius!"

The class was bored with her eulogy; they had heard it all before, many times, but fortunately for them she was interrupted at this point by the bell.

"Saved by the bell," someone breathed at the front of the class. She did not hear that because of the immediate action of people pulling bags from below desks and shifting of chairs that naturally followed its signal, but she still had an ace to play.

"Well, as we seem to have been denied the opportunity to finish our investigation in class," she shouted over the furore, "I do believe tonight is English homework!" That caused an immediate lull in activity, so her next words came out rather too loudly. "And this looks like it might be fun."

"This is fun?" someone snorted. "What does she do for serious stuff?" Assorted groans and complaints along the lines of "Aw, Ms Chadwick, it's Christmas!" illustrated the general dissent.

"I thought we had already covered that point. '*I must be cruel only to be kind.*'" Those who recognised the quote groaned again. "You do have two weeks that are not officially Christmas to complete this assignment. I do not require any of you to do this on Christmas Day, unless you really want to."

"She's mad!" someone ventured a little too loudly. This time she did hear.

"Maybe, Richard, maybe. *Though this be madness, yet there be method in it.*"

"Does she quote Shakespeare in her sleep?" the girl sitting next to Marcie Hadley asked crossly.

"Probably," her companion replied. "Have to ask Mr Cole to be sure." Both girls sniggered. Unfortunately they were too near and Ms Chadwick's sharp ears had caught the reference to Len Cole. She glared hard at both offenders who had the grace to return to packing their bags in silence.

"Come on, be quick, stop moaning! Copy down the question and as much information as you need from the board. This is your opportunity to write about how you really feel. I do not mind which side of the discussion you take, but I do mind sloppy work. I shall expect clear, reasoned arguments backed up by relevant quotations and references. This is light relief from all the revision you are going to do, and to show you how generous I am, I will expect this in a week Monday after our return to school. Satisfied? When you have all you need, you may go. Have a great holiday. Merry Christmas. See you in January, ready for the mocks."

There was another chorus of groans followed by several muted seasonal greetings as they started to leave. "Jonathan, can I see you for a minute please?"

As the others filed out in twos and threes, he stood awkwardly by her table preparing to defend himself. Several people smacked him on the back as they passed, and others pulled sympathetic faces in an attempt to reassure him. Kevin, the note passer, was one of them; he felt secure enough now to grin as he thumped Jonathan's arm, but his confidence was misplaced because retribution was waiting for him by the door. As he approached his nemesis, she extracted his note from her pocket and scanned it again quite deliberately. His colour drained: Providence was not going to be kind after all. She looked him directly in the eye which caused him to swallow hard as he coloured rapidly from his collar to the roots of his bleached hair. Ms Chadwick folded the note carefully, held it out to him, and observed mildly, "There are two e`s in meet, Kevin, not an ea. Might I also suggest you read some of Romeo's conversations with Juliet, because he could remind you of some of the nicer expressions in the English language – words you might find are not quite so embarrassing should you be foolish enough to commit your thoughts to paper in my lesson again. Next time, I may not have a balcony for you, but you will deliver the content aloud. Understood?"

Kevin nodded and grabbed the note, anxious to make a speedy exit, thankful for Christmas mercy, such as it was.

Ms Chadwick closed the door after him and returned to her table to pack her things. Jonathan was waiting impatiently but neither of them spoke until she had finished. "I was sorry to hear about your parents," she said slowly, trying her best to establish whether her concern was registering. It was impossible to tell because he did not look up once, even when she bent her head down in an attempt to connect with his eyes. She tried several more times without any more success before her persistence registered sufficient to divert him from his investigation of the floor. He looked up, confused. He could not avoid meeting her gaze so he returned it defiantly for a second, before looking away again.

It was an encounter that had left him more confused. He had been expecting retribution, but he thought he saw only concern. Battle alert seemed a trifle hasty after that, although he was by no means convinced that all defences were unnecessary - Ms. Chadwick had a tough reputation. He had never crossed her before but he had heard tales of those who had. He felt that silence must be his best defence, so he returned his gaze to the spot on the floor and said nothing. Fortunately it was a very interesting spot. The hole in the worn vinyl bore a remarkable resemblance to Italy, and he was trying to locate Rome while deciding how she knew about his parents.

Ms Chadwick observed, "We share a bad habit."

"We do?"

"Mm-mm, trying to find difficult answers on the floor. It doesn't work. They are never there. Please look at me, Jonathan."

He nodded and shuffled some more, covering Italy with his left foot in case she guessed what he had been doing. This conversation was going nowhere, and it was embarrassing to him, if not to her. Making eye contact was even worse. "That was an interesting observation you made in class." He nodded and blushed scarlet as he recalled the term "idiot". He was almost sure she must have forgotten he had flung it at her too, because she would not be so nice to him now if she had remembered. It was the other reason he had been prepared for battle, not conciliation. In truth he was ill equipped for anything other than battle. Negotiating skills and diplomacy were not in his current arsenal; sulks and tantrums were all he had right now, but neither seemed to fit this bill. She continued. "Interesting, but perhaps more fuelled by your current situation than by your real feelings."

"I don't think so!" He had not been able to stop himself saying this any more than he had been able to control his previous outbursts. The passion in his voice was as unmistakable as the pain. The sulks had let him down, and the tantrums were all he had left to express it. Neither approach fitted the bill, as he had thought. In the silence following this outburst, he shifted uncomfortably. He had been lucky once; expecting clemency twice was expecting too much.

Ms Chadwick resisted the urge to respond for a couple of reasons. She was no longer on view, and so it was no longer about control, also, she really did want to help – even though she was not sure how to do that. She waited to see what would happen next. She did not have long to wait, and when it came, it was not the apology she had been expecting. For one who had been excused twice, it seemed downright foolish or plain ungrateful, but to Jonathan it was explanation.

"Maybe when life has robbed you of your happy ending, you will see things differently, too," he spat at her.

She was shocked by the venom in his accusation and so it was more difficult to ignore the immediate urge to defend herself than before, but she nodded slowly and weighed her words carefully as she pointed out quietly, "I am trying to understand how hard it must be for you right now, Jonathan, but being rude to me when I am trying to help is not helping me much."

This time he did not respond at all and instead retreated back to Italy. "I know sometimes nothing seems to go right. In fact, sometimes things *always* go wrong at the worst possible time." She looked at him and dropped her voice to a whisper. "And then you pick up a book, and well, I can see why today's little outburst happened. I know it can't be easy for you right now because nothing is happening the way it should, except in books, and that must be frustrating." He lifted his head slightly and she smiled at him, "I think Shakespeare and I took the flak today, but I reckon anyone with a happy ending would have got it from you." At least this time she didn't get an insult as reply. That had to count as some sort of progress, and it encouraged her. "Maybe you don't know this, but you are directing your anger at people who could really empathise with you."

"How come? Did his father run off with their next-door neighbour, leaving his family to face huge debts or lose their home? Have you had a husband like that?"

At any other time she would not have ignored his complete lack of respect, but there was more at stake here than her hurt feelings. She knew this was different; she remembered this territory, and so she ignored his insensitivity and launched into relating the troubled events of Shakespeare's youth and the stories about his father that she had heard debated so many times over the years.

"So you see, I reckon he would understand what you are going through. Check it out and read up on it. As for me ..." She looked him directly in the eye. "If it helps you to know, then yes, it did happen to me. It wasn't the next-door neighbour, but everything else happened to me, too, Jonathan. The lot."

Now it was his turn to tread carefully. "I didn't know that," he stuttered, momentarily forgetting about Italy.

"No reason why you should. And I didn't tell you now to have it made public knowledge, either," she warned.

"So why did you tell me?"

"So you can see that both Shakespeare and I really do know what you are going through. And that means you are not alone. And another thing: both Shakespeare and I survived. So can you. You are capable of dealing with this."

"You're saying I'm feeling sorry for myself!"

"Am I? I thought you said that. I am saying ..." She stopped to gather her thoughts, to make sure she got this right. "I am saying that I know it hurts, and I can't take that hurt away, but it's okay to hurt as long as you hold on, because it will pass. Sooner or later, it will pass, I promise you."

Finally her certainty made a chink in his armour and he shifted his gaze back to her face. There was no animosity in his face this time, just plain beseeching that exposed his pain. "Will it? Will it really pass?"

She nodded and put a hand on his shoulder. "Maybe not this week or the next, but yes, I promise you that it will pass, eventually." He stared at her without moving, and she smiled sadly; contemplating the enormity of his heartbreak, none of it of his making. "Now just one more thing. I would appreciate it if you could give me advance warning if you feel like making such radical statements in my class again, especially when you do not follow class protocol. I cannot allow today's performance to be repeated – ever! Do you understand that?"

He mumbled his understanding and added an almost incoherent apology. "I'm sorry about calling you an idiot."

"Apology accepted. Off you go, before you are late for your next class." He was at the door before she called out to him again – one final attempt to provide something for him to hold onto. "Jonathan, there are happy endings, even when it seems impossible, but it usually takes time, and even then it might not be the ending you expected. Do you remember what Hamlet said to Horatio? *'There is a divinity that shapes our ends rough-hew them how we will.'* Well, I don`t know about the divinity, but I do know that life can, and does, provide solutions for apparently insurmountable difficulties. I am sure Shakespeare didn`t care much for some of the things that happened to him and his family. But do you know what? I like to think those things helped him to become our greatest writer. You see, the end wasn't really the end – it just looked like it at the time."

He nodded and then was gone.

She checked that no one had left anything behind and then she removed her glasses, put them away carefully, and closed the classroom door just as carefully. She tried to put the memory of Jonathan's challenge away also. "No happy endings?" she repeated. Her response to him had pulled her back from almost starting to think the same. What was it about an ill wind …? "Okay, so what if I *have* been a bit of a pessimist lately," she confessed to herself. "I had better find a way to live up to my advice now."

Chapter Two

The drama underway in the staff room was more predictable than the one in the English class because it was more like sterile old newsreel footage than the raw, hot anger of the last lesson. Sure, the scene had emotion, but it scored less on anguish and significantly more on frustration because it was the struggle between the awkward and the determined, and the main protagonists were more Laurel and Hardy than Montague and Capulet. Admittedly, the crowd scenes did still pull everyone in as extras on a regular basis. Sarah Chadwick stared glumly past her friend Elinor Farrington, who was leading the fray, to the sign hanging innocently on the on the wall behind her head: *"Human history becomes more and more a race between education and chaos."* Some wit had written a postscript and stuck it to the frame: "Here, chaos wins!"

It seemed to sum up her last lesson, her day, and this school for that matter, and although the postscript was now yellowed and fading, no one had removed it because it was more than mere sarcasm – it was truth, and everyone knew it. Everyone except Elinor, that is. Everyone else understood why this room was chaos, the cause of more staff arguments than any other issue, but Elinor had to keep battling on in her no-win cause because John Anderson, the head and the other combatant, wouldn't back down, either. He stirred the conflict regularly, upsetting Elinor in the process and providing North Green's pupils with a plentiful source of ammunition. One famous commentary on the staff room had made so many appearances over the years that its reflection on the remarkable similarities between staff room residents and the inmates of the local psychiatric wing had earned its own place in school history, elevating its amusing observation about both groups consuming vast amounts of tea, coffee, and cigarettes, and both places containing tortured human beings, to the status of required reading. Naturally the psychiatric wing had fared better, but because of that lampoon, this beleaguered outpost of state education with all its human and professional troubles had become public property, or at least material for juvenile scorn, to be ridiculed regularly with glee.

The mountains of junk pinned or stuck to every inch of the walls betrayed its occupants' worst nightmares: things could get worse! Suicide rates for the teaching profession mocked government recruitment campaigns promising solid careers; old exam results and new exam schedules competed with angry missives to the press about falling academic standards; and the odd but highly prized complimentary letter from a parent compensated for public announcements of criminal proceedings against wayward colleagues. That infamous lampoon might have had some validity in its comparison except this bizarre edifice was more a cross between the Berlin Wall and the Wailing Wall than any hospital for the afflicted, because this place offered no hope of cure for the residents' maladies, just plenty of opportunity for supplication. North Green's very own icon to the frustrations of twentieth-century teaching was impressive, and the devout improved on it daily.

At some point the contents of the room must have been new and may even have matched, but those days were long since passed. They now consisted of a random collection of battered desks and faded chairs, none of which would have fetched a very good price in any reasonable second-hand shop. The desks were always occupied by souls trying to mark work or prepare lessons – a difficult enough task at the best of times, but one often made impossible by the volume of noise generated by less diligent colleagues. Hence the perpetual war! Everyone was agreed on only one thing: it could not meet both sets of needs, work and social. Finance had decreed that it must, and because money was more articulate than even the most erudite, finance had won. That was how the long-running and bitterly contested battle for supremacy between the two sides had begun.

Elinor was head of geography and chief protagonist for one side of the argument. Her mission in life was to promote the debate, keep the matter on the boil, and not allow the head (the other chief mischief maker) any rest. She tackled this assignment with a level of determination that was only to be found in those truly dedicated to the rise of the underprivileged. Thanks to both of them, the staff room could never be a peaceful sanctuary or a calm work place; because it was their combat zone, and their battle raged between nine and four, Monday to Friday, every week of every term of every year.

From this shabby bunker John the commander dispatched his troops on desperate missions, only to have them trudge back forty minutes later as shell-shocked casualties anxious to report fresh skirmishes. As a resuscitation room, the staff room regularly contained truly gruesome sights with folks smoking themselves senseless as a means of recovering from classroom trauma. They were only outdone by the caffeine addicts knocking back five or six cups between classes. And all of it had remained private until that lampoon had exposed their plight. Despite that, these war-wearied souls remained responsible for holding civilisation together in these parts. The only thing never in dispute with any of them was that teaching in North Green High was never going to feature in any of those glamorous government recruitment campaigns.

No one could actually remember the beginning of the conflict; no one had been there long enough. Elinor had sort of inherited it, and though war wearied the soul, long-lasting peace had been promised by so many, for so long, that no one seriously believed it was possible anymore, so without any credible means of resolution, the sniping continued on a daily basis -his semantics and her histrionics orchestrating constant altercations over trivialities, tit-for-tat skirmishes, and poorly executed ceasefires that barely held total anarchy at bay.

Apart from all that, Elinor was generally acknowledged as one of the most popular members of staff, whereas John Anderson was without doubt the most hated. Outsiders might consider him a successful head but insiders knew better. Elinor called him a skunk, the worst sort of vermin: a stench trader who was always willing to trade on anyone else's success to make himself smell good. He was always willing to settle for the best deal he could get today, but he was also always on the lookout for a better deal tomorrow, and he didn't care who he had to use to get it.

John Anderson did have some good points, but they were generally ignored because when everything else was running smoothly, and staff and pupils were coexisting reasonably well, he could always be relied upon to do the totally unnecessary. He had done that this lunchtime because the cleaners had informed him they would no longer be risking life and limb by cleaning "in there" next term. Being well used to these dramas and realising that everyone had their regular roles to play in them, Sarah tried her best not to be drawn by her friends current provocations; refusing to get worked up about this particular crisis because she had long since lost interest in any of their little war games, or their inevitable outcomes. She reckoned they were more like medieval passion plays than regular battles anyway: they came round on a regular basis, everyone got excited for a while, and then it was all put away for another season. Nothing ever changed; this was just the latest episode. It would be no different than all the others. It had started the same way, and it would end the same way.

"Look at it this way," Sarah contributed when her friend eventually climbed down from the distinctly rickety-looking chair from which she had been urging insurrection. "At least staff room issues will stay private. Have you seen some of the stuff on these walls?"

No tongue-in-cheek comment was ever going to work on this.

"Know what the trouble with you is, Sarah Chadwick? You are never serious about anything! Well, besides you-know-who!" Elinor observed sniffily, allowing herself the pleasure of a flash of real anger.

"How hard is it to wash a few cups?" There was no reply, so Sarah changed the subject, adding a plea to be ready for home as soon as the last bell went. "I have a splitting headache that's resisted all the tablets I have offered it."

Elinor waltzed off, not caring two hoots about mere headaches when there were bigger things at stake. She left the headache sufferer muttering something about tolerance while she searched for some missing homework for her last class, the infamous five alpha.

Sarah was crawling out from underneath a desk, clutching the missing essays tucked under one arm, when Len Cole called her. It was too late to duck back under the desk, but she did bang her head for the second time that day in the attempt. She muttered some Shakespeare under her breath as she started to cram the books into her already bulging briefcase. Len's hovering presence meant she jettisoned what vestige of patience she had left. He smiled nervously and twitched his nose in that way she hated: it reminded her of rabbits. Twitching did nothing to improve his chances of being heard.

"Just a quick word about Michael Davies," he said apologetically.

"Can a quick word cover such a subject?" she asked, quite overlooking that not five minutes earlier she had been castigating Elinor for her dramatics.

Len ignored her sarcasm or missed it; sometimes it was difficult to tell which it was with him. He had been practicing all afternoon, searching for the right words to convey his concerns without giving offence, but as he stumbled around repeating himself without communicating a thing, his listener grew more impatient. It would have been easier for Len if there had been a formula for this; words were such difficult things, imprecise and open to misinterpretation. Formulae, on the other hand, were beautiful, cool, clean, and precise communication. One knew exactly where one was with a formula. He thought it a pity there wasn't one for this.

"Well!" the virago repeated impatiently.

"I was having my little end of term chat with Michael earlier today." Len stopped and looked across at his heroine ponderously. The sigh that escaped him summed up his complete lack of understanding.

She sighed, too, but not for the same reason. Then she dismissed his thoughtfulness with an abrasive, "Look, Len, I think we should do this some other time."

"No," he said, cutting her short. "I think it will be better said now."

That was unusually assertive for him, so his bad-tempered heroine conceded mostly from shock. "Then please get on with it, whatever it is," she bullied as full-colour nightmares of five alpha running riot made her less than happy with all this waiting around for whatever it was he had a mind to say but could not utter. From this exchange no one would ever have guessed that these two were anything other than two colleagues – two rather distant colleagues at that. But the headache, five alpha, and other things were playing a large part in the lady's behaviour, and as she reckoned the first two things were reason enough to cause anyone to behave less than perfectly, she felt no need to justify herself.

"We were discussing exams," Len finally managed to say. "He knows that English is not his best subject."

"I think that is just a tiny bit of an understatement," the headache sufferer pointed out sarcastically, wholly unable to stifle her true feelings on the matter.

Len ignored her again. It was obvious to her, if not to him, that this was another of those bizarre conversations that would achieve absolutely nothing. She had become something of an adept at these in the course of this very long, very traumatic day. Better take a deep breath and start again. While she was struggling to act on this advice, Len stooped to pick up a coffee spoon from the floor – another wrong move. At that precise moment, she was not sure what it was that stopped her from yelling, "Pay attention!" When he did straighten up to the task in hand, she had not curbed her bad temper, but she had managed to restrain her tongue.

Explanation would have been easier for Len if Sarah had responded the way he had imagined, but she hadn't. Real women were always more awkward than his mental version of them. He never remembered this until he was having problems, and so he remained completely oblivious to the fact that his biggest problem with women was timing, or a lack of it. There was no point in stopping now, difficult or not, so he took a deep breath and got it over with.

His breath was a little too deep so it caused Sarah to drop her remaining anger and ask with some genuine concern, "Are you all right, Len? Are you unwell?"

"No, of course I am not unwell," he complained, red faced. "I am fine! The truth is ..." He took another deep breath, and this time she waited if not exactly patiently, then certainly with increasing curiosity. "The truth is ... The truth is ..." How many more times did he need to say that? "The truth is Michael Davies has been making some pretty nasty allegations about you!" His words had finally tumbled out in a mad rush, underlining how inadequate he felt in getting this awfulness aired.

A lengthy silence followed, until finally Sarah asked, "What sort of allegations?"

"About you."

"Yes, yes, you have said that. What about me?"

Len nodded miserably. "He said you were terrorising him, that you had a personal vendetta against him."

Last lesson's bombshell must have used all her reserves for dealing with the ridiculous because she stared wildly at him, half expecting him to recant of his madness any second. He simply stared back. Then suddenly all of her rising panic was subdued by one single thought: this is Michael Davies we're talking about here! It was a simple truth followed a second later by a dozen others. She smiled and spluttered. The splutter turned to laughter and did not stop until it bordered on hysteria.

"Oh Len, I am sorry," she offered contritely, wiping her eyes and trying to look apologetic. The fact that she kept on laughing, did not exactly make it look like her apology was for real, and to Len it looked like she was anything but sorry, so he found it impossible to hide his displeasure. He had agonised over this all afternoon, and all she could do was laugh! His face assumed a look of perfect indignation that ill-concealed sharper feelings.

"I don't see what there is to laugh about," he offered testily as he took her by the elbow and steered her into a nearby corner. "Smaller allegations than this have got some people into very deep water." She offered her thanks, but he continued with his dire warnings monologue as if he had not registered it. "I would hate to think of any trouble coming from this. We all tread on eggshells with this lad. I'm afraid it's very thin ice."

He looked so genuinely concerned that she even allowed him to indulge his second most annoying habit, mixing metaphors, without feeling duty bound to correct him. She was grateful he had bothered to tell her about these allegations but it was her regard for him –because he was a nice man who cared about her – that stopped her from laughing again.

Len was blissfully unaware of any of these things, so he continued gravely with his warnings. "I know these fifteen-year-olds are a bit of a handful. Well, let's face it: they're a *lot* of a handful at times, and where Michael Davies is concerned, it's always a lot, isn't it?" He sighed noisily, sounding strangely like a deflating balloon before it came to rest, and then he resumed his best thoughtful, puzzled look – the one that was meant to convey concern but usually betrayed resignation. "Do you know, I don't remember there being any kids like Michael Davies when I started teaching? And that isn't all that long ago, whatever some people say." She knew this was his attempt at humour so she smiled and patted his arm to show she did not disagree. "I will say one thing, though, once some of them get an idea fixed in that sawdust they have for brains, you have a devil of a job shifting it. Pity it doesn't seem to work with the things we *want* them to put there."

By now she had lost track of his ramblings. "What are you getting at Len?" she asked patiently.

He cleared his throat and shrugged. "This Davies lad is a load of trouble, and I don't want him causing any of it for you."

Her headache receded a little, and she smiled warmly at him. Her very real pain and her equally real frustration were both temporarily softened by gratitude. For a fraction of a second their eyes met and then he coughed and looked away as she picked up her bag. He recovered by placing both hands together on his chest, flexing his fingers forward in a strange, bone-cracking gesture to underline the seriousness of the moment. It was a ritual he saved for the most delicate situations. She considered it the final touch to rendering their conversation almost Falstaffian in its absurdity, but she could hardly give way to laughter again without upsetting him even more. In the absence of any sane alternative, they both stood nodding at each other, trying to look sensible, but in reality bearing more than a passing resemblance to a pair of nodding toy dogs. In a day filled with minor upsets of one sort or another, this was tragedy of a new dimension, but instead of dwelling on what her informer had just divulged, Sarah was contemplating some of Hamlet's lines and wondering whether this qualified as "*pastoral-comical, historical-pastoral, tragical-historical, or tragical-comical-historical-pastoral.*" Wonder what would have happened if Falstaff had made a guest appearance in Hamlet? These delightful ruminations were interrupted by the other nodding dog calling for her attention rather sharply. "Oh, I am sorry! I was just thinking."

"About what to do about all this?"

"Something like that," she said, banishing Falstaff's ghost back to his more usual haunts and hoping her comment was sufficiently ambivalent for Len to read into it what he wanted. It was a little devious, but it would have to do for now because any attempt at explaining the Michael Davies allegations would mean that she had to take Len through all the school gossip about the two of them. That was bound to be embarrassing as well as time consuming –and there was no way she was about to do any of it right now. He would have to wait.

All of North Green's staff did agree on one thing: Michael Davies had to be a descendant of Machiavelli, and even Sarah had to admit the timing of these latest allegations was distinctly Machiavellian. The probability of five alpha's sweet, dulcet tones reverberating down every corridor in the school settled the issue for her. "I have to go, Len," she reminded him, displaying her watch under his nose. "Like, right now!"

Not to be so easily deterred, he made no effort to move, although by now she was trying to edge past him clutching her bulging briefcase in front of her, ready to use it as a battering ram if necessary. Just before it came to the point where she might have to do that, she offered a compromise. "Well, if you must discuss this now, can we talk as we walk?"

The staff room was joined to the main corridor by a smaller one and this opened directly into the main hub of the school. Everyone crossing the school had to use this space. It was always busy, and right now, some ten minutes into this last lesson period there were still plenty of noisy stragglers around. They were almost bowled over by one girl who was attempting to run backwards while continuing her conversation with a group of girls huddled outside the cloakroom area.

"Look where you are going, Sophie Hadley!" Len admonished the flying figure in navy blue as she collided with him. "And walk!" he threatened as she rushed away. "Don't know why I bother," he muttered as seconds later the enforced walk of the navy flier accelerated again. "Just like her sister, completely uncontrollable. So I suppose we should be grateful Michael Davies is an only child, eh?"

Sarah had not registered Len's droll comment as she was busy attempting to disperse the group outside the cloakroom. They were more interested in exchanging gossip than getting to their lessons, so her interruption was not popular, but they moved grudgingly. Their innocent looks and coy, behind–their-hands sniggering meant she did not have to try too hard to guess what one of their subjects had been – and here they were, coming out of the staff room together so very late. More fuel for the gossips. She glanced across at Len, but he was oblivious, confirming what she had suspected: he had yet to discover that the two of them were the subject of the latest, most colourful scandal on the school grapevine. She rather wished that she was as ignorant of it as he was; today might have been very different if she had been. It was an attractive thought, but even as she was condemning Elinor for telling her, she recognised that if she had been in the dark about that, then this business with Michael Davies would have been nigh impossible to understand, and Jonathan would still have had his problems. No, it looked like today was always going to be another difficult day to add to her growing pile.

Elinor had shared the gossip about the two of them this morning partly because it was the last day of term, but mostly because she had decided it would provide the sort of light relief Sarah clearly needed after not getting the vacant head of English post. Sarah had not seen the funny side of Elinor's news. She had been embarrassed by it, and then angry, and she knew now was not the time to compound that embarrassment by discussing any of it with Len. He would have to remain ignorant a little while longer.

Len shook his head. "This week has been sheer madness, even for here." What had started with the third years at the beginning of the week had spread like wildfire through the whole school, and the result was total chaos! All 1,059 pupils doing their level best to fulfil the staff room witticism as if it had been prophecy.

Sarah said, "Now, where were we? Oh yes, Michael Davies." She realised she would have to say something, and so she concentrated on his work. "Between you and me, Len, I would say that our Mr Davies needs a miracle! Forget the mocks. On present performance, he hasn't got a chance. Stop looking at me like that! I am not saying he lacks the intelligence, just the will, and maybe that can change. Miracles *do* still happen sometimes. But don't you dare ask me whether or not they will. I am a teacher, not a clairvoyant -or a miracle worker." Len's frown looked too judgemental, so it earned him yet another rebuke. "You are doing it again! Stop looking at me like that! All I am saying is that right now Michael Davies has no idea of self-discipline, and his motivation – well, what can I say about that? At its best it's probably only 'Do the minimum'."

"And at its worst?" he questioned.

"At its worst? I would say that he actually enjoys disrupting my classes. *He* sets out to make *my* life as difficult as possible. I think there is a line in *Henry IV* that describes him perfectly."

"What's that?" The question had been asked dutifully because Len knew the question, if not the interest, was required of him.

"'*Rebellion lay in his way and he found it!*'"

Len's thin, watery, polite smile and nodding head conveyed nothing, and so she shrugged. She had thought the quote quite clever; obviously he didn't feel the same. Why did science teachers always have to be so matter-of-fact? Did nothing move their souls except a collection of strange squiggles on a blackboard, or a mass of scientific apparatus? She paused only long enough to chastise herself and draw breath, and then she continued before he could have a chance to interrupt her.

"Having said that, please understand that I am no more against Michael Davies than I am against anyone else who persistently disrupts my lessons with their corny wisecracks. I warn you, Len, an awful fate awaits this lad if he persists! I haven't quite worked out what it will be yet," she admitted, "but it will be awful, I can promise you. *Then* you can come and tell me I have a vendetta against him!" Her facial gesture dared him to disbelieve her. A moment passed in silence before she added, "Do you know, I think I might …" She paused, looked upwards as if receiving sudden revelation, and then laughed as she proclaimed, "I think I have decided what I shall do with our Mr Davies."

If Len had been a little more perceptive he might have noticed the devilish glint in her eye, but her laugh was sufficient distraction and he noticed nothing else, so he remained visibly worried. She let him stay that way. "I think I might," she continued unrepentantly. "I think I might marry him off to Marcie Hadley, an older woman with a tongue like a viper's nest! Mm, that should do nicely for both of them! It might not count as a happy ending, but it's definitely just desserts and all that."

As Len was unaware of the last lesson, this black humour did not clear the air, but it did produce another catalogue of dire warnings from him, none of which impressed her any more than the last lot. The only remaining strategy seemed to be outright dismissal. "Anyway, *I* won't have to do anything because he has already designed his own awful fate: complete and utter failure!" Normally she might have exercised a little restraint instead of unburdening her soul so, but not today, and not on this subject. He had been the one to insist that they discuss it now, and so she felt little if any remorse. It was actually a relief to vent her frustrations on the subject, so there was nothing to be gained now by being faint-hearted. "Come and inspect his work, if you don't believe me."

"I didn't say that."

"The look on your face said that," she pointed out bluntly.

It was obvious as they opened the corridor door that her premonition about five alpha had been spot on. The child posted as look-out darted back inside to warn the class that she was coming so the noise level had subsided and was almost peace and tranquillity by the time they arrived at the door. She purposely opened it then held it closed, hoping her silhouette through the frosted glass was sufficient to ensure their continuing compliance, and then she turned to give Len her last thoughts on the matter.

"Unless you want me to give this boy top grades for the most appalling work, there is really nothing more I can do for him - until he is prepared to meet me halfway," she whispered, well aware that there were listening ears just the other side of the door.

"Oh no! I wouldn't want you to do that," Len confessed. "I didn't even realise you felt so strongly about him."

"Len, it's impossible *not* to feel strongly about him."

He nodded miserably. "Yes, I know. And you are not the only one," he added confidentially. "There are others who are concerned, too. Perhaps I have need of further words with our friend."

Finally she offered some concession. "I have tried, Len, time and time again – ever since he came to me in September – and I will keep trying! But not now. Next term, eh? Even I have had enough for now."

"Leave it with me, then," he announced condescendingly, much as if he were capable of resolving the entire situation with a mere word. "I will speak to him again next term. I am sorry if I have upset you." She nodded politely and tried to look equally serious, but her frown concealed a less respectful response. She turned away to hide it, but he called her back. When she had gained sufficient control she turned around, and by now his manner was different, too. "I got us tickets for that concert," he whispered. "The one I was telling you about. You still want to come, don't you?"

From one trauma to another! She double checked the door was shut. If five alpha should hear this, it would fuel even more rumours. This was probably how they had got started in the first place, though according to Elinor someone had seen them coming out of Len's one evening, and of course the only possible explanation for that was that they were having a mad, passionate affair! The truth was a lot more mundane: they had called to collect an umbrella before going to a concert, but that being so, she had no doubt that news of another date could be embellished in exactly the same way. Knowledge of the existing rumours should justify her saying no, but she had expressed some interest in this particular concert earlier in the week, so it seemed impossible to decline it now without giving offence. Elinor's theory about her being a regular sucker for a hard-luck story, or a sad face, was always hotly disputed, but whoever was right generally, this time Elinor would have won. Could Len really be her happy ending?

"I need to fix a sitter," she said slowly, mulling over this proposition. Len assured her his niece would be available to sit, then smiling gratefully for her easy agreement, went on his way with a wide grin adorning his face. She watched him bounce festively down the corridor humming "Jingle Bells," before turning her attention to addressing the equally daunting task of teaching Michael Davies and five alpha.

For the first time that day all her worries were unfounded, and the last lesson of the year passed off without a single incident – neither Shakespearian disasters nor even Orwellian chaos threatening her bit of education. All the same she greeted the last bell with as much relief as anybody because it signalled not only the end of the lesson but the end of the day, the week, and the term – and that meant she had survived another year!

School went predictably wild. It had been preparing for this moment all week and now it had arrived; it was going to live up to it, so it was almost four o'clock before she had pushed her way through the crowds of pupils blocking the corridors discussing Christmas parties.

"Merry Christmas, Ms Chadwick!" a youngster yelled to her. She returned the greeting.

"Merry Christmas, Mrs C!" She whirled around just in time to see Michael Davies raise a cheeky arm as he escaped through a convenient door.

"Do not call me Mrs C." she hissed at him. He had already fled, but she said it all the same. The result was not much different when he was in front of her.

She was fastening her coat when Elinor came into the staff room complaining loudly about her being late. "Sorry, I got delayed. Do you know something?" she said pulling on her gloves with grim determination. "Friday at three thirty is sheer delight!"

"No, you joke me! That has to be the biggest understatement I've ever heard you come up with, and I have certainly heard you come up with some." Elinor raised her eyes heavenwards in search of suitable inspiration and offered her own version of this wisdom. "Friday at three thirty has got to be the nearest thing to blissful release for tortured souls ever to be experienced by mortal man – or woman for that matter... oh, apart from you-know-what!"

Even Sarah had to laugh at that, but then she held her head. "Ouch. It hurts more when I laugh."

"Shakespeare didn't say that, did he?"

"What? 'Ouch, it hurts more when I laugh'?"

"No, idiot! Friday at three thirty," and Elinor repeated the rest of her little gem.

"No, I don't think he did."

"That makes a change. He has a bad habit of pinching all the best lines. Come on, let's get out of here.

"Just one thing: I am not an idiot, okay?"

Chapter Three

The day had already slipped into evening when two heavily laden figures left the shelter of North Green's building. The school was typical of the concrete school buildings introduced as 'exciting new educational architecture' in the sixties, but like most of its kind, by the mid-eighties, it no longer looked exciting, simply grey and grim. Staff and students hardly noticed that anymore. It was what it was. Both had bigger things to worry about.

The pair leaving so late were no different. Tonight they did not even notice the winter sky was filled with snowflakes descending by the billion like the hosts of heaven, every one doing its best to cover North Green's greyness with a sheet of white. Both heads were down and they were so absorbed in their conversation that they missed all of the strange, silent beauty around them. Huddled inside the paraphernalia of winter clothing only their short, snappy breaths managed to escape collars and scarves to chase the wannabe snow storm in the cold air. When Sarah did eventually notice, she only sighed, and that produced another rebuke from Elinor.

"Come on! What is wrong with you now?"

"Nothing,"

"Yes, there is. It can't still be the headache?"

"Maybe."

"What does that mean?"

"It means maybe."

Elinor sighed. "Okay, so this is going to be one of those stupid conversations! Which came first, the head or the dumps?"

"Don't know, and right now I don't care. I want to go home – analysis can wait."

"You should say that more often," Elinor advised peevishly, pleased that she had found something to say that could convey some of what she really wanted to offer on the subject without seeming to give more offence.

Sarah looked at her blankly, hearing but not understanding, "Analysis can wait?" she asked dumbly.

"Well, yes, that as well. But I was thinking more of the 'I want to go home' bit." There was a moment's hesitation before Elinor continued.

"There *is* something wrong, isn't there? You don't have to tell me about it if there is" she pointed out with indecent haste, "but if it helps, and if you need an ear, then I suppose mine is doing nothing else right now." She had already forgotten that analysis could wait, or that she had agreed.

"It's nothing serious. I am just having a bad day. It will pass," Sarah said dismissively.

"You don't have bad days!"

Sarah blinked. Her head still ached, and Elinor's was beginning to. "That makes me sound like a saint or very boring."

"Same thing, ain't it?" Elinor replied, waving at some colleagues in a passing car as emphasis. "See, even John's dotty secretary is leaving before us now."

This was a very familiar pastime; it had no name, but the gist of it was that the shop steward in Elinor felt compelled to regularly point out to her friend that she worked too hard too often, and that allowed John Anderson to abuse her good nature by giving her too many extra classes. Naturally, Sarah denied this. From there it generally escalated into an all-out attack on how badly she managed the rest of her life. It had been funny at first.

Rather than get dragged into another fatuous round of accusation and denial, Sarah admitted defeat early tonight and promised that all would be well after she had had a break.

"Looks like we are last again," Elinor repeated sweetly as they reached the car, neither content with her earlier success, or used to it.

It was one sarcastic comment too many, and though she was struggling to open the car door with both arms full of books and a briefcase, all of which were preventing her from achieving her objective, Sarah snapped, "No, we are not! Phil's car is still here!" as she dropped her keys.

"So? He is nearly as big an idiot as you are."

This time there was no reply; the victim knew she was not going to win, and being called an idiot three times in one day did nothing for her self-esteem, so she gave up gracefully. Better to save her energy for getting home.

The frustration was real on both sides. Elinor knew that, but she was not going to be denied giving vent to hers because they would never succeed in backing John Anderson into a corner while people like Sarah not only consistently refused to be drawn into the battle but actually helped the enemy. Elinor`s sense of betrayal had been simmering all afternoon since the earlier encounter in the staff room and she was well into airing these frustrations as she walked round the car to retrieve the keys. She was more intent on getting all her complaints in than looking where she was going, so she slipped in the slush and banged her leg hard against the wing of the car. Her cursing was neither quiet nor slight.

When it had been established there were no bones broken, she hobbled back only half listening to the chastisement following her outburst. "Sorry, it just slipped out," she grumbled. "Some friend you are! I nearly kill myself. And all you go on about is not swearing!" That didn't earn the response she wanted so she went on meanly. "But then, you are always going on about all sorts of daft things like some stupid old woman. Just look at you: you are the one that looks half dead, not me! You look old and decrepit! How old are you?" she demanded malevolently as she eased herself gently into her seat. "Thirty-seven? Thirty-eight? Fifty-five?" There was nothing in any of Elinor's rule books that said she had to argue fair, or stick to the point. Her current victim was used to these sudden changes in tactics.

"I take it you *do* want a lift home tonight?" she said sweetly. "And I seem to remember that *you* are thirty-eight. I am not *thirty-five* till March."

"That's very nearly thirty-five," the antagonist pointed out ruthlessly as she adjusted her seat belt accompanied by only the slightest of groans. Sarah simply smiled at her through clenched teeth. No reply was deemed as good as an admission by Elinor. "So the age thing is a sensitive spot, after all," she probed, almost forgetting her damaged limb for a moment. More silence gave more away. "Thirty-five." She chortled unrepentantly. "And look at you! You are the one that looks thirty-nine. No, I am joking," she said, throwing up her hands to defend herself from the expected blow. When she was sure it wasn't coming, she added sarcastically, "You *do* look fifty-five!" Still no blow, so she tried again. "Did you hear what I just said? I said you look like an old woman!"

"Is this a pep talk?"

"Come on, be serious!"

"A minute ago you said I was *too* serious! Make your mind up! Anyway, if you really want to know, I am neither old nor worn out: I am just plain old-fashioned exhausted."

"Stop trying to be funny. And stop twisting my words! You know very well what I mean. Besides, who jokes about looking rotten?"

"After a day like I have had, I reckon it's obligatory."

"I thought it was only me who had days like that," Elinor confided, returning her attention to her injured leg. "Whatever happened to Super-teacher?" she mused aloud.

"Figment of your imagination," came the swift reply.

At least that penetrated, because the opposition glanced up from her task and measured her next words very carefully. "It can't have been that bad."

"Want a bet? I slept late and burned three lots of toast before we got to eat breakfast. The dishes got left, then the girls argued all the way to school, remember? Then you told me about the gossip about Len and me – and all of that happened before nine o'clock."

"I told you for a laugh," Elinor pointed out, "not to stress you out."

Sarah either did not hear or chose not to pay any attention, because she continued. "Then I lost my temper with the third years first lesson this morning, developed this thumping great headache by break, had a heated difference of opinion with Stella at break, and was awful to the upper sixth this afternoon and gave them homework on top of revision. To cap it all, I was really rude to Len before the last lesson."

"Oh, is that all?" Elinor sighed. She thought they had been talking about something really serious, but this was tame stuff. "Seems a fairly average day by my standards," she yawned.

"Well, it's not by mine! I must have rated an eight or nine on the disaster scale so far, and it's not over yet!" A lopsided smile turned out better than expected despite the doleful commentary. "But less cheek from you would really help. See, I have got into analysis after all. Change the subject – I need to forget it, put it all behind me ASAP."

Neither of them had done anything so far about getting home, but as they were almost certain by now that there was nothing seriously wrong with Elinor's leg, Sarah switched on the engine and announced with a comic grin, "Then, '*Hence home you idle creatures, get you home. Is this a holiday?*'" It was her favourite form of retaliation for Elinor's bullying. The response was neither comic nor amused, and feigned innocence was only going to make matters worse.

Elinor complained, "Do not quote Shakespeare at me! It's wasted on me – I don't recognise it! I never know where it comes from, and it annoys me!"

"Ah, but you're learning."

"What makes you think that?"

"I didn't say it was Shakespeare!"

"Well, it doesn't take a genius to figure it out," Elinor responded thunderously. "You quoting someone else would be like pigs flying, and how often have you seen that happen in these parts recently?"

"Classified information," Sarah said with a chuckle, almost forgetting her headache for a minute. "But I do quote others. Who would you like? Hardy, Yeats, Donne, Elliot, Austen?"

"Wells?" This was Elinor's ace card.

This insistence that she must be responsible for the staff room witticism irritated Sarah more than most other things, but today she looked Elinor calmly in the eye and shook her head. "Sorry, my dear, still no Wells."

"Just drive. I thought you had a headache."

Despite the weather, groups of pupils were wandering at a snail's pace towards the gate. Sarah commented on one particularly large group believing she was saying something harmless.

"Were you never young and stupid?" Elinor asked with some irritation. "Do you not even remember that when you are fifteen, home time has got nothing to do with getting home?"

Sarah`s ignorance was matched by Elinor's derision.

"Did you really go straight home after school?"

"Always."

This strange possibility demanded some contemplation before Elinor confessed, "Well, I guarantee no one else did. Home time has always been about catching up on gossip." The face that met hers was not amused. "Sorry," she muttered, concealing the smirk that recorded another point to her brand of common sense. "It's true, honestly! Home time has always been about catching up on gossip and flirting. You know; getting fixed up," she explained mischievously.

"That's obviously why I thought it was about going home then," Sarah said smoothly, refusing to rise to Elinor`s provocations. There was a longer silence as she concentrated on slowing down to negotiate the blind bend immediately beyond the school gates and then thought of ways to add to her argument. It was just as well they were silent because several pupils were standing in the middle of the road with no thought for their lives. The Shakespeare quotation was no more successful on them than it had been on Elinor, so Sarah finally resorted to the plain, unromantic modern idiom, and the offenders sauntered grudgingly to the side. "Is that better?" she inquired of Elinor as she wound up the window and drove on.

"Infinitely."

"Nowhere near as pretty, though." The group reconvened in the middle of the road as she passed. "I don't know why I bother sometimes," she admitted, unconsciously mimicking Len. Elinor nodded her head vigorously in agreement as she lit a cigarette, and though the driver swallowed her point about aspirin for pain, she did allow Elinor to smoke her cigarette in peace. So much for giving up! Five minutes later, Elinor took up at exactly the same place she had left off.

"Of course if you want to throw your life away worrying about mixed up-kids. That's your affair. Me, I take it all at face value. No use getting all worked up about them. It's wasting my breath and my energy, so I don't. I save both for better things – things that do *me* good!" The next question was offered in a more conciliatory manner. "How long will it take *you* to realise that this is just another job?" There was no answer, and so she answered it herself. "Too long, I reckon! Why can't you see this is simply another means of keeping body and soul together, and when we walk through those doors at night, that's it, finito! Well, except for a bit of prep, and then no worries till the next day." After a short silence she added significantly, "And it took me all of three months to figure that out. All you get from over-involvement is ulcers if you're lucky, and nuts if you're not! Don't laugh! I have seen it plenty of times. Three teachers at my last place had serious breakdowns, and I only worked there six years. None of them will ever work again."

Sarah nodded her head seriously as required and then she smiled generously. "Real little ray of sunshine aren't you?"

"Maybe not, but it's true! How you have survived here so long is beyond me! How long have you been here? Eight, nine years? You must be due anytime."

Laughter bubbled forth from Sarah despite the pain in her head and despite the fact that she knew she wasn't meant to think it funny, but it neatly disguised the urge to cry. She summoned enough sangfroid from somewhere to divert the conversation one more time. "It is really comforting to know that your best friend has you down for a padded cell," she managed bleakly, "but too soon!" She choked back the emotion and added, *"I am but mad north north-west; when the wind is southerly I know a hawk from a handsaw."*

42

"You are still doing it!" Elinor threatened as she went off again into her own rhetoric. It provided enough time for Sarah to regain a hold on her emotions.

"I am sorry to disappoint you, Elinor, but I have no intention of ever stopping, or ever needing the breakdown, and the quotation just sort of tripped out on its own," she announced defiantly.

"That's exactly what I mean!" Elinor screeched. "You do it now without even thinking about it. This is a serious affliction, Sarah, and it could be a fatal one if you carry on without treatment!" She raised her hands to show her intention, whereupon the intended victim gave a fake scream and then groaned as her head hurt again. "All right, joking apart, admit it: there is no point whatsoever to dedication." She waved at some bedraggled youngsters outside. "They don't want it, don't recognise it, and aren't worth it. These are kids with problem lives! Their parents screwed up, and their kids will do the same. Leave 'em to it. It's easier all round. You can't still believe that they appreciate your efforts." Without allowing any opportunity for an answer, she added, "Do they hell as like! And no, I won't apologise or recant for that. Hell is what North Green is, and hell is what it should be called, whether you like it or not!"

This was another regular diatribe, so it did not affect its listener unduly. Sarah knew she was not the only one who did not know when to give up.

"Come on," Elinor wheedled, suddenly adopting her best conciliatory manner. "You know very well what I mean. Stop playing the innocent with me. So many years in a dump like the Green has to have taught you something."

"It has taught me that I am in the right job. Well, most of the time I am. I will allow you today as an exception."

"Is that supposed to be funny? You are a good teacher, a dedicated professional. Heaven knows there aren't many of them left."

"Thank you."

"What for? Stating the obvious? You are wasted here! Get out while you still can! Go somewhere better!"

"What for?"

"So you can do what you are good at – and just maybe get a life as well."

"I do that here, and I have a life, thank you," Sarah said defensively.

"Some life!" Elinor barked, backing up her disapproval with a list of facts and more head shaking.

The lecturer was in no mood to cope with other people's lectures and so she begged, "Let's not get into this again, Elinor. Not tonight, please."

Elinor considered that request for a whole minute. Even if she was prepared to forgo the assault on her friend's private life in the interests of friendship, the shop steward in her felt that this same friendship demanded she have her say on the subject of Sarah's working life. "Okay," she said sulkily, "But I bet you next month's salary that there aren't more than two or three kids in each class you teach who really want to learn, so why waste all that effort?"

"Except my A-level group."

"You and this blessed A-level group! Why are they so different? I thought you said they were a pain today!"

"Doesn't mean they don't want to learn," the defendant pointed out carefully, more than half certain that Elinor did not understand this. "Most of the kids in this class have made plans for their future, and that means they want to learn. And I want to be part of that, I enjoy teaching them."

"Even Marcie Hadley and her pals?"

"Especially Marcie Hadley and her pals. Marcie may not be my easiest student." Honesty demanded she admit this much. "She may not even love Shakespeare the same way I do," she added, remembering the finer points of today's discussion, "but she is my benchmark: if I have her on board, I have the others." For once Elinor said nothing and so Sarah thought she had made her point and queried, "Do you know that no one in her family has ever stayed on at school before? Marcie Hadley is one of my heroines! I admit she tries my patience to the bone at times, today included, but she knows as well as I do that she needs all her grades to get the college place she wants. I don't need to tell her there is more to life than what her parents and brothers have. She knows."

"You mean the younger brother earning a thousand pounds a week by dealing?"

"Even him. She is not going to repeat his mistakes or let go of what she wants, however hard it gets. That is vision, and I applaud that every single time. It's the ones without that sort of vision whom I worry about."

"Okay, well apart from the A-level crowd, the rest just look on you as their jailer until they are sixteen. Everyone else seems to understand prisoners do not owe their jailers anything – other than making their life hell as often as possible. So how come you don't understand it?"

"Pass. So why does it not bother you?"

"Because I don't care!" Elinor had articulated this so slowly and precisely that there could be no mistaking her meaning this time. "I do not give a damn about any of them, so they can't hurt me, disappoint me, or frustrate me. They can't do anything to me because I clock in and clock out, just like them. They have my presence, that's all. Besides which," she added significantly, "I have a life outside of that hell hole."

"You are too cynical."

"It's healthier!"

"I don't know about that," Sarah said. "If I am to rest in my bed at night, I have to go there knowing that I have done my best for each and every one of them – the Michael Davies's and the Marcie Hadley's included. Whether or not they appreciate it is irrelevant."

"That's exactly what I am getting at! That's why you need to get out of this place before you go completely doo-lally, ga-ga. Call it what you want. I am serious, Sarah – stop laughing! You are just another teacher, just another woman. You cannot save all the deprived kids in London, not even all the deprived kids in this school. What can one person reasonably expect to do against all that? I'll tell you what: absolutely nothing! So if you must be dedicated, go and do it somewhere else, somewhere it will be valued, somewhere you can get something back for it." A moment passed, and then she said in a much more amiable tone, "I happen to know they want a head of English at that private school in Hampstead where my cousin works. Nice school, nice area. Head of department – *promotion*. That is what you want, isn't it? *More money?* And you get nice kids with regular parents, standard uniforms, and legible homework. Think about it! Education heaven, no problems! Sorted lives and sorted pupils! Maybe even a decent staff room, too," she muttered, suddenly rather taken with the idea herself. "Go for it, kid!"

Sarah stopped laughing. "Oh Elinor, it's not that simple," she pointed out with some kindness.

"Why not? You tell me why it's not that simple."

"It just isn't."

"How do you know it isn't if you haven't tried? And you haven't tried, have you – except for John's poxy little job, which he was never going to give you. You *do* know that, don't you? Have you tried elsewhere?" Silence was as loud as admission though Elinor did at least wonder whether she had crossed the line again, so she offered explanation as well as appeasement. "You had nothing to trade," she said kindly. "You must know that at least.

Trader John knows he gets your best regardless of your position. Why should he give you a promotion when he needs it to buy someone else's devotion?" There was still no retaliation. "I reckon you could get a job anywhere with your exam results from here. Miracles always impress, even old cynics like me."

"But maybe that's why I stay here," the miracle worker offered. "I am vain enough to think I can do a better job here than most. See, it might have nothing to do with money or altruism. That's a shock to you, isn't it?"

"No, of course not."

"You are a lousy liar, Elinor. For some reason you always credit me with the noblest motives, and I am not noble – well, not nearly as often as I would like to be, or you think I am. I am doing this because I know I am good at it, and it gives *me* satisfaction." Elinor provided some suitable background noises, and Sarah smiled at her benignly. "I don't think you have ever considered that this could be about something as base as vanity, have you? See, you haven't - but it is! I stay here because my vanity tells me I have a talent for working with our kids. Numbers don't matter; one in a class makes it worthwhile. Another thing: have you ever considered that in a school full of really outstanding teachers, like this private school probably has, I might not be anything special at all? Insecurity, as well you see."

"Maybe, but I doubt it."

"That's my line," Sarah said with a smile. "Anyway, whatever, I cannot simply switch off at three thirty, so please stop asking."

"Why not?"

"Too big a responsibility." Elinor was neither convinced nor amused by this. Sarah didn't really care, though she did concede. "But maybe I will make tonight an exception just to please you. Marcie Hadley has used up all my reserves of tolerance for one term, Michael Davies is currently bottom of my list of favourite causes, and I have a pile of ironing that needs doing as well as the usual mountain of marking."

"I dare say you will have recovered by next term. I know you well enough to know you will be back all bright-eyed and bushy tailed, raring to go again. Sick, sick, sick," she complained thrusting her fingers down her throat to show exactly what she meant. A minute later she asked, "So what's happened to dull our Mr Davies's favoured position as the delinquent most in need?" Elinor actually asking anything about Michael Davies was sufficiently unusual in that it was rewarded with a blow-by-blow account of her conversation with Len, including Michael's accusation, before she realised what she was doing, but by then it was too late to recall her words, and Elinor naturally demanded to know why she was treating the whole thing so lightly.

"Because I know him," Sarah said thoughtfully. "After three months of teaching him four times a week, I know him very well."

"Don't we all, unfortunately."

"Yes, I know that. But think about what you told me this morning."

"You mean about you and Len having an affair?" Elinor asked, desperately trying to find a connection between that and this when they seemed so totally unconnected. Sarah nodded, so Elinor sat back for a moment trying to think it through again. After giving it more careful consideration, she had to admit she still could not find any connection. "You are way ahead of me here! What has *that* got to do with *this?* This is serious, Sarah!"

"You are as bad as Len. No, it is not! It wasn't, it isn't, and it never will be, I promise. This is about Michael and me, about him finding something to rattle me. Why else would he tell Len? Anyone else with an accusation like that would have gone straight to John, with parents for backup." She looked at Elinor's troubled face and smiled. "Michael is a manipulator; he plays on people."

"Tell me something I don't know."

"He is bright and clever, but it's not harnessed, and so it becomes something …"

"Dark and devious?" Elinor volunteered.

Sarah laughed. "Maybe. Anyway, what matters most to him is that I don't play his games. I will not ban him from English, or excuse him from homework, or scream at him in class. Maybe his tactics worked with Danny – I don't know – but they don't work with me, and that bothers him. Correction: I think that bothers him a lot."

"So like I said, you have more patience than is good for you."

"Then along comes this great piece of ammunition." That was sufficiently interesting for Elinor to forget her grumbles and inquire what that might be. "My affair with Len?" Suddenly Elinor's interest in this conversation was greater than her interest in her injured leg until Sarah clarified, "My *supposed* affair with Len then. Is that better?"

"Only you know that," Elinor said sarcastically, slumping back in her seat again and returning her attention to her wounded limb.

"I bet you next month's salary that Michael has heard the rumours and thinks they could provide him with a bit of fun and a perfect way to cause some trouble between Len and me. He plants the seed with Len, who just happens to be his form teacher." She sighed and then grinned. "He doesn't know me well enough though, or else he would realise that the rumours are exactly that. Poor boy."

"That's a very devious scheme."

"And he's a very devious lad. You just said so yourself."

"I know, but …"

"But what?"

"Sarah, you are becoming obsessed with this lad. Let it go. Let *him* go!"

"I can't."

"Why not?"

"Because he deserves a chance."

"He's had *thousands of chances*," Elinor pointed out emphatically. "What makes you think you can succeed where everyone else has failed?" There was only one word in the reply. "Vanity?" This tongue-in-cheek attitude did nothing to appease the opposition. "I give up!" Elinor said as she tossed her second cigarette away. "And so should you, if you have any sense left at all!"

"Not only will I take this horse to water, Elinor, but I will find a way to make it want to drink, I promise you."

"This horse does not need water!" Elinor wailed in utter exasperation. "This horse runs on…" She searched around for something suitably dramatic and finally came up with it. "Poison! Get this into your thick skull: Michael Davies is no challenge. Michael Davies is suicide – your suicide! He is Lady Macbeth's nearest and dearest, and everyone else but you knows it. Wake up! He is already banned from chemistry, and whatever he says about that explosion being an accident, I believe Martin's claim that it was deliberate. This lad is dangerous. For once Len is right, so listen to him!" This ardent plea produced nothing but a sheepish grin, and Elinor, who was used to fighting hopeless battles, finally recognised that this was another one, though she ended doggedly, "Personally, I think we should cut out all the messing and just expel him. The next time he is in trouble, I shall say so. I don't suppose I will have long to wait."

"And what would that solve?"

"It would solve *our* problem about how to control him. And it would send a powerful message to the rest of them: keep in line, or else!"

"We are not running a prison camp."

"Grow up. That's exactly what we are running. We are jailers. Haven't you been listening to a word I've said?" There was an uncomfortable silence before Elinor added, "No wonder his mother goes off and leaves him to it. I'd strangle him if he were mine. Devious little devil."

"Oh Elinor, how can you say that? It is not as simple as that. This is not just about plain naughtiness, is it?"

"Oh Sarah," Elinor responded in a stinging parody of her friend's plea. "Spare me the bleeding heart! We are talking about a juvenile delinquent here with a criminal record, not a high-spirited lad playing a prank." She had long since lost patience with this whole conversation, and it showed in the tone of her voice, "so before you tell me the 'he's been abused by his criminal father and rejected by his drunken mother' excuse, I know it. I know it all in every tawdry pathetic detail, and it does not impress me anymore."

Michael Davies's defence refused to be intimidated and calmly stood her ground. "It is not an excuse, Elinor. It is a reason, and it explains a lot. I completely agree with you that Michael Davies is a pain, but I am not sure that I would be much different given his circumstances. The details of his background make me want to weep, so I will not give up on him without a fight. Every human being deserves that. You seem to think I love him. Believe you me, I most certainly do not! And I certainly do not condone his shocking behaviour, but it hasn't stopped me from wanting to help him so far, and it won't in the future – if he will let me in. Somewhere inside this monster has to be someone worth helping."

"You should have been a social worker," Elinor said. "Then you could have wasted your breath on all the no-hopers you could find."

Sarah had to stop at traffic lights, and by now the atmosphere in the car was anything but friendly, so she tried a smile to reduce the tension. Elinor simply glared back. "Do you know what percentage of the children we teach come from broken homes like Michael's?" Sarah asked quietly.

"Nope. And what's more, I don't care." Elinor offered without remorse before remembering something else that seemed relevant to her argument. "Your kids come from a broken home, so how come I don't hear about them terrorising their teachers?"

Sarah refused the goad and replied quietly, "I know they do, Elinor. Not a single day passes that I don't regret that. Maybe it's part of the reason I care so much about the kids like Michael. My girls don't have a perfect life, but they do have the best I can give them. It seems like Michael Davies has never had anything – well, nothing except stolen goods and chips outside some pub or amusement arcade. I wonder who helped him learn to read. Who tucked him up in bed? Who supervises his homework now? Who sets the standards for his behaviour, the father in prison he hasn`t seen since he was six, or the alcoholic mother? Or maybe some moronic television programme or violent movie? Who *really* cares about Michael Davies and what becomes of him? Not the people who make the TV programmes or the movies, that's for sure. They are not interested in the Michaels of this world, only in making money. Maybe his mum and dad do care, but they don't know any better themselves." Elinor was not moved by any of this, and she signalled her disgust with the whole subject by turning to look out of the window. Sarah continued to address the back of her head. "Maybe I should have asked you how many of our children come from emotionally damaged backgrounds then, because some of our damaged children do have both parents at home, like the Hadley girls. Is that better?"

"No! Because I still don't know, and I still don't care. But you are the social scientist, so I suppose I am going to get to know whether I want to or not. So, just get on with it, and then I can have some peace."

"It's over 30 per cent and rising. Does that not alarm you?"

"No!" That seemed fairly categorical.

"Why not? It should."

"I told you, I accept that this is a rough area. The people are rough, so it figures the kids will be the same. They pay me to teach 'em New York ain't the capital of the United States, and that's what I do – and that is all I do. I am not here to be a social worker. Neither are you."

"How can you say that you teach them geography when the problems they have mean that some of them cannot, or will not, learn? We have to do more."

"Back to Michael Davies, I suppose," Elinor said in such a menacing tone that it should have been impossible to overlook the fact that she had finally had enough of this topic.

Sarah had ignored all of her previous signals, and right now she was so busy responding to the man behind her who was sounding his horn impatiently, that she missed this one as well. She did acknowledge her error to the driver behind; Elinor was not so lucky. She did admit, "Okay, Michael is the extreme example. Do you know Jonathan Spicer?"

Surprisingly, Elinor's head stayed connected to her shoulders and she nodded as she said grimly, "Nice lad. One of the few." As Sarah started to recite details of Jonathan's current situation, Elinor interrupted her, "Listen, when you tell me gossip, at least makes sure it's news, not history. I told you all that on Tuesday."

"Sorry. Well, here's something you don't know: Jonathan lost it in English today," Sarah said bluntly, noting that a degree of interest was surfacing in Elinor, so she provided the necessary explanation. "…because *Twelfth Night* has a happy ending." It was a simple enough statement but it drew an immediate inquiry because even Elinor and her well-advertised dislike of Shakespeare could not quite grasp why anyone should react so strongly to a boring old play. "Exactly! It beggars belief, doesn't it? But if you think about it, it isn't that strange." Elinor could not fathom that either and though the explanation naturally went into some detail, it had no more success. "Oh come on, Elinor, use your common sense. He is seventeen; five months off taking his `A` levels, and working hard. Then wham! Ten days ago his dad walks out, and today he finds out about all sorts of problems he did not know existed a week ago. No wonder he is causing problems in class for the first time ever. Come on, there has to be a connection! He cannot handle this! Did you know they have huge financial problems?" Elinor shook her head." Well, they do. He told me they might lose their home! These are not the sort of problems he needs right now."

"Calm down! Tell me again what actually happened?"

The repeated version spared none of the detail and finished with the beginning of the outburst in class. "He just yelled, 'Shakespeare is an idiot!'"

Elinor smirked. "Hey, that is revolutionary stuff for your class! Good for him."

"He said I was, too," Sarah said seriously. "Is that good?"

"No, of course not. Hey, I'm sorry. I was being funny."

"Jonathan wasn't. He was deadly serious. I lost control for a while."

Elinor grunted. "Well most of us can remember the last time we lost it, though I don't suppose many of us can remember the first time, so think yourself lucky it's your only time."

"He could have disrupted the entire class for the whole lesson the mood they were in today."

"Disrupted the wonderful sixth? Good heavens, what will happen next?" Elinor's expression of facetious alarm at such a dreadful prospect as this did not warrant any lessening of the tension between them. Sarah stared hard at her, though Elinor was not to be so easily cowed. "So did you give him a detention?" she demanded. It was a solution that seemed reasonable to only one of them.

"What would have been the point of that?"

"Teach him not to do it again - hopefully before he gets used to the idea that it's easy to cause trouble."

The blanket of frustration now covered both of them. Sarah felt obliged to point that out, "This conversation is pointless! Do you realise I have had an entire day of pointless conversations? Everything I have said today has been completely wasted. Am I convincing you of anything?" The opposition shook its head. "Thought not. And as you are not about to change my mind either, I suggest we drop it and talk about something else." Elinor said nothing, but Sarah remained annoyed with herself for getting embroiled in this very old argument all over again. Her desire to convince Elinor that lads like Michael Davies were the real litmus test of their teaching ability had dragged her into it. "Okay, so maybe I am pigheaded," she said as a peace offering.

"Maybe you are right," was the sulky reply.

"I wasn't looking for agreement," she said softly. "More for support."

"Get a good bra, then!"

Silence lulled Sarah into believing that their latest truce had been agreed and that the subject was put away for another day. Elinor did not think the same because a few minutes later she grumbled, "Anyway, what are we discussing kids for? It's the holidays, and even you must take a rest from shouldering their burdens. No, do not tell me that thoughts of Michael Davies eating chips on Christmas Day will ruin your Christmas dinner! I do not want to know. Besides which, all of that was a very clever diversion from our original subject."

"Which was?" Sarah questioned.

"You! And I refuse to be put off by that irritatingly innocent little girl voice. What was I saying? Oh yes, I remember: about you being too serious. I think what I should have said is that you are too dull."

"That's the gospel according to Elinor Farrington and it differs significantly from the gospel according to Sarah Chadwick," Sarah pointed out. She felt that Elinor had yet to realise this.

"I don't mean to upset you," Elinor pointed out sincerely.

"Would it really matter if you did?"

"Of course it would." There was only a brief pause. "But just look at yourself! You are nearly thirty-five, nearly halfway there! Yes, you are! Thirty-five is halfway to that three score years and ten. And what are you doing with your life? Nothing! What have you done with it in the last twelve months? Nothing! That's bad enough, but what have you done with it in the last five years? The answer is still the same: nothing! Do you get my drift? Your life is passing you by! You are getting older just like the rest of us, so stop dawdling around as if you were here forever. What you need is a lot more excitement and adventure right now. I'll bet you the highlight of your Christmas is going to be carving the turkey on Christmas Day, isn't it?"

"So, what's wrong with that?"

Elinor's answer came in the form of a withering look that was generally used on recalcitrant fifteen year olds, but Sarah made allowances for the fact that whether Elinor realised it, or not, she too had difficulty in leaving the schoolteacher behind at home time.

"Get out," Elinor said as she gestured enthusiastically. "Get out and live it up. Put the sparkle back in your eyes, or whatever it is they say that means you are having a good time. And I don't mean marking exercise books either, so stop marking so bloody many. Sarah, I promise you that there is more to life than an empty locker!"

For once, this particular wisdom did not fall on Sarah's usually deaf ears. Jonathan's "no happy endings" had disturbed her because she had been considering something not entirely dissimilar recently, and now Elinor had hit the nail home with this. She knew both these things had some relevance to her present predicament, but she was unwilling to admit to either, and her conscience was easily appeased because of the inevitable remedies that would follow if Elinor knew. The fact that she was still wondering about the point of it all must stay classified information because it exposed her vulnerability as a human being – the other thing she had worked hard at concealing for the last ten years. Admitting to any of it seemed tantamount to giving Elinor grounds for having her committed to that padded cell. She didn't need anyone to tell her that she was daft -mad even, because she had thought it herself sometimes. Worst of all, Elinor's solutions would involve men, because all of Elinor's solutions for everything always did. If Shakespeare and her dad had been unable to come up with any effective remedy between them, she was absolutely certain that Elinor's brand of men could not do any better. The fact that both her men were dead and Elinor's were always very much alive was irrelevant.

Despite not knowing any of this, Elinor was already into her third solution for this sorry state of affairs by the time Sarah picked up on the conversation. A third set of men – three sets too many.

"Tis a truth universally acknowledged these days that a woman in possession of a good salary need not have a husband," Sarah pointed out archly.

Elinor guessed she was being sent up. She just didn't quite know how, so she muttered, "Who said anything about husbands? And since when did you get a pay rise?"

The audacity of the answer deprived Sarah of the opportunity to educate her friend about the provenance of her line, but she shrugged off the temptation to pursue the thoughts that Elinor had stirred, to concentrate on finding a way to return the conversation back to her friend's injured leg, because she had wrestled with her demons too often to be attracted by the mere mental exercise they provided. She knew examining them could fill any amount of time, and she did not need any further proof of that, or of her intelligence. She knew that her brain was capable of dealing with abstract concepts – it had done nothing else over the last few months. What her brain needed right now was practice with a few physical realities – substance, not surmise; testing out the methodology, not setting up the theory. The trouble was she was no scientist; she was a wordsmith tantalised by the power of the thought process, an addictive dreamer easily diverted by some alluring verbal picture, a philosopher. It was hardly a good basis for a scientific inquiry. But dreamer or not, she now understood that an answer was needed in order to save her sanity, and she had thought about it often enough to accept that thinking was not going to produce one. New knowledge would have to come from somewhere else. But where else was there besides thinking? That was why it was easier to talk about Elinor's leg, except Elinor was not going to be put off so easily.

"If you had given me the chance," Sarah finally conceded in a saccharin, sweet voice that belied the complexity of her thoughts, "I might have told you that I am going to a concert with Len on Tuesday. Though I am not sure if it will replace carving the turkey," she teased. This friendship with Len was her best attempt yet to find that new knowledge.

"Wow, that is really living!" Elinor said disparagingly. "Though I suppose it's a start. But with Len Cole of all people? Did you not listen to a single word I said to you this morning? The gossip, remember? If you are going to be gossiped about, at least do it with someone that's worth being talked about! You might as well be guilty of what they're saying." Upon seeing Sarah's frown, she changed her mind. "No, well maybe not. But no one else knows that. No one else knows about your strange ideas." Sarah ignored her. "I told you this morning what everyone else thinks. They all think that Len Cole is getting …"

"I do not want to hear this Elinor!"

Elinor wagged her finger. "You didn't say that this morning. You had to ask this morning! And the fact you had to ask was bad enough," she pointed out baldly. "But the fact you needed me to spell out what everyone else thinks Len Cole is getting was pathetic! This is not naiveté, Sarah – this is gross negligence of life! They all think the same: they all think Len Cole is getting private lessons, and I am not talking Shakespeare, either."

"Oh."

"Is that all you are going to say?"

"What else do you want me to say?" Sarah shot back. Elinor shook her head because for once she was lost for words. "You keep telling me that I should go out more, and now that I am, it is *still* wrong! You are impossible to please. Just what do I have to do to get this right?"

"Drop the sarcasm, for a start. Didn't you say something to me only this afternoon about sarcasm not being becoming?"

"Wasn't that cynicism?"

Elinor doubted it. "Was it? Oh well. Is it not the same thing? As for Len, well, what can I say except that he is definitely not what I had in mind when I told you to get out more. I want you to fall in love with someone nice, have a good time, and—"

"And I would just have people thinking the very same things they are thinking now," Sarah pointed out with remarkable equanimity.

"With one important difference! It would be with someone worth being talked about. I cannot imagine anyone having a good time with Len Cole, let alone falling in love with him or wanting to be the brunt of tasteless jokes because of him. He is so boring! I daresay he would send you to sleep at the vital moment!" Then as an awful possibility dawned on her, she grabbed hold of Sarah's arm to get her attention. It did that alright, but it also caused her to swerve dangerously.

"Let go of me before you get us both killed!" Sarah yelled.

"When you tell me you haven't!" Elinor demanded frantically."

"Haven't what?"

"Haven't gone mad altogether and really fallen for Len Cole." Until now she had never really considered that there could be any substance to the rumours that had her friend almost panting for the amorous attentions of their colleague.

Sarah looked at the anxious face beside her and grinned. "Would it be so awful if I had?"

"Don't be stupid – of course it would! Falling in love with Len would be even worse than sleeping with him, though I daresay that would be bad enough," Elinor said distastefully, shuddering at the thought. "I know you have been on your own for a long time, and that does funny things to people. And you haven't had any men friends except that Stuart bloke you went out with once. What was wrong with him? What is wrong with you?"

"Are you trying to find excuses for me?"

This was not the answer to Elinor's question, but she appeared not to notice that and launched into her reply without grasping that the tactic had been deliberately employed as yet another diversion. "I am so glad you said 'trying'. Come on, Sarah. Len Cole? You can do better than this! It's cruelty to women! This is not your knight in shining armour, and it's no fairy-tale romance either– it's a nightmare! It's ... it's ..." She waved her arms around, still trying to find words of sufficient abhorrence. "It's Cinderella in reverse," she declared triumphantly. "One kiss from him, and you would want to go to sleep for a thousand years."

"Not only have you got your stories mixed up, but I actually find that quite offensive. Len is a very nice man, and I can't recall ever specifying a knight in shining armour. I thought that was *your* downfall, believing in fairy-tales."

"Okay, I'm sorry. Maybe Len is a very nice man. Maybe the moon is made of green cheese. I grant you that life can be very happy without some adventures, and he is one of them. Believe me, he may be fine for someone's Aunty Gladys, but not for you."

"Why not?"

This was the most challenging accusation of their conversation so far, and at least Elinor appeared to award it some degree of consideration. Still, she did not have to think very long before she came up with her answer. "You cannot seriously be contemplating throwing yourself away on Len Cole. Even Wills didn't write such awful tragedy," she remonstrated. Sarah smiled at that despite herself. "See? Even you know it's true. And anyway, Len must be at least fifty."

"What has age got to do with it?"

"He is an old man. I would have thought that had a *lot* to do with it."

"Well, he is not an old man, and he is not fifty."

"He's fifty–five?" Elinor shrieked.

"No, of course he's not. Len was forty last month, if you must know."

"Well, he looks at least fifty," Elinor countered, unable to give up her argument.

"Didn't you say I looked fifty-five? That makes us a fair match."

Elinor stared hard at the perfectly serious face that was apparently concentrating on driving, Sarah had to be joking, so why wasn't she laughing? Elinor`s struggle for words to express her horror was fruitless, because there were no such words – well, none she knew of, or none she dared use that could express such revulsion. She finally said, "I suppose you know that he is a fisherman!"

"What has that got to do with anything?"

A most exquisitely distasteful sneer: the one Elinor practised a lot, preceded her explanation. "It means that he gets kicks out of sticking great big hooks into poor, defenceless fish! Ugh!" Her shiver of disgust more than adequately conveyed what her vocabulary had failed to do.

"Well, if it will save you from sleepless nights worrying about me being hooked by Len Cole, you have my solemn assurance that despite all rumours to the contrary, I am neither in love with Len, nor sleeping with him – or anyone else for that matter. And I am not likely to do either in the near future. I do not want a husband, and I will not have a lover. I do not need a relationship. I am perfectly okay on my own, full stop! Will that do to end all of this ridiculous speculation, or do I have to put it in writing?"

"Okay, okay, no need to be so touchy. I am glad to hear it, especially the Len Cole bit. It might take more to convince everyone else, though."

Sarah was about to give in to an emotional response but she managed to control it at the last minute. "I think you worry unnecessarily, and you use the word 'love' far too often," she said calmly, "a bit like the fifth form, really. They use it for anything more than a nodding hello. If you understand me, I can live with the rest of them thinking what they like."

"You sure about that?"

"For now, yes. I'll sort the rest out after Christmas," she conceded wearily, desperate to close the entire conversation.

Elinor sensed her moment. "Listen, I know you think that it's none of my business, and strictly speaking you are right. But if you will take a bit of friendly advice, you will dump Len Cole and find yourself some philandering, virile, madly handsome Romeo to sweep you off your feet – preferably into the nearest available bed. Then it doesn't matter what the others think, because you will be too busy to care." Sarah shook her head vigorously as an attempt to end the conversation before a real row could erupt, but Elinor was unrepentant. "No, hear me out. Throw caution to the wind, have a mad passionate love affair, and grab some fun while you are still young enough to enjoy it. Put the colour back in your cheeks and the sparkle back in your eyes. Have I said enough to give you the general idea? Good! And if you do happen to find one as described, either get me one as well, or pass him over when you have finished with him."

Sarah said simply, "Be serious."

"I *am* serious. Stop wasting time. Get out there and enjoy yourself. Stop being so dammed responsible – it's killing you! There is plenty of time to be good when you are too old to be naughty." North Green's newest philosopher was mightily impressed with this bit of wisdom. She considered it carefully and then repeated it a second time, just in case her pupil had missed it the first time round. "Get yourself a man. Well, not just any man. I suppose even Len qualifies on that count."

"Elinor! That is enough."

"I mean one that will do you some good. One that knows a thing or two." The reply that Len was knowledgeable about fishing and jazz, as well as physics and chemistry, was of course dismissed. "Not the sort of physics and chemistry I have in mind, or the sort of fishing or jazz, come to think of it! Why do you always have to be so awkward?" Elinor demanded. "You know damned well what I mean. I mean a man that knows about life and about women. And don't you dare tell me that Len knows about any of these things, because I will not believe you. He is a duff, sandy-haired, forty-year-old bachelor. Worse still, he is a duff, sandy-haired, forty-year-old bachelor who still lives at home with his mother, and he is only interested in test tubes, fishing lines, and trumpets. No way!"

Len`s defence enquired innocently, "Am I wrong, or was it only last week in this very car that you were giving up on men because they were all the same, all out for one thing? Well, Len is different. He is not only out for one thing. He is a good friend, and I value that."

"Okay. That was last week. You know why I said that: I was upset and irrational. This week I am more normal, less emotional, and I can see that I can't blame all men for the failings of one rat. Neither can you.

People recover Sarah, and so should you." Sarah tried to answer, but Elinor interrupted. "Just tell me you've been getting some."

"Elinor!"

"I am not going to say sorry, if that's what you want. Why should I apologise for telling you the truth? Whether or not you like it, what you really need is someone to share that double bed with. You are frustrated!"

Whether or not she was, being labelled as such was not easy, even after this conversation, so Sarah looked away to obscure the fact that she needed to control her emotions. She hoped Elinor had not noticed that. When she had recovered some, she launched into a story about her mum and dad's early marital squabbles, and Mary's inability to realise that the peace-offering dinner that she thought was so wonderful was something her husband actually hated. "It was her idea of what he should like; she never thought to ask him. It wasn't reality. It was an illusion – *her* illusion."

"Yes, yes, I get the idea."

"My having a lover is an illusion. *Your* illusion. It's not my answer," Sarah said seriously.

Elinor looked at her and sighed. "Why do you always have to be so different?"

"No reason. I just am. It's me. Take no notice of me. I'm okay, honest." She nodded her head even more vigorously to emphasise that she really was and to disguise the emotion that was threatening to overwhelm her once again. There were only so many ways of doing that safely when one was confined in such a small space and had to drive and had just committed yet another sin of omission. Good job she wasn`t Catholic. "But I am glad that you are feeling better," she said cheerfully, struggling to regain her composure.

Elinor was only slightly mollified by this. "Did I tell you about the guy I met at the sports club on Tuesday? He is so fit! I can't help feeling better when he's around. He seems a really nice guy as well," she added hurriedly, noting the sceptical look.

"If I had a pound for every time you have said that I would be a very rich woman."

"Okay, so I've been wrong a few times."

"How many?"

"*Now* who is being cynical?" Elinor shot back.

The point was conceded with a sigh. "I told you, take no notice of me; I am out of it today. I am just shocked that you have been dating someone for three whole days without telling me!"

The introduction of this new man into the conversation made it easy to focus on Elinor's life, and Sarah did that gratefully, forgetting for now about the things that plagued her own. She listened patiently as Elinor got into her stride on the merits of her new conquest. He had a lot of merits. "How many times have you seen him since Tuesday?"

"Just last night. Why?"

"Nothing. Except here's me thinking that a good psychoanalyst would be hard pressed to discover so many good points in that length of time. People don't generally get to know other people that fast, Elinor. It just doesn't happen."

"Okay, joke if you want to, but he has made me feel great again. Whatever you say, it's what you need, too. Honestly! I bet your dad could have liked that dinner if he hadn't been so determined not to," she added hopefully.

After taking time to negotiate a particularly busy junction, Sarah felt composed enough to risk a reply without adding comments about short-lived attachments – or short-lived celibacy – because she knew saying either would not help, though it was tempting. "Elinor, I am touched by your concern for me," she admitted, forgoing the jibe. "But I do not need romantic adventures to complicate my life. It's complicated enough. I am one of life's plodders," she added with a grin, forestalling Elinor's open mouth and its contribution. "I love you dearly, but I do not, and never will, subscribe to your outlook on life. In fact, I can think of nothing worse than having some canoodling, chain-store Casanova hanging round me. Besides which, if I ever did get the urge to paint the town red, I do have two very real drawbacks, as you know." Elinor looked at her expectantly, so she explained. "My girls!"

By this time they were stopped at the next to the last set of traffic lights before Elinor's road. Sarah was relieved because her ordeal was nearly over, Elinor was quietly contemplating what Sarah might have been inferring with that phrase "canoodling, chain-store Casanova," and wondering whether it could have been a reference to Tony, the guy from the squash club because he was a supermarket manager.

"You see, El," Sarah said suddenly rather apologetic, "I have never been one of your social butterflies, and it is much too late in the day to start now. But I wish you well with this Terry."

"Tony," Elinor corrected morosely. "How could you forget that name?"

"Well, the current model, whatever he is called."

This time Elinor allowed her real disapproval of such levity to surface. "See, you can't even say his name, can you?" she wailed. "Ten years after the event, and you still cannot say his name." It was one jibe too many.

"Yes, I can. Tony!" Sarah exploded. "Are you satisfied now?" she asked as she lapsed into sulky silence.

"Okay, I give up! Remember that I did try telling you! Just because one man was a lying drunk who cheated on you and then hit you and abandoned you, it doesn't mean all men will do the same."

"I know that!"

"Then don't come moaning to me when you are sixty and past it. Don't tell me then that you should have got your act together when you were younger. Just remember that I tried to tell you!" For a moment the silence was acceptable to both parties. Then Elinor dared one last try. "People are beginning to think you are ..." She shrugged. "You know." Sarah turned to face her friend. "I mean, people are beginning to ask if you are, you know, different."

"I don't believe you! People really think that? No, I don't believe you!" Elinor would have recalled her words instantly if she could, but like all other hasty disclosures, this one was as indelible as the most considered. She tried to change the subject, but this time her victim pursued the point. "Who said that? Who thinks I am?"

"Leave it alone."

"No! You tell me who it is that thinks this about me."

"A couple of people have asked."

"What, at school?"

Elinor nodded glumly. "They didn't know about Len, naturally. And I didn't think I had the right to tell them. Why are you so surprised? It's not natural, living as you do. People are bound to get curious and make assumptions."

Sarah's head had scarcely stopped shaking for one reason or another the whole of the trip home, so it seemed okay to continue now, except now it was prompted by anger and disbelief. Today was clearly not going to end any different than it had started. "It's not natural because I have the nerve to act how I believe? Forget it! I don't want to know these people, and I don't care what they think."

"Listen, I put them straight. I am just telling you," Elinor offered apologetically, realising too late that this was one piece of information she should have kept to herself.

Sarah swallowed hard and stared out of the window, biting on her lip to stop the tears from flowing. Elinor did the same. One saw nothing, the other too much.

Across the road, a man was wrestling with huge panels of paper as he tried to get a new poster in place on a hoarding. He had an advert for foreign holidays that wanted to show a sleek white jet taking off into a vast expanse of blue sky but it was a daft thing to attempt in the current weather. He currently had nothing more than the tail end of a jet in place and a mass of paper wrapped around him. It was so comical that it was easy to get absorbed in his struggle. Most people would have laughed. Sarah didn't, but she did miss another set of lights, much to the chagrin of the man waiting behind. He was less patient than the man at the last set, so he sounded his horn angrily to register his disapproval, and she waved an apology.

"Now *that* is something I could do with," she said, trying to force some cheerfulness into her voice to mask the distress she still felt.

It was a brave gesture but did not fool Elinor, "Look I am sorry."

"Forget it, Elinor. Just forget it."

Elinor could not do that, so there was nothing to do except regret her disclosure. And though it did nothing to improve her frame of mind Sarah continued to concentrate on watching the man and his advert until the lights changed again. The man behind sounded his horn again just to make sure they weren't here on a camping trip. "Wish it was paradise, next stop," she mumbled at the bill poster as she put the car into gear. Eager to promote any conversation that could conceivably get her out of her difficulty Elinor asked what that meant. Sarah pointed out the poster to her and read the strapline aloud. "Paradise, next stop. If only it was," she sighed. "But I don't even require paradise anymore. I would settle for a good holiday – well, *any* holiday right now."

"So have you made any plans yet?" This was that ideal opportunity to get the conversation back onto safer ground.

"No, and I am not likely to, either."

"How come?"

"The school play starts rehearsals next term."

"So what has that got to do with holidays?" It was a reasonable enough question. Sarah's answer was not.

"I get involved in making the costumes."

That reply rekindled all the old frustrations in Elinor. "This is exactly what I have been going on about! School takes over your life. Tell them what to do with their stupid play!"

"I can't do that."

"Why not?"

"Because I enjoy it, and anyway, I can't afford a holiday at Easter. The girls want to go to Sweden with their school in summer."

Elinor was not one to be defeated so easily and demanded, "What is wrong with taking a holiday in the summer, then?"

"Nothing at all, except that the roof needs fixing, and I could do with a new bedroom carpet, to say nothing of—"

"Stop it, stop it! All this domestication drives me dotty."

"Doesn't do much for me, either," Sarah agreed wearily. "But it's no use ignoring it, because it ain't going away."

As they approached the last junction before her home, Elinor turned in her seat and confided earnestly, "Well, whether or not you spend the entire summer up on the roof, I am going to America. I have been thinking about this for the last three or four years at least. This summer there's no more thinking – I am going for the entire six weeks at least, seven if I can manage it." How one could manage a seven-week holiday in a six-week vacation period was not clear to Sarah, but her question was rewarded with yet another piqued answer. "You do it by telling John it is a trip of a lifetime, a long-held ambition about to be realised."

"He might be impressed but he will remind you very politely of the term dates."

Elinor screwed up her face, in her heart she knew this was true. "I am going to write a book," she confessed.

It wasn't immediately clear whether Sarah really was addressing her own eyebrow, or whether she was merely scoring points by being doubly irritating, but she did call out aloud to her reflection in the mirror. "Elinor is going to write a book! Now, *I* am impressed!" She added, "Unfortunately, it's not me you have to convince."

"Please don't laugh at me – I am serious! Okay, so I loathe writing most things, but this isn't most things. It's not your sort of book," she added hurriedly, just in case Sarah should be disappointed to find she had no intention of becoming a novelist or a playwright. "This is a useful book, a guide book. I have researched the market and there is a definite need for mine. It will be aimed at people who want to do it alone, don't want the student guides, and aren't loaded. A sort of middle-of-the-road, economy guide for serious adults interested in exploring real America, not just Disney and Hollywood." Her nodding was supposed to encourage Sarah to agree with her, but she had given too much offence to be let off that lightly.

Sarah resisted the urge to get drawn into the same argument about fiction for the second time that day on the grounds that she had even less chance of winning it this time. She also avoided pursuing whether Elinor was qualified to write for serious adults. She merely observed, "I thought Disney and Hollywood *were* the real America!" It was followed by a swift apology before a blow could be delivered, but she only lowered her arm when the expectation of retaliation was past. "I didn't realise you were a budding author."

"Well, I am! See, there's probably as much about me that you don't know as there is about America."

"And here's me thinking I know you well. Sounds like a great idea, though. Good luck with it."

"Does it really?"

The approval and encouragement were sincere, though the conclusion was less so. "Who knows, perhaps there are a lot of people out there that don't know New York ain't the capital of America!" This time Sarah stood no chance of escaping retribution; a road map whacked her mercilessly on the head. "Ouch! You are hitting someone with a headache!"

"Then behave like someone with a headache!" A moment later the last bit of Sarah's earlier comments registered with the would-be travelogue producer. "Hey, I just had a great idea! Why don't you come with me?" she suggested enthusiastically.

Sarah's blank expression conveyed some of the amazement this suggestion inspired. "What, me go with you?" The tone got the rest across nicely.

Elinor nodded. "Why not?"

"Well, for one, you might get people saying funny things about you, too," Sarah taunted.

"Give it a rest, eh? I have apologised twice. Go on, come! You can help me with the text; grammar was never my strong point. And if you are really helpful, I might even let you get 'a you-know-who' quote in. Come to think of it, that might not be a bad idea. It could really impress the Americans – they are pretty fond of old Will."

"I thought you said this was for the English?"

"Did I? Does it matter? Just think about this. We could have a ball, see all the sites, get a great tan, write the book and earn some money. The bonus is all those millions and millions of American fellas."

"You are man mad."

"So what? It's healthier than work mad," Elinor retorted.

"Haven't you forgotten something?"

"What's that?"

"The millions and millions of American women."

"Trust you to come up with the disadvantages! Will you come?"

"I can't, Elinor. I'm sorry."

"Why not?"

"I told you, I have two children to consider. I can't just pack up and leave them for six weeks."

"I know that," Elinor said dismissively. "But they're not babes anymore. Send them to Sweden then board 'em out." If they had been discussing a dog or cat, this might have been acceptable advice. "Better still, I bet your mother would have them for free, wouldn't she?"

"Maybe she would, but won't you want to take Terry – sorry, Tony – with you?"

"What on earth for? He might not even be around by then. Besides, we could have more fun together."

"Don't count on it!"

"Well, think about it," Elinor cajoled as they pulled up outside her flat. "You do have a right to take a holiday, you know."

"I also have responsibilities." But despite all the responsibilities that Sarah could list, Elinor managed to extract a promise from her that she would at least consider it before dismissing it. Then Elinor happily waved farewell, believing that the decision had already been made.

"We can discuss it some more when I bring your prezzies round next week."

Chapter Four

The car parked on yellow lines at the height of the evening rush hour was deceiving. It was not some juvenile being rebellious but a sensible adult trying to fend off disaster, and a whole army of traffic wardens could not have prevented her from doing it, because it was the lesser of three evils – the other two being passing out, or crashing, neither of which should happen to sensible school teachers in public places. Once she felt reasonably safe from all these eventualities, Sarah closed her window very carefully. She still felt awful, and the reflection in the mirror denied none of it, so Elinor was right about that as well: she did look old and haggard, and with her face currently doing a fine imitation of that ghastly grey pallor normally reserved for the seriously ill or the newly released from prison, it was all authentic. She hoped most of it could be put down to the seven-hour headache. There was certainly no happy ending for this day yet. "Just do not die here," she threatened herself as yet another motorist sounded his horn when she tried to re-join the fast-moving traffic. Others took up his cause until there was a mad cacophony of frustration all around her. "Okay, I am sorry!" she bleated defiantly. "I am having a bad day, too! Is there no chivalry around these parts?"

At the very next traffic lights her language was less ambiguous when the car chose to die right in front of the busiest set of traffic lights in the area. Calamity had never been so unkind. A few motorists shouted obscenities, much as if she had done this on purpose just to ruin their day; others honked their horns in some sort of ritual greeting. Neither approach was helpful. If Elinor's knight in shining armour really existed, this was his big opportunity. Predictably, he didn't show up. "Good job *I* am not counting on you," she muttered grimly as she set out in search of a phone to organise her rescue. By now the snow and sleet had given way to rain. "All this rain would probably rust the armour, anyway," she mused.

Rescue eventually came in the form of a distinctly un-chivalrous knight who fixed her car muttering barely veiled threats about maintenance. She signed his form, more interested in getting home to a nice hot bath followed by eight hours of unconsciousness in a warm, dry bed, than heeding warnings from such a miserable prophet of doom.

"And drowned rats do not die of pneumonia in their sleep," she promised herself heroically before sneezing violently. "They die from drowning." Fortunately there had not been quite enough water for that.

In her heart she knew that the bath and bed would have to be downgraded to a shower, two paracetamols, and a five-minute nap, if she was lucky, because whether Elinor understood it or not, children took precedence over everything - even pneumonia. She ordered herself to think about something else for now and Elinor's dotty scheme seemed to fit that slot nicely. Both Elinor and her pupils were way off track in thinking her secret vice was Len Cole; it was much less physical than that, far more cerebral, and she would have defended it as more virtue than vice had anyone ever guessed what it was. But as no one ever had, she had kept the pleasure of daydreaming all to herself. She credited it with saving her sanity, if not her life, several times over the last few years. Daydreaming had supported a nice, simple lifestyle without any risks, and given that her knowledge of psychology had always been pretty basic, she had never even had to worry about the threat of self-programming until recently. Instructions for this guilty pleasure had been predictably precise: *Use sparingly. For amusement on rainy days, or tedious journeys.* There was a cautionary caveat thrown in for good measure: *Not a rehearsal for future events.* And this was a very rainy day, and as it was fast becoming an extremely tedious journey, it seemed okay to air this newest addition to her range right now.

Until today, her most daring daydream had been the one about telling Elinor to mind her own business and succeeding. The most dangerous had been a brief consideration of what it might be like to be married to Len Cole. That particular indulgence had been followed by swift repentance. Even Elinor's American scheme could be nowhere as dangerous as that, so she indulged in the latter with as much abandon as any seriously wet headache sufferer could be expected to muster. Her interest lasted exactly ten minutes before she lost patience with it and abandoned Elinor somewhere in Arizona. That had been happening a lot lately, losing patience, and she knew that was down to the strange restlessness that had crept into her life. It had taken over and spoiled all her simple pleasures. Even daydreaming had lost its usual ability to satisfy her. This unwanted visitor had provoked some interest in psychology, and that of course had initiated the relentless analysis. The analysis had spawned the depression, the depression created the headaches and all the other pains had galloped along in swift succession, just like Shakespeare's battalions had always promised. Like most other uninvited guests, this restlessness had refused to be easily satisfied or removed. She had built her entire life to this point around just getting on with it, so it had been puzzling, and then worrying, to discover that was no longer an option.

A new member of staff had recently asked her what she did in her spare time. That question had worried her and earned him a blank stare. Did people still have spare time? She didn't! There wasn't one moment when she was not mother, daughter, neighbour, teacher, or friend; it was a state of affairs that seemed to indicate somewhere along the way the vivacious being of her daydreams had turned into a frump – and a robot frump, at that! No one needed to tell her that a robot frump's sole ambition was to go to bed each night with a completed worksheet full of nice big ticks against all the required tasks of the day. She had lived that programme for the last nine years at least, and fat lot of good it had done her! How she could have arrived at such a place, when she had only been trying to do was what was best for everyone, was beyond her. Elinor's sarcastic remarks about empty lockers had merely underlined this predicament, and though she had not replied, she had finally understood because Jonathan's little bombshell had found its mark.

All of that would have been bad enough on its own, but an even worse discovery had been made during a recent evaluation of her parenting skills. Two simple facts had illustrated the depth of her problems: first, the person who had laughed a lot was now too busy to smile most days, and second, that person spent so much time on regimental duties that there were precious few moments left to simply enjoy life. The guilt trip that followed these discoveries had only been appeased by a sincere promise to do something to resolve the mess she was in. Like most hasty promises, it had been much easier to articulate than effect; practice still eluded her a full two months later. Elinor's little homily had reminded her of that as well, but the Christmas holidays had always seemed as good a time as any to undergo this miraculous transformation, and she had successfully disarmed all reminders up to today with this platitude. Obviously that could not work for much longer because Christmas was next week, and she was no nearer knowing what to do, or how to do it, in order to achieve her transformation. Revelation clearly didn't come like the mail. She sighed loudly. There were still too many other things to do before Christmas, there was hardly time to plan for, let alone undergo, transformation. Maybe she was a lost cause like Elinor said, because any change that could be conveniently scheduled to happen somewhere between Christmas shopping and carving the turkey had to be pure daydream stuff – the impossible item on this year's to-do list -but if she did get the tick to show she had done it, it had to be more than ritual robotics. This time her shiver was more disgust than chill. A silent pledge renewed her dusty intentions, it would have to do for now. Come January, everything would be sorted! She would be sorted. Everything would be back to normal! After all, this could hardly be as difficult as some of the things she had faced during the last nine years.

It was a bitterly cold September day with hailstones backing up the biting north wind. Few people were out because of the weather. That was good; it meant no one would see their method of moving. A new life started in three days' time with a new job, but first she had to get through today, the end of the old one. She bundled up the girls in their pink jumpsuits and hats, the only bright things in a day of unremitting greyness, and then she strapped them in their pushchair with their favourite toys for company. Hopefully they would play while she loaded the van.

A box van was ample for their move because they only had one piece of furniture left besides beds: her father's desk; everything else had been sold to pay off debts. A passing stranger helped her move the desk, then she struggled alone with the rest. Common sense told her the day would end, but it could not tell her that after it ended, there would always be a third day locked away in a cupboard that rarely got opened. Today could only have twenty-four hours, like any other day, but today was the day she was losing her home, her last shred of respectability, the last solid thing from her old life. Its passing had to be measured in hours, its effects would not. It was hard for her to grasp that every day, someone somewhere, was feeling this bad, because she had never noticed any of them, though she knew people did lose everything. It had simply never happened to her before and now that it had she pledged that it would never happen again. She would never allow herself to be this vulnerable again.

It was late and she was exhausted by the tasks of the day before she collapsed into bed in her new room in their strange, new house. She closed her eyes and waited in vain for sleep to claim her; there was only a myriad dancing images of filthy, bare, floorboards adorned with thousands of dead wood lice lying belly up amid the faded, peeling remnants of long-forgotten decorating trends, to torment her. Worst of all, the pungent smell of stale nicotine embedded in the fabric of the building nauseated her. She wrapped herself tightly in the folds of her duvet to try to shut it out before tears could claim her. Both turned out to be inescapable.

Monday morning the twins start nursery. That was what the calendar warned her in big red letters, though probably nothing could have prepared her for leaving her babies screaming in the arms of complete strangers. Tuesday should have restored her spirits because she started her new job. She had not foreseen it would also double her guilt. There was something writ in the fabric of her being that decreed it might be okay to have to work to support them, but enjoying it was another thing entirely.

That was just as well, because North Green High turned out to be a desperate place even by inner-city standards. Schools in such notoriously tough areas shared a common dilemma: no one with any sense wanted to work there yet they needed the best teachers to make any impact on their students. Unable to afford the luxury of choice, she had secured the North Green job with just twelve months post-qualification experience gained in a nice girls' school in a middle-class area of London. It was no preparation for the harsh realities of life at North Green.

The staff greeted her arrival with a mixture of dismay, alarm, hostility, and black humour. Despite her age, she was the equivalent of a probationer, and they definitely did not need any sort of probationer who needed nursing and supervising; they needed someone who could cope and take on some strain. The head had to be mad for employing her, and by the end of the first week the cynics were already placing bets on how long she would last. The general consensus was a term; the most generous thought no more than a year.

She had thought about walking out nearly every day that first term, but somehow or other she had resisted the lure, mostly because of how much money she owed – and she had no hope of paying any of it back if she failed here. That was the dilemma: insanity or insolvency yet again. What a choice! Was there a choice? One seemed certain, but the other could perhaps be avoided if she could only find a way to stick with it.

Sarah smiled. See, she had done difficult before. No, she had done near impossible before! The pressing question right now was, could she do it again? A wanton thought suggested she should drive and not stop – escape and leave everything behind. It was tantalising for a split second before she dismissed it, sighed wearily, and brushed away the emotion as she forced a reluctant smile in its place. However awful this got, that was not an option. It was not any sort of happy ending at all.

She did at least smile genuinely as memory reminded her she had found a way to stick with it, to cope, to survive and then somewhere along the way that the battle for survival had mellowed into challenge, then opportunity, and then a full-blown love affair. Now she was well into her ninth year at North Green, she still loved it – well, most of the time she did. She would allow today to be an exception, but otherwise she had thrived, and if she had been childless, she knew she would have been content to devote herself to the cause of North Green High for the rest of her days. But the girls were an even deeper love. Lately, it had seemed like these two loves were pulling her apart mentally as well as physically. Elinor did not understand any of that, and chances were she never would. She expected all teachers to be the same as her: being different was outside the rules for teachers as well as adolescents.

Back at the beginning of this tug of war, Sarah remembered thinking the pain would never go out of her life, but it had, and so there had been some sort of happy ending for a while. A line from a poem reminded her of that; it was a line she had repeated so many times over the years that it had assumed the importance of a mantra: "*You must live through a time when everything hurts. You lived through it. It passed!*" It is what she had tried to tell Jonathan today: everything, however awful, eventually passes. One might never understand it, but it passes; it simply has to be endured. She knew you could lose your husband, your home, your good name – everything, in fact – but you could survive. And it was still possible to get a happy ending! However, she had stopped feeling like that recently, so whatever it was she had found back then, she had lost it again but at least she now understood that life wasn't a one-fix event and needed constant attention. That worried her. Constant attention might demand more than she had to give. She could already fill 168 hours a week several times over, but she did understand that transformation and her new happy ending would take time, so she would just have to find the time from somewhere.

Her first attempt at transformation had been going out with Len Cole. It had not provided an answer to her problems. At least she had recognised no one else could provide her answer: she had to be the answer because she was the problem! Even so, accepting that she was regarded as an oddity in an age when conformity was sacred, and prudish when permissiveness was hallowed, was not easy, but it was why everyone else, except Len, thought she was fair game for their personal improvement theories. At least he didn't seem to mind that she was not exactly Miss Popularity. He didn't even seem to mind that she was frequently written off as strange – but then, she thought, perhaps that's because he is exactly the same.

Before the start of this relationship with Len, her social life had consisted entirely of things built around children, either her own or the ones she was responsible for at school, so it was easy to see why the undisputed highlight of each year's social activity was taking the exam classes to see a performance of their Shakespeare texts in town. The girls were too young for this sort of treat, her mother was too canny, and she knew no one else who would watch real Shakespeare with her. Going alone was not an option for her, so these yearly trips had assumed unwarranted importance in her social calendar. Going out with Len had not remedied the lack of Shakespeare, but it did provide an occasional trumpet concert, and if that wasn't perfect, it was a start.

No good thinking about any of it now. She wanted to be rid of her headache, not make it worse, so she drove for a few minutes with a mental restraint fixed firmly around any subject remotely involving happiness. Then her concentration drifted again. Those fleeting images of America had brought to mind the only American she knew, but thinking about Shelagh Phillipson, or Shelagh O'Leary as she had been then, finally resurrected some happier memories. The two of them had shared so many happy times during Shelagh's exchange year in England. Where else but college would an English farmer's daughter meet the upwardly mobile, illegitimate offspring of a dodgy Los Angeles bar owner? Shelagh O'Leary had possessed everything she lacked, and in abundance. And being five years older and therefore five years wiser, she had readily taken to the idea of having an acolyte over which to exercise her superiority. Their very first meeting had established that.

"Where you from, kid?"
"Warwickshire."
"Where's that?"
"The Midlands."

The Midlands was nowhere near California and so it could reasonably be expected to be primitive. "They don't have washing machines in Warwickshire?"

"Of course they do."

"Then how come you can't use one?"

Sarah hadn't replied – she hadn't known how to – so had just shrugged. The American had guessed, "Because Mom did it for you?"

"Maybe."

"No maybe about it. It sticks out a mile. Newly released from the apron strings."

That`s why Shelagh had taken her under her wing and shown her how to work washing machines and taught her other essential student skills – things like how to get a tutor to extend a deadline, how to arrange world peace (which was a regular obsession), and how to live on four pounds twenty a week (which was a permanent necessity). The one thing that Shelagh could not show her was how to keep a boyfriend. "Listen, Sarah," the oracle would urge, "loosen up, honey. This is how it happens these days."

The clipped English reply was predictable. "It might be for others, but not for me!"

"So don't fret if you stay home most nights. Go get yourself on the pill and enjoy yourself. A little romance doesn't have to last a lifetime you know. You are only here three years, so enjoy it! Time enough to start thinking about serious relationships when you have your degree. Might all have been blown up by then anyway. And if we haven't, it's still best to wait, because it's difficult to pick the winners at this stage; they've only just set off. No good catching one with no money prospects, is it? A good marriage depends upon a good bank account." They had agreed about saving the serious relationships for later, but nothing else. "Gee I didn't think anyone our age still thought like you. You are a moral eccentric!" It was a tart remark that seemed to have been pulled out of thin air, though it had stung just as much as if it had been well-considered; ridicule from a friend always hurt more. An open textbook had provided the saving explanation.

"If I didn't know that George Elliott said that first, I might just be impressed," she had responded, and then read aloud, "'Deronda was a moral eccentric.'"

"So what? I recognise a good line when I see one."

"Plagiarist!"

"Not so. Stick around, read a few good books, learn a few useful lines, and then improvise," the unrepentant cribber advised as she bowed to a make-believe audience.

"See, Elinor?" Sarah explained to the empty car. "That's how my little affliction got started." Another fond smile preceded the next deliberately measured comment. "But maybe I won't tell you that!" She almost laughed at that, though she could not laugh at the memory of Shelagh's other big piece of advice that intruded at that moment.

"Forget Tony Chadwick! If he isn't sleeping with you, then he is sleeping with someone else. He is one creepy guy."

Her reply to that advice still haunted her. "He is a perfect gentleman!"

"The prince of darkness is a gentleman."

"Hamlet. And just what is that supposed to mean?"

"Which act? He's no good, believe me," Shelagh said.

"One? No, oh, I don't know. How can you possibly know that? You can't, so I would appreciate you either being quiet or telling me what evidence you have."

"Shit!"

"Whose line is that?

"Funny! I don't want to fall out with you, kid, but ... "

"Then don't. And please stop calling me kid. My name is Sarah."

"Sarah, he got a girl pregnant last year, and ... "

"And what?"

"And abandoned her!"

"I don't believe you. He's not like that. He is the—"

"The only man who has not wanted to take you to bed?" Her nod had been supercilious enough to warrant the reprimand. *"That's why you should be asking yourself, 'Why is he like this with me?'"* she hissed. *"That's why I am telling you to be careful. I know him. He is in my class, and he is a first-rate slime ball."*

"That is Shakespeare?"

"Funny! He will have a reason for doing this. I may not know what it is right now, but I am pleading with you. Don't be stupid."

"I thought I told you, I am not."

"There's more than one way to be stupid, kid; and that's not a quote, just a fact!"

It had turned out to be prophecy.

"I wonder how many more there are?" This sudden proposition brought her back into the present with a jolt – as did the truck driver in front of her slamming on his brakes. She stopped a couple of inches from his bumper. "A lot of them! Pay attention!"

Tony Chadwick had gone home with her the following Christmas. That was not a pleasant memory either. Both her parents had voiced their misgivings, and that had made her angry. She would never take him there again.

She scolded herself. "Okay, stop this now." She switched off the radio and pulled over again. She was less than two miles from home but it was far enough for her to really get into some deeply forbidden territory at the rate she was going. What was happening here? "No happy endings" had done this? Okay, maybe he had a point. Maybe she should think some more about Elinor's dotty American scheme then! Or was that how she had got started on this stuff in the first place? She wiped her hand across her head and examined her face in the mirror again, hoping to find explanation printed there, or at least to discover that she looked a little better. Neither thing was apparent. Maybe she was running a temperature; that would explain this maudlin autopsy of her life. People did strange things when they had a temperature. "It is absolutely no use raking over the past," she told herself gently. "It doesn't change a single thing. And you do have a happy ending." She almost believed it.

She had been a useful girlfriend, of course. Somehow she had kept Tony to his study timetable, helped him with his assignments, read his thesis, and corrected his drafts. She had been so useful that she had failed her own exams. The other factor influencing her failure – the one that had won her the

resit – was her father being killed in a road accident only two weeks before the exams. That had devastated her. Suddenly, and without warning he was gone – no reason, no preparation, no good-bye. Before she could reorganise her thinking her mother was in hospital following a heart attack. Two short weeks had destroyed her safe world.

"That's how the stage was set for my own Shakespearian tragedy, Elinor," she explained sadly, "and the actor waiting his cue played his part to perfection. It was only me who had him cast as the hero." There was no Elinor there, but she said it all the same because she thought it was justification for all the things that Elinor had ever accused her of. "Fortunately for me, my mother recovered," she said soberly, not daring to think what would have happened if she hadn't. She tried once again to force the memories to stop, but they continued to push themselves forward, tumbling from their restraints like men stumbling from shackles: pictures of the first eighteen months of their part-time married life spent renovating their house, scenes of the hard work keeping up at college during the week, and then working all weekend a hundred miles away. She could not deny the memory of how she had allowed no doubts to intrude, because it was true. She had been happy. Nothing had the power to touch that happiness – until Tony had lost his job as a reporter after missing too many assignments. That had plunged them into a spiral of drink-sodden rows and short lived jobs. The day she graduated and managed to get a job immediately had been the day he chose to tell her that he had decided to put their house up for sale. She could still recall that row almost word for word, even though it was so very many years ago. It had been delivered with such practiced cruelty that it had inscribed itself indelibly into her memory. She had loved that house and had mistakenly thought he felt the same, basing her assumption on how he had acted when her mother had bought it for them. The day she had found out she was pregnant, he was telling the truth though.

"Are you crazy? I thought you loved me, and you do something like this at such a time?" The witty reply had died on her lips as he decided. "Well, you will just have to sort it out. Get rid of it. We can't afford it!"

The end had arrived unannounced on a bitterly cold February day, and though it was now more than ten years ago, it too was etched as precisely in her mind as the moment it happened; suspended like some fossil in a frozen landscape, only to be viewed as a relic. She could never allow herself to feel the heat of its emotion again. It was better frozen.

She fastened the twins in their pushchair and set out for the local market. She did not have sufficient money for the bus fare and dinner, and dinner was more important, so the walk was unavoidable. She would not try to persuade herself that she needed the exercise because the evidence of frozen face and fingers begged differently. The house had been cold, but now she really was freezing. She kept on the move. A shortcut through some side streets would cut fifteen minutes off her journey, and then without warning, he was there, sitting in the window of a backstreet cafe holding another woman's hand.

"Please stop this now," she whispered. Jonathan's comments must have resurrected this in defence of his charge. But what if he was right? What if there *were* no real happy endings? Tony was supposed to have been hers, and he had been anything but that. She could never risk that degree of unhappiness ever again. The girls deserved better. She deserved better. Was Len Cole better? That was the crux of this dilemma. Trust Jonathan to rake all this up today of all days. She shivered as she turned the car into her drive. "Forget it! It's Christmas, so just try to enjoy it!"

Chapter Five

Number forty-three was the best lit house in the entire street. Every light in the place was ablaze, but though the effect was very welcoming on such a cold, wet, miserable night, it was not without cost, and it was the cost that bothered its owner, who muttered to herself about "free electricity" and "money growing on trees," as she marched up the drive. She was at the front door before she realised she was on the point of storming into the house all wound up again – yet another bad-tempered outburst in a day already filled with them. It changed her anger to tears. She allowed herself a moment's indulgence because nothing else would suffice, and then she swallowed hard and chastised herself much as she would a naughty child at school. She tried to believe it was not worth getting worked up about a few lights. A nasty memory of last year's winter fuel bills begged to differ.

Alison ran to meet her mother the instant she opened the door and then America, electricity bills, headaches, and all other troubles (including happy endings) had to be shelved as a deluge of information poured forth. It only ended when interrogation took over.

"Is the car fixed? How will we get to swimming in the morning? Are you wet?"

"Just hang on a minute, pet. Yes, I am wet. Yes, the car is fixed, so we can get to swimming just fine. Let me take my coat off. Where is Edna?" Usually Edna was waiting in the hall ready to go home. Tonight she was conspicuous by her absence.

"She had to go home. Jim rang. They have an emergency, a burst or something. We told her we would be okay till you got back. She has only just gone," the child added timorously, sensing that this was not going down too well. Sarah's best frown adequately conveyed the feelings that she was about to spell out, but when she saw Ali's worried face, she closed her mouth. It was better to deal with this later, when she was calmer.

"Letter for you on the desk. Think it's from Nan," Ali said hopefully as she hung around trying to win a smile from her grim-faced parent. She won only the heavy briefcase, but she gamely followed her mother through into the front room while she collected her letter. "Help! Where do you want this thing putting?" she pleaded, almost collapsing under its weight.

"Anywhere. Just put it down." Another irritable instruction, but this time it was followed by swift repentance so Ali got her smile and a kiss before she opened her letter.

"That Mum?" the other twin asked as her sister returned to the living room. Julie was sat at the large dining table surrounded by an enormous pile of magazines, which she was carefully destroying for the cause of collecting suitable material for her latest project. Glue and sticky tape were major supporting acts. Being a perfectionist was not easy, and there was plenty of evidence of Julie's current striving in the vast amount of crumpled rejects scattered around her. Alison looked at her and then at the table.

"Better clean it up, Ju. Mum doesn't look too happy."

A dark scowl met her stare and its owner was about to register protest, so Ali went across to the table. "*We do* want to watch this concert, don't we?" she hissed, staring menacingly into her sister's face.

"Yes, of course we do."

"Then you had better clean it up," she retorted smartly.

"Help me?" her twin pleaded, surveying the mess.

"No way. You made the mess; you clean it up."

The Chadwick twins were ten years old and identical. What made matters worse was that they both had the same short-bobbed hairstyles, which completely ruined the chances of anyone telling them apart who did not know them really well. Since they were first old enough to realise this unique advantage, their favourite game had always been standing side by side absolutely silent, watching various people struggle to decide who was who; alternatively they'd both answer to the same name. This last version of the game only worked with people who did not know them at all, because anyone who did could tell them as soon as they spoke. They might be as near identical as identical gets, but even the same face and hairstyle could not disguise the different personalities underneath. Alison and Julie were only ever known as that by their head teacher, or occasionally by their mother when they were in trouble. Ali and Jules were what they preferred, and so that was what everyone called them. Ali had taken to calling herself Al of late and referring to her sister as Ju, because she reckoned these were more sophisticated titles now that they had reached double figures. But whether one called her Alison, Ali, or Al, she was the eldest child by twenty minutes, and Julie, Jules, or Ju was the younger.

Ali was as boisterous and assertive as befitted her image of what an oldest child should be. She was also the highly creative one and the one who could be moody and difficult to love. By contrast, Julie was quiet and methodical, and she was almost everyone's idea of an ideal daughter because she was loving and kind and very easy to love. She was the serious child, the one with patience and application. Ali might have the dazzling flashes of inspiration, but Julie usually achieved more through sheer persistence. Naturally enough, school had always regarded Julie as the clever child and Ali as the average performer, though their mother knew all too well the restricted perspective that encouraged this attitude: it was the attitude that passing exams and tests mattered more than anything else. At ten years old it had already had a detrimental effect on Ali, who was so used to teachers singing her sister's praises that she had become prone to the odd outburst of jealousy. It was difficult enough explaining the place of academic performance in the grand scheme of things to teenagers. It was nigh on impossible to convince a sensitive, prickly ten-year-old that she was not worth less than her sister because they were different; they simply excelled at different things, and at ten, art counted less on this grand scale of things than did mathematics.

"So why can't I be good at maths as well as art?"

"Maybe you could if you worked harder at it."

Ali had dismissed this advice without a second thought, as her mother knew she would; working harder at things was not the answer she was looking for, and it was a typical teacher's answer. Sometimes it was very obvious that they had this really big disadvantage: their mother was a teacher! "Well, think how boring it would be if we were all good at maths naturally," Sarah had said and Ali had accepted that. It had seemed reasonable. She had no real desire to be good at maths, but it was still difficult for her to understand why teachers found Julie's maths and English more praiseworthy than her drawing and painting. Sarah had tried her best to reassure her on more than one occasion. "I know teachers don't always see the value in being different or doing things differently," she had said kindly, secretly wondering why she always ended up apologising for the entire teaching profession. It was an imperfect world, so why were teachers not allowed to be imperfect on occasion?

"Did Leonardo earn more than you do?"

"Probably. Some artists do and some don't."

"What's the difference?"

"Try and find out," Sarah had suggested, even more kindly.

"Aw, Mum! You tell me to ask questions," Ali pointed out with the sort of impeccable ten-year-old logic that beats most adult reasoning.

"True. Now I am telling you that finding out the answer for yourself is good as well. It might even be fun," Sarah advised, realising that there were some practical advantages to practising on the likes of Michael Davies after all.

"It might be, but I bet you it isn't," Ali had grumbled.

"I dare say you will never know, if you don't find out, will you?"

The struggle with Ali was acceptable because Sarah knew she was right, the same as she knew she was right about the likes of Marcie Hadley and Michael Davies. But then, her job with all of them was essentially the same: to help them develop some balance to their exuberant natures. Being a parent and a teacher had taught her all this, besides which teaching the Jonathan Spicer's of this world was about as difficult as teaching Ali to ask questions!

The girls were in the middle of the silent sulks when she walked in scanning her letter. The noise coming from the television set masked their silence for a short while but when that was switched off the silence became more apparent until Alison protested that she had been waiting for Blue Peter to begin. "It's very educational," she pointed out emphatically, well aware that Blue Peter would score considerably higher with her mother than the pop group she knew would be on the programme.

Sarah forgot about the sulky silence as she dispatched Julie to fetch headache tablets and a glass of water. She swallowed them as the group came on. "I think I will fix dinner," she said resignedly. "Even quiet TV is unbearable."

"You are so square, Mum!"

"I know," she said, kissing the bent head. "And I am glad I am, and so are my ears. Anyway, have you no homework? I thought we had agreed homework first."

"Done it!" Ali declared triumphantly, finding it impossible to disguise the smug note of satisfaction.

"You *have* done it? All of it already?" Sarah asked. Her incredulity was well founded in painful reality. Alison doing homework without any hassle was about as rare an occurrence as snow in the Sahara. "You have done all your homework already?" she repeated, thinking she must have misheard.

"You have said that once already, you know," Ali pointed out in her most offended tone.

"So I have," her mother agreed, still struggling with disbelief. "Are you sure you are being straight with me?"

Ali laughed as she admitted the truth. "But you should see your face," she promised. Then, before Sarah could open her mouth to reprimand her, she explained, "Oh Mum, it's Christmas! No one gives homework at Christmas, ever! So we don't have any."

Sarah's cursory nod was a cover for what she had just heard about Christmas and homework. It was different for eighteen-year-olds. Everyone knew that.

"So …" Alison wheedled, threading her arm through her mother's to delay her entry into the kitchen. This generally meant she wanted a favour. "So, we were thinking that you might let us watch this pop concert at eight o clock tonight," she pleaded waving the newspaper under Sarah's nose.

"I might, eh? Why?"

"Because it's the last day of school, and because it's a Christmas special. You know, the 'once a year' sort of thing, but mostly because you are the best mum in the world."

The best mum in the world was smothered with kisses before she could disagree. She had been outmanoeuvred by a ten-year-old.

Two hours later, dinner had been eaten, the dishes were washed, and both girls were bathed and ready for bed. They sat down to watch their concert as Sarah escaped to her den.

"Okay, you two, I am going to do some marking. Pop concerts do not hold the tiniest bit of appeal tonight, but if I hear any arguing, you will both go to bed immediately. Understood?" Both nodded in unison and settled more comfortably on the sofa with their arms wrapped around each other, an obvious declaration that peace and friendship had been restored. Giggles and whispers provoked her most natural smile of the day. Who could have guessed deliverance would come in the shape of a pop concert?

Sarah's sanctuary from the noise was the front room of their house. It was the only place in the entire house where a body could find guaranteed tidiness and peace and quiet, so she valued it very highly. This room had always been declared off limits to messy activities so they could fool visitors that they led organised lives, but as they didn't have many visitors, and she *did* have a lot of lessons to mark, it had soon assumed the appearance of an academic's study rather than a family living room, and the period writing desk that had belonged to her father had pride of place. A large collection of books, two nearly new armchairs, and a comfy if rather battered sofa completed the décor. It was hardly Ideal Home, but it was comfortable. Ali had christened it Mum's Retreat, and tonight she was definitely in need of one.

Sarah stretched out in her favourite armchair by the fire for a while, her eyes closed as she worked on summoning up enough resolve to tackle the pile of homework calling to her from the desk. A remnant of the mammoth headache still lingered, so it took a lot of resolve to get up and go collect it. This would tick one of those last two remaining boxes of the day. If she had anything left after finishing it, she would tackle the pile of ironing, and if not, it would have to wait until morning. That wasn`t good, but it was the best she could manage after a day like today.

She had barely started on the first book when the phone rang. "Hi, you busy?" Elinor queried, though she continued without allowing time for any answer. "If you really want to come with me, we should start planning right away."

It took a moment for Sarah to place the context of this conversation, but as memory supplied the missing details, she smiled and with some justifiable measure of exasperation pointed out facetiously, "Elinor, I have hardly had time to do anything since I left you!" This was only a slight exaggeration. "I had a breakdown - car, not mental – though it was very nearly that as well I suppose! Anyway, I have had no time to think about your scheme." She wisely chose to leave "dotty" out of it.

Elinor was unimpressed by the breakdown and clung tenaciously to her point. "So how long does it take for you to decide yes or no?" Explaining to Elinor about this was on a par with explaining to Ali about maths and art. When it seemed Sarah might have succeeded, there was a short silence while her friend reconsidered her strategy. "Tell you what: think about it some more over the weekend, and then we will discuss it when I bring your prezzies round Christmas Eve." This would coincide with Mary Reid's arrival for Christmas but as the two things seemed unconnected, Sarah did not object. Her mother was fond of Elinor and Elinor was fond of her, and this might be the only chance the two of them would have to catch up with each other over the holidays as Elinor would doubtless have her usual exhausting social schedule. The call ended with Elinor issuing yet another warning about empty lockers and wasted lives when she realised what Sarah had been doing.

Saturday started out as planned. Sarah took the girls into the city to do their Christmas shopping. They had six people to buy presents for: Nan,

Edna, Rachel their best friend, Jen Wade their next-door neighbour, each other and A. N. Other. Their mother was grateful it was only six because by the time they had reached the third person on their list, she was ready to desert them. Arguing about what to buy for each person took time! When they left the restaurant after a late lunch, she warned them that next year they would shop earlier, and they would shop differently because her nerves were not up to this. She sighed with real relief when they announced they had finished but that turned out to be a bit premature because they had some money left, and that meant their last port of call had to be Hamley's to dispose of it.

Hamley's had become such a firmly established part of the girl's Christmas ritual that it could never have been omitted. It was as important to them as Christmas dinner was to the adults, so Sarah could only plod along wearily in their wake, laden like a human pack horse and grunting and puffing like one, while they skipped and pushed their way through the crowds on Regent Street. Even greater crowds thronged the toy store, and if they had procrastinated in all the other shops, in here that paled in comparison, because here they acted as though they were conducting a major shopping survey, with everything needing to be tested. And Hamley's had a *lot* to test. After an hour Sarah was ready to leave; her feet ached and her head matched. Pleas to hurry up had no effect whatsoever, and it was only when she threatened to abandon them that they made their choices. One mammoth queue and two purchases later, it was finally back to the tube and home.

Her recovery was by no means complete when Len rang to check the arrangements for that evening. She could hardly tell him she had forgotten all about his concert! She did rather hope his niece would not have been available at such short notice, but Len had sorted that out as well, so she had to finalise the arrangements or admit she didn't want to go. She finalised the arrangements. He called for her a little after six thirty, and though she was a little more recovered, she was still heartily relieved they were going someplace where she could sit down, relax, and listen to some soothing music. It turned out to be anything but soothing; though that was probably just as well because it kept her awake.

They arrived back much later than he had promised but that provided her with a real reason to not invite him in: it had been a long day and she had to get up early in the morning, etc. He looked less than pleased, but he did not pursue the matter; simply waited sullenly in the taxi while his niece collected her things, so that he could drop her off at home.

Sarah locked the front door behind them just as she remembered she had forgotten to discuss the school gossip with him. Too late now. She could do it before next term. There was no hurry.

Chapter Six

Father Christmas arrived early Christmas Eve in the shape of Elinor wearing a daring black party frock and a funny hat. It was freezing cold but she had only a thin wrap and gloves to keep her warm. She was carrying an enormous bag of presents. The hat and presents were disposed of in seconds. A small file took longer; it contained brochures and pamphlets about every place in America that Elinor had ever dreamt of, so even though she had not planned on staying long, the girls easily encouraged her because this was her number-one obsession, and her pursuing it left them free from the threat of bedtime for a little longer. Their reprieve had lasted a full ninety minutes before they were careless enough to make too much noise.

"Hell, is that the time? I should have been in Wimbledon an hour ago," Elinor said, and after wishing them all a hasty Merry Christmas she whipped her wrap around her shoulders as competently as any magician about to perform a disappearing trick while producing a last-ditch attempt to convince her chosen travel companion about the merits of her scheme.

Explaining to Elinor why *wanting* to go was not the same as being *able* to go was impossible so Sarah patted her benignly much as she would the girls when she wanted to show sympathy for one of her tough decisions.

"Well?" Elinor demanded, brushing off the pat. "Will you come?"

This time the answer was delivered with no frills. "No."

"You don't want to come to America for six weeks? There's even more wrong with you than I thought!" Elinor exclaimed, wagging a warning finger.

"I did not say that! It's not that I don't *want* to come," Sarah admitted, chancing another attempt at the explanation. "I'd love to come, if—"

"If, if, if!" Elinor's patience had never been great. "Do you know how many times you say that? No? Well, it's a lot," she muttered sullenly. "A fraction ahead of 'maybe', and that should be banned as well." Then she brightened as she added, "What did old Will say? *'If all the world were paper.'*"

"Nice try," Sarah said with a grin, patting Elinor's shoulder again. "But I think you've got a mite confused. *'If all the world were paper'* is not

Shakespeare. '*Talkest thou to me of ifs*'" she offered hopefully. "Now that's Shakespeare. Richard III. But keep trying –you are getting there."

Elinor glared at her and snatched her bag from the outstretched hand. "Well, whatever it is, I don't need Will or anyone else to tell me there aren't any 'ifs' or 'buts,' or even 'maybes' for that matter, that you can't deal with, *if*," and she stressed the word, "*if* you want to. What is it you are so fond of saying? No can'ts, just won'ts! And it would be good for the girls to have some time away from you. I bet your mother would love to have them stay, wouldn't you, Mary?"

Mary Reid was startled into life by this unexpected inclusion in the conversation. She dropped the brochure she was looking at and nodded. "Of course, but that would depend on whether Sarah wanted to go, or not," she added thoughtfully. Mary was no academic, but she did possess the sort of wisdom that sometimes eludes those who are more cerebrally focused, and she did not want to ruin Christmas.

"Of course," Elinor agreed calmly, her heart pounding all the same. The three of them looked at each other.

The schemer closed her pitch carefully. "See, that's the first 'if', and the rest can be sorted out just as easily," she promised, nodding at Sarah while pulling on her gloves. "I bet the next 'if' is, '*if* I had the money,' right? And that's easily solved, too. Get a bank loan, like me. At least then you will have a legitimate reason for staying in all next winter while you repay it."

"Go to your party!" Sarah admonished firmly.

"Promise me then that you will think about this seriously."

Mary Reid offered her farewell to Elinor as she left to take a drink upstairs for Julie. After Mary was out of earshot Elinor hissed, "And apart from all that, the best reason I can think of for you coming is simply that you need a break – a *real* break, not an afternoon out with Len or a day away from marking exercise books!" This familiar rhetoric continued all the way to the front door, and though Sarah was still nodding, she was trying to nudge Elinor through it, so that if her mother came down, she would not overhear any of these references to Len Cole. Once Elinor got started on this subject it was impossible to predict what she would say next, and there were some things Sarah would rather not have to explain right now. She gave one push too many. "Will you stop doing that!" Elinor protested.

"I am agreeing with you!"

"That's what's making me nervous. I am only used to you being plain awkward."

"Are you going to this party or not?"

"I'm serious, Sarah! Have you looked in the mirror recently? Don't bother – I'll tell you. You still look awful!"

"Thanks! There's nothing like flattery from your friends to feed your ego!"

"Well," Elinor continued, unabashed and unrepentant, "those are either big grey bags under your eyes, or you have taken to wearing eye shadow in some very strange places. It's Christmas, Sarah. You are supposed to sparkle!"

Despite the instruction not to, Sarah peered in the hall mirror.

"She's right love," Mary observed, catching the tail end of the conversation as she came downstairs.

"Whose side are you on?" Sarah asked sternly.

Elinor beamed at Mary, hoping to encourage further support. She had been counting on this intervention all along.

"No one's. I'm just saying Elinor is right, love: you do work far too hard, and you do need a break, just like everyone else."

"Before you two start falling out," Elinor said quickly, sensing Sarah's growing disapproval, "there's an even better reason why you should come." They both looked at her curiously. "I don't want to go alone," she laughed, then turning towards the door waved with a last *swoosh* of her wrap, and shouted, "Merry Christmas!" Then she was gone.

Sarah closed the door behind her and shook her head. She threaded her arm through her mother's and led the way back into the den. "Is she not the most precious person we know? Well, perhaps except the Lady Marion. Do we collect these people, or do they collect us? What do you think?"

"I don't know, but I do know Elinor is right, love. I didn't say it in front of her, but you really don't look at all well. I am worried about you. If you think this holiday would do you some good, perhaps you should think about going." Mary had offered this bit of counsel while plumping up some innocent cushions: it gave her comment a certain studied innocence. Shakespeare devotees were not the only ones with dramatic ability. "And you must know that I would be absolutely thrilled to have the girls come and stay. You do know that, don't you?"

Now there were two people pushing her. It seemed impossible to give in to either after making such a determined stand against the whole thing: daydream material should not translate into reality; it should not, could not materialise!

Elinor was back Boxing Day armed with fresh ammunition. She produced this out of her handbag much like a magician might produce a pack of cards and although hers landed on the floor in an untidy pile, the drama value was equally high. She followed that up with a landslide of information about must-see attractions until she had scattered literature across the entire floor.

"I don't recall ever saying I was going," Sarah protested, concerned that Elinor was still not grasping this rather important detail.

"You will. Believe me, you will. Not only is this the greatest opportunity to ever come your way: the holiday experience of a lifetime, but it is also going to be one of the cheapest holidays you ever had as well. Now beat that!" she dared. "I don't think you can!"

Sarah moved to her favourite armchair; she had no need to watch her back from here. She kicked off her shoes and curled her legs up beneath her, "Fine, you carry on, but I am telling you the same thing that I tell all double glazing salesmen: my listening does not mean I am buying."

A half hour stretched into an hour and when Mary knocked on the Retreat door over an hour later, Elinor was still busy scribbling figures and attempting vastly complicated calculations without the aid of a calculator. Sarah waved for her to come in and she managed to clear enough space on the sofa for her to sit down just as one of Elinor's vast computations was coming to an end. They both listened respectfully.

"So what are you waiting for?" Elinor pleaded with all the passion she could muster: all magic tricks having failed. "Say you will come. Please!"

"For once I agree with all you have said. *But*, agreeing with you still doesn't mean I can," Sarah said quietly, "end of story." This limited explanation did not satisfy Elinor and she pushed her point until she earned Sarah`s snappy admission. "Because I cannot possibly afford it, that's why – even at this remarkable bottom-drawer price! This is just another holiday for you. It would be the only holiday I could afford to take until I was fifty! I am sorry, but it is simply impossible. There will be other years and other trips. Write a book about Scotland or Wales - I might be able to afford that. Thank you for thinking of me, but it is quite out of the question, so forget it, please?"

Elinor nodded miserably.

"Would you go if you could afford it?" Mary Reid asked suddenly. "If the girls didn't want to go on this school trip, and if you could afford it, would you go?"

Sarah was taken aback by the seriousness of this unexpected question, though she answered it as evenly as she could, "I might … apart from the roof needing fixing." It seemed a reasonable enough reason to her.

"So if the roof were to last another year, would you go?" Mary persisted.

"What is this about?"

"I am saying, if it is only a matter of money, I will give you the money." Elinor nodded delightedly; this was better than even she had hoped for. "Because Elinor is right, love," Mary continued seriously. "You *do* need a holiday."

"Perhaps I do, mother, but there are holidays and holidays. What Elinor is suggesting is likely to cost an arm and a leg – no, make that *both* arms and legs – and I will not take your money for that. The same amount of money would take all of us on holiday to Devon for a week, and do the roof, and …"

"Sarah," her mother said raising both hands to her face and shaking her head to communicate her frustration with her daughter`s intransigence, "I am not offering to pay for the roof, or a holiday for all of you in Devon. I am offering to give you the money to go on this trip with Elinor, if you want to go."

"But why?" she asked naively.

"Because Elinor is not the only one who is worried about you, and because I am a selfish old woman who would love to have her granddaughters all to herself for a whole summer." Mary's waspish wit made the more difficult parts of her reason sound acceptable.

Her daughter kissed her cheek affectionately. "You don't have to pay me for that!" she pointed out. "But you are a treasure for offering, you know? A serious treasure."

Mary shifted in her seat and looked a little embarrassed by all this praise in front of an audience. "The trouble with serious treasure is that no one ever seems to use it! Folks put it in bank vaults or lock it away somewhere safe. I don't want to be serious treasure if you do that to me. Please use me. Let me have the girls for the summer – if they will come, of course."

"Of course they would come, but are you sure? Six weeks is a long time, and two ten-year-olds can be quite a handful. My two can, anyway. They are not angels all the time."

"Then I have some relevant experience! Now, you had better give Elinor your decision."

"Much against my better judgement, and providing you can keep this below £1500, *and* if Mum will lend me the money – no, I am not accepting a gift – then I will come."

Mary nodded her immediate agreement. Elinor threw a whole pile of leaflets in the air; victory was never going to be a quiet affair for her. "Ready or not," she shrieked, "America; here we come!"

Chapter Seven

Elinor fully expected that being back at school would be boring, so it should not have depressed her when she found it was, but it did. "Nothing ever changes here," she moaned the very first day back. "Well, nothing except the faces, and they only change once a year. Nothing else *ever* changes! Nothing exciting ever happens. Just endless, boring days in another endless dull year! Every single day the same! I guarantee you the only different thing that will happen this term is that we both get a year older! Depressing, ain't it? Everything else will stay exactly the same: same boring old subjects, same boring old problems, same boring old staffroom, same boring old John."

Sarah risked pointing out that America would not be the same, or boring, but Elinor dismissed these reassurances on technical grounds. "I am not talking about holidays here – I am talking about all the time we waste in this dump! The holiday isn't till July, and you are thirty-five before then. Worse still, I am thirty-nine before then! Our life is passing us by! Why do we have to waste it being bored here?"

"I am not bored here."

"Well, I am! Terminally! Why do I have to suffer like this?" Sarah`s reply had not been offered maliciously or even facetiously, but Elinor glared at her as balefully as if it had. "Thanks for the support! You were depressed last term, so what made you feel better?"

"Was I? Did you really think that? I just thought I was …"

Elinor pursued this sudden reticence, thinking that it might conceal something but not for a moment guessing the importance of the *something* so hurriedly censored at the moment of disclosure.

"It's not important," Sarah mumbled, not concerned about misleading information for once, simply overanxious to cover her blunder. She had never told anyone about her restlessness, or the "meaning of life" inquiry, so she saw no reason to now, when it had all been sorted. "You wouldn't believe me if I told you," she added evenly.

"Why not?"

"Just wouldn't," she promised, knowing that Elinor would be expecting it to be the same sort of malaise that she was prone to when there was neither a man in her life nor Christmas parties to look forward to. Explaining her problem might take some time – in fact, it could turn out to be a whole re-education process. It was much better to save it for another day when she was not so tired but Elinor was not about to be denied her education so easily, so she added irritably, "It really is nothing dramatic I was confused for a while."

"Confused? What does that mean?"

Sarah supplied the dictionary explanation mechanically.

"I know that! And so?"

"So, I was getting pretty stressed about my life."

It was too much to hope that Elinor could resist saying she had known as much, but it was her determination to know how Sarah had resolved this difficulty that produced the shocking disclosure.

"I think I prayed about it," Sarah finally replied. She might as well have said she had consulted a large standing stone in the middle of nowhere.

"You think you *what?*" Elinor sneered derisively. Sarah repeated her answer more slowly.

"Yes, yes, I heard you. Whatever possessed you to do such a thing? I didn't know you were religious."

"I'm not. But I had tried most other things, and someone suggested it might help. It seemed worth a try. I needed help from somewhere, that's for sure."

"And did it work?" Elinor asked a mite curiously.

"Do you know what? I think it did. Well, I was able to think straight again, that's for sure. So, when I had reorganised my life and changed my priorities, it seemed only natural to count my blessings."

Elinor looked at her in amazement. The extended explanation had been offered without emotion or apology, but it had rendered her speechless all the same. That gave some momentum to the imparter of such wisdom to add more.

"Reorganising helped some, but do you know what? I think it was counting my blessings that helped most, so I made myself count them over and over again, until I felt better."

"That's really it?" Elinor did not have to say, "I don't believe you" – it was implicit in her tone. Why she had ever thought Sarah would have anything sensible to say on any subject, other than her blessed Shakespeare, was beyond her. She gestured that she considered Sarah to be seriously short of something in the upper reaches department and added, "Right now I don't have any blessings to count; so maybe that's why I am so fed up," she grunted in disgust.

"That's not true."

"Yes, it is! I am as bad as you are right now: no man, so I'm boring like you, and no parties to go to so I'm as depressing as you."

As this was the term of mock exams, the school play, and the run-up to the real exams in May, Sarah felt that should be enough to prevent anyone from being bored. She was trying to hint at something along these lines when she suggested, "Why not concentrate on school, then?" As encouragement it failed miserably; as fuel for an explosion, it worked admirably.

"Are you mad? Why would I want to do anything so stupid?"

"Because the exams will be here before you know it, and summer will be right behind them. And if exams come so quickly, then so will our holiday."

Elinor shook her head in total disgust while the other half of the duo gave some serious thought as to how they could possibly survive six weeks together without war breaking out.

The reorganisation that had been achieved with such little disruption over the two-week Christmas break had simply been called "things to improve my life." That had sounded slightly better than just another list of things to do, and remarkably she had felt lighter with every item she had ticked off. Bedtime reading with the girls had been a big hit from day one. She had also made a promise to take time to exercise more regularly. Regular adult social life had definitely needed more work, so Len had been awarded three more dates during the break. And then of course there was the unexpected item of the American trip to plan. The girl's disappointment about the school trip to Sweden had lasted only as long as finding out about a possible summer with Nan.

"What, at her house? Not here?"

"Yep, at her house."

"And we can all sleep in the sky room?" Ali sang, dancing around the kitchen.

"Well you two will, unless Nan builds an extension before then." The difficult bit had been telling them she wasn't going.

"But what will you do, Mum?" Julie wailed. "We can't leave you here on your own." Information on the American trip had not yet been declassified. But when Sarah informed them she would not be coming it was greeted with glee by Ali.

"Of course we want to go to Nan's," Ali shouted, swinging dangerously on the back of a chair as a way of expressing her delight at the thought of any trip anywhere minus her parent. "And the sky room will be ace!"

The admonition for Al to stop swinging, because they didn't want any broken bones preventing this visit, went as unheeded, as did the reminder about occasionally using something other than `ace` to express approval. Julie merely conceded, "We will love it, Mum, if you will be okay."

Even so, the disclosure about the American trip met with a mixed response. "We don't mind," Julie said, threading her arm through her mother's in her customary way. "You go with Elinor."

The balancing act wanted to know where they would be going, and after she had sat down with some dignity on the very same chair that had been in danger only a minute earlier, she had her answer. Her mother`s confession, "All over the place," was greeted by a thoughtful silence.

"Great! Do you think Nan will let us ride every day?" Julie asked, filling the space left by her sister. She was far more interested in the riding stables at the end of Nan's lane than any trip to America.

"If you save your money, she might," Sarah offered absently, watching the struggle in the silent twin.

"Are you going to Disney?" Ali finally asked bluntly.

"No. We are only going to the Everglades in Florida."

"That's okay, then." she declared cheerfully. "I never wanted to go there."

Sarah was so grateful for such easy compliance that in a moment of excessive generosity, she promised them that next year, their final year in junior school, she would find the money for both of them to go on the school trip, wherever it went – Disney included. That satisfied even Ali. They rarely got such unconditional promises from their parent, and she had every intention of making the most of this one. Until then, they had Nan's to look forward to this summer.

As city dwellers all their lives, any chance the girl`s had to visit their Nan in her tiny cottage was like a trip to their very own Magic Kingdom, a kingdom with hardly any traffic but lots of very old, odd houses – to say nothing of rolling fields to walk through, stiles to climb over, and woods to explore, none of which was available to them where they lived. Nan's kingdom was populated by people with funny accents and odd clothes, but impressive as all these things were, none of them could compete with the special room in Nan's attic and the riding school down the lane. Despite this, Nan always came to them simply because they had three bedrooms and she had only one, other than that very special room in her loft. In reality this sky room was not a room at all; it was nothing more than a basic loft conversion minus the stairs, and it had stayed a half-finished project since Sarah's divorce until an enterprising village joiner had come up with the novel idea of a fixing an upright ladder against a wall as a means of easy access, provided one was nimble enough. It was a bit like climbing into a tree house. All of existence was ordered differently in this sky room. Adults had to walk stooped over to avoid the sloping walls, or risk banging their heads. And even they had to fold their clothes into treasure chests, or else leave them scattered on the floor. Everybody had to sleep on mattresses on the floor, or the floor itself, because there was no space for a proper bed. Best of all, Ali reckoned if they pulled the mattresses under the skylight, they would be able to lie in bed and look up at the stars. Not that they had ever done that, but she was eager to put her theory to the test, and she even volunteered to give it a trial run in the half-term holidays.

"Bet you don't get to sleep anywhere near as exciting as the skyroom," Ali pointed out one night as Sarah finished the bedtime reading. "Hey, Jules, we can play Peter Pan! Jules, you awake? You can be Wendy, and I will be Peter fighting the pirates."

"I don't like pirates," came the sleepy reply from the next bed.

"Al! You haven't been listening to a single word I've read, have you? You have been daydreaming!" Sarah protested, tickling the offender mercilessly until she begged her to stop.

"Yes, I have! Stop it! Hook has just captured Wendy and the Lost Boys, so stop, please!"

"I spend half an hour reading to you both. Jules falls asleep, and you spend it daydreaming about Nan's skyroom!"

"Only some of it," Ali said, snuggling down beneath her duvet. "The rest I listened to. I like the bit about walking the plank best. Perhaps I can make Julie walk a plank across the skyroom hole!"

"Ali!"

The bedtime reading turned out to be the most popular of all the changes she had made during that Christmas makeover, and by February it was still working so well that it seemed like it had been part of their life forever. The only downside was the intrusion of Nan's skyroom into every story they read: Peter Pan, Heidi, and most recently the Water Babies had all ended up as a potential source of new games to enhance their summer adventure.

Expectations for the adult trip were not so straightforward. Elinor had been sure it would be easy to hire a motor home, the reality had turned out to be a little more complex.

The Chadwick doorbell rang insistently late one freezing February evening, and Sarah rushed down to answer its demands, anxious to prevent whoever was out there from waking Ali, if not the entire street.

"Where have you been? It's freezing out here!" Elinor demanded petulantly as she stumbled over the step.

"Was I expecting you?" Sarah asked as she took the proffered cold coat from her unwanted guest at the same time as she reminded Elinor that there were children in bed here. Both matters were dismissed peremptorily.

"No, you weren't expecting me, but this is important. We have a problem." Elinor confessed, handing over her scarf and boots as well. It already looked like more than a five-minute chat.

"Is this a quick visit? I am trying to mark my papers," Sarah enquired, hoping to make that clear, but she had left the door open to the den, and Elinor had already settled herself in an armchair by the fire before she could stop her.

"Oh, is that all. Well forget papers," Elinor observed as she drew her chair nearer to the flames to warm her hands. "They can wait. We have a *big* problem."

It turned out no one would let them drive a hired motor home across the country from one coast to the other and leave it at the other side. Some of Elinor's solutions were plain scary. "One, we take a tent and hike across ..."

"No way! I am not, under any circumstances, taking lifts from complete strangers. Forget it! It`s daft and it's dangerous. It's just plain stupid!"

"Okay, okay, calm down," Elinor said soothingly. "I get the message. There are alternatives."

"Good! If they don't entail hitchhiking, I will listen. If they do, forget it – I am not interested."

"Option number two," Elinor said calmly, "is that we work out a network of half a dozen hire firms to get us from New York to California."

"Are you mad? I thought this was supposed to be a break. It sounds more like a recipe for a nervous breakdown. Let's forget the entire thing. It's impossible."

"Wait a minute. There is one more option." If Sarah had been looking carefully, she might have seen the smirk of triumph before Elinor exclaimed, "We buy a camper!" She made it sound as simple as if she were suggesting they buy a newspaper.

The coughing and spluttering this idea provoked were self-explanatory. "Have you any idea how much these things cost?" Sarah demanded.

All opposition was dismissed on the grounds that it was going to cost a lot to hire one, and this way they might even save money. That seemed highly unlikely to Sarah without further explanation. "Hear me out, huh? You mentioned you wanted to get as far as northern California to visit what's-her-name. Shelagh Phillips, from your college days?"

"And?"

"And didn't I hear you say that her husband has his own business, his own *used car business?*"

"Oh no, we can't," Sarah said, shaking her head, realising exactly where it was that Elinor's train of thought was heading.

"Why not? I presume he knows about cars if he sells them, and motor homes are almost cars. Come on, Sarah, he must have some contacts in the trade. Yes? So, we ask him to help us buy a second-hand camper, at trade price if possible. Then if we finish our trip there maybe he will help us sell it as well. And that's how we will get across the states without any hassle, or lifts." She emphasised the last point. "And we might even undercut the cost of hiring."

Sarah hurriedly explained that when she had said she would like to visit her friend, she meant call one day and take them out to dinner, nothing more. Elinor sighed and looked at her much as a biologist might examine a strange specimen under a microscope. "Have you told her about this?" For once the answer was what Elinor wanted. "Then isn't it worth just checking it out? This woman might be waiting for you to visit her. It could be all she prays for, day and night, year in and year out."

Despite having been manipulated, Sarah agreed to write and ask if they could visit, because she did remember the numerous occasions Shelagh had invited her to do exactly that.

"And the van?" Elinor prompted.

"That as well, I suppose. But no mention of getting it at trade price, and if he says no, we forget all about it? Agreed?"

"Agreed!"

"Do you really understand how much these things cost? Even second-hand ones cost the earth. How on earth do you propose we raise that sort of cash? And don't you dare mention my mother."

"As if I would. Finance is all taken care of. I shall take out a second mortgage on my flat. I owe virtually nothing, and it's worth far in excess of what I paid." Seeing Sarah's alarmed expression, she continued. "Calm down, it's only a short-term loan. When we get back, we will have the cash from the sale, so we can work out what it has cost us, split that in half, and pay back the entire loan in one go. Might even make a profit. See? Simple."

"What if we write it off?"

"That's cheerful!"

"It's called being realistic!"

"No, it's not. It's called being pessimistic! You are supposed to be the optimist. If we write it off – which we won't – but if we do, we claim on the insurance like everyone else. That's what insurance is for, isn't it?" For once this seemed like such impeccable logic that there was no argument. "Nothing is going to stop me going to America this year, even if I have to walk."

By the middle of April when Summer Term began, Elinor owned a motor home, and most of the arrangements for its disposal were also in place. They were to collect the camper in New York, and Dave would sell it for them in California. Shelagh had turned out to be almost as excited as Elinor had forecast, and as Elinor was happy to spend a few extra days with the Phillipson's to enable these transactions to be carried out, everyone was more or less happy. Sarah still had days when she had her doubts.

"The girls really want to go to Mum's."

"So that's good, isn't it? What's wrong?"

"Nothing is wrong. It's just that six weeks is a long time." She looked across at Elinor's serious face and managed a half smile. "I am not sure I can do it now," she admitted wryly. "I have never been away from either of them for as much as a night before."

Elinor snorted derisively. "You are joking me! Your children are ten years old and you have never been apart from them for one single night? *Never?* Do they not stay at friends?"

"Ali would, but Julie won't, so they don't. Their friends stay here."

"And Julie wants to go to your mother's?" Sarah nodded. "Then it's going to do them both good, and you as well! They are not babies anymore, and they are going to your mother's in Warwickshire on a fully supervised holiday, not a do-your-own-thing, self-catering package to Timbuktu. What can happen?"

Sarah shook her head. She was quite sure Al might rather like the self-catering package to Timbuktu, but she didn't say anything. Elinor would not understand her worries about her mother coping with Al.

"You are seriously weird!" Elinor warned.

"No, I'm not! I am a mother."

"Same thing, isn't it?"

By June the stress levels in the Chadwick household had been running at danger level for a couple of months. Those extra exam classes Sarah had taken on when Danny Massey died had exacted a heavy toll on her patience. The twins knew all about exam pressure and its effects, because both visited their home every year, but even they thought this year was worse than usual. Ali had been keeping a low profile for weeks, including doing all her homework without argument, hoping to save herself from the increasingly unpredictable consequences of her mother's stress levels. Perhaps predictably, most of the Christmas changes had been jettisoned by the beginning of the exam season; only the bedtime reading remained, and even that had suffered. It was usually Sarah who fell asleep after two or three paragraphs these days; Ali had to wake her.

It was this extra pressure Elinor was moaning about during the drive home after the last of the A-level exams. "You are never going to make it to America if you carry on like this! We still have GCSEs to go yet. Damned inconvenient of Danny, packing it up like that!"

"I don't suppose he had much choice."

"How do you know?" Elinor demanded. Sarah felt it was fairly safe to presume no one actually wanted to die – well, no one as young as Danny; he was only fifty-four. "If I was teaching Michael Davies, I might," Elinor pointed out truculently. "Like I said, it was damned inconvenient of him. If he hadn't died, John would not have been able to impose on your good nature. You are a pushover for a hard-luck story, you know! You should have told him what to do with his classes."

"Too late now. Besides which, Michael is not my biggest problem right now."

Even Elinor could not mask her surprise at such a declaration. "So who is?"

Sarah obligingly explained her concerns about Jonathan Spicer and his declining performance, and the fact that nothing she had said or done had made any difference.

Elinor had asked, "And why is Michael Davies better than that?" before she realised she was breaking her own rule here – the one that said, never ask about Michael Davies because it always ends in a dispute.

"Michael is much better than that. In fact, I don't really have any problems at all with him right now. He is a reformed character."

"That's why he was in detention last night, I suppose?"

"I didn't say he had become an angel," Sarah corrected. "Just that I didn't have any problems with him. Neither does Geoff Slater, Hazel Shore, or Ben Shepherd."

"Geoff hates him. So why you four?"

"Just brilliance, I suppose," Sarah said with a laugh. "Sheer brilliance."

"Maybe that covers you and Geoff, but come on – Hazel and Ben, brilliant? I do not think so. There must be some other reason, so come on, give."

"I thought you didn't like listening to tales of woe about Michael."

"I don't, but you said this wasn't one, so get on with it. Put me out of my misery -persuade me that Santa Claus lives, fairies dwell at the bottom of your garden, and Michael Davies is a model student."

"I didn't say that, either." Sarah admitted laughing, but she went on to explain how she had confiscated a photograph of a bookcase that Michael had insisted he had made for his mother last Christmas.

"Michael Davies's mother reads books?" This was even more shocking than fairies at the bottom of the garden.

Sarah disregarded the sarcasm and continued the tale of how she had shown the photograph to Geoff, his woodwork teacher, who had been sure that this was some sort of wind-up because the bookcase looked very good.

Elinor said, "Now that sounds more like Geoff."

"He checked it out with Mrs Davies, and it was exactly what Michael had said it was."

"So how did that develop into the entente cordiale?"

"Geoff got permission to fix him up with a work placement. It's not usual before exams, but it could hardly damage his chances; the mocks proved he didn't have any. I suppose we were offering John the equivalent of three weeks of Utopia," she mused. "Three critical weeks without Michael Davies in school. How could he refuse?"

"Geoff wasted a good contact on him! So did he blow the place up?"

"If you really want to know, he was good! He got there on time every day, and he worked hard. They were so impressed with him that they have offered him an apprenticeship, provided he passes four GCSEs. He needs them for the day release."

"Of which English is one?" Elinor said, finally slotting all the pieces of this puzzle together.

"Maths, woodwork, and ADT seemed to be the most appropriate others."

"Proper little Machiavelli, aren't you too?" Elinor jibed. The response was the denial she expected. "Could be a one-day wonder," she warned, "How long has he been back?" A snort confirmed her position when she heard it was his third week. "I rest my case. Come tell me he has changed when he has managed a whole term! I won't be putting any money on it! Anyhow, if he is that good, how come Geoff had never seen any evidence of this talent in class?"

"Because even Geoff admits that making the simplest of shelves is not going to test anyone's skill to that extent. Maybe he was bored in woodwork, the same as everywhere else. Maybe we have all failed Michael; we have all written him off as a failure, and he isn't. Admittedly he has some big problems, but we have failed to show him the relevance of education to helping him use his talent. I think education has failed Michael Davies all along the line."

"And now it's not?"

Sarah had to admit she couldn't say that. "All I know is now he has a vision, he might just produce the work to make the vision a reality. That has to be an improvement. Can you not allow him that?"

"Will he pass, though?" Elinor's question was both harsh and unrepentant.

"I don't know that, either. I can't read the future, even though you keep expecting me to. I am a teacher, not a clairvoyant. Michael has an awful lot of work to make up, and not much time in which to do it."

Elinor snorted again and looked away in disgust. "And you have been helping him?"

"Isn't that what we are there for?"

"Like I said, we'll see if it lasts first."

The evening following the very last exam, Elinor invited herself to dinner on the pretext of finalising their itinerary. It was a little more than three weeks to the holidays and they were still debating what to include and what to leave out, so agreement on the itinerary was now a matter of some urgency. At least Ali went to bed happy, having established that Disney had still not been included. Julie had simply kissed them both goodnight and followed her sister upstairs, half listening to the plans for a new game in the skyroom based around Alice falling down the rabbit hole, and half dreaming about riding ponies every day for six weeks.

"So how did the kids do today?" Elinor asked as she flopped on the sofa in the living room, waiting for Sarah to serve up dinner. There was no answer, so she walked to the kitchen door and repeated her question. "Today was English, wasn't it?" It disturbed the cook's contemplation of whatever it was she was thinking about, but she looked up a little bemused as Elinor repeated her question for the third time.

"Okay, I think; wonderful, I hope. The paper was a gift! We had covered most of the stuff on it. We even did a similar Shakespeare question in class last week, so I hope they all managed that one, at least. The poetry question was the hardest, but it was an option."

"And Michael?"

"I don't know. I didn't see him."

"Is that why you are so miserable?"

"Am I? Sorry," Sarah apologised, attempting a smile.

"That, or you just lost a million pounds. Okay, let's get all the misery over in one. How's Jonathan?"

"I don't know that, either. He has not been in school since his exams. Someone said he had a job."

Elinor was nodding even if she wasn't listening; she was far more interested in sampling the pasta. "Mm, that is so good! Just have to wait for the results, then, like everyone else."

"Except we won't be here, will we?" Sarah grumbled. "I didn't think about that when I agreed to your trip. This will be the first year I have missed them."

"So that will make it the first year you don't disgrace yourself by crying all over everybody. See, there's a positive side to everything." Elinor could tell by the silence that greeted this assertion that it was not as amusing as she'd thought it was. "I suppose we can always ring school if you must know on the very same day. Seems like a waste of good money to me."

"It won't be the same as being here."

"No, but it's no good worrying about it now ..."

"No. The deed is done; the die is cast."

"If that is Shakespeare, don't you think it's time he had a rest for the summer?"

"It's not – it's me."

"Even more reason then why he needs a rest," Elinor emphasised without the slightest trace of humour. "You are beginning to sound like him, even when you are not quoting him."

Dinner was served up in silence, and Elinor easily abandoned school matters to concentrate on their itinerary, offering as an inducement, "We could go north first to Vermont, if you want."

"Do you think there might have been some improvement in Jonathan's home situation? He must be feeling okay to be working."

Elinor put down her fork and looked across the table. "You haven't been listening to a word I've said, have you? Stop worrying about Jonathan Spicer and all the rest of them," she insisted. "They are not your responsibility any longer – not that they ever were." She loaded another forkful of pasta into her mouth, which prevented her speaking for a minute. When she did, it was only to deliver another sharp reprimand. "I told you months ago, it's all sorted. His dad is not going back. Stop hoping for a miracle!"

"What makes you think I am?"

"Because I know you! Happy ever after queen. It's a shame; his dad seems like a great guy, but some things just fail. Accept it."

"Can't be such a great guy to run off with a neighbour and leave his wife and child to face losing their home and thousands of pounds of debts to pay."

Elinor's patience was never that great, and Sarah had just used up the last bit of her entire night's supply. "Grow up! It happens. People drift apart. It doesn't mean he's not a great guy."

"Sorry. We must have a different understanding of the word *great*."

"What is it with you tonight? What is wrong?" Elinor threw down her fork with just the right amount of impatience to underline her feelings on this matter. "Whatever it is, go ahead and get it off your chest now, before we go anywhere."

"There is nothing wrong," Sarah protested; aware that even as she said it, she was thinking of all the leftover, unresolved bits of school that still bothered her – things that could not be dropped so easily. "Nothing is wrong. It's …"

"Fine. Then let's eat before this food gets cold." Therapist had never been on Elinor's list of desired occupations: too much angst and not enough action.

"I am sorry Elinor, I suppose it's just the end of year blues. You know, the feeling when all the pressure is off. I will be better by next week."

"End of year blues? I never heard of such rubbish! End of year relief! End of year euphoria! End of year freedom! But *never* end of year blues! What is there to be blue about? Exams are over, and we shall shortly be free for a whole six weeks!"

"Is that really what it's all about?"

Elinor checked out her lack of understanding of this statement with a look of undisguised disbelief. "Exams?" she queried.

The philosopher looked a little bit flustered by that, and in a rather sheepish whisper confessed, "No, I mean life."

As an attempt to clarify confusion, this statement failed on every conceivable measure known to man; Elinor's glass just managing to connect successfully with the table before she choked on the mouthful of wine she had been in the process of swallowing. "You are joking me? Here's me thinking something serious is wrong, and you are just sorting out the meaning of life. You are a gem, do you know that? An absolute, bloody gem! Sorry!" she offered, leaning across to pat her friend's hand, which was withdrawn quickly.

"Don't patronise me!" Sarah objected.

"Then don't be so stupid. It doesn't matter what it's about," Elinor confided seriously. "Normal people do not bother what it's about. Normal people do not even care what it's about! Normal people certainly don't ask what it's about! Normal people just get on with it. Who the hell knows, anyway? Probably only some egghead with jargon that I understand less than Shakespeare, if that's possible." Her listener was not amused. "Sarah, even if the meaning of life is $E = mc^2$, or some other mathematical puzzle, I do not want to know – and neither should you, if you have any sense."

"Can I ask you something?"

"Sure, ask away. It doesn't mean I'll know the answer, though."

"Who is this 'normal people'? Sorry, I mean who are these 'normal people' you keep going on about? "The slip had happened because frustration was getting the better of her. Elinor did not answer, so Sarah repeated her question. "These 'normal people,' these mysterious average citizens. Who, or what, is a normal person?"

"How the hell should I know?" Elinor answered honestly. Then she added mischievously, "It's certainly not you!"

"Exactly! And it's not you, either! I don't believe normal or average exists; it's a statistical unit, that's all! We all go about quoting it; comparing ourselves to it, seeing ourselves as odd if we don't measure up against it, and it's rubbish! I am not average height, IQ, waist, bust, or shoe size. It doesn't say a thing about me, and what matters to me is Jonathan and Marcie and Michael and all the rest of my students -even if it means I'm not normal!" She had got this upset very easily, so she had not recognised the part of what she had said that was funnier than she had intended.

"Hey, okay! Hang onto your hat. I didn't mean to upset you, but you do realise you just admitted to not being normal?" Sarah shook her head and tried to smile. It covered the pain. "Sorry, I didn't realise it was such a sensitive spot. I'd watch it if I were you, though. Twice in one day is dangerous. Three times you turn into ..."

"A human being?" Sarah suggested. An accusation that was delivered with a grin, but it handed out more than humour.

Elinor sniffed disdainfully and waved her fork. "Okay, point taken. But please tell me next time philosophy is on the menu. I can go elsewhere for my stodge!"

Chapter Eight

The last day of school eventually arrived. Elinor had been waiting for it since December. The girls had been counting off the days on a calendar since January, and even Sarah had been counting down the days for the last week or two, so it should have been a happy day for all. It wasn't. The twins argued all the way to school, Elinor was bad tempered because of it, and Sarah was fractious because of all three of them. A longer, more wearisome day could not have been imagined, but the last lesson did finally end.

In the middle of all the excited chatter about holiday plans, one young pupil remembered the teacher and wished her a "smashing holiday too." Sarah returned the greeting and added brief details of where she was going.

This information prompted a second pupil to advise, "Well, mind you don't get shot if you go anywhere really wild!"

"Indians do not shoot people these days," she responded knowingly.

"No, but Americans do," the first child informed her seriously.

She was denied the opportunity of correcting them by a third child joining in the debate. "It's true, Miss. They are shooting English tourists! Murdering 'em!"

"Who says?" she asked, only a trifle nervously. This had to be some sort of a wind-up.

"Me' mum saw it on the ten o'clock news last week. This tourist got stranded somewhere and ended up getting shot dead! Murdered for real!" This alarming commentary came complete with appropriate sound effects.

"That was one tourist, not all of them," Sarah pointed out, recalling the incident. "One tourist in one city, and she wasn't stranded. She was lost. It was unfortunate, but it wouldn't have happened if she hadn't got lost." Her advisors did not appear convinced. "Maybe you will wish they had shot me when I have you writing about America every lesson next term," she added with a grin. She prudently withheld the delicious quip about not needing to worry about her getting lost, or getting shot at for that matter because she was exploring with Elinor Livingstone, on the grounds that pupils did not need to be taught how to make fun of staff. It already came effortlessly enough.

Elinor was in a jolly, expansive mood by the time they reached her flat, so she extended an invite for Sarah to join her and some friends the following evening after the girls had gone to Warwickshire. "We won't be late back," she promised. "Get some practice in," she teased. Her offer was declined because Sarah had to confess she had yet to start packing so Elinor felt obliged to admit that she hadn't started hers either. "It doesn't take long," she grumbled. It didn't change Sarah's decision.

The twins were busy finishing their packing when she arrived home. They were arguing about which music to take with them. "I have to take Madonna," Ali pleaded, "but I can't because we agreed five each."

"Swap it for one of your other choices." That was logical to Julie.

It was not at all logical all to Ali, who folded her arms in front of her and swayed her head from side to side like a snake; this was her deep thinking mode. When she stopped, she declared sweetly, "I thought you might want to take it. I'll let you," then she wrapped her arms around her sister as evidence of this generosity. Julie did not resist the embrace and appeared to think about the offer for a moment, but then she kissed Al's cheek, released her arms, and declined.

"Don't involve me in your arguments," Sarah protested as Ali looked to her for support. "Sort it out between yourselves. Just promise me that whatever you take, you will not play it as loudly as you do here. Nan was never much of a music lover."

There were no pleas for extra time at bedtime, not even a tiny one from Alison. It was one of life's little ironies that on the one occasion that the girls were actually keen to go to bed, she was loathe to send them there, because apart from a few hours in the morning, she would not be seeing them again for six whole weeks, and right now that seemed more like a prison sentence than a holiday. It was the equivalent of half a term! She finished the last few pages of Alice in Wonderland very slowly even though Julie had already fallen asleep.

The two people up bright and early the following morning did not include the usual early riser. In a total reversal of all normal morning procedures, *they* rushed into *her* bedroom, pulled back the curtains to reveal a bright sunny day and admonished her to abandon her bed and get up and get ready. Being on the receiving end of this ritual felt different than delivering it, but Sarah obediently dragged herself out of bed. The car was already loaded and so they were ready to leave for the station right on schedule; it was the last thing that happened according to plan all morning.

Half way to the station a sudden howl of distress at least similar to a lone wolf caused Sarah to swerve. Trying hard not to think about the possibility of a cancelled holiday she slowed down to investigate which twin was in pain. Her solicitous enquiry as she checked their pallor through her mirror, was rewarded with an admission. It was only Ali. If it had been Julie she would have presumed appendicitis at least but as it was Ali, she felt sure it would be nothing so serious.

"I have forgotten my wellies!" All explanations why they could not go back to collect them were to no avail. "But my wellies!" Ali wailed again. Her temper was sometimes frayed by little things, and this was a huge thing.

"I daresay Nan will be able to get you some wellington`s from somewhere," her mother urged, too stressed to have much sympathy for mere wellington boots. "She has dealt with bigger crises than just a pair of missing boots, you know."

Peace had been restored by the time they were settled in the train carriage under the supervision of Edna's youngest daughter, Lynsey, who had been happy to accompany them to Warwickshire in exchange for the price of the train fare to Manchester to see her boyfriend.

"Make sure you give them personally to my mother before you leave them. She will be waiting for you on the platform." This warning had been repeated at least a dozen times before the train pulled out, "Bye, be good! Be careful! No accidents Ali! See you in September. I love you both. Bye."

Sarah returned home with something important missing. It was not unlike the feeling she had experienced when the girls had graduated from needing a pram. No thoughts of America could compensate for it. The phone started ringing as she closed the front door behind her, its timely intrusion helped stem the threat of tears. The ring sounded incredibly loud.

"Hi, Mum, train left on time," she muttered automatically.

A sheepish little voice answered. It took a second or two for her to realise who it was, and then, though she did momentarily consider if anything could be wrong, she dismissed that idea as easily as she had Ali`s wail. She knew that Elinor's little voice would be hiding nothing more than a bad hangover.

"I have broken my leg."

"Sure you have and I am going to stand in for the pilot." At this point some recurring pips interrupted their conversation and helped Sarah admit the first small doubts because wherever her prankster friend was calling from, and however she was, she was in a callbox somewhere.

When they were reconnected they exchanged numbers with a warning, "If you are joking me, Elinor, I need to warn you, I will not be amused. Not today!"

Elinor was not joking, her leg really was broken so it left Sarah apologising for the predicament Elinor had got them into. If this accident had been a combination of desperate circumstances and bizarre coincidence it might have made it easier to bear, but Elinor had simply lost her footing and tumbled down the sports centre steps last night. It was too easy to go back over all the things that had happened since then, and Sarah did just that while Elinor was contemplating the degree of her misfortune.

Elinor's voice interrupted her thoughts. "I wanted to ring you last night," she said miserably, "but it was gone midnight by the time I got to the ward, and you know what these places are like. Trying to get hold of a phone at that time in the morning is like trying to get information out of KGB headquarters. Even E.T. didn't have this much trouble calling home." Neither of them laughed. There was a short pause before the casualty asked the obvious question – the one that neither of them had asked so far. The one which neither of them had an answer for. "So what do we do now?" A minute's silence marked the passing of her dream before Elinor declared bravely, "You will have to find someone else to go with you. If you can't, then there's nothing else except …" she paused to gather strength to utter the words, "except cancel the whole thing." If self-reproach were ever to achieve status as an art form, it would have some of its finest moments in the weeks to come, and this was Elinor's first awkward rehearsal; sympathy for Sarah's situation already overcome by sheer despair at her own. Sarah expressed some doubts about their cancellation rights, it was not exactly what Elinor wanted to hear.

"Of course you can cancel," she insisted, "we are insured."

"And what about the van in New York?"

Elinor held the receiver out in front of her and stared at it blankly. This was not the time to come up with awkward, unanswerable questions? There was silence at the other end of the phone also because for once there were no satisfactory answers there either. This needed thinking through sensibly, and right now Sarah was hardly capable of thinking sensibly about any of it. She needed a quiet space and a rational approach, then she could sort out the issues, make a list, deal with each one methodically and tick them off one at a time. None of that was possible on the phone to Elinor. "Forget what I said. I will sort it."

"Promise?" Elinor said.

That sounded so much like Alison pleading for a favour that Sarah replied in exactly the same manner. "I promise," she said with more conviction than she felt. "I will sort everything out, and then I will come and see you. Don't worry, it will be okay."

She was still sitting on the bottom stair, stunned, when the phone rang again. This time it was her mother, so this conversation was as brief and cheerful as the last had been long and dismal. Then she returned to her ruminations. Under the circumstances, odds of twenty million to one seemed excessively generous -she needed to find someone who could just drop everything at twenty-four hours' notice to waltz off to America for six weeks. The odds were not just high, they were impossible.

Elinor awoke in a panic, disorientated by her unfamiliar surroundings, then the throbbing in her leg reminded her where she was and why she was there. She lifted her wrist; her watch said six forty-five. A nurse stopped by her bedside to check her pulse and inquire how she was feeling. Her head said lie -tell them she was fine - no aches, no pains, nothing. Admittedly that would be fairly remarkable for someone with such a badly shattered limb, but she was prepared to tell them anything to be awake when Sarah arrived, even if that was awake and in pain. It might even have been easier to bear her misfortune if they had left her writhing in agony. The nurse reassured her there had been no visitors yet, so she lay staring up at the ceiling, going over the events of last night as if repetition could, or would, change the outcome. However much she cursed and berated, she had a broken leg, and like all other broken limbs, this one would not heal by regrets. Like it or not, she was stuck in this hospital bed until someone said she could go home, and even then she had no doubt it would take months to heal completely. The doctor last night had told her there were two fractures, one in the femur and the other in the ankle. One of them had a fancy name, tri-malleolar fracture or something like that, and she had known instinctively that it meant awful. It changed nothing of course -except now she had a fancy name for it. America was as far away as ever.

The visitors for the ward came in together; a motley collection of humanity having little in common except a liking for flowers, fruit, and paperbacks.

"I brought you some grapes," Sarah announced as she pulled up a chair and tried hard not to react to Elinor's thunderous face.

Elinor swept aside all inquiries about her leg with demands to hear Sarah's latest news. It was useless trying to avoid the topic because it was plain that sympathy was not what Elinor needed. Unfortunately, what she needed most, barring miraculous recoveries, was not what Sarah had to say, and she was considering how best to break her news when Elinor confessed, "I've been an absolute idiot, haven't I? Stop being so bloody nice about it. Sorry, I know a broken ankle and leg is no excuse for bad language, but what is, according to you? Losing a holiday? Surely that must excuse the odd swear word? No? Well, come on, then, tell me the alternatives, and I will try not to offend you anymore."

The way that Sarah patted her hand made Elinor hope, for one small moment that she had performed the equivalent of pulling a rabbit out of a hat. Her visitor knew there was no point in dressing up her answer – it was always going to be negative, but Elinor had to review the entire list of people she had approached before she could accept it. This done, both sat pondering; one thinking about a wild idea, and the other thinking about the one person that had not been mentioned – the one person who Elinor was almost sure would be free to go. She tried hard not to sound too precious about suggesting it.

"Have you thought about asking Len?"

"No, I haven't, and I am not going to – and neither must you. I am serious about this, Elinor. Promise me!"

"Why not? He's single, no ties."

"He is a man! That's why not."

Elinor swallowed the answer that all too readily sprang to her lips, and with some effort she simply said, "So? Think about it. Hear me out, huh? You are an adult, and so is he. Well," She pulled a face that was meant to make her friend smile, but it failed, so she changed tack and tried another way. "You know him and you like him, don't you? Hell, you've been out with him enough, surely!" Her voice faded away as she registered Sarah flush with something resembling anger. "Sarah, this is too important for your strange ideas," she pleaded taking a firm grip on her arm.

"Nothing is too important for my strange ideas, as you call them. Len and I do not have that sort of relationship."

"I sometimes wonder what sort of relationship you *do* have."

"Well, don't worry about that, either! I will tell you: friendship, and that's all, Elinor. Friendship, nothing more."

Elinor chewed this over for a minute and then said, "I thought you said he was a gentleman."

"He is."

"Then it should be possible ..." Her voice trailed away under the withering scrutiny. "If you really *are* just good friends, then he should be able to sleep one end of the camper, and you the other and never the twain shall meet." She added, "It is only six weeks you know, not a lifetime commitment. I am not asking you to marry him!"

"You just do not know when to give up do you?"

Elinor shook her head. "I am trying to save your holiday!" she pointed out soberly.

"Listen to me, please! I am not sharing a camper for six weeks with Len, or any other man. One, there is no real privacy in there, and two, however much of a gentleman Len is, everyone has their limits. Three, can you imagine the gossip if this should get back to school. Four, what would I tell my mother and the girls? Five, Len might get ideas about our relationship that do not exist. Six, we would argue the entire six weeks, or he would drive me crazy. And seven, just because of my strange ideas. How many more reasons do you need?"

"We argue," Elinor pointed out in one last desperate attempt.

"No, Elinor! Just no! How much of that do you not understand? No!" The woman sitting by the next bed turned around to investigate. Sarah smiled apologetically and then turned back to Elinor to hiss, "Forget it. Promise me?" Elinor nodded reluctantly but there were tears in her eyes. "Don't get upset."

"Why not? Why shouldn't I get upset? I have ruined your holiday as well as my own."

"No, you haven't, I am going ... by myself." Elinor stared at her, not sure whether she had heard correctly. "I have decided to go alone," Sarah repeated earnestly, though still trying to get used to the sound of it.

"You sound as if you are referring to a daytrip to the seaside."

"Don't be so patronising. Why can't I go alone."

"I am not being patronising – I am talking sense. You cannot go alone because of the obvious dangers. Stop looking at me like that. You forget I know that look; I use it myself, and it only works on kids! The fact that you need to ask the question is one reason, and second, a trip to America is not like going to Brighton for the day. America is not like Brighton Sarah – it's not even like England." Sarah did not respond and just sat nodding obediently. Elinor was never sure which was the most infuriating, Sarah's agreement or her disagreement, but right now that nodding agreement won hands down. "There is some dangerous country out there, to say nothing of the animals and the people," Elinor continued.

"Come on, even I know Indians don't scalp people these days!" Sarah said, recollecting memories of yesterday's debate with the third years.

"Are you trying to be funny? There are all sorts of weirdoes out there."

"They wouldn't be the same ones who were desirable Americans a few months ago? Or are they just your plain average weirdoes, a bit like the plain, average, British weirdoes I manage to avoid every day of my life."

"I give up!" Elinor declared vehemently. She straightened her bedspread because she didn't know what else to do.

"Good!" Sarah declared equally vehemently, removing an extra crease that Elinor had missed.

Elinor hit out at her hand impetuously. "Okay, forget about the people," she conceded. "I am still serious about the animals and the territory."

"I promise not to walk down any strange garden paths without checking whether they have a rabid dog or cat. What else?"

"You are going to America, Sarah!"

"Yes, I believe that's what it says on the tickets," she said with a laugh, trying to lighten this increasingly acrimonious atmosphere. She was beginning to realise she should have said nothing about her plan and just gone.

"Sarah, listen to me, please! For once in your life, just listen! Stop thinking you are the only person on the planet who knows anything."

"I do not!"

"Yes, you do, all the time. Well okay, sometimes," Elinor said boldly. Then instead of telling her when those times might be, she went on to use the opportunity now that she had her undivided attention to educate her about some of the perils. "There are crocodiles and alligators in Florida, bears in California, mountain lions in Utah and California, and poisonous snakes all over the place. Did you know any of that? No, you did not! Don't tell me you did, because I can tell by your face that you didn't, and I know *I* was prepared to go alone, but please credit me with having a little more knowledge and expertise about the place than you have. Can you read a compass?" Sarah had to admit she could not. "A map, then?"

"It is civilised, isn't it? Road signs and things? Oh, and don't they speak the same language?"

Elinor pulled herself up on her pillows as best she could without attracting any unwelcome attention from her guards, and then she stared hard at her friend. "The itinerary we have planned goes into some really interesting bits of America," she continued. "And interesting is always more challenging than boring! Who knows what will be necessary? And didn't you tell me you didn't do risk or adventure? That's why I am trying to get this into your thick skull now: America is nothing like here! Sarah, are you listening to me?"

"I think you are over-dramatising this a wee bit, don't you think?"

"Go ahead, you think that – as long as you remember that I did try to warn you when you are wrestling with an eight-foot grizzly." There was a sullen silence for a moment, and while Sarah was thinking, Elinor registered her final point. "And besides all that, what about all the driving?"

"What about it? I will have to amend the itinerary a bit, that's all. Longer hauls, fewer diversions and shorter rest periods."

"Sounds great," Elinor said sarcastically, "Tell you what: I will fix you up with a long-distance driving job for six weeks. I know a guy with a haulage firm; he is always short of drivers, and that way you can get all the long hauls and short rests you need, and there will be no obligation to do anything as frivolous as enjoy yourself. What's more, you'll get paid for doing it."

Rather than attempt to change Elinor's mind about the wisdom of her plans, Sarah concentrated on the choices she had available. There were only two: she went alone, or she stayed home alone. "If I cancel both flights," she continued, "we would get yours refunded, but I don't know about mine. The travel agent suggested I ring the insurers, so I did, but they were shut. It's Saturday, so back to the travel agent. If I were your husband or wife, it wouldn't be a problem. The trouble is, I am neither! This is different. And there is no way of finding out for sure until Monday, and that's too late! I have to be on that flight tomorrow. Honestly, Elinor, it is the only sensible thing to do. I can imagine how you must feel being stuck in here after all our planning, but there is nothing I can do to remedy your situation. I know you must hate the idea of staying home, but …"

"I know, you don't have to say it. I got a busted leg through my own stupid fault."

"At least give me credit for having the tact not to say that!"

"I do. Doesn't mean it's not true, though. You could go to your mothers," Elinor suggested morosely.

"I could, but you said this would be good for the girls and me, and I have just started to see that. They have loved planning this time with my mother, and I can't spoil it now. This is their time together, and if I go there, it will be different. Everything tells me to go to America. I want to go," Sarah said simply. "You have spent the last six months winding me up for this. Now that I am fully wound up, I have to go. I promise I will eliminate all the dangerous bits, first cut. What else do you want me to cut? This is your opportunity to say!" They both attempted a grin, but it came out as a sigh from one and a groan from the other. "When I have collected the camper, I reckon the best thing is to take the most direct route across to Shelagh's. I will ring her when I get home, I am sure she will be happy to put me up for longer when I explain what has happened. That will get your van to Dave as quickly as possible and cuts down on the dangers of being alone and the chances of having an accident. I am protecting your interests here, and I also get to spend more time with Shelagh, so all is not lost. How long do you reckon to drive straight across?"

"It's not what we had planned," Elinor mumbled.

"No. But I shall take next year's texts with me and read them while I relax at Shelagh's. See, some good will come of it: I will start school better prepared than I would if we had spent six weeks rushing all over America. I really need to brush up on Lear; it's been a while since I've read it. One of next year's O-level books is *All's Well That Ends Well*," Sarah added hopefully.

Elinor looked up from her sombre contemplation of the unremarkable green bedspread to warn, "But it won't!" she moaned. "You mark my words, it won't!"

"It will. I promise you it will," Sarah said, patting Elinor's hand for the umpteenth time. "I will be fine, and you will be fine as well – eventually."

Elinor responded to this with a great sigh simply because the threat of tears forbade her from speaking. When she had regained sufficient control, she said, "I never thought of you as the intrepid explorer type."

"I'm not. Told you, I don't do danger, and that includes animals, strange geography, and weirdoes. No risks. No adventures. No talking to strangers. Satisfied?" she asked gently. Her refusal to be goaded broke the tension, and they both smiled. A minute later the bell sounded for the end of visiting. Sarah sat until she was the last visitor left on the ward.

"I should go; that nurse is staring at me so I think I have out stayed my welcome. I will write to you, I promise." Elinor was so overcome with grief that despite the nurse continuing to stare, her visitor delayed her departure. "Come on, cheer up. I hate to leave you like this. It's not that bad."

"How can you say that? It couldn't be any worse!"

"Of course it could. You have missed a holiday, that's all. There will be other holidays, other years. The main thing is that your leg and ankle gets better, isn't it?" As condolences went, it was not the most successful.

"The best laid plans of mice and men, eh?" Elinor mumbled. "Bet you didn't think I could quote old Will, did you?"

"No," Sarah admitted with a tender smile. "And I would be right. That's not Shakespeare – it's Burns."

Elinor nodded. "Oh well. I don't need either of them to tell me I wish I was coming with you." Sarah agreed wholeheartedly with that. "Then why me? Why me now? Why not me in September? Tell me why right now, of all times?"

Sarah swallowed the lump in her throat and sat down again. This time she sat right on the edge of the bed, to signify to any nurses that she did not intend this to be a permanent arrangement. She took hold of the hand lying limply on the cover and patted it. She tried to say, "I don't know," but it was an incoherent whisper, so they sat together in silence, doom and gloom united, until Sarah found her voice. "I don't know, Elinor," she finally managed. "I really do not know."

Elinor nodded; it was all that she could do. Words would have breached the tide of emotion that was swelling up inside her again. One word could have opened a gap wide enough for the torrent to rush through, and she did not cry – she *would not* cry, not at this, not in front of Sarah. Maybe later, when the lights had gone out and it was dark. Maybe when all the others were asleep, she would cry then, but not now.

A nurse was advancing down the ward towards them to chivvy this last visitor on her way, but she stopped at the end of the bed looked at Elinor's pinched face, and nodded to Sarah. "Five minutes, no more!"

It was like allowing the condemned man one last cigarette.

"Maybe there isn't a reason," Sarah admitted softly, hoping that she sounded more convincing than she felt. "It just happened. That's what accidents do: they just happen. They don't check if it's convenient."

"You say there is a purpose for everything," Elinor pointed out miserably.

"I never realised you listened to everything I said," Sarah jested.

"Can't help it. You say some things so bloody many times."

Sarah nodded, and they both muttered a contrite sorry. What else could she do? She was guilty as charged, and now she couldn't even supply the necessary explanation, so for once she overlooked the swearing. She tried to summon up words of sufficient comfort or explanation from somewhere, willing them to spring into her head, but they didn't. All she could think about was the door that was banging repeatedly somewhere in the background. It distracted her. *Bang, bang, bang.*

"Maybe it's about doors," she said finally as her mind grasped hold of something in the amazing way that only thought can, connecting two completely different things in the space of a millisecond.

"Doors? What sort of doors? I fell down steps," Elinor pointed out testily, thinking that her advisor must have forgotten that.

"Just doors. Any sort of doors."

Elinor looked up from under a thunderous brow; Sarah had obviously gone quite mad.

"What can you hear right now?" the mad woman persisted, quite animated now that she had found some sort of explanation.

"Jessie snoring, same as she did all last night," Elinor grumbled, nodding at the old lady in the next bed.

Sarah followed her gaze and smiled. "Forget Jessie. What else?"

Elinor listened. "The curtain drawing round that bed down there?"

"What else," came the impatient demand? "Listen!"

"A door banging somewhere?" They both listened to it for a minute. "It's only a door banging somewhere, that's all. Somebody left it open."

"Exactly!" Elinor looked thoroughly bemused by now. "Before the door can bang shut, it has to be open." Elinor was completely mystified by this inane logic, but Sarah continued. "And all you see right now in your life is a door that has banged shut in front of you,-just as you were about to go through it."

"When I need a lesson in the use of metaphor, I'll send for you," Elinor said wearily. She pulled the bed covers over her head and slid down as well as she could. Her actions conveyed, I have had enough; go away.

Sarah grabbed at the one hand remaining visible and held onto it tightly before it also disappeared beneath the blankets. "Maybe you should be looking for the door that is about to open in front of you," she suggested to the raised rim of the blankets.

"You mean the operating theatre door?" came the muffled reply.

There really was no adequate answer to that, so Sarah didn't try to give one, but she conceded, "Well, besides that." But what else was there besides that? "Oh Elinor, I am so very sorry," she said suddenly, and she leant forward to awkwardly embrace the half-hidden figure as best she could. It looked like tears were going to win out on both sides as she mumbled into the blankets, "Maybe we all spend too much time agonising over closed doors when we should be looking for the open ones. Open doors are adventures, and maybe we all need some adventure to stay alive. You have been telling me that for ages. Well, thanks to you I have found one. I know it was yours, and it's only mine by default, but there will be another one for you! You just have to find it. Elinor, are you listening?"

Such a totally unexpected confession of honesty was sufficient to cause Elinor to peer up from beneath her blankets and into the serious face addressing her. She restrained herself from saying what she really thought, but she couldn't resist commenting, "You are nuts, you know!"

Sarah nodded slowly, biting her lip to avoid replying. For once she would allow Elinor her opinion.

"The doors stopped banging," Elinor said thoughtfully "Someone shut it."

"Maybe, maybe not."

Elinor was not so distressed that she couldn't demand, "Will you stop saying that! It's driving me insane too! What do you mean?"

"I mean you automatically thought someone has shut it. Maybe they have, but maybe they haven't. Maybe someone has propped it open." Elinor absorbed this information carefully while Sarah watched her face cautiously. "It's just your supposition that the door is shut. We don't know that. You think it's shut; I say it could be open. This is the same. It looks like a devastating blow, but maybe it isn't. Find out. Don't be so miserable over this that you miss something else." Wisely, she chose to keep "something better" to herself.

Elinor sighed heavily; philosophy on top of broken bones was more than she could handle. "We'll see," she said glumly. "You go and have a good time – and be careful! Don't go getting *too* adventurous. Be sure to keep me informed of everything. Write to me, send me postcards, and ring me at home. I won't be stuck in here the whole six weeks, I hope."

Sarah kissed Elinor's flushed cheek one last time and then rose to leave again. "I will! I'll do all those things, I promise."

She was halfway to the door when Elinor shouted after her, "No talking to strangers, remember!"

The car park was quite deserted when Sarah reached it. It was starting to rain but she stood paralysed by a sudden, blinding, flash of possibility. No challenges -so no risks? A sterile life? Was that really what had been wrong with her? Nothing to push against. Nothing to overcome, well, nothing if you overlooked the constant challenge of paying bills. She smiled grimly. This was no time for sarcasm. She nodded several times as reflection digested this insight and then she awarded it some importance by pledging she would not forget it again, before she celebrated by jumping over every puddle in the car park. It was quite intoxicating. "Not as useless as some folks think, old girl! Life in you yet," she puffed. She was soaking wet before she reached the car, but instead of frowning at the sorry spectacle that confronted her in the mirror, she grinned and promised it seriously, "Jonathan, my lad, you are wrong. I am definitely right. There are happy endings. Lots of them. This is one" As she was alone she was safe from being contradicted –or certified. That 'no happy endings,' might have been powerful enough to rent room in her head for the last seven months, but this would surely clear it out. "And you have to savour every single one of them, not rush breathlessly through them on your way to your next bit of misery," she said slowly as that dawned also. "So, America -here I come! Ready or not, I am going to enjoy you!"

Chapter Nine

Dear Sarah and Elinor,

Welcome to the land of opportunity! Hope you get plenty of opportunity to enjoy yourselves. I can't wait for you to get here! Ring me now, and then hurry over. Forget the rest – we are by far the most interesting bit! Hope that the camper is up to expectations. Dave says it should be fine for two of you. Bonus is it's easy to resell this model. (Thought you might like that!) But please make sure you have all the documentation before you leave. Now that I have passed on all that information, I have no room for anything else except to say, Have fun! See you soon.

Love Shelagh

P. S. I was not joking: we do live in the best bit, but the rest is okay, too!

Elinor's accident was already history by the time Sarah was reading Shelagh's note. Its sender had only been deterred from flying out to New York because it would have meant sending all her children to stay with other friends. Sarah had managed to persuade her she should stay home, even though it did seem a much bigger thing she had undertaken now she was actually sat in New York and not in Elinor's hospital room. Fortunately the motor home was rather like a playhouse for adults, so novelty diminished her anxiety a little as she examined the cupboard-size kitchen and diminutive bathroom facilities.

"I wouldn't cook onions," the salesman joked as he handed over the keys.

The most worrying feature of this plaything was the claustrophobic-looking bunk over the driving cabin and although she tested the ladder for strength, she decided against the climb because she didn't want to get stuck there in public. Besides, the man promised her the seating around the table would convert to a bed. That would prove to be an engineering feat beyond her capability, but at this point she had to admit that having one of these things was pretty neat, or at least after a whole day in New York, she did. Last week it would have just been a great idea. She didn't actually clap her hands like Ali when she acquired a new plaything, but her delight measured about the same.

That delight lasted right up until the minute she had to drive the thing, and then all her courage deserted her. The salesman sensed what her problem might be and solved it by taking her out for a spin. After half an hour of him calling out at each junction which way to turn, she felt more comfortable, and being spurred on by his declaration of faith, she dropped him back at the garage as he said, "You'll be fine, lady. Just get out there and drive! Get out of the city; all the roads in America are not like this." That was a relief. So far it had been worse than nursing a jumbo jet across the Atlantic! "A word of warning," he shouted after her. "Watch out for the bad guys!"

"Don't worry. No need to send for the cavalry," she said with a laugh, signalling to turn left. "I won't need them." But her words were lost in the traffic noise.

A week later she was still in New York State! There was just too much to see, but she did understand that if she continued at this rate, she would be lucky to reach Shelagh's by late October. Her itinerary needed some urgent pruning. By the time she finished, it was clear that Elinor had a valid point about the distances: this new schedule looked remarkably like a long-distance lorry driver's rota. Despite that, over the next few days the rest of the cares of the previous twelve months evaporated and any remaining vestiges of that black cloud were banished by the warmth of American sunshine and the hospitality of its people. Adventure suited her after all. Homesickness didn't! She was still making at least one call a day to the girls at the end of the second week. It was better that Elinor was not around to witness this.

In the middle of all of this, there were two other concerns, both of which were called exam results. Late in the afternoon of the day following the A-level results, she called Elinor. She had reckoned that even if Elinor had not been able to get into school, the results were always in the evening paper, which she must have by now. Initial polite inquiries about Elinor's leg and ankle, the weather, and anything else she thought was required, were dispensed with as swiftly as she could. Elinor guessed why, so she prattled on and on about the problems with her ankle and her flirtation with the consultant, until finally Sarah pleaded,

"Elinor! Please stop teasing me – every second is costing me money! Just tell me, please!"

"You are supposed to be on holiday," Elinor declared breezily. "I am sure that I wouldn't be in the slightest bit bothered about exam results if I was in…. Where are you by the way?"

"Almost in Vegas. Come on; get on with it before I die of suspense. This is the first year I haven't been there!" Sarah wailed in frustration.

"Vegas, eh? Wouldn't have thought it was your sort of place."

"Elinor!"

"Okay, okay! You sound just like a kid on Christmas morning."

"No, I am not! Children on Christmas morning get to find out what presents they have been given! What does it take for you to tell how my class did?"

"Ah ha! Self-interest. Not how did your class do Elinor, or even how did the school do? Just how did your blessed English class fare?"

"Elinor please!"

"Oh okay. They all passed," she said as if it was nothing. There was a necessary silence while this news sank in.

"What, all of them?" Sarah finally queried. "Every single one of them? All seventeen? They all passed?"

"I thought that was the generally accepted meaning of 'all'," Elinor said with a yawn, feigning disinterest as Sarah erupted into simultaneous laughter and tears.

"They all passed," she sang between her tears. "They all passed!"

"I presume you are disgracing yourself in a public place, from the din I can hear."

Sarah admitted she was before she remembered passing was not enough for some, so she banished euphoria until she could hear the other vital information. She needed to know grades, and she knew that finding this out was not going to be easy, but she did eventually persuade Elinor to read them out from the paper line by line.

"Marcie got an A?" Sarah repeated stunned, "Marcie Hadley got an A, and Jonathan only got a C?" She had half-expected one but not the other.

"That's what it says here. Isn't it enough?"

"I don't know."

"Well, you will just have to wait till you get back to find out," Elinor pointed out hastily, "because there is no way I can go round there to ask, not even for you. So forget it!"

That said, their attention turned to discussing Elinor's class and then the school results, for as Elinor wittily pointed out, they had all done better than expected, because no one else had been expecting anything at all. North Green did not have a large sixth form, and the school was in a very deprived area, but this year, their few kids had done better than ever before, and three of them had gained straight A`s in three subjects – another first. The three were Jason the lawyer and two more of the seriously studious crowd.

"They all took English!" Sarah said stupidly, by now punch drunk.

"Sure did! So you will be even more in favour now," Elinor pointed out, remembering the extra O-level group. "And even more will be expected of you next year. Just think of it: you can give extra tuition to all John's dear little Marcie Hadley's. Who knows? Maybe he will even arrange for you to live in some of the time. I daresay the girls will be able to visit, but only on weekends of course."

Sarah laughed. Nothing Elinor could say right now could upset her, and she paraphrased Mrs Bennett`s line from *Pride and Prejudice* that said exactly that. As expected Elinor did not recognise the quote, and she seriously doubted the content anyway, but none of it seemed to matter right at that moment. After all the trauma of the past year, everyone had passed.

She kept repeating this amazing fact to herself all the way back to the camper. She continued with the odd, giddy little repetition for the rest of the day. "They all passed!" she told the moon as she closed the curtains that night. If there was such a thing as a perfect day, today would qualify.

Two days later, on the Thursday afternoon of the third week, she arrived safely in the outskirts of Los Angeles. She had actually been heading for the Joshua Tree Park, but somehow or other she had ended up heading in almost the opposite direction, and though Shelagh and Elinor had both gone to great lengths to advise her to stay clear of LA because she was alone; she had only *nearly* promised them. *I may never pass this way again,* and all that. Her first stop was a small market for groceries. It was in a nice, leafy suburb, and her thoughts were already beginning to suspect that all the fuss everyone had made about this place was over rated. It was just like

Basildon. Well, perhaps not all of it, but this bit certainly was. One of the nice, ultra-polite store lads carried her bags back to the camper for her.

"You English?" he asked deferentially. She nodded. "Here on holiday?"

"Yes." This much she felt was fairly obvious.

"Just arrived?" She paused from taking her bags from him and looked at him curiously, wondering where all this questioning might be leading. "Wanna see the sights?" That invitation earned him a hard stare. He was hardly older than her A-level class, and she was just about to say so when he pushed a card into her hand.

"Maestro Movie-land Tours," she read aloud, "You've seen them at the movies – now see where they live. Visit the homes of some of Hollywood's most famous residents with the people who know them best. Leaves every afternoon at 1.30 and 3.30."

"They're real swell trips," he informed her seriously as she produced a beaming smile to conceal the embarrassing error she had just avoided.

"I am sure they are," she replied equally seriously.

"My uncle runs them."

Well, what more could one want she thought as she tipped him but declined the trip. "I don't go to the movies very often, and when I do, it's usually Disney, so your tour would be wasted on me – unless of course you happen to know where Bambi lives?" He looked at her blankly, so she rescued his confusion by confessing warmly, "Better save your seat for someone who will really appreciate it. I wouldn't know whose house I was looking at."

"But they *all* live here," he pointed out hopefully. "All of them."

She looked at him closely. "That's really nice," she said gravely.

Despite the boy's best endeavours on his uncle's behalf, both tour buses left without her that afternoon though she *did* catch a bus into the city to do a few touristy type things. She didn't get to do as many as she had planned because she got absorbed in the art gallery on Wilshire Boulevard, before finishing her day off at the nearby tar pits where she hoped to find some suitable ammunition for the long, chatty letter she intended to write to the girls that evening. Letters were the new way of coping now that she had been dissuaded from ringing every day.

She checked in at the very first campsite on her way out of the city because she was tired after a hard day's sightseeing. Over dinner at the site diner she tried her best to stay awake by working out how to reach the Joshua Tree Park the following day. It was less than a couple of inches on her map, but translating two inches into real miles was beyond her navigational ability. Getting lost had become an almost a daily occurrence, and inquiries of the natives usually produced such a wide variety of opinions that she felt it unsafe to follow any one set of directions without a corroborating second opinion. As to how far this particular two inches was, she was no nearer knowing for sure when she gave up asking and went back to the van. The most common opinion was somewhere between a hundred and two hundred miles so she made an uninformed decision to go anyway, however far it turned out to be. With letter and journal completed, she climbed up the ladder and into the skybunk, repeating her newly devised explorer's prayer as she closed her eyes.

"Survived another day. Thank you. Now, can I please sleep well and get up early."

Ali had been the first to comment on the similarity between the sleeping arrangements in Warwickshire and the motor home. She had christened the cabin in the motor home the skybunk, after their skyroom and Sarah had adopted it because the girls were not the only ones who needed to think that they were sleeping in similar accommodation.

Tonight sleep eluded her, so she lay for a while watching a particularly bright star that was just visible through the corner of the small window in her roof. She wondered if Ali might be watching the same star from her mattress beneath the window in her roof until she remembered the time difference. Strange to think the girls were still enjoying the afternoon. Probably different stars visible in England anyway.

She picked up *King Lear* and turned her attention to catastrophe instead of cosmology. Lear had become her new nightly challenge: could she read a full page before falling asleep? Some nights she did, but most nights she didn't. Tonight her eyes had scarcely scanned the first speech before the book fell from her hands. Shakespeare might not have been flattered at becoming a sleeping tablet, but he served his purpose well. The book woke her as it fell, but only just long enough for her to switch out the little overhead light. "Tomorrow night I will read a whole act," she promised as she pulled the covers over her head.

Chapter Ten

Night replaced day across the vast sprawl of downtown Hollywood with the swiftness of a magician's hand and then the city's daytime hustle was easily outshone by the vibrancy of its night life. It was gaudy and glamorous, but it bristled with excitement and noise and action, and if it seemed too ecstatic in its approval of life, this illuminated city didn't care because it always endeavoured to hold onto the life of the day almost gone with a fervour that both thrilled and frightened those more used to timid living. It was never "just another day" here – it was always *the* day, and as most everyone was prepared to live each day to its utmost limits, the electricity was never wasted. Some people said this was a city with style; others said that attitude was nearer the mark.

Not far away, in the best residential suburbs of Beverley Hills, darkness adopted a more subtle approach than downtown. This was home to some of the world's most dedicated hedonists, so it was bound to be more padded, than prickly. Out here everything that money could buy *had* been bought by somebody or other, sometimes several times over, and like all glossy toys those of the super-rich were displayed to their best effect under subtle (rather than glaring) lighting. The compulsory shining hardware that adorned the driveway of virtually every pastel mansion with its pampered lawns and seductively lit swimming pools might be the sort of things most people could only dream of, yet they remained the stuff of universal ambition, and here they were every bit as plentiful as the flashing neon signs downtown. Such displays necessarily demanded more advanced security than downtown's efforts, but both venerated the freedom to aspire.

In one discreetly lit drive, on a hot summer's night, some of the most desirable possessions on earth were being stacked with suitable reverence by a small army of uniformed valets. Any downtown showroom would have been proud of their efforts; it amounted to automobile heaven, and though competing with the light show from the house was hard work, this hardware managed it beautifully.

Light and loud music drifted out from the house on the night air, but it was nothing compared to the ear-popping celebration going on inside. A few people were still arriving, and others with early morning assignments were already starting to leave, so the hosts were as busy as the valets: both were permanently engaged in a dizzying mix of greetings and farewells. The cause: the Enderleys were celebrating. The largest group of their guests were crowding into a marquee adjoining their marble-floored hall because champagne was flowing freely in there from a fountain. Only connoisseurs thought that a travesty -and they changed their mind when they had tasted it. In the middle of the marquee, a young man was gyrating wildly while trying to instil some enthusiasm in his audience for more activity than downing glasses of bubbly, but he was dressed in a spacesuit resembling baking foil, and as it was a very warm night and the air-conditioning was erratic to say the least, he was fast approaching well-baked status. He was dressed like this because the contract had made it a non-negotiable condition. He would definitely have been better occupied thinking of his own welfare than his disinterested audience.

This gathering was supposedly the wrap party for Jake Enderley's latest venture – well, that was how it had got started, it was now unrecognisable as that. The evening had been themed to fit in with the movie, a thriller about the murder of an astronaut in space and a vast amount of dollars had been invested in the movie, and in this party, but few thought about that; free booze was free booze, free champagne was better. Lots of free champagne was better still. It bought happy guests. Because of that no one had mentioned to the DJ, the likelihood of astronauts being murdered in Beverley Hills, even if that was by frying alive, or complained about the place being adorned with an annoying number of larger than life cardboard astronauts and mammoth posters -they were all too happy grazing at someone else's expense.

Even casual moviegoers would have recognised the face on the posters; it was a very famous face, but this production – which had run over schedule, over budget, and over most everything else – was almost as famous as the face by now because it had hogged the popular press headlines from its inception, and not always in a positive way. The only thing never in doubt during its long and troubled life had been its director's persistence that it would be a blockbuster if they could just get the damned thing finished. Every problem known to movie making had hit it: illness, accidents, mayhem, weather troubles – this project had all of them in plenty. Now Jake Enderley was expecting to be rewarded by making millions, and this was his way of saying "I told you so" to the cynics.

Tonight was actually the result of one particularly frustrating moment when he had sworn in front of witnesses that if he ever did get it finished, he would give the biggest party of the year, the Oscars included, and get absolutely legless. He was never going to get away with forgetting that; there were too many people with scores to settle. It might not have been quite Oscar standards, but it was pretty impressive, so it looked like he had stuck to his word. Jake was counting on that. It was how he had made his money: creating illusions.

By using some of his darker arts in the real world Jake had convinced the money guys that this little bit of hospitality should go on the film's promotion budget and he would donate the use of his home for free. It was an impressive bit of manoeuvring even in a place renowned for it, but that was how he had delivered his party without it costing him very much. Better still, he was well on the way to achieving his second ambition without it costing him anything at all.

Jake's partygoers were an odd assortment, they included everyone from the slenderest of nubile young women clad in the skimpiest of dresses, to the most rotund of middle-aged men in dinner suits and others who looked for all the world as if they had just finished a day's shoot. In the middle of them Greta Enderley was holding court. She looked fiftyish, though she was nearer to sixty-five, and if she had lived anywhere else, she would have been forced to admit to at least sixty, but not here. Biological age was an irrelevancy here, even though aging (or not aging) was most folk's prime preoccupation. This community's obsession with youth was only matched by its obsession with wealth, but as both caused endless lies to be told, declared age was always as disregarded as acknowledged riches, and always judged by how much one liked someone or not. It was a form of assessment that was standard for journalists, and the main reason most people were nice to them: they broadcast their views.

Jake was about the same age as his wife, but somehow he carried it better. He was a little man of five foot six inches, and he was round and balding, but he was saved from insignificance by his larger than life personality and oversized voice. They were an odd couple, she tall and tanned with the unnaturally taut skin caused by too many visits to plastic surgeons, and he round and short and wearing very naturally with rolls of loose flesh hanging from any place they could hang onto. Despite the difference in their appearance, they were most odd in that they had stayed married in Hollywood for over thirty-five years.

Jake was tonight's hero because he had saved the day – well, he had delivered the movie, which was pretty much the same thing in these parts. In fairy-tale terminology, it would shortly be happy ever after if one overlooked any potential difficulties with post-production, but as virtually no one had expected him to get this far, everyone was prepared to overlook such a trifle. He had protected the investors' money from bankruptcy, and he had enhanced some very precious reputations, made some new ones, and damaged a few others. Now he was the recipient of much hand shaking and back slapping from the previously awkward financiers, the bolshy crew, the temperamental actors, and even the plainly sceptical media people; only those with damaged reputations were missing. Somehow he had managed to keep most of the others happy while getting his own way – a remarkable feat he could never repeat at home, because here he was outnumbered by women.

Jake's wife had not been in on his scheming for the party; he knew better than that. She would never have handed over *her* house to PR nobodies. As far as she was concerned, this was just a personal thing to celebrate the completion of a very troubled project, and she always ensured they did everything in style. This party was no exception. She had personally invited everyone who was someone, which meant she was hostess to some pretty impressive folk, and she was playing up to that for all she was worth. Best of all, Jake's star was here in flesh and blood, and this was a coup that she had pulled off.

Rick Masters rarely turned up at parties; his reclusive nature was almost as well-known as Jake's parsimony. Unfortunately for Greta, there were also dozens of gossip columnists, movie critics and other media people here -none of whom she had invited. In fact, half of tinsel town's PR machinery seemed to be here. She had not reckoned on Jake's party being this big, but then she had no way of knowing that the team who had been cornered into footing the bill had simply added their own guest list to hers: post-production might not have got started yet, but as this had turned out to be their first official promotion, they were determined to make sure everyone was here even if that meant spending big bucks to get them.

"Greta, darling!" a middle-aged woman cooed over the din as she pushed her way through the throng in the hall. "How sweet of you to have us over." She knew what Greta didn't and couldn't resist her sly remark. It was wasted. "I was promised Rick would be here," she said, sucking the olive from her third canapé like a bird did a worm from its hole and juggling a cigarette lighter and a full glass of champagne. "*He* is the only reason I came."

If Greta was annoyed by this admission, she did not show it. Instead she answered sweetly, "He *is* here, honey," as she waved to a handsome young man across the room. The man raised his glass to her in a silent toast, and she smiled back. She would have died sooner than give the woman the satisfaction of her insult. She mouthed something back to the young man before turning her attention back to the woman who was about to drift off in search of the man she wanted. Greta caught hold of her arm. "Hold off half an hour or so, eh? He is busy right now."

The woman curled her lip. No one would have called it a smile. "Really? Who with?" she asked, blowing a perfect smoke ring in Greta's face.

Greta waved the smoke away, and smiled back. "Would I tell you if I knew?" she teased. "Just have to wait and see."

Masters was a magnet for journalists. Most would go anywhere and do almost anything in order to get a shot at any sort of interview with him, and though Greta had been clever enough to realise that her party was ensured the sort of success that translated into reams of press coverage the instant she could persuade him to come, she hadn't exactly reckoned on *them* being present at the time. They could scare off her prize guest because he had a famously difficult relationship with them. She had persuaded him to come because she had worn him down by reminding him almost on a daily basis that he was planning to be in town on the night, and this would be fun – a little get-together for a few people from the set that would help them all unwind. She stressed that Jake had said how hard it had been, and this was his way of saying thanks for the support. At least, that had been Greta's interpretation of Jake's version of the story. If his version had omitted some significant details, hers had omitted whole chunks of truth, including motive, and that was currently in danger of being thwarted by these media hordes. Her cosy little soiree had turned into a free for all, and all her hard work would end up being wasted if he left.

Greta's winning ways were less effective with the journalist, and after being unable to get anything else of any interest from Greta, she moved on, cutting her way through the crowd like a shark in a shoal of small fish.

"Stupid bitch," Greta muttered after her. It was much the same sort of language the woman was using about her. She was smiling sweetly again by the time Jake pushed his way through the crowd, spilling champagne over anyone in his path. It took only a few souls getting very wet for the path ahead of him to clear like magic.

"How's it goin', honey?" he bellowed, chewing on the end of a cigar. He was more interested in seeing it was properly lit than in any answer she might give him.

"Where have all these columnists come from?" she demanded. There was no reply. "Jake, I asked you a question! Do you think it's okay? There are a lot of press here, and I don't remember inviting them."

Drink had already started to impair Jake's thinking, and when he spotted a young woman in the corner whom he was interested in having in his next movie, he was anxious to leave because he didn't want to get drawn into any sort of discussion with his wife that would lead to her discovering things he didn't want her to know. Greta repeated her questions and then followed his eyes across the room to the scantily dressed young woman. "And don't you think she is a bit young for you? She will kill you."

The cross-eyed stare was an indication of how much he had drunk. "You reckon?" he slurred, "well, how come that tennis coach hasn't killed you yet?" Greta looked him in the eye and swore, but he merely laughed and slapped her bottom. "Party's fine. Don't fret." He was about to move off in pursuit of the young blond when he remembered something else. "Where's Susan? I haven't seen her all night."

Greta answered lightly, trying to feign disinterest. She had once been a passable dancer, but she had never been anything of an actress. "She's around." She was not a convincing liar.

"Around where, exactly?" he growled.

"The last time I saw her she was outside, talking to Rick, if you must know."

Jake exploded champagne. People turned to look at him.

"Calm down – you're drunk," she admonished. "And stop shouting. Everybody is looking at you. Susie was only talking to him." She had to provide him with details of when and where that was, before she pointed out, "Our daughter's got great taste," as she inspected her nail polish for flaws. "Do you like this shade of dark red? She chose it for me."

"Correction," he said, ignoring the comment about the nail polish and cutting straight to the important bit, "our daughter's got great taste in everything *but* men. She has lousy taste when it comes to men! Or have you forgotten," he threatened as he grabbed a new glass of champagne from a passing waiter, "she just got divorced for the second time!"

"You *are* drunk!" Greta warned heavily.

"I know, and I aim to get even drunker – when I've sorted out Masters," he raged, swallowing the contents of the glass in one go. Greta's pleas for him to stop shouting were wasted. "So what? Let 'em hear me. Then they won't be surprised when I thump him, will they?" It seemed unlikely he could thump anyone right now, least of all someone twenty years younger, even if he deserved it.

Greta thought better of saying so and instead said soothingly, "Stop being such a tyrant! Susie is twenty-two, not twelve, and she is divorced, like you say. She is a free agent, and whatever she does now, it's her business, not ours."

Jake said nothing until he remembered something that seemed relevant. "Would have thought that last divorce might have taught her something, even if the first didn't," he mused, plunging into melancholy for a moment. "Four million dollars. Shit! Still can't believe we paid that jerk four million dollars!"

"We didn't. Susie did."

"And where do you reckon her money comes from? Santa Claus?"

"She knows what it's about," Greta pointed out, pouting, "so stop treating her like a baby."

"When she stops acting like one, I will! Hell, why can't she be like everyone else in this house? Why can't she be satisfied with being discreet?"

"Like you?"

"No," he said coldly. "I had like you in mind."

"Let's not argue about this now," she pleaded. "Rick isn't after her money."

"Maybe not. It's what *else* he's after that bothers me."

"Honey! They are probably just having a nice conversation – offering each other some support, you know. He's just split up, too, hasn't he?" The look Jake gave her in reply was as good as thunder. "Come on, honey. He must be nearly old enough to be her father," she added dismissively, reading her husband's mind perfectly.

Jake grunted and puffed on his cigar. "Since when has that mattered in this town?"

"Mm, he *is* still quite a catch, isn't he?"

"So you tell me," he said darkly. "I see now why you went to such lengths to get him here."

"You know that had nothing to do with it, darling," she purred. "I was trying to help you, honey-bunch," she cooed, pinching his cheek.

He might have believed that last week. There was a moment's silence before he continued in a cold, menacing tone. "Master's reputation with women stinks. He stinks! He's bankable material only on celluloid. So I'm telling you now, if you're looking for a new husband for our Susie, leave him off the list. Find some guy who is manageable, not this head case. He screws women like joiners screw cupboards."

Greta rubbed his cheek again and repeated her assertion. "I told you, he's old enough to be her father."

"Why do you keep saying that? Is he?"

Greta laughed but did not dare say what she wanted to. Instead she said, "Look at her, Jake. Whose daughter is she?"

It was appeasement, but he pushed her hand away roughly. "Question is, does he know that? And does she care?"

"Don't worry," she offered as Jake walked away. "Susie will be fine as long as she follows my advice." Then she watched in silence as her husband swayed across the room, spoke briefly to the young blonde who was much younger than Susan, and then went off in search of his favourite daughter. Business could wait a while longer now that he had set it up. Family came first.

Susan Enderley was an opportunist who had been well prepared for this chance created by her mother, who was a master of the art. If the gentleman in question had not been in such a foul mood, the ladies' plans might well have succeeded. But Rick Masters *was* in a foul mood, and because of that Susan Enderley's schemes were bound to fail because when he decided he would rather be elsewhere, he meant exactly that. He was on his way back into the marquee in search of a drink as Jake was going out in search of him. Despite all his recent threats, Jake merely nodded as they passed, and then he turned round and headed back to the young blonde while Rick stopped to chat to a couple until he spotted the gossip columnist Greta had been playing with, heading his way. He moved on a second before she joined them. Third close encounter! This place was crawling with columnists of one sort or another. He had been here less than an hour, and he had spent most of it avoiding people. That was how Susan Enderley had managed to hold onto him for so long: she had saved him from one particularly hated columnist. It was definitely not the sort of gathering he had been led to expect, so he decided to make a run for it and was on his way towards the door when Wayne Crowther spotted him

Wayne was a powerful figure in the business. His presence underlined what Rick realised he should have recognised an hour ago: this wasn't about pleasure, this was about business. Crowther had spent the last half hour selling his man to an English producer, when by stroke of luck, the guy himself walked in at the crucial moment. The god of great deals was obviously smiling on him tonight. He could do real gratitude for that. His man might have been listening as he made the introductions, but it was difficult to be sure because he was loosening his shirt collar and undoing his bow tie.

"It's like an inferno in here," he complained, removing his jacket as Wayne tried to hand him some champagne in an attempt to focus his attention. The fixer nodded and explained there was a problem with the air conditioning, then he waited. Rick let him wait. Kindness was not one of his most noticeable attributes, and right now it was even less than usual. "Shouldn't take too much notice of what Wayne says," he offered to the English guy, leaning heavily on the sarcasm and mimicking Wayne's desperation perfectly. "He has a dangerous list to starboard too. It`s called money. It affects all his judgements." Then he knocked back some of the champagne before picking up his jacket and preparing to leave.

Wayne knew he was being mocked, even if he didn't quite understand how, because the English guy laughed and noted that Masters obviously knew more about his intended project than Wayne. Pretty smart guy. But that was no more than he had heard: the word was that Rick Masters was a smart guy. He was also known to be touchy and bad tempered, but cash registers rang when he was in a movie, and that was really all that mattered. Working with him might be more interesting than he had thought. Black humour was better than none.

"I'll send you the script. Read it and see what you think. If you are interested, we'll talk again." Then the man was gone.

Wayne looked at his man and shook his head in disbelief. "I've worked my butt off on him for the last hour," he pointed out sullenly. "He wanted Ford till I persuaded him you could do a better job." Expletives hardly helped, but he dropped a few choice ones anyway. "You only just got here? Loosen up and enjoy yourself – you've been working too hard. Here." He handed Rick another drink. "Find someone to cheer you up. Where's Susie Enderley gone?"

Rick stared hard at the older man and noted the vacant and rather bloodshot eyes, then he shook his head. "I don't know, and you shouldn't care. And I don't want another drink," he added, handing back the champagne and spilling a generous measure as he did.

Wayne sighed. "Thought we had this sorted," he said sourly, throwing in another couple of colourful expletives to underline his point. This time his man did not even look at him.

"You might have it sorted, but obviously *we* don't," he observed as he turned to leave.

Wayne grabbed his arm. "Susie Enderley is keen," he suggested hopefully, his beady eyes narrowing with expectation as he wiped the perspiration from his forehead with a large hankie. "Greta tells me she has been divorced for three weeks, poor kid. She needs someone to offer her some support."

"You go console her, then. I'm going."

Wayne stared morosely into Rick's glass. There went his gossip coverage as well as his movie deal, but there was no point wasting champagne, so he downed it in one. Was it his fault this guy didn't know a cert when he saw one?

Greta caught up with Rick by the door, and though she tried her level best to get him to stay, there was nothing she could do to stop him. It was cooler outside and he needed the air to clear his head. He fished in his pocket, hoping to find a light. Fortunately for him he located a battered book of matches with someone's telephone number on them in an inside pocket, so he conveniently forgot the "I quit" promise he had made again only yesterday and lit the cigarette Greta had handed him on the way out. A few puffs later, he stood on the rest and dismissed the valet's offers to get his car for him. He had scarcely covered fifty yards when someone else called his name. He recognised this voice too and its tone; he was not in the mood for either.

"Rick! Wait!" He didn't turn because he thought Paula Mallin might take the hint that he wasn't in the mood for company, however, she was operating on a different principle – the one that said persistence plus opportunity scores every time. She caught up with him at his car, by now genuinely breathless. "Are you going?" she gasped as provocatively as she knew how.

"Seems to be the idea."

"You going my way?" It was impossible to refuse without seeming churlish, but he could do churlish with ease. He was tired, and it had been a long day. "Because I just happen to live right where you are going," she said coyly, "but, even if you're not, you could be a real pal and take an old friend home. It wouldn't take you a minute in this." She stroked her hand along the hood. "I have to be on set by six."

He realised that he wasn't going to get out of this without being unpleasant, and he did not have sufficient energy or interest to be that again. He nodded to the door, and she folded herself elegantly into the passenger seat. "This is real nice. Is it new?" she asked, running her hand along the console.

"Sort of." He didn't disclose it had been on order so long it that it felt as if he had owned it a lifetime already.

"It's gorgeous!" she purred. "Ferraris are always so sexy, aren't they?" Her conversation rattled on effortlessly, leaving him to wonder why he hadn't bothered to be rude. Didn't matter now – he was lumbered with her, but he did not feel any obligation to be a conversationalist as well as a cab driver so he drove off in silence, completely occupied with the devils of his own discontent so that he soon forgot about hers.

Paula had arrived at the party on her lover's arm, aiming to get noticed by Jake Enderley, but she had ditched that in favour of leaving on Rick Master's arm, one obsession easily exchanged for another. It had only taken a manufactured row over nothing, for her to be able to rush out in tears seconds after she saw Rick leave alone; simple stuff for someone who earned her living this way. The tears had dried on her cheek long before she reached his car – her make-up still intact. No point in ruining an opportunity like this.

"You are very quiet tonight. You didn't even say hello when we met earlier."

"My loss."

"You'd never guess," she teased.

"Okay, sorry. Hi, Paula, it's nice to see you. How're things?"

"It's a bit late now, don't you think?" she reproved coyly, stretching her saucer-sized eyes even wider and fluttering the most expert set of lashes on the planet.

In between changing gears as he accelerated out of the drive, he flashed her a smile. Some critic had once said in a moment of unmitigated generosity, "On film this guy's smile must be worth every dime of a million bucks because it has an effect on women similar to what full production in a nuclear plant has on the grid." Whether or not that was just the rhetoric of the trade, this smile was sufficiently powerful to make his passenger feel confident enough to snuggle deeper into the leather seating, fold her legs more seductively, and work those lashes again.

"I was beginning to think that you and I weren't friends anymore," she said.

Rick pulled up smartly outside the apartment block she indicated, and then he leapt out to open the door for her. It was not gallantry: it was manipulation. He reckoned this way she wouldn't have any excuse to sit and talk for another hour before she made a move. The strategy backfired on him because climbing out of such a low-slung car with any degree of style was not easy, but Paula could accomplish it beautifully. She'd had plenty of practice, and none of it was wasted as she held onto his outstretched hand, swung her legs out first, and then drew herself up effortlessly to stand only inches away from him. There was no way he could miss the perfume or the cleavage. The perfume was marketed as intoxicating, and at this range it was positively lethal on its own, but with the special effects thrown in as well, he didn't stand a chance.

Neither of them moved for a second, and then she smiled and said huskily, "Come in for a coffee, or something?"

"I thought you had an early call."

"I do. I just don't feel sleepy anymore." It needed no further explanation.

He really was about to say, "Sorry, another time," when he looked into her flashing green eyes and lost it. The next minute he was questioning what he had to rush away for anyway. There was nothing except an empty hotel suite or a long drive home, and though he had left Jake's party intent on doing one or the other, both had suddenly lost their appeal. No empty house or hotel room could compete with this. Neither of those other things could satisfy his ill-tempered boredom, whereas this just might. Perry could wait. He had promised to be home by Saturday, and tonight was only Thursday, so he drove his car into the basement parking lot and they rode the elevator together with the perfume still talking.

She asked, "Are you trying to get me drunk?" as he handed her a full glass in her kitchen.

"Do I need to?" The irony was lost on her, but she smiled as she touched his face.

"You look worn out," she purred. "Five weeks over is enough to wear anyone out. You work too hard, and are too much of a perfectionist. You need to relax more, unwind."

He grunted. She wasn't sure what that meant, but she was not put off by it. She was a stunning young woman, and she knew he was no more averse to beautiful young women caressing him than most other men. The fact that he had dated some of the most beautiful women on the planet had never dulled his appetite for more. There was no reason he should change now.

Paula rose early before it was properly light. This was part of her life, but the alarm that was routinely programmed to repeat its warning beeps until she was sufficiently awake to crawl out of bed and switch it off, was not needed today. She had been roused instead by someone stirring in the bed next to her, and despite it seeming like only minutes since she had closed her eyes, she had slipped out to prevent the clock from disturbing her companion. She had showered and dried her hair before she heard her name, then she abandoned her routine, made coffee, and perched on the end of the bed concentrating all her energy on being fascinating. Rick lay back and listened to her chatter, only interrupting once to warn her that she had better hurry.

She had just finished dressing as the car arrived to take her to the studio. The doorbell rang impatiently as she checked her bag. "I am coming!" she shouted to the man six floors below as she left her apartment key by the bedside, saying she would see him later, much as though they had spent a great deal of their lives together.

Rick took a drag of a cigarette and then stubbed it out. Smoking in bed was a habit he abhorred. He had picked it up from Sherri, but though she was long gone, her habits were proving more difficult to break. He ground the cigarette to pulp in the ashtray and lay staring up at the ceiling. It was a pretty unremarkable ceiling, just plain white with no lumps, bumps, or cracks. He followed the path of a tiny spider attempting to cross its vastness and then grunted sympathetically when he recognised the tiny insect had not covered a fraction of the distance needed to get to the other side; it was still stuck there right in the middle, stranded. "If you're heading for the other side, pal, there's a lot of walking ahead of you," he advised, wondering if the spider could have any idea of the size of the task that faced it. Without any possibility of an answer, he dismissed the spider's plight to consider his own.

Why he had got started on this particular journey was pretty unfathomable. And what lay ahead of him? Paula had been as keen as he was last night, but he had guessed from this morning's conversation that that was where their expectations parted company; she clearly expected more. Last night it had not been mentioned, but this morning had turned out exactly how he knew it would. It didn't help one bit to know that she had engineered the entire situation. "I guess I am just like you, pal," he said to the spider. "A lot of walking to do." With a last glance at the tiny black speck he got up and went to shower.

He was still figuring how to resolve his dilemma as he dressed. Okay, so he had taken easily what she had offered lightly, but that didn't help much because he had realised years ago that most women were incapable of a no-strings relationship, even when they did the offering. That sort of exonerated her, even though it left him without a plausible excuse. It was a shame he had stumbled on that particular truth, and he had regretted finding it ever since because it had spoiled his ability to take what was on offer without recognising the cost. Paula was just the latest to wring this weird sort of guilt from him. Someday some jerk would make a fortune telling everyone that women were different than men, but until that happened there seemed little chance that anyone would accept it in this day and age.

He stared hard at his reflection in the bathroom mirror. "Keep to practicalities," he advised as he set about searching for a disposable razor. The place was a mess, and when he did find a packet buried beneath the jumble of all sorts of pots and potions, there were no new razors in it. He frowned at the empty packet and then screwed it up and threw it away, knocking over a sign by the side of the basin. He set the sign upright. The message on the tiny sandwich board read, "Take whatever life offers you; it may never offer it again."

He shook his head and straightened the sign gently. A faded memory of an old man who had paraded around the bus station of the town in which he had grown up, came into his head. The man had worn a much larger version of the same sort of board. What was it the old man's board had said? "Hell is here and now." He had never understood that or thought of it since; funny that he should be remember it again after all these years.

It was nine before he left the apartment, but having decided his course of action, he carried it out without any further deliberation. After driving round the block, he stopped by the janitor's office to leave the key Paula had supposedly forgotten. It was the best he could do. The janitor thought nothing of it. "Sure thing. Or shall I call her? Then you can return it yourself."

Rick shook his head and thanked him, saying that he was running late. The guy weighed up the unshaven face and less than wonderful appearance and nodded. Folks generally didn't realise movie stars never looked quite the same in real life. They were quite ordinary really.

Rick bypassed breakfast because he had a thumping headache, probably due to last night's champagne. That annoyed him, though regret was fleeting. "Should have known Jake would only give away cheap stuff!" he grumbled. He shaved, changed, and then checked out of his hotel. Home was a good three hour drive away, but depending on traffic and how often he broke the speed limit, it could be a lot less. This morning it would take longer because he needed to avoid the law, so he would have to stay within the limit all the way.

An hour or so later, he pulled off the freeway to make a call because the car phone was out of order again, and no amount of cursing and banging was making any difference. There was no point in having a phone that only worked on certain days! Did no one deliver anything perfect these days? This was the second time in three weeks the thing had packed up. He had no more success with the payphone at the gas station either, and so instead of wasting any more energy cursing, he swung the car around in a parking lot and then joined the freeway headed in the opposite direction until he hit the coast road heading north. Going home would solve nothing. Sure, he knew there were things he had to do there, but he also knew he lacked the patience to do them right now. He had put off going home last night because he had needed distraction. He still needed it – the hangover simply multiplied the need. On an impulse he decided to go and visit friends; it might help, and it was less troublesome than picking up women. Was that why people visited friends? He dismissed such inconvenient speculation and chanced the police by putting his foot down. Driving helped his mood, occupation generally did as long as he could find things that were sufficiently interesting. At present the only things that seemed interesting enough, for long enough, were work and driving, and given that there was no work available to him right now, he allowed himself the other pleasure, hoping that it would at least occupy all of his attention for a couple of hours.

He tried the car phone a second time an hour later, but the thing was still not working, and he slammed it down hard as he pulled over to the next diner. The call box there was working. It rang out for a minute before someone answered. "Hi, Laura, it's Rick. I'm not far from your place. Are you going to give me lunch if I call by?"

Laura Der Witt was more than happy to offer him lunch. It turned out she and her husband, Jon, were both home, which was even better. Then of course there was Nina, and at the thought of her, Rick`s face crumpled into the nearest thing to a smile it had managed for weeks. It would be real nice to see them all again.

Chapter Eleven

Sarah was up at her usual time of six o'clock on Friday morning so she had showered while most of her fellow campers were still dreaming. While they were thinking about getting up, she was already waiting impatiently for her breakfast. That was the end of her perfect day! The diner staff sabotaged her schedule by being young and unconcerned about the value of the precious minutes they were allowing to slide so carelessly past them, but then, most of them were still half asleep, whereas she was wide awake – and cross! Unfortunately she had ordered before she realised their problem, and so all she could do now was urge them on with fixed smiles and a not so discreet glance at her watch every time one of them was within range.

Every bit of this frustration was rooted in performance anxiety. She would not have admitted to that, but punctuality was too ingrained in her psyche for it to be discarded simply because of the shortcomings of one diner's dozy staff. Obviously, they did not understand it was the only day she had to fit the Joshua trees into her holiday. Or, how determined she was to fit them in! But that's why the early start was essential. According to the majority opinion of last night's customers the Joshua Tree Park was a couple of hundred miles in the opposite direction to the one she was meant to be going. And four hundred miles in one day was a lot of miles, even by her recent standards. It would be impossible if she didn't get started until nearly lunchtime because she just had to be where she was meant to be, by tonight. No excuses. And on top of all that, the weather forecast this morning had warned of potential storms so even more reason why she needed to get a move on. She tried to convey all that to a passing waitress in the hope that it might inspire some action, but the girl merely shrugged her shoulders, shook her head and pointed to the cloudless blue sky outside. Clearly, the weather did not concern her at all. Sarah nodded and tried to feel as confident. Maybe the weather forecasts here were no more accurate than they were back home.

That's how she arrived at the park much later than planned, and that's why she set off to explore immediately she arrived. She was anxious to make up as much lost time as possible. However, that made lunch so late that it qualified as afternoon tea, and then fatigue hit her so hard, that she had to sit down in the shade with her sketch pad to try to capture an image of the strange trees because she had insufficient energy for anything else. She had not allowed for the heat or for her tiredness. Concentration soon capitulated as the last remnants of her energy evaporated, and then motivation melted away in the searing heat.

She awoke with a start. Another schedule malfunction! The nap had sapped what strength she possessed, so she could quite easily have stayed there all afternoon, lazing in the shade, baking like a fat lizard on a hot rock, except unlike any of the resident lizards, she had only another hour or so to see this place. After having travelled so far to get here, she had no intention of spending it all frying in the sun, however attractive that might seem right now. Habits could not be abandoned for sheer indulgence; *work* beckoned, and that meant there were boxes to be ticked, so she struggled to her feet, trying to salvage enough enthusiasm to get started. Cold water provided the necessary motivation.

It had been a good summer even by California's standards. As far north as Santa Barbara, the temperature had been soaring for days, and although today's fresher breeze from the Pacific had not been strong enough to cool the interior, it had helped to make the coastal areas a little more comfortable. Rick Masters drove his car through the gates of a discreet Pacific coast residence just before lunchtime. His friends, the Der Wittes, lived in this secluded house set high into a cliff face a few miles from Santa Barbara. It was a splendidly isolated spot with only the coastal highway linking it to the outside world, but as that road led to all the places a rich Californian might reasonably want to get, life here was very pleasant.

The house had been designed by one of the giants of modern architecture back in the thirties, and it had featured regularly in all the notable design journals ever since. Both its previous owners had been overwhelmed by this pedigree so had embraced the role of custodian of a national treasure with almost humiliating subservience. Its present owners were less easily impressed because they were *really* famous, whereas the house was just well-known in design circles. Nothing of its presence was visible to travellers along the road linking it to the highway and it only appeared like magic to those who survived the sharp bend in its drive, but even then it blended so effortlessly into its surroundings that it was difficult to tell where one ended and the other started. First-time visitors were always impressed by this engineering feat. Some frequent guests remained impressed, and Rick was one of them. This house was the most luxurious troglodyte dwelling imaginable because it was literally carved from the rock, but one had to stand on the beach or be out at sea to fully appreciate how that worked. The whole structure had such a deeply intimate relationship with sea and land, that the terrace that wrapped itself around its exterior like a great sea serpent seemed intent on reclaiming it for the sea, with only the rock face maintaining its equilibrium and holding it firm on the land.

To the east the house looked out over wild breakers crashing on the rocks below, but on the western side the ground fell away more gradually, allowing a staircase to be cut into the rock face that led down from the drive under the house until it reached a boathouse in a small bay. This was the best place to admire how the different levels had been cut into the rock, and see how the house depended for its survival on the mountain protecting it from the unrelenting force of the ocean. In spite of all of that, it was the ocean, not the rock face that was the main attraction here; all the main reception areas and some of the bedrooms faced out over the Pacific. It was a serious piece of modern architecture, but it was no museum. A child's toys and the paraphernalia of its owner's latest hobby invariably adorned its fashionable interior. The child was currently into bikes and plastic tractors, the owner sub aqua diving, which was marginally less messy than the old jukeboxes which had been his last passion.

It was well over a year since Rick had been here, and he felt a quick stab of guilt that it was only a selfish whim that brought him today. He did not have time for much reflection before the lady of the house ran up the rock steps waving an enthusiastic welcome.

"Hi, you. We were beginning to think you had forgotten us!" Laura chided, kissing his cheek lightly. He made the usual excuses about pressure of work. "You're forgiven that, but you are still in trouble about the Oscars," she warned. "Did Molly not tell you? I rang you nearly every day for four weeks. I even got you a formal invite to the party."

"Sure she did. What can I say except I'm sorry? I was away." The look on her face signified some measure of doubt. "Hey, if I had been here, I would have been with you, I promise. Did it go well? Did he get my message?"

Her frown melted as she threaded her arm through his and nodded. "It went brilliantly, and he's got your wicked wit framed on the wall. He is so proud of that lump of glitz. He said it's even better than the hundred-metre javelin cup he won at school. Don't tell him I told you, but I caught him polishing it the first week he had it."

Rick laughed. "It was a great piece of work, and he deserved it. The best doesn't always win, so it was good that he did."

"Talking of trophies, this is new, isn't it?" she asked, turning her attention to admiring the car.

"Consolation prize," he said lightly as they went back towards the steps.

She looked directly at him, trying to figure out what that might mean, but he was difficult to read – always had been. "Jon's working on the terrace, it's a bit cooler down there," she added, changing the subject without warning. "He doesn't know you're coming yet."

"How come?"

"Because, I haven't told him yet," she answered simply, pressing her fingers to his mouth and indicating for him to be quiet. "I am warning you, the Oscar euphoria has had plenty of time to wear off – he has been in a foul mood all week. I think I stopped asking Tuesday, and it hasn't got any better since then. Worse, if anything!"

"Are you two speaking?"

She stopped and turned to face him, pouting demurely and putting her hands on her hips as she sighed perfectly. "How come you always know everything?" she asked in the tone that conveys, why do I always give everything away so easily?

"Well, are you or aren't you? Just tell me which it is before I walk into the middle of it and get shot at from both sides."

"I might, now that you are here," she conceded. "But only because he might not bite my head off every time I say something now that there is a witness."

"That bad, eh?"

"Worse," Laura said grimly. "When Jon has a lousy week, we all do. This week has been the pits, so I am glad you came to save me." He wanted to ask more, but she went on chatting as they walked down the steps, and he put it aside, realising he would know all too soon if it was anything really serious. "You don't look that good, either," she said after scrutinising his face. "You okay?"

"I have a hangover, if you must know."

She frowned but withheld her comment because she knew her silence would be as eloquent as censure. His genuine groan made her smile, and she tapped his arm playfully. A quick succession of well-understood gestures was about to achieve what a week of sulks and silences had failed to do: she was about to laugh. It was good to have someone around who could make her do that. Jon had been a pain all week, and that was never a laughing matter. He might be accepted as a creative genius by movie people, but that did not make him a domestic angel – rather the opposite. Others brought work home with them. With Jon, work never left home except when he did.

"The Enderleys' bash?" she asked curiously, recovering her composure. Now she had him intrigued, and he asked how she knew that. "Well, let me see, how do I know that? Is it because I have my spies everywhere? Or maybe because I am tuned in on your frequency and can read your mind? Or even because you told us you were doing Jake's movie, and I knew about last night?" When she had his full attention, she confided dully, "It was none of those things, though I am quite attracted to the reading your mind bit. We had an invite."

"Didn't know you were buddies with the Enderleys," Rick interrupted.

"We're not. Hardly know them, but Jake's been trying to get Jon to work with him on something or other for months. I don't know what it is. But Jon's not that keen, so he didn't want to go, so we didn't go. End of story. And I didn't believe Greta when she said she had persuaded you to go. I might have gone alone if I had known you were really going to be there. I could've left old grumpy at home."

"Wouldn't that have made him grumpier still?"

"What, that I had gone to meet you?"

"No, that you had gone alone."

"Yeah, I suppose so," she admitted reluctantly, "but it's not my fault he's had a bad week, and I hate staying home."

"I remember."

Laura swung her blonde hair back from her face and lifted her sunglasses onto her head. "That's why I didn't believe Greta," she said a little peevishly. "I figured you wouldn't go. It's not like you to go to these sort of things, but I suppose men are allowed to change their minds just as much as women. Though it's a pain," she warned him, "when a girl can't work out a man's whereabouts because he changes his mind!"

"I haven't changed my mind about anything. I was in town for the Cavendish dinner, and Greta had been calling me for days. In the end I said I would call in just to get the damned woman off my phone. Satisfied?"

This time his companion stepped out in front of him and blocked the narrow path completely. Her hands had gone automatically to her hips, and she used her most offended tone to complain, "*I* called you for weeks before the Oscars, and you never answered *my* calls."

"That's not true. I always return your calls, except when I'm not there. And I wasn't there then."

"Molly said so every time I rang," she said sullenly.

"So why keep ringing? She passes on messages."

"I have a better idea. Why don't you just leave us a number when you're away? What if there is an emergency? This *was* an emergency."

Instead of answering her questions, Rick said, "I rang you as soon as I got the message."

"Or get one of these cell phone things."

"No way. I have enough problems as it is without adding to them."

"I would be adding to them?" she demanded innocently.

She had asked this spontaneously, so he answered it the same way. "You are going to change the habits of a lifetime?"

Her gasp of horror could not be controlled, but she followed it with another sharp tap on his arm. It was never unsatisfying to touch him, and this exchange had provided her with another acceptable reason to do exactly that. "You horror! I'm sure that I can't be in the same league as Greta Enderley and her plotting." His innocence prompted the explanation. "Come on, Rick! I said we didn't know them well, not that we had just landed from Mars. Greta is a schemer – it's all she does. Don't tell me you don't know that, or why she went to all that trouble to get you there, because everyone else does. You don't, do you?" She laughed out loud. He had to admit he didn't have a clue what she was talking about. "And they say women are naive," she cooed while taking hold of his arm. She had to watch his face for a moment before she grasped he was never going to ask what she meant, and she didn't want to be denied the pleasure of imparting this particular piece of wisdom. "Oh, Rick, you can be so tiresome! Susan Enderley needs a new husband!" After not getting any response, she slid her hand down his arm and took hold of his left hand. She looked up and half smiled as she explained. "She must have been on her own all of a month, poor lamb. Being on her own does not suit her. Will this be number three, or is it number four? Either way, it's a lot for a girl her age!" Rick still didn't answer, but he reclaimed his hand as she got to examining his ring finger. "Everyone else knows Greta is drawing up a list of possibles, and you might be on it. Hey, you might be top of it." This time he shook his head and pocketed his hand as she jested, "Still not the marrying kind, huh?" This last comment held something more than plain teasing, but he ignored that, too.

They reached the spot where the path opened out onto the terrace, and Rick looked around to locate the man they had been discussing. It wasn`t difficult, he was seated in the middle of a long expanse of stone seating following the terrace curve. Jon was protected from the fierce sun by a huge red canvas umbrella that clashed perfectly with his vibrantly coloured shirt so that even his Bermuda`s seemed dull by comparison. He held a phone to his ear with one hand, typed with the other, and manoeuvred a mobile trolley containing a mound of paperwork and a pile of directories with his right foot – the perfect way to work. He had been completely absorbed in his task all morning, but the sound of voices and laughter had distracted him. The house had been deathly quiet all week, so the sound of chatter and laughter had cut through such well-established silence like a knife going through butter, reinforcing the fact that he and Laura hadn't spoken for days. What was worse, they hadn't laughed together like that for … well, he couldn't remember how long. The situation was so bad right now that he knew the house help tried to keep out of his way and say as little as possible when their paths did cross; even Nina had been quiet this week. The pair were still out of sight when he recognised Rick's voice, but his grin was replaced by something approaching a frown as they came round the corner arm in arm. He pretended to be working when they stopped on the corner, but he was watching from behind his shades as his wife swung on his friend's arm, her body teasing him just as intently as her smile. His expression froze a little; Nina did this with him, laughed and pouted in his face to tease him. He loved it with Nina. He continued watching, mesmerised by his wife repeatedly tossing her hair back over her shoulder as she pirouetted around Rick. He knew these moves and he knew what they meant, and although in his heart he understood that she was only flirting, testing her powers over a very attractive man – and she could no sooner resist doing that than she could stop buying new frocks – his head strangled some enthusiasm for their visitor. He could overlook all Laura`s other foibles and make allowances for this one - with anyone other than this man. Too much history, too much pain, and too much to lose. The look on his face settled into a deeper frown.

"Rick, ol' buddy, it's good to see you. Where you been hiding?" he shouted as he headed towards the two of them. The discussion about not hiding was repeated for his benefit as they all sat down, and then Rick's inquiry about him being too busy was brushed aside in like manner. "Nothing I'm not glad to have a break from," he quipped. "You timed your arrival well, I think lunch should be about ready."

"Think I'd have come all this way just to see you two if I had not been promised some of Maria's cooking?"

"You knew he was coming?" he asked Laura abruptly. She nodded and turned away without answering him. Rick looked from one to the other, but neither spoke or looked at the other, Laura's smile had gone from her face, and there was an uncomfortable silence.

"Listen, you guys, how about you call a ceasefire? At least till I leave."

Jon considered this carefully and looked at Laura's back. Then he took her hand and pulled her towards him, she resisted and continued to sulk until he kissed her and apologised sufficiently that her smiles were restored.

Five minutes later lunch was announced by a simpering, blushing, middle-aged Maria. "Do you have to make love to every woman you meet?" Jon demanded sulkily as she left. "I think I object to my cook making special favours for anyone but me."

"Did Laura never tell you about me and Maria?"

"Laura tells me nothing, least of all about you. Like your visit this morning, I am last to know! The whole house knows, but not me."

Laura kissed his cheek. "It was a surprise, Jon. You know surprises – nice things that cheer you up!"

He accepted her kiss. "I still object to your relationship with my cook," he said to Rick. "I hope it's not intended to lure her away to that fruit farm of yours."

"Would I dare? Besides, Molly would never tolerate another woman in her kitchen. I'm just like you, buddy: I do as I'm told."

"Good! Remember it stays that way! Good cooks are not easy to get hold of in this place: Movie stars are ten a dime, but good cooks without tantrums are worth a million bucks."

"You pay her that much?" Everyone knew Jon had only two financial weaknesses, Laura and his hobbies, so this was no innocent remark. Only someone as close to Jon as Rick could get away with saying it. They went in to lunch still discussing catering and the worth of a good cook. Jon was not satisfied until he had heard the full story of Rick's last visit when this "special arrangement" had been made.

"Hey, a guy has only so much willpower and this was her special pasta that was on offer. Come on, what do you take me for?"

"So what happened about the weight?"

"Didn't do it. Fattest POW on record."

"No wonder the bills always go up when you come!"

Laura said, "Okay, you two, quit the war, let's eat."

Over lunch Jon pushed Rick for a game of squash after they had eaten, and all his protestations were dealt with ruthlessly - by the time they got to the club their lunch would be digested and they could find him some shorts that would not be totally offensive to his sense of style.

Laura caught up with them in the hall as they were leaving. "Maria wants to know if Mister Masters will be staying for dinner."

"I usually wait for an invitation from my hosts."

Laura grinned, "Not here, you don't. You should know by now it's a standing invitation. Come when you want, stay as long as you want, do what you want. So, are you staying for dinner? Can I tell her yes?" She took his silence as agreement, kissed Jon lightly on the cheek, and then turned to kiss Rick, too. "I'll even get Mai to wash you a shirt if you don't have any clean ones. What more can I offer you?"

Rick laughed easily. "Okay, dinner will be great. Bag's in the car. The shirt deal sounds good, too."

Jon ended the niceties. "Come on, are we going or not?"

"Listen to him," Laura complained. "I have been trying to get him to do something all week – play golf, go to the club, anything. I am so glad you came; at least you've managed to get him to move. See? He's almost in a good mood now! He has been awful all week." The culprit's earnest denial was dismissed. "You *have* too," she insisted, kissing him again. "Not one of my charms has worked on you all week."

Jon frowned but kissed her neck gently. "Oh yes they have. Don't tell lies!"

It wasn't difficult to see who the performance was for.

"Okay, you two, cool it. Are we going to play squash, or can I just flop out there like I really want to?"

"No, you take him out and make sure he has worked off the rest of his bad temper before you bring him back," Laura replied.

As they walked back through the house Rick asked about the cause of their difficulty. His answer was preceded by Jon`s look of undisguised disgust. "Who are you, a knight on a white charger coming to the rescue? Come on, pal, this is no damsel – this is Laura we are talking about here!"

The lady in question overheard that as she returned from the car with Rick`s bag so she let them know she was within earshot; Jon`s sarcasm leaving her free to make a point of her own. "Rick, a knight?" she laughed wickedly, "I doubt he has a chivalrous bone in his body, but I guess we can make allowances for him as well," then she turned to Rick and explained confidentially, "you will have to forgive Jon, he has knights on horses on the brain. Perhaps not on white chargers," she mused, smiling benignly at her husband, then, like the skilled actress she was, she delivered her punch line without hesitation, "more like knights *not* on black chargers."

Jon winced and turned to say something, but she had gone. Rick just looked mystified and asked, "What the hell is going on with you two?"

"Nothing. Just a disaster with some damned horse. Your car or mine?"

"Mine's out."

"Okay, yours it is, but drive slow, okay? Like inside the speed limit all the way."

They discussed the saga of the black horse all the way to the drive until Jon stopped dead in his tracks when he spotted the black Ferrari. He whistled as he walked around it, admired it, and then admitted, "Pity it's not a real horse," he joked as he brushed his hand over the badge.

"Is that all you're going to say?"

"No. Nice car."

"Don't you want to see what it will do?"

"No! You know I hate speed. Save it for the girls; they will be much more impressed with your performance. Is this the same car I saw in Paris last month?"

"Well, not this one, but yeah, one like it was there."

"Must be good for the image. How long did you have to wait for it?"

"Long enough."

They were almost at the club before Jon asked, "Do you know who said the line about kids and animals?" Rick shook his head. "Neither do I, but whoever it was, they sure as hell knew what they were talking about. They're nothing but trouble!"

"Is that kids or animals?" Rick asked, knowing full well that Jon's Oscar movie had starred a particularly difficult thirteen-year-old who had plagued him for the entire shoot.

His answer was reward enough. "Both!" It was a declaration of undisguised, desperate emotion, "Though right now I guess it's animals – and horses in particular. We have one week's location work left, and the damned thing gets colic. Why now? I thought only babies got that. It's why I have been home all week. No point going without the damned thing. Give me a car chase any day." The suggestion that he get another horse was greeted with sarcasm. "Gee, I'd never have thought of that! What do you think I have been doing all day, every day, this week? It's not that easy. Folks who say we get money for nothing should try dealing with the money men when something like this happens. I have had nightmares about black horses, and my ulcer is doing long multiplication sums on what it's costing. We're already over budget."

"Didn't know you had one!" Rick quipped.

"Who doesn't?"

"Me!"

"You don't? Luck, pal. Sheer luck!"

"Well, all this searching for black horses will not have gone unnoticed. It will probably increase their going rate next time anyone wants one. I think I might get Perry to train some of ours. I can't believe we haven't thought about that before now; it could be real profitable. I'll suggest it to him. Thanks."

"Any time! I'm glad my problems are helping you make money!"

Jon belonged to an exclusive sports club on the coast. It took an hour to get there but by the time they did they had caught up with each other's news. Perhaps it was the banter, or perhaps it was his frustration, but something increased Jon's appetite for their game, and he soundly thrashed Rick, who could not generate sufficient interest to fire his competitive streak. The hangover wasn't helping any.

"Would have expected you to be fitter," Jon jibed as they came sweating off the court.

"I don't play much anymore," was Rick's only excuse.

"Maybe you are just getting old like the rest of us!"

"Come on, let's get changed, and I'll buy you a drink."

The clubhouse was full, and they stayed longer than they had intended because Jon's ego was sufficiently inflated by his win over the younger man that all his previous bad humour had disappeared; he even bought a round of drinks when it was his turn. One drink became two, and two easily became three as they chatted to acquaintances. Then Jon concluded some business with a man he had been trying to get hold of for a while. "Glad we came," he said as they finally dragged themselves away. "It's been a profitable afternoon." And he continued repeating the details of the deal he had just set up as they walked back to the car. It was a good deal, and he was glad that Rick had been there to see it; in a town like Hollywood, one was only ever as good as one's last deal. The fact that they weren't officially in Hollywood escaped him, but then, everyone knew Hollywood was not about geography; it was about a way of life based on a philosophy whose main tenet was, "The reason for all things is power."

"Do something for me," Jon bargained as they stashed the gear in the car.

"Sure. What's that?"

"How about going back, you stay inside the speed limit all the way! Besides the usual reason of I have a wife and child to support, there are at least three insurance companies depending on me to stay alive. Yours might not bother, but mine would be upset. In other words, your car is nice – correction, your car is very nice – your driving is lousy!"

It was late by the time they got back, and Laura was nowhere to be found so the two men disappeared down to the boathouse to inspect some new diving gear Jon had just acquired. They were trying to come to some agreement about when they could test it out when Laura came down to remind them Maria had been slaving away all afternoon over a special dinner, and she would not be impressed if it went cold before they ate it.

As promised, Mai had washed and ironed the unexpected guest's only spare shirt, the dress one, as well as pressing his trousers, so Rick looked rather formal compared to his host, who had simply opted for a dressier pair of shorts and a louder T-shirt. Laura had changed into a dazzling silver cocktail dress by the time she joined them on the terrace at six. Her appearance sparked more of Jon's sarcasm. "Is this an award show?"

"Ignore him," Laura advised Rick. "I love men in gorgeous clothes. Who made the shirt?"

"Come on, be honest! You just love men!" her husband said, kissing her neck. "Especially me – even though I don't have on a formal shirt."

"So I do," she said smoothly, taking him by one arm and Rick by the other. "But seeing as how I have two handsome men tonight, I'll let you both take me in to dinner."

Dinner lived up to everyone's expectations: the perfection of the evening providing a fitting backdrop for Maria's famous cooking and Jon's excellent wine cellar. It was easy to feel pleased with the whole world on such a night, and the conversation reflected that right until the very last of the coffee was being drunk on the terrace nearly two hours later. Rick stretched back in his chair and shook his head as Laura offered him another sort of drink. "I'm fine," he said. And he was. In the company of good friends, enjoying great food and with the unparalleled beauty of the shimmering, silver, evening ocean and sky, it was impossible not to feel at peace with the world. Maybe he just needed to buy a house on a beach.

"Don't go in," Laura pleaded as Jon headed for the house.

"I'm getting us some scotch," Jon said as he disappeared inside. He re-emerged a minute later carrying a bottle of his favourite single malt. "You can finish the wine, but we need a proper drink." Rick declined that as well on the grounds that he was driving and must be going soon. "Stay over, then. We can finish this off, then if we're half sober in the morning, we can take the boat out early and do some fishing, maybe even try out the new gear."

It was tempting, but even as Rick screwed up his face to consider it, he remembered his previous promise. He couldn't do this and keep that as well. "I thought you had to find a black horse."

"I do, but even owners of black horses are in bed at five, aren't they?"

"And you are seriously suggesting we won't be if we drink all that? No way! Anyway, I have to get back," Rick said as he struggled to his feet. "Perry has been ringing me all week. It seems pretty urgent, and I promised I would be there by tomorrow at the latest. He has a week off, and I said I'd see him before he goes." He glanced at his watch. "That means I ought to be making a move right now." He drained the last of his coffee. "Thanks for the offer, though. Maybe we can get together some other time."

"Sure. Give me a bell whenever. As soon as I get this week's work out of the way, it's all studio stuff. Call me."

"How's Perry working out?" Laura asked out of politeness rather than any real interest. It was also a ruse to avoid talking about black horses again, as well as an excellent delaying tactic. Rick turned to face her. "He had only just started work last time you were here," she explained.

"He's fine. A good sort of guy to have around. He knows his stuff, so I just leave him to get on with it."

"Isn't that a bit risky with someone you don't know that well?"

"I hired the guy to run the estate Laura, so that's what I expect him to do," Rick said in as neutral a voice as he could manage. "And as he's already turned a huge operating loss into a small profit, I can't complain. He gets his share, too, so I presume everyone's happy."

"You share the profits with him?" There obviously hadn't been anything so scandalous in these parts for a long while. Rick nodded and watched with grim amusement as Laura struggled with this information. "I thought you said you financed the horse business to get him."

"That too, and it's not all for him. It's a partnership: my money and his skill. I benefit as well as him, so we're both happy. Happy workers are good workers, or something like that." He watched her digest this new piece of information; it was even harder than the last.

"That's the trouble with staff," she said flippantly. "Motivating them is always such an uphill struggle, and then when you do, they always want more – or someone else comes along and takes them from under your nose."

"Didn't you always want more every movie? I certainly do." Rick countered.

She batted her eyelids. "Is it the same?"

"I reckon so. I pay my people what they are worth: Perry's good, and so I pay him well because I intend to keep him."

Conversation dried up at this point as Laura recalled the row she'd had earlier in the week with Nina's nanny over a ten–dollar-per-week rise. This couldn't be the same as that though. Thinking about her daughter reminded her of something less unpleasant, so she changed the subject.

"Nina should be home soon – please don't go till you have seen her. Mai let slip this afternoon you were here, and she wanted to wait for you then. The only way I could get her to her appointments was by promising her you would wait until she got back. I did expect her back by now; Mai has gone to collect her."

"In that case, I reckon I'd better stay a bit longer."

Less than ten minutes later, Nina came rushing in like a miniature whirlwind, demanding breathlessly if Uncle Rick was still here. "If you are referring to me, yes, I am," Rick growled from the lounger where he was hidden from her view. She greeted her parents dutifully, brushing her lips quickly across their cheeks, and then she threw out one of her cheekiest, cutest smiles as she hurled herself across his lap, wrapping both arms around his neck and smothering him with kisses. He returned her hug and tried to disentangle arms and legs, but she was not to be moved from his knee. "Hi, princess. Where have you been hiding all day?"

"Piano lessons. Ugh!" She pulled an exquisitely ugly face to show her disgust. "Then, when I got back, you and Daddy had gone out, and then I had to go to Marianne's birthday party." She sighed heavily. "I thought I would never get to see you. So I am very happy that you are still here!" She kissed him again to prove that, and then she remembered something that made her frown. "I thought you had forgotten me!" she declared petulantly.

Rick shook his head. "Not possible. Why did you think that?"

"Because you haven't been here for *ages*!" she said. Everyone laughed. "I know so!" she remonstrated, pouting. "He hasn't!"

Rick nodded and tried to sympathise. "How do you know so?" he asked.

"Because I have had one Christmas and two birthdays since you came last time," she said seriously.

He considered this information carefully. It was correct. "Well, I'm here now, aren't I?" He offered no explanation for his lengthy absence.

"So have you missed me?" she asked in her best grown-up voice.

"What do you think?"

"I think …" she started. Then she stopped, reflected, and changed her mind about whatever it was she had intended to say; instead she slid down from his knee, stood in front of him, and looked up at him through lashes which she batted expertly even at six years old. "Are you staying for ages now?" she asked, suddenly serious.

He regarded the waiting little face and smiled again. What was it this kid did to him? "I'm not staying at all, princess. This is a flying visit. I only stayed this long so I could say hello."

"Oh!" Her face fell. She had taken it for granted he would be staying, because he always had before. She handled disappointment poorly. "We could go fishing. I have a new rod and net and Daddy has some new diving stuff, and—"

"Too late, honey," Laura interrupted briskly. "We have already tried that. Uncle Rick has some business to attend to."

Nina was well used to business, and she knew there were two sorts. "Movie business or the other sort?" she demanded.

It was tempting to laugh but Rick controlled it when he saw Laura's thunderous face and heard her sharp chastisement. "Nina! That is not polite. Apologise, please."

As compensation and consolation, Rick reached out and tousled the dark head of curls. "I feel just as bad as you about it. Tell you what: I'll come again real soon, and you can show me your rod then, okay?"

"When's soon?" she asked sullenly. "It's been ages since you came last time, and if it's as long till you come next time, I will have broken my rod by then." This time everyone did laugh. "It's true!" she said dismally, thrusting her hands down to find pockets, except there weren't any in this dress.

"I'm sure it is," he said drawing her gently back towards him. She sulked a little more and resisted his hand until he lifted the chin that was stuck to her chest and said softly, "You, my girl, are definitely your mother's daughter."

"Is that good?"

It was impossible not to smile at that, and as he looked up, he caught Laura's eye. "Let's just say it's pretty interesting," he said with a reasonably straight face.

Grown-up talk, Nina thought. Its meaning was lost on her.

Rick saw her plunged back into disappointment, and so he added, "But I promise I will come again real soon. Well, before you get to have either Christmas or another birthday. Okay?"

Nina digested this slowly, trying to work out how long that could be, and then she nodded. "And you will stay for ages?"

"I don't know about ages, but I will stay."

"Promise!"

"Scout's honour," Rick said solemnly. "And we can fish or do whatever you want to do, okay?"

"Hunt crabs?"

"That as well, although I always thought little girls weren't into such things."

Further discussion was denied her because Laura took hold of her hand and marched her indoors. "Come on, young lady. You have had a busy day, and I believe it's already way past your bedtime. I don't know where Mai is, but let's you and I go find her. Then you can get ready for bed, and you can come and say goodnight before Uncle Rick goes."

It was obviously not what Nina had in mind because she was led away still protesting. Within fifteen minutes she was back, freshly scrubbed, ready for bed, and peddling a large, multi-coloured plastic tractor containing a soft-bodied doll almost as large as she was. Both these things had been presents from Rick, and she wanted to show him they were still intact. The rebellion was not through, she was just deploying new tactics. These new tactics turned out to be no more successful than the old ones, and so with a long face she dutifully kissed everyone goodnight before Mai hauled her off to bed.

Rick pushed the abandoned tractor to one side, dismissing Laura's apologies as Jon disappeared indoors to take a call about a possible replacement black horse. This seemed the obvious place to take his leave, but instead of getting up, he stretched out in his lounger and closed his eyes, ignoring Laura's curious scrutiny. For the last half hour or so, since Nina's arrival, he had seemed lighter, almost normal. Instead of reassuring her that she had been imagining his mood earlier, this last half hour had merely confirmed what she had been thinking most of the day, and right now she had to decide whether she had the nerve to ask about that outright, because no opening for a natural inquiry had presented itself.

"What are you looking at?" he asked as he rearranged his back cushion.

"You."

"Any particular reason?"

"Apart from the fact that you are good to look at?" she teased.

He leant back and closed his eyes again. "Apart from that," he concurred dryly. "And as long as it's not because I have sauce on my nose."

She laughed at that, which was his intention. He didn't want to discuss anything heavy, and she had that 'hey there's something serious bothering me' look, the one he knew only too well. Making a joke of it seemed the easiest way to get the message across to her: not tonight, Laura!

She ignored the hint. "No, you don't have sauce on your nose. That would be easily remedied." The way she said that made him realise that what she had on her mind probably couldn't.

He turned over to face her and prepared to stand up and leave if necessary. "Okay, give with what's bugging you? But I'm warning you now, I will not take sides. You need to sort this thing out with Jon, not me."

"Oh, it's not us. We are okay. It's you I'm worried about."

"Me? What on earth for?"

She didn't exactly know what for, but saying so was difficult. After a couple of awkward attempts without her saying anything in particular, she got bolder, though she knew that doing so was likely to produce a rebuke any time now. Jon was not the only man she knew who could be difficult. It was rather ironic that here she was, prying into his life without even so much as a mild reprimand so far. When they had been lovers, she would not have risked this much. Now they were just friends, she obviously could. It didn't make much sense.

His reply was neither harsh nor sarcastic; it was not even a put down, just humorous indulgence – the same sort he had shown Nina earlier. It told her absolutely nothing. Intuition advised her quit now while you are ahead. She didn't listen. She never listened. "But ..."

"But what?

"It's just ... well, I've had this feeling all day."

"You're going in for crystal ball gazing now?"

"No of course not." She laughed nervously.

"So what sort of feeling have you had?"

"Call it women's intuition. I don't know, just a feeling. That's all."

"So what does your women's intuition tell you?" he quizzed only a little impatiently.

She answered with a question. "Is it Sherri?" she asked quietly, half afraid that if she said it any louder, he would explode.

The smile froze on his face, making it fairly obvious that he did not want to discuss whether it was Sherri, or anything to do with her. Fortunately he held his temper, though she could tell it was an effort, so she allowed the conversation to drift onto other things. Despite his intransigence, she remained convinced that she had been on the right track. By some slow, skilful manipulation she eventually managed to steer the conversation back to Sherri.

"Have you seen her since she left?" she asked innocently. Without waiting for an answer, she informed him, "I saw her last week at a charity lunch. She looked real pale." He still didn't answer. "She asked about you." she said cautiously. "I said I hadn't seen you."

It was one statement too many. She had pushed through his patience without realising it, and it had snapped just as easily as the tape that a runner cruises through at the end of a race. This time there were no congratulations. He had never given voice or name to the feelings that were bothering him, half believing that if he refused to recognise them, they would eventually go away. Talking about how he felt would be a major step towards accepting his state of mind was for real. It was a major step he was not ready to take yet.

He simply said, "Tell me something. Why do all women think that men cannot live without them? Why must I be heartbroken?" Fortunately it didn't seem as if he expected an answer, which was just as well because she wouldn't have dared offer one right now. Then he added bitterly, "No, I haven't seen Sherri since she left, and if you see her again, you can tell her I didn't ask after her." She was wondering about that when he continued in the same strangled tone. "How I am feeling has got nothing to do with her. It's over. She has a new guy. Good luck to them both. It's okay. I'm okay."

"Okay," she acknowledged meekly, "I get the picture. What can I say?"

"Try nothing!"

It was good advice, but she was going to risk one more try. It was a brave gesture in the face of such a complete shutdown. "So it's not Sherri. I'm sorry, I was wrong about that." She hesitated, and he looked up and met her gaze. "But there *is* something, isn't there? It's been there all day."

Whether it was the curiosity in her voice or something else, his patience ran out, and he stood up ready to leave. He didn't need an interrogation right now, and if not for the fact that she put her arm out to stop him, he would have left without saying another word.

"Rick, don't shut us out. Don't shut *me* out. We are your friends, and we care about you. I care about you."

It was more than she had said in ten years, but it received no encouragement. He nodded abruptly; it was still a split-second decision whether to walk or stay. He wasn't sure what it was that made him stay, but he sat down again and looked her straight in the eye. If he was staying, he needed to hold his temper. A scrap of bright pink paper caught his eye as it tumbled past him on a sudden gust of wind, so he picked up it up and examined it closely. It was a sweet wrapper, a recognition that caused him to smile a little as he smoothed out its crumpled surface. He concentrated on folding it into ever smaller pieces until he could make it no smaller, all the while battling with his temper until he could confess almost without irritation, "I'm tired, Laura, that's all. Nothing's wrong with me. Nothing serious, anyhow." He looked up from his completed task. His interrogator was watching him carefully. Their eyes met again briefly.

"That's not like you, either," she mused fondly.

"Yeah, well, like Jon said, I am getting older." He shrugged. "Tired is the nearest I can get to naming it. Tired of being here – well not right here; you know what I mean. Tired of being me. Tired of life I reckon."

"*Temporarily* tired of life, I hope."

"Maybe." She withheld her response but came and sat next to him, hoping that there might be more to come. "So is that good or bad, d'you reckon?" he asked cheerfully.

"I don't follow you."

He grinned. "Why should you? I don't follow myself sometimes."

"Now you are playing games with me."

"No, I'm not. I am just asking you if a serious problem with life is good or bad for the soul. You said you wanted to help!"

"I suppose it depends," she said slowly, trying to sort out what he meant as well as her answer.

"On what?"

"On why you are tired."

He nodded and smiled, then he sighed wearily as he patted the hand she had lain on his arm. "Laura, if I knew that, I wouldn't have the problem, would I?"

Laura had been a very successful actress, and persistence was a core requirement of that craft. She was sure that persistence was about to pay off right now and so she chipped away at the last bit of his reluctance until he unwrapped his troubles. It was way past irony what he told her; his present state almost perfectly parodied her own just before they had split. At an earlier time she might have even thought, what goes round comes round, and been glad, but tonight she didn't think any of those things. She was well past payback time, though she did find herself reliving the things he was describing, and what had happened next still haunted her dreams. It seemed beyond her ability to communicate any of it easily or painlessly because it meant she would have to talk about them as a couple, and they had never, in all the years since. Maybe it wasn't absolutely necessary now.

She tried another way. "Maybe you've just been working too hard," she said reassuringly. It sounded like a platitude even to her ears. "How many movies have you made this year?"

"Only Jake's."

"And Scott's starts when?"

"Next month."

"That's two. What's next? What about last year?"

162

He wasn't sure where this line of questioning was heading, and he had to think for a moment, but his answer was exactly what she had expected. "Three."

"See? I'm right, you have been working too hard. Why don't you take some time off, go travel somewhere, go paint something? Unwind."

He stood up, walked to the terrace rail, and gazed down on the ocean pounding the rocks below them. "The truth, Laura, is that I can't stand my own company," he confessed, flinging his words out into the emptiness in front of him. "Suppose that's why I've been working so hard."

"Any other reason?"

"To pay for Box, of course," he said with almost a smile as he turned around briefly.

She resisted asking what sort of hold the damned place had over him, but it was hard. What do you want all that land for? That was equally hard, equally unimaginable. Not disclosing any of her real feelings about the place that had taken possession of his wits over the last few years was great strategy, so for once she contented herself with a simple inquiry. "And have you?"

"Yep. Last year."

"So why not slow down now?"

"I told you why not."

"No, you didn't. Anyway, work can't be helping if you still feel so bad. How long has this been going on?"

He shrugged, "A few months, maybe, a year perhaps. Well, maybe a bit more. Hell, I don't know – I didn't think to keep a record."

"One thing's for sure: if it's that long, you need to do something about it now!" It was an answer motivated by those secret painful memories. He didn't know that, but something about the way she had said it penetrated his indifference, and he turned back to face her properly, spreading his arms out behind him and leaning back against the rail as he regarded her with interest.

"I mean you have to find a solution," she said more evenly, "while you still can. Do some re-evaluating, but promise me you won't carry on ignoring it, please. It's not healthy to feel like this for so long. Rick, are you listening to me?"

He had turned back to the sea as soon as he had realised she was not going to say anything remotely helpful. She had to walk across to his side before she could be sure she had his attention again. She put her hand over his and pleaded, "Don't wallow in this. Don't drown it in drink, either. Do something positive, eh?" He nodded as she lifted his hand and put it under her arm. "Most things have a solution, you know. Right now, I'm desperately thirsty, and the solution is I need a drink."

He took the hint and poured her the last of the wine. When he returned with it, she smiled and held on to the hand giving it to her. "See? I told you, everything has a solution."

"You sure about that? Is this positive?"

"Maybe not, but the rest is, at least give it a try. Pack a bag and go someplace. Don't come back till you feel better."

"Are you suggesting I break my contract with Scott? I just told you, we start work in a month. You are telling me to go find myself -that could take years."

Laura shrugged. "You don't have to take my advice," she pointed out. "Just remember I didn't tell you to break your contract. That was your idea."

"You told me to go and not come back till I felt better. I can't imagine feeling better in three and a half weeks."

"Why not?"

He shook his head. "Just can't. Three and a half years, yes. Three and a half months, maybe. But three and a half weeks? Never."

"I want you to be positive."

"Listen, the only thing I am positive about right now is the fact that I have to be on that flight to Harare on the twelfth. Work is the only thing that's keeping me going."

She frowned, "I understand why you think that, but it's not true."

"And you know?"

"Yes, I know." These words were small, everyday sort of words, used a million times a day to mean very little … but this time they communicated so much more. She checked out his disbelief with her gaze. "Work is like aspirin to toothache, Rick: it simply deadens the pain. Like gin, or vodka, or whisky, or all of them." A statement that posed a whole set of new questions. "Sooner or later that tooth is going to need a dentist to take a look at it and either fill it or extract it. Right?"

Gin, vodka, and whisky rang some bells he didn't care for, so he didn't reply immediately. When he did, it was a quip. "Is that a plug for your dentist or your shrink?" he asked sarcastically.

"Neither. Why not just take the three weeks and go try it? Go home and sort out whatever it is you have to sort out with Perry, and then just go. Take someone with you if you can't go alone, or go somewhere you know people. Come here if you want, but please, Rick, believe me that I know what I'm talking about. I have been there, and I know it's no joyride." Her blue eyes promised a full measure of conviction. "I think I put it down to an identity crisis when I was through it, but at the time I thought I'd lost my sanity for good." She had finally said enough to make it clear what she was referring to. "It's scary territory, and just thinking about it makes me go cold, even now." She shivered as if to prove her point.

Rick deliberately ignored this reference to their painful past. He did not want to start discussing that, or accepting blame for it now -especially not now. For once Laura's perception was spot on. It made it seem as if she was able to read his mind when she urged, "Don't be embarrassed – that's not the reason I said it. I said it to make you think."

He snorted derisively. "Thinking is not my problem, Laura! *Stopping* thinking is my problem. That's why work helps: it stops the thoughts – well, blocks them out anyhow."

"Have you never thought that the real way to stop them, if they annoy you so much, is to accept them? Say, 'Okay, my life sucks, I give in', and then do something about it."

"We're back to the shrink guy?" he asked cynically.

"So?"

"So!" He repeated her interrogative with more impatience. "Everyone's in therapy."

"Then it's okay for you as well."

"Everyone except me."

"I can recommend a good guy. He's really helpful."

He placed his finger over her lips to stop her talking. "Laura, I don't want a therapist, and if I did, I would find my own. Right now even I don't think I am worth listening to, so why should anyone else – even someone who is paid to?"

"Perhaps there are some things in your life that are worthless, but you're not. Dissatisfaction with self is always a great spur to improving things." He looked at her rather incredulously and then smiled broadly. "What's so funny?" she demanded, offended he should think her so.

"You. I never knew you went in for philosophy."

"I don't; it's the sign over my gym door, but it's true though," she replied, still offended by his levity. "And even if you don't know what needs changing, finding out could be interesting."

"Are you on commission for this guy?"

She laughed outright at that. "I wish I was. He has a client register that leads like a who's who of the Hills."

"Not very professional of him to say so."

"He doesn't. People want to say they see him."

Rick wiped his brow and looked at her comically as he shook his head and said, "It's nice to know that I'm not the only one that's nuts around here."

"You're not nuts, maybe a bit lost. Maybe the cost of being a movie star finally got to you." The enquiry about what that meant produced the explanation. "Come on; don't treat me like an absolute idiot! I know you know what I mean. It's either that, or your life needs a new direction. Maybe you should quit acting and go back to law school. Hey, listen, I'm prescribing solutions here that might not fit the bill. Now I *do* sound like him, don't I? Maybe you should just think about taking that break and finding your own solutions. It would do you good, even if you don't get anything monumental sorted out." She meant, "Even if you don't decide to sell that stupid obsession before it bankrupts you or kills you," but he had no way of knowing that, and so he misinterpreted her meaning.

"I know. That's why I need the three hundred-dollar-an-hour guru?"

"If it gives you the opportunity to talk and find some solutions, then why not?" she countered.

"I told you, I don't need a therapist," he said leaning heavily on his next words to make his point. "In my experience, most of them are more screwed up than the people they are supposed to be helping, and that goes double for the ones in the Hills. The answer is no way, forget it. And I wouldn't go back to law school at forty – correction, forty-one in three weeks. See, it's just a minor dose of the middle age blues." He howled out loud till she dug him in the ribs to stop.

"Forty-one isn't exactly senile," she said, tracing a teasing, questioning finger down his arm.

He stopped her by placing his hand over hers. "Don't do that," he said quietly, and she nodded and removed her hand. "Forty-one might not be exactly senile, as you say, but I bet there's not many that go back to law school successfully." His last remark had deliberately filled the awkward moment before she could fill it with what he definitely did not want to hear.

"You are just like Jon!" she exclaimed in a flash of sudden irritation. "Why do you always have to be successful? Why can't you just do something for fun? Pleasure, even?"

He ignored her irritation because he thought he knew its source. He answered calmly, "Don't know about Jon, but I have to be successful because that's who I am. And I wouldn't go back to law school for fun – I hated it. Acting is where I get my pleasure."

"So if it's not the job you are dissatisfied with, then it's you."

He kissed the top of her head and smiled at her as he checked his watch. "Laura, you have just taken half an hour to tell me something I already know," he pointed out patiently.

"I'm sorry. I was only trying to help."

"I know. Thanks." He stifled a yawn and took one last look out to sea. "Better be on my way; I'm shattered now, and it's a long haul back from here. One thing to please you: I never get bored here. I'll get home, and I guarantee you I will be bored by lunchtime tomorrow, but then most things bore me these days – even acting sometimes. Being famous is the biggest bore of all." He stopped, completely astounded by the magnitude of the words that had slipped out among the other smaller confessions. He tried a laugh to cover the exposure. "I never thought I'd say that." He paused. "It's true, though, isn't it? Acting is real, but fame is …" He couldn't put a name to it, so he shrugged and dismissed it. "I guess everything has a price, like you say. Fame's is pretty high. It seems to be responsible for a lot of my troubles these days, and *I know* you are the only person I would risk saying that to! So seeing as how you now know it all, can you tell me what I mean by that, too?"

Laura nodded obligingly but didn't say anything immediately, because she wasn't sure that she *did* know, or even whether she would agree with him if she did. Still, she was so amazed by his revelations that even her usual remedy of 'just sell the damned place,' was forgotten. She asked him what he thought fame's price was, but that was more to keep him talking than anything else. At first he simply shook his head, then he grunted and walked off ahead of her. "Never knowing the real motive for people's actions," he threw back at her.

Laura digested this slowly. He had a point.

Rick concluded, "I guess we don't know that until we experience it, or say it because there are millions of poor sods out there who would willingly swap places with us anytime, and when you see some of their lives, you think, what the hell am I blabbing on about? Maybe that's what makes the problem worse." He ran his hands through his hair distractedly. She had never seen him do that in all the years she had known him. It worried her. "Hell, I know I'm lucky to have what I have, and I wouldn't want to be without any of it. But it's not enough anymore!" He added an expletive under his breath, it was directly linked to his frustration. "I feel guilty even thinking that, let alone saying it. I wanted Box because I thought it would solve everything, but it hasn't."

"So what do you mean by 'more' now," she asked quietly. "You have fame, wealth, success, good looks, property, cars... You can have anybody you want, anytime you want them – come on, I know so," she added when he opened his mouth ready to protest. "What more is there? What else is on your list?"

He wondered whether she had heard what he just said about fame. He was not about to repeat it. "Truth, Laura? I honestly do not know. That's my problem. I find myself watching people and then watching myself, and usually what I see doesn't impress me. We're mostly a greedy, money-grabbing lot with one focus: self. Pitiful, ain't it? You know I said I was bored? That's the nicest way of describing it; there are others. If you really want to know, I have this weird feeling of looking in on my life and it's ..."

"Worthless?" she ventured tentatively, speculating on the word he was about to say.

He looked across at her and met her gaze, "I`m real glad you are being helpful," he said stonily. She apologized, and asked what he would have said. "Pointless maybe, hell, I don`t know, I haven`t thought about putting a label on it." She asked him to try. "Like I`ve lived in the same meaningless bubble forever."

"Africa's not the same bubble."

"Of course it is. A set in Africa is much the same as one anywhere else. Temperature might be different, but ten hours a day on a set is the same wherever you are. Do you understand what I'm getting at?"

"I'm still listening," she said, taking his hand and leading him back to the deck sofa despite his protests. "Blow Perry for now – you are more important. Rick, listen to me." She sat down next to him and took hold of both his hands in hers. "I wish this had been a bit of grief over Sherri because it might have been easier to solve. But whatever it is that's got a hold of you right now, I do believe what you are saying. You are scaring me because I *know* it's real. My advice is still the same: do something about it!"

"But what? Buying a Ferrari helped for exactly three weeks. Working helps for ten, twenty weeks at a time. Going home hardly helps at all. Going to bed …" He paused.

"Well?" She said this so smoothly that the implication could not be avoided. He looked at her. "Going to bed?" she reminded him.

"Everyone has to wake up sometime," he said brusquely, and he carried on talking before she had a chance to say more. "Going to a party didn't help at all," he joked.

She smiled at that. "At least you haven't lost your sense of humour," she said softly, "even when 'Hands-on Greta' has you in her sights." He laughed with her. Both of them knew they needed to lighten this up.

"Doing things is not a problem, Laura. It fills a space. It's when I'm *not* doing things that I start to look at myself and wonder what the hell I'm doing. What is the point of my life?"

She shook her head. "I don't know the answer to that, but I do know there's something you haven't tried doing for a long while, something that always seems to help everyone else. Maybe you should try it as well."

"What's that?" He searched her face more than half dreading her reply because he knew she had him cornered.

Finally she answered him. "Go back to your roots. Go home. Why don't you go see your folks?"

He laughed outright, and it was only partly from sheer relief. "You are beginning to sound as crazy as your therapist guy."

"I'm serious," she protested.

"Then you have a twisted sense of humour. You know that wouldn't help me at all."

"You say that. I don't know that. How long is it since you last went there?"

"Couple of years, I guess."

"Then give it a go, please."

He looked at her serious face and grinned. "You always did have a twisted sense of humour. It's not changed."

"Maybe I do, but I am still serious about this. Even if you can't understand it, please just go and give it a try. I do know what I'm talking about here. Getting a bit of earache from someone who loves you will be a small price to pay if you also find some peace."

"Peace! The last place on earth I expect to find peace is at my folks'! A day is usually long enough for us to be on the brink of World War III. I could handle it if it stopped at earache, but it won't. I nearly thumped him last time I was there." Despite her protests that it couldn't be so bad, he hardly relented, except to concede that he would think about it some more, but no promises were given, however hard she tried.

"I wish you would go," she said at last. "At least it would get your feet back on the ground for a while, and you would be with some real people. We're not real, you know – we're playing some other game."

"Reckon I was right about the philosophy bit as well," he said, kissing her cheek lightly before stooping to drag the plastic tractor along with him as he walked off.

"I'm not joking," she said trailing behind him. "Rick, I am serious. Will you put that thing down! Mai will move it tomorrow." He did as he was told, so she caught hold of him and took hold of his arm again. "I do know what you mean about the price to be paid. I know it, because I paid it, too." It was another more obvious reference to her breakdown. He nodded and patted her hand. He was even surer he didn't want her to talk about this now, but he was even less sure about how to stop her. She started with, "When I met you …"

He groaned and walked ahead, hoping his action would send out the right signal, but there was to be no avoiding it. She caught up with him again. "Rick, listen to me! Okay, I know I am talking ancient history here, but they still teach college students about ancient Rome, don't they? If we can learn from their mistakes, why can't you learn from mine? Just hear me out, huh? Remember where we met?" He started to walk away again, but she caught hold of his hand and followed it round till she was facing him and blocking his path. He was not going to escape that easily. "When I met you in that detox clinic, I already had the famous face; you simply completed the package. Then I thought, Hey, I've made it, I have all these big ticks in all these big boxes – fame, fortune, success, youth, good looks. And sex? Well, now I had the handsomest, sexiest guy in town." He shook his head to protest, but she carried on. "These were big and important ticks, Rick, against big and important things. I reckoned that most people would be satisfied with them, which didn't make it easier when I realised I wasn't. I despised myself for not being satisfied. Sound familiar yet? I told myself everybody else would be satisfied with this. It didn't help me one bit – just made me worse."

Rick opened his mouth to say something, but she touched her finger to his lips. "Let me finish, please; I may never get the courage to say this again. If you tell yourself now what I told myself then, then you will end up following the same path I did, with the same result: disaster. I knew I was going under again, so I grabbed at everything, thinking if I had more of it, everything would be okay. It wasn't. I should have known about the drink of course, but I didn't, so I had to find it out all over again. More booze didn't make me healthy, just sicker. More drugs didn't make me a better actress, just doped. More houses didn't make me available everywhere; I was completely lost. More clothes didn't make me desirable, just in debt. More money didn't even make me rich; I became more wasteful. More attention sure didn't make me secure, just petulant. And more lovers didn't solve our problems – it just lost me you." He met her gaze. "You know I saw other men, don't you? Had one-night stands?" He nodded. Now it was her turn to sigh heavily, and she turned away to hide her distress. "Is that why you let me walk out on you?" This question could not have been asked facing him, but it would not now be denied the asking. It had taken ten years to get this far, and it had waited too long.

"Partly." That much answer hurt. "And partly because I thought you must want to go."

She turned back to face him, gaining a little courage from his answer. "You and I never said what we meant, did we?"

"Maybe not, but now is not the time."

"I know. I guess what I'm getting to is this: it's easy to get carried away thinking more is the answer. Nowadays I don't ever think it is. Nowadays I always think it's less. Less of all the things on that list, anyway. Less money, less possessions, less drugs, less drink …"

"Less sex?" he asked mischievously, anxious to avoid facing the emphasis she had placed on drink.

"Less sex with people you shouldn't be with, certainly," she said seriously, refusing his attempt to trivialise this. "And more of the things you and I forgot about: more sex with the right person, more family, more time together, more restraint. Nasty word, that. It still makes me shudder even now because I have had to learn to respect it the hard way. But I do, because I remember the lesson it taught me."

He looked at her serious face and nodded. "Okay, you made your point."

"Rick, it's not a point – it's a plea. Don't be stupid like me! Don't wake up in detox again wondering what the hell happened, or in someone's bed wondering what you are doing with this person. Worst of all, don't wake up in a psychiatric clinic wondering how the hell you got in there. Wake up now! That's why you need home, some real people who care about you. Because they *do* care! They will keep your feet on the ground. As a group of people, we should be bottom of everyone's 'most useful' friends list – too much introspection and not enough contribution. We all are so used to putting on our faces that we miss the damage we are doing." She paused, shifted slightly, and then looked around, checking to see they were still alone as she pulled the terrace door shut. Then she said quietly, "I have never said this to you before, but maybe it still needs saying. I am sorry. I was a fool." After ten years it had been difficult to admit it, because she still meant it. It was the natural conclusion to the other long-buried feelings being given an airing.

It triggered a response no less genuine or generous. "Maybe it should be me saying sorry to you. I didn't know what was going on with you. I guess I was too interested in myself." How come he hadn't been able to say that back then? He knew he should have.

Laura took it as he offered it now. "We both were," she concurred. "I will accept your apology, if you will accept mine. Deal?"

"Deal," he said, smiling faintly and hoping they could now close the entire subject. It even looked like that might happen as she took his arm to walk him back through the house.

"If you really have to go, then I guess you should be going now. It's a pity you can't stay, though. A few days messing about with Jon's new stuff might have helped some. But hey, I should know these pressures by now. Please come back soon." She stopped and turned him to face her by the hall door. He could tell by her face the lecture was not yet over. "One last thing to remember. You just hit the roof about your dad. Do you know what my dad used to say about me, at least when he was sober enough to say anything? He used to say, 'Our Laurie's a visitor in other people's lives because she can't bear to be in her own.' He said I was different than anyone else he ever knew. I guess he was right in a way: some of us are insecure in our own skins. But he was wrong about us being different, Rick – we are exactly the same as all the other humans on this planet, all mixed up together. I didn't know it then – and I guess I still don't know now – what it is we are looking for, so you will have to find that out for yourself. I do know most of us think we're interested in finding out, but we're a fickle lot and get easily diverted. You don't have to be a Harvard professor to work out how many of us really sort it out. You see, maybe my dad didn't realise this, but I do now: it's not just movie stars that louse up." She squeezed his arm and grinned. "Though you must admit, we do it magnificently! I suppose if you are going to lose it, you may as well lose it in designer clothes and Rolex watches and Ferraris." There was a moment's reflection before she teased lightly, "Ever thought they could be part of the problem? Who knows? Anyway, all this wisdom cost me five years in therapy and a helluva lot of money."

"That was your cure, then?" Why couldn't he just learn to keep his big mouth shut? He had already said it before he thought to ask himself this.

"No, it was Jon mostly, I suppose."

"Jon was your cure!"

"Don't sound so surprised. Jon was my cure because he was level-headed and knew what I needed. He still does. Why do you think he's so good at his job, Rick?" She asked this in such an offended tone that it seemed like a total departure from their previous topic.

Although it had taken him by surprise, he answered it without even querying what it had to do with anything else. "Disciplined vision that pulls all the pieces together?"

"Guess he just did the same for me."

"He helped you pull it all together? Did I help you pull it apart?" He was even getting embroiled in the unwanted autopsy now.

"No."

"I don't think I helped, though, did I?" Was that another attempt at an apology of sorts?

Laura did not understand this attempt any better than his last so she answered smoothly, "Maybe not, but this was my thing. I was going to have this breakdown; I was heading there on my own. You just said it: you didn't even know." She paused and reflected. "Isn't that sad? We had lived together for two and a half years, and you didn't even know.

"Why didn't you tell me?"

"You mean in that once-a-month conversation we had between making love when we crossed in cities?" That was cuttingly sharp. He looked away, and Laura softened her tone, aware that this thing could get out of hand if she didn't. "Hey, that wasn't all your fault; I was as much to blame," she whispered, patting his hand. "I was just as crazy as you." No one said anything for a few seconds, and then she continued in a more cheerful tone. "I don't really think I knew where I was heading myself until I got there. Even then I only learned to identify the markers on the way back." She shrugged and explained, "They were all on the wrong side of the road going, so I guess I missed them."

"So how come Jon helped you where I couldn't? He lives the same life we do."

She looked him straight in eye and shook her head slowly. "No, he doesn't, Rick. Jon does not live like you and I at all. He made me feel safe because he *is* safe. No more living in anyone else's skin; he made me face myself, live in my own skin, warts and all." Rick shook his head in disbelief. Jon the lap dog had done this? How? "I guess he put down some limits," she said simply.

She watched his reaction. "I know what you are thinking, and I know it seemed like he would do anything and be anything I wanted him to be, and he did while I was with you. He said that was because it was all he could do at the time. He reckoned being there whenever I needed him might help – he couldn't do anything else, could he? You were his friend. He did tell me after we married that he could always see where you and I were headed, but he couldn't do anything about it. He couldn't save us, but he wouldn't harm us either. You do know that, don't you? He was the only guy who ever said no to me. I asked him lots of times when I was mad at you, but he wouldn't. That was because of you. He cares a lot about you, but I guess you know that, too. I really envy you that, you know – a real friend. I never had one. Anyway, when we were over, things changed between Jon and me. Did you know it was Jon who found me stoned out of my head at the studio? He told everyone I was ill and got me into a very discreet hospital – you know the sort. Then he kept me there till I was better, paid all the bills, visited me when he could, phoned every day, and wrote me letters." She looked up. "He was the only one who came. When I asked him why, he said he owed me something for introducing him around. He owed me nothing. When I came out, I tried to repay what I owed him. The money was easy; the rest was not so easy. We saw each other a few times before he said, 'I love you, Laurie, but I won't watch you do this again. If you want to go back in there, you do it on your own. If you want to stay out, you and I can make this work together.' See, I still remember his exact words. I moved in with him, and he taught me discipline – you know, work, eat, play and sleep stuff. Routine stuff. Disgusting word, discipline, but I started to feel better, and then everything was great – except the work wasn't acting, it was housework. I still miss the other sort, even after all these years," she added ruefully.

"He made you give it up?" Rick asked, thoroughly amazed by these disclosures.

"No, of course not. He gave me some choices. When I was better, he said, 'Laurie, if you marry me, I'll take care of you.' Do you know he is the only person besides my dad who has ever called me Laurie? Funny, isn't it?"

"And has he?"

"Yes, I suppose he has, though I'm still working on the acting bit," she confessed grinning. "Jon's old-fashioned, like his parents. His mom stayed home, so he expects me to. That's why he didn't marry me straightaway, he said he wanted me to be sure, to know I could do it. Why am I telling you all this?"

"You amaze me."

"I think I amaze myself. The last ten years have been the most stable period of my entire life, and if I could just get Jon to see sense over the acting, my life would be perfect."

"People think you retired."

"People think what they want! But you should know better than that. I know most of them think I wasn't offered any roles after the breakdown. Not true. I still get offers, and some of them are good ones."

"But what would happen to Nina if you went back to work?"

She looked at him a little differently. "Now you sound like Jon again," she said peevishly. "Nina would stay home with Mai, just like she does now. Or perhaps go to school. Let's not talk about this now. It's you we are talking about. So, will you go home?"

"I told you I'll think about it."

Rick found Jon in his den still immersed in his conversation. He interrupted only to signal he was leaving. Laura walked him to the car. She watched him throw his bag in before she grabbed his arm and pulled him reluctantly towards her. She kissed him the same as usual, though after all that had been said, it felt more dangerous. "Remember what I've said, Rick. I meant all of it. Get out there and find an answer. Don't just go from one set of kicks to the next – and that includes women as well as drink!" Her next comment was delivered jokingly as he climbed into the car. "I know you won't believe me, but we are not all like Greta."

Rick didn't reply immediately because he was busy sorting through some music, but having found what he was looking for, he held it up for her to see. "Ever heard of *Cosi Fan Tutte,* Laura? It's an opera by Mozart."

"I didn't know you liked opera."

"Some of it was part of the soundtrack for *Lives and Deaths.* I liked that, so I bought the whole score. It's good stuff. You should try it." She wrinkled her nose to show that his suggestion was not that appealing, and he laughed. "Do you know what the title means?" She shook her head, wondering where all this could be heading and whether she was being set up. "It means something like, women are all the same, and if Mozart hadn't written that Laura, I could have done." With that cryptic remark ringing in her ears, he drove off.

Chapter Twelve

After a long, hot day it wasn't difficult to get into automatic driving mode, and Sarah had been driving for a while before she realised that was exactly what had been happening. Monotony was robbing her of any semblance of alertness. She hoisted concentration back on duty by pointing out the possible consequences of such behaviour: death being the worst, and at the very least it could have something to do with why she had seen so few road signs recently. Her speculation only graduated to dilemma when the very next sign mentioned places she had never even heard of.

The guy at the gas station was helpful even if she did walk in and ask, "Excuse me, can you tell me where I am, please?" as if getting lost was a completely normal occurrence to her. He continued chewing on his gum and stacking his shelf, much as if adults not knowing where they were was completely normal for him, too. But then, this *was* California, the designated home of ninety nine per cent of Elinor's weirdoes, so maybe it was.

Despite the man's clear instructions, two miles down the road she missed the exit he had said to be sure to take. What had started out as a rather irritating but little bad habit first thing this morning when she was fresh, was upgraded to downright upsetting, major character flaw stuff at eight o'clock at night now that she was exhausted. It deserved the whole repertoire of Shakespearian sayings, the ones she reserved specially for occasions when a little emotion was needed. Though that ventilated her annoyance, it did nothing to find her another exit, because like all other missed exits this one turned out to be the maximum distance from the next. As far as she knew, Shakespeare had never commented on that.

She was tired, cross, and totally lost for the second or third time that day before she finally came to a stop. It was now impossible to even think about retracing the miles back to the gas station because it was completely dark, and she knew with that awful sense of certainty only known to truly lost souls that if she had been trailing a ball of string behind her all day, she would have tied a pretty impressive knot by now, and there was no Greek hero to unravel it for her – not even an American one. Memories of Elinor's thinly veiled threats about driving such long distances did nothing to improve her disposition, but as she was unable to come up with any credible plan B, she had to keep following Plan A, while reciting every known bit of Shakespeare as an aid to alertness, though it still solved nothing.

Midway through act two of *Henry IV,* a white picket fence caught her eye and excited her like nothing else could. "Signs of lost civilisation coming up!" she promised Henry as she pulled over smartly by the very first building. It was a small farmhouse. She knew that much because there was a barn adjacent to it, and she knew all about barns: they came with farms. Thank goodness! A good chance of finding some common sense here, I hope.

She reminded herself about asking sensibly as she jumped down from the cabin and went in search of her sensible residents. There was no one at the front or round the back, and no one answered the very loud doorbell. She waited patiently for another minute or two before banging on the door as hard as she could and shouting up at the windows in utter frustration. "One house! Correction, the *only* house! And you let them all go out. What sort of farmhouse are you!" This regrettable outburst smacked of desperation if not insanity, and it was too embarrassing to consider what anyone overhearing might have thought, but her only reply was the wind blowing round the eaves and the distant rumble of thunder, which she dismissed without a second thought because there were far too many other things to worry about – things like whether she should wait for these farmers to come home, or whether she should continue driving in the hope she might find someone else to ask. She reviewed the pros and cons of both courses of action several times in the next few minutes. She had almost decided to wait when she realised waiting could be foolish if these people did not come home tonight. Was that in favour, or against? Farmers must come home – everyone knew that! The job was three hundred and sixty five days a year, and all that. What if these farmers didn't know that? "Well, if they don't come home," she consoled herself, "I shall park here overnight and sort it out in the morning. Things are always better in the daylight. If I keep on driving now and can't find the highway, I might end up in the middle of nowhere for the entire night!" The house withheld its counsel, and the depressing thought that this was the middle of nowhere did nothing to uplift her.

She was still ruminating on these choices when a male voice made her jump. "You want something?"

She tried hard not to look or feel stupid, which was difficult, because she knew only seconds before she had been talking to an empty house. She nodded and swallowed hard, hoping the owner of the voice had not been privy to that. She whirled around just in time to see a young lad clambering over a tractor by the barn. He repeated his inquiry. She ignored the temptation to ask what he was doing at this time of night doing that by subduing the school teacher in her and concentrating on her own issues. Explaining her predicament was easier this time, except the lad had never heard of the interstate.

In a moment of sheer desperation, she asked, "Is anyone else home then? Mum? Dad?" It might have seemed an innocent question to her, but she had to hold up her road map for verification that she really was a lost motorist and not some alien investigating the planet for takeover, to stop him scampering away.

The flapping map seemed to calm him a little, and he finally replied, "Only granddad, but he's deaf."

Deaf or not, granddad was able to draw her a map and tell her how to cross country and pick up the road she wanted. It turned out she was nearly sixty miles off track and heading in the wrong direction yet again! What else was new – this was a country full of wrong directions. According to the old man's instructions, this road forked about eight to ten miles further on, and then she needed to take the left-hand fork, which would eventually bring her to a junction with a small road. That would lead to another local highway, which in turn would lead her to the highway that fed back into Route 5, and there was a campsite about twenty miles along Route 5.

"Easy! Even I can manage this," she told herself as she waved farewell, determined to get as far as that camp site tonight. She turned up the radio and hummed along to the music until she could stand the inane adverts no longer so switched it off just as it came to another break, supposedly for the news. "One minute of news and ten more minutes of adverts? I do not think so! Thank you very much!" She forgot about the adverts and everything else as the road forked exactly where it was meant to, and she got excited about that instead. "Everything, stay exactly where you are meant to be for another hour or so," she commanded.

Sure enough, the little road ran into the other road as promised … and then there was nothing. No sign of the local highway or Route 5. And twenty miles further on, there was still no sign of either one! There was no sign of anything in fact. No people, no cars, no houses, no shops, no factories, and just the odd side road now and then. Mostly it was row after row of fruit trees disappearing into the darkness beyond her lights. The doubts returned, multiplied. Had the old man really meant turn right at that junction? Had he sent her out here deliberately? That thought, and every other conceivable variation danced around in her head.

Although she had not seen another vehicle for many miles, she automatically checked the road and signalled before she pulled over to try and establish where she was for the fifth time that day. "Just my luck to have asked the one farmer in California who can't tell left from right," she grumbled as she tried to align the old man's diagram with the corresponding part of the official road map. It was no easy task. Half an hour later she was still no nearer discovering where her little bit of the universe fitted into the overall plan; in fact using a map here was no easier than it had been back at home; the skill was still beyond her.

She made a hot chocolate to calm her anxiety, deciding as she drank it that as there was no way she could sort it out, she had no other option but to continue following the old man's instructions; they had to come out somewhere, eventually, and anywhere had to be better than right here. A little clear-headed reflection had been all that was needed. She climbed back into the driving seat intent on doing just that. The ignition clicked as she switched on, then nothing.

She tried again. Nothing at all this time.

Panic waited until she had tried four more times and then it flooded her body as effectively as the oil had flooded the engine. "Do not do this to me, please!" she wailed. After several more equally unsuccessful attempts, she finally acknowledged this was no temporary hiccup. This was your genuine breakdown -and it would definitely need a different kind of person than her to remedy. Being an optimist, she grabbed a torch to go and take a look anyway. She was still hanging on to the vain hope that whatever it was that was wrong, couldn't be that serious - after all she had just driven the thing all day. Maybe it would be her day for a miracle!

In her heart she knew pleas to the skies were likely to be at least as effective and a darn sight more satisfying, because the intricacies of the internal combustion engine meant nothing to her, but perhaps this lump of useless metal would not know that, and if it turned out to be a distant relative of the school photocopier – the one that generally responded to a well-placed kick – then she could deliver that. She marched to the front of the van prepared for both. "Play acting!" she snorted as her fingers twiddled with wires she knew nothing about in the vain hope that it was her day for that miracle. It wasn't. Expectations exhausted, she slammed the panel shut with such ferocity that she had to lean back against the van to recover. Further contemplation produced nothing but an urgent desire to cry, but she stifled that because it would solve nothing. Even Shakespeare had nothing to say for once. A whole trainload of awkward questions queued up neatly in her head, the persistent theme being, "Why did I not think about something like this happening before now?"

She had no answer for that, but she had almost reassured herself that it was no big deal when a loud rumbling noise, accompanied by an occasional chunky raindrop, made her reconsider. She abandoned stoicism, administered the kick to the van, and pleaded with the sky, "Not now! Please, not now! Rain all day tomorrow and the day after, but just show a bit of restraint and do not do it right now, huh? It's not convenient, and besides, you might scare the wildlife." A little alarm bell sounded somewhere in her head. What was it Elinor had said about wildlife? "Stop it! Stop this right now," she told herself, "It will not help!"

The line about sorrows not coming as single spies sprang into her head, but because she lacked an audience, she kicked the van tyres again instead. "Stupid, stupid machine!" she cursed, which wasn't exactly Shakespeare but got across her feelings nicely. Unlike the photocopier, the camper did not respond to kicks. This downright awkward piece of mechanical wizardry – correction, *junk* – was not going to play fair.

The problem with rain right now was that the ground here was pretty soft, and she didn't need Elinor to tell her what happened to soft ground in the rain. Visions of sinking slowly wheel by wheel into a muddy grave could do nothing to raise her spirits, so she tried several times during the next hour to push the camper back onto the road. Each time she had to admit that it had not moved a single inch despite all her grunting and groaning. After three more totally exhausting and futile attempts, it had confirmed its status as a pile of "useless junk", and after two further attempts she gave up completely and went inside to sulk. She was too tired to do anything else now, besides the thunder seemed nearer, and those niggles about wild animals had become a little more relevant because she had remembered something about bears in California – or was that Utah? Whether bears were nocturnal seemed a good question. She had a real talent for asking these good questions. It was a pity the talent did not extend to supplying equally good answers.

That was how the shivering got started. She made another chocolate and drew a blanket around her. It was meant to stop the shaking, but it increased by degrees until even firm, loud, uncompromising instructions to stop, failed miserably. "Go to bed. Lock the door. Stay dressed." She did at least carry out these instructions to the letter, only deviating to add a large kitchen knife for protection. Had people stabbed bears before they were able to kill them? The thought that she might die out here no longer seemed unduly melodramatic. No happy ending at all! But that was where all this had started – Jonathan and his "no happy endings" had got her into this, as if she had something to prove! The memories queued up neatly after that, waiting to be viewed as part of the inexorable chain of cause and effect leading right up to this moment. That "no happy ending" possibility bounced around in her head for a while before it was upgraded to a probability, and then her teeth started to chatter, and it had become an absolute certainty by the time her whole body started shaking. In a last-ditch effort to regain control, she offered up some words to whoever might be listening. After that some yoga meditations helped a little, but bears crept into every scenario, and even one where she met William could not keep them at bay.

Rick glanced at the clock on his dashboard and cursed. It was almost 1.00 AM. Another fifteen minutes and he would have been home, but he knew he might not make it so quick if this storm moved in before then. He should try to outrun it. He put his foot down hard, and the Ferrari accelerated with ease. The sheer pleasure of speed needed appropriate sound to accompany it, so he turned up *Cosi* till it filled the car and his head. He had intended to give the score some serious attention on the way home, but he had been into "E la fede delle femmine" for the second time without having noticed any of it. A particularly vicious streak of lightning sliced across the night sky, distracting him again. "Wait another fifteen minutes," he ordered as the lightening flash died and darkness reclaimed the night. His only answer was a mightier rumble of thunder. The speedometer told him he was already doing over a hundred, but that was nothing in this car, and he slammed his foot down as hard as he could. He had seen these summer storms before, and he had no intention of being caught up in this one if he could help it. There was nearly forty miles of highway between the Interstate and the estate. That was nearly forty miles of racetrack with no reason to waste any of it.

Sarah was trying to sleep. Well, that was her instruction, though she had no way of guaranteeing compliance. She had hid her head under the blanket and was, in between shaking bouts, trying to sing "Somewhere over the Rainbow" as inducement. That song usually worked, even on Ali. All reserves of whatever qualities were needed in emergencies such as this were thoroughly depleted by now, so she failed to recognise the connection between sleep and the ability to relax: survival was all that mattered. She had been closely monitoring the thunder for a while now, checking that it was not coming any nearer, and her ear had become so finely attuned to its sound that she missed the new sound for a whole minute. When it did finally register, she fell out of the skybunk in her haste to get down, and hoping against hope there were no such things as auditory hallucinations – or if there were, she was not having one, she scrambled to her feet, rubbed her knee, grabbed her torch, and switched on her headlights as she struggled with the door. Damn – she had locked it to keep out the bears!

Ten clumsy fingers fumbled frantically to unfasten the lock she had fastened so carefully two hours earlier. Then she tumbled out of the door, trying to keep her limbs in the right order so that she could jump up and down and wave her torch as she yelled, "Stop! Help!" at the top of her voice. It was not a sensible sight. Fortunately, by the time the occupant of the vehicle was near enough to see her properly, she had calmed down and was stood calmly waving her torch like some solemn boy scout on routine exercises. Ever the optimist, she was hoping this vehicle would be the breakdown truck for which she had been praying, but even she accepted that the odds on that must be pretty impressive. Maybe it would contain a Good Samaritan who would call out the breakdown truck for her. Either way, salvation seemed close at hand until she remembered, 'they're murdering English tourists out there, Miss.' In the few remaining seconds it took for the vehicle to assume a shape, her thoughts became macabre enough for her to lose control again. If part one of "the very worst thoughts you can imagine" had been about man-eating wild animals, part two was definitely about her chances of becoming California's next murder victim and like the unwanted thoughts about bears had escalated into an in-depth examination of the entire wildlife species of southern California, Nevada, Utah, and Mexico, this observation now snowballed into multi-coloured, wild speculation about the likelihood of this approaching vehicle containing a murderer or rapist or kidnapper. It seemed important that she should cover all eventualities because felons, like wild animals, couldn't read maps. Neither of them took any notice of boundaries or signposts, and just like a mountain lion in Nevada, could easily get lost and stray over the border into ... wherever Nevada was next to, everybody knew about travelling serial killers and the like.

"You are ranting again," she warned herself. Reason and hope had done their very best until now, but it was optimism that had almost persuaded her that there were unlikely to be any really wild animals out here, wherever here was, because there were normal fruit trees. She had remained unconvinced about the plain wild ones. Murderers and rapists came in a different category to wild animals, and optimism, reason, and hope together could not provide sufficient reassurance right now, however hard she worked at it. There were stronger forces at work here, the strongest of which was self-preservation, and that told her to be scared! Though she had been following that instruction before this vehicle had put in its unexpected appearance, her alert level was now hiked to critical, imminent danger. This might not be the cavalry at all – only the Indians! The pupils at school were right: bad things were happening everywhere. Imaginary headlines danced in front of her head. *"English Tourist Found Raped and Murdered!"* That more than convinced her she didn't want the vehicle to stop. Pity she had been waving her light around to attract its attention. Dying of fright, and even being eaten by a mountain lion after being mauled by a bear, suddenly seemed infinitely preferable to being raped and murdered by Indians. "No way am I accepting help from strangers, No way, ever!" She breathed deeply to try to reassure herself, but she only succeeding in frightening herself more. Was it foresight or hysteria that caused her to recall such things at the very worst possible moment? "I am an intelligent woman, I can cope with this."

Rick had less than twenty seconds to compute all the possibilities before he had to decide what he was going to do. It didn't make any sense for the law to be out here at this time of night, but someone was definitely flagging him down. As he picked out the solitary female figure behind the dancing light, he dipped his headlights, eased off the brake, and thought some more. It was not the police – no logos, no lights, no sirens, and no uniforms – so maybe it was a breakdown? But hardly any one used the road, except the people from Box and occasionally the people from Wilson. But what if it were a hijack? It was a crazy place for a hijack - unless - she was waiting for him? Maybe there were hidden heavies, and she was bait. Even if she was on her own, she could still be bait. Hands-on Greta could even have updated her story and left Susan stranded out here. Something approaching a smile contorted his features, but he started to accelerate again. He had lived out here for five years and had never seen a single breakdown; this had to be some sort of trap, and tonight was not the right night to be finding out.

As he roared past the woman he registered a moment's hesitation, and then the thunder crashed right on cue. What if it wasn't a fix? What if she was a local woman on her way home? What would she do in the storm if he drove past? No one else would come down the road tonight. He hadn't recognised her, but then there was no reason why he should; he never mixed locally.

He switched off the music, swore softly at the figure in his tail lights, and braked hard. The car screeched to a halt several hundred yards down the road. His lights illuminated the darkness, and his exhausts continued polluting the night air as he considered what to do next. This was the stuff of movies, but without a script it was a whole different ball game, and he didn't feel nearly as confident as he would have expected. He watched through his mirror for another minute or so for any signs of sudden activity - knowing he could be away faster than anything else on wheels helped. He hoped the continuing revs would send out a clear message to any heavies: he was on his guard.

Sarah remained rooted to the spot, staring at the strange craft much as if it was an alien spaceship dropped in from some hostile planet, and she was dreading it disgorging its hideous crew with every bit as much terror as the young lad back at the farm had greeted her appearance.

Inside the craft an equally suspicious attitude was earning its occupant approval for his reticence. What was going down out there? A minute passed, and then another. Nothing moved inside or out. He was just about to drive off when for some reason he ignored all his own advice, opened the window, and yelled, "Hi there. You having some trouble?" He wasn't exactly sure what it might establish, but he said it anyway.

To the woman outside, it seemed a totally stupid question. Of *course* she was having some trouble, and she wrapped her arms more tightly around her for comfort, wishing she had grabbed a jacket before coming out. "No, I usually stand around here freezing at this time of night," she muttered ungraciously before yelling back, "Yes, I'm afraid so."

The thunder crashed on cue as the vehicle reversed back to within ten yards of the van. Those fanciful hopes for a car mechanic had been downgraded to wishing the cavalry would turn out to be female. Only a man got out, and she could see he had no passenger. Drat! But whatever it was that had kept her rooted to the spot suddenly lost its power as he came closer and she smelt alcohol. It was not the cavalry at all – it was an Indian! She backed up hastily till she bumped into the van. And this Martian Indian is drunk, she thought. The fact the alien had driven at speed and in a straight line right at her, and still missed, should have been some sort of evidence he wasn't that drunk, but it was overlooked because nothing else was as relevant as the fact that drink loosened inhibitions, and any rapist or murderer would need little encouragement if they were already drunk.

The alien Indian was completely unaware of this detailed examination of his sobriety as he was checking to see that no one was waiting to jump him. Sarah noted these actions also. Why would anyone need to look around like that, unless they had something to hide? Both parties were less than satisfied with their observations.

"You alone?" he finally asked.

"Yes." The answer was distinctly squeaky. There was no use denying it, because he could find it out easily enough. He peered into her van as she tried to crane her neck to double-check if there was anyone else in his car. Neither party was totally reassured, but he nodded briefly before walking back to his car to switch off the engine. She remained rooted to the same spot in front of her ailing craft. This charade did not make any sense.

The Indian indicated for her to shine her torch while he took a look inside her hood, and so she tried to concentrate on that. Her breathing was being seriously hampered by fear, and her heart was beating so fast that she was sure a heart attack must be imminent, so speech was probably not wise in such circumstances. At the very least she was expecting a panic attack. How did one handle panic attacks? Slow, deep breaths, or quick, shallow ones? She didn't know because she had never considered having one until right this very minute. She took a wild guess and took some slow, deep breaths. They were relatively successful in staving off the heart attack but had no effect on the panic, so she kept her head down, breathed some more, and concentrated on his hands -that was where the danger lay.

He had nice hands. That more or less sealed his fate and his intentions, so she tightened her grip on her torch, never once stopping to consider that millions of men had jobs that meant they had nice hands – Len for one, and she had never considered him particularly sinister because of it. She increased the need for alertness, and watched closely as the Indian checked wires, pulled things apart, and put them back together again. She was almost beginning to consider he might be that Indian mechanic, except for those hands. No respectable mechanic had hands like that; their hands always came with oil slicks and dirt under their nails at least, and his hands had been immaculate when he had started. He lifted up and held his arms up, she could see they had plenty of grease now because they were covered in black streaks. It took her a moment to work out that his surgeon's pose was not a signal he intended to dismember her, just an indication for her to undo his shirt sleeves. She obeyed hesitantly, it was not pleasant touching him because it meant relinquishing her cosh for a precious few seconds. Explosives could not have been handled more carefully.

The Indian sighed rather like Len did, and then he nodded impatiently to signify that was enough. "Take it off," he said.

Maybe she would have that panic attack after all!

He clarified. "Take my watch off. I think I know what's wrong, but I need to get down there, and I don't want to damage my watch." What was wrong with this woman? Was she some sort of idiot, or was she simply worried he might find out that she had deliberately sabotaged her camper? Either way, he was determined to find out what was wrong with this van. The idiot fiddled nervously, trying all the while to avoid touching him any more than was absolutely necessary, much as if he were a leper and she didn't want to catch anything. It made her task that much longer than it should have been. "Don't lose it," he barked as she finally released it, and he bent back over the van with a smirk, having completely misinterpreted the reason for her fumbling.

"Don't worry, I won't," she said more calmly than she felt, and immediately examined it for any inscription or any other means of identification. There was none, but she did discover the make and that it was numbered. She was inordinately pleased with this superior bit of detective work. I can now identify his watch and his hands in a line up, she thought triumphantly. Maybe it would be a good idea to get a good look at the rest of him, too, but the rest of him was currently hidden in the inwards of her camper, and so there was little else to take note of except the back of his head and his back. She turned to get his registration plate because that seemed the next best thing to have. That produced an immediate yell for her to hold the light still, so that had to be abandoned for now as well. She could get both later.

The Indian had very steady hands for a drunk. That observation should have cheered her up, if only that annoying little voice had not informed her ever so sweetly that steady hands would be more capable of strangling or raping her. Clearly this was a no-win situation! Absolute inebriation suddenly became the most desirable condition. Remaining rational with such competition was no easy task. The lack of conversation gave her time to develop a survival strategy, and it was simplicity itself: forget about mending the van – just get rid of him as soon as possible, -stay alive!

She was absorbed in perfecting this strategy when he yelled for her to hold the torch closer, so she didn't hear him. "Do you want me to find out what is wrong with this thing or not?" he demanded irritably.

"What? Oh yes, of course." That wasn't in her strategy.

"Then hold the light closer!" He waited a second. "Well?"

"I'm sorry," she mumbled, reapplying herself reluctantly to her task and recognising that she had just missed a perfect opportunity to tell him to go.

A moment later he asked something else and got no reply again. This time he straightened up and regarded her vacant expression with much less tolerance. "I asked you how it happened," he repeated -neither patiently nor politely.

"I stopped for a drink and to check my map." She was about to add, "because I have been lost so many times today," but she stopped herself in time and shrugged to show that she didn't know exactly how it had happened.

He tried to assess what the shrug meant but couldn't, and so he went back to checking a few more wires before declaring with an impressive note of irony, "So it sort of broke down without warning, I suppose?" Was that a crime? She handed him the cloth she had left under the hood from her earlier attempts. It was supposed to be encouragement for him to abandon her and the van, and go. "So, how come this lead was in entirely the wrong place?" he asked, indicating the errant lead.

"I don't know. Oh, unless …" She blushed furiously and hoped he wouldn't be able to see that in the dark.

"Unless what?"

"Unless I put it back in the wrong place when I had a look to see if I could fix it," she admitted quietly.

"You know about engines?"

"No, not exactly."

"Then messing with things you know nothing about is stupid and dangerous," he warned. "And I suppose you have no idea of what happened to make it break down *right here*?" That emphasis also eluded her.

"No, of course not." *Stupid* was the silent bit she added in her head.

"Well, something is wrong with it."

"Wow, that is really clever." She coloured and regretted the words immediately they passed her lips. She made an attempt at an apology. "I'm sorry, I didn't mean to sound rude. It must be the strain of being stuck out here so long. I am sorry." She was rapidly becoming an acceptable version of a total nervous wreck.

He ignored the apology, put the lead back in place, and slammed the hood shut with such a resounding thud that it made her jump again. "So what do you do now?" he asked.

"You haven't fixed it?"

He shook his head. "Can't even say for certain what's wrong with it. All the usual things check out, except the points and leads, and I haven't checked the tank. I presume you have gas."

"Of course I have gas," she retaliated indignantly. She might not be a mechanic, but neither was she an idiot! Spending the night out here alone did not seem nearly half as bad as it had a short while ago, and one night terrified was a whole lot better than a lifetime dead!

She was plotting on how best to implement her strategy when he enquired, "English, aren't you?" It was a simple enough sort of question; she had answered the very same question dozens of times already. This time it made her feel vulnerable, so her affirmative came out as that tinny little croak again. "Here on vacation?"

She nodded, unable to lie about that either, though she rushed to explain, "I am on my way to a campsite to park up for the night." Her vigilante voice screamed full volume that she had done the wrong thing yet again. Without much effort he had discovered she was alone, a stranger in a foreign land, and was heading for a campsite. The odds were no one was expecting her, so no one would miss her if she failed to turn up at all. If he were a murderer or a rapist, he could hardly need more encouragement than that! He now knew he had plenty of time to do whatever he wanted, dispose of her body, and be clear of the area long before anyone even suspected she was missing. Elinor was right: it *had* been dangerous to come out here alone. Dangerous and stupid. She added extra information in the hope it would undo some of the damage -well at least make him reconsider about murdering her. "Actually, I am on my way to a friend's house. I should have been there tonight, but I got delayed, that's why I am going to the campsite. I shall have to ring her soon, or else she will have the cavalry out looking for me." His laugh embarrassed her. Why couldn't he have been a woman? She dismissed the thought that most women were no better with cars than her, in favour of feeling smug that he had not been able to fix it either. Right now all she wanted was for him to go — oh, and ring the breakdown truck. "Ask Indian send smoke signals," she mumbled under her breath. That would provide the necessary incentive. "I am grateful for your help. Thanks for trying to fix it. Can I ask one last favour of you? Will you call out the breakdown when you reach a phone?" She pulled a crumpled card from her shorts pocket and offered it to him. "It's the second number on the back, the Los Angeles one," she explained. "The one below is my registration number."

Rick took the card without looking at it or mentioning that he might have worked that out for himself. "Los Angeles is a long way for a truck to come," he pointed out bluntly. She simply nodded, not feeling obliged to explain anything else. "The next call box is Wilson. My place is nearer."

"Well, if you want to be going, perhaps you could call them from there. It is a twenty-four-hour number, so if you would ring as soon as you get home, I would be very grateful."

"No rush," he added quixotically.

What did that mean? "I think I would go if I were you," she advised, looking up at the rapidly moving storm clouds overhead. Obviously he wasn't her, because he ignored the advice. Both were deliberating what should come next, but two very different agendas were being considered. Hers was whether being really rude to him would make him leave, or murder her; his was more metaphysical: she had been enterprising enough to get him to stop, and the crossed wires proved the breakdown was a fix, but to what purpose? Hell, she had even admitted the meddling, but most women lost no time in telling him what was really on their minds when they had him to themselves. Ironic, really. The loudest clap of thunder yet reminded him they didn't have time for games.

"Okay, lady, your luck's about to run out," he concluded calmly as the thunder was followed by a vicious streak of blue-white madness hitting the ground not that far away. She was no oil painting so she was going to have to work a whole lot harder fast if she wanted entertaining tonight. The brutality of his observation was adjusted quickly as a very large raindrop hit him hard on the nose, followed by another and then another. The sky, which had been content to look threatening for the last hour or so, looked ready to deliver on all its warnings. There was no chance of escaping any of it now. Damn the woman! He could have been home by now without this. As it was, he was still at least ten minutes away at speed. Another almighty thunderclap right over head reinforced the need for some immediate action. Pity. "Points sheared," he said simply, as though it were apparent to all the world.

"What?"

"You broke down because the points sheared," he explained slowly, articulating every syllable as if addressing a child. He saved the heaviest sarcasm for his next comment. "I don't know why. It could be anything, or something I know nothing about, but that's all I can find. It's enough. You ain't going anywhere in this."

"I do realise that," she observed dryly. It was a remark prompted by exasperation.

Thankfully, he neither reached for a knife nor attempted to strangle her. He simply laughed and said, "Get what you need."

"What?"

"Get what you need. Are you deaf? I'll give you a lift to town."

"No!" Her refusal was immediate and more than a little offensive, but she didn't regret it at all. *I am not accepting lifts from strangers*, played in her head right on cue! She swallowed hard and then softened her tone, "No, thank you, I can't. I can't go and leave the van."

"Why not?" He was rapidly running out of patience.

"Because I can't!" she said emphatically without any attempt at explanation.

The lightning flashed twice in quick succession. "You got a rope?" he asked.

"What!" she spluttered, indicating the extent of her mistrust. The exposure made her colour from the neck up. After clearing her throat, she repeated her request in such deliberately measured tones that it could only convey even more suspicion. "What for?"

"Tow you in, of course."

"Tow me in where?"

"Well, it's certainly not going to be Los Angeles, not even Wilson, but seeing as how it's going to get a whole lot worse when this rain starts any minute now, and seeing as how you are parked on some pretty soft ground here, and seeing as how it's thirty odd miles to the nearest motel in the other direction, I was thinking I might be doing you a favour. Just a small one," he added sarcastically. If she wanted to continue this game, he had no objections; he would no doubt get some reward for his patience later.

"Thank you for the offer, but I think I will stay here. I will be fine. I would appreciate the phone call when you get home."

He could hardly believe his ears. What did this woman want? Walter Raleigh? Or was it Walter Scott? His knowledge of English history was sketchy, and he couldn't be sure who the guy with the cape was, so he said nothing because he didn't want to chance correction. He didn't have any doubt that if he went back to his car, she would soon come running if she thought he was really going to leave her there. One last try. He sighed impatiently. "Listen, lady, I have a phone at home, and if you are sure you want me to go, then I'm more than happy to do that. I will call the truck out for you, but even if this place sends out a local truck tonight, it will be at least an hour before it gets here, and I reckon by then you could be in serious trouble."

"What sort of serious trouble?" she asked, a mite curious.

"Ever been stranded in a flash flood before?" She had never been stranded anywhere, least of all in a flash flood. She didn't even know what one was, but it sounded impressive. No answer indicated she was worried.

The hand clamped to her mouth confirmed it. "You reckon?"

"I reckon." Even though he had said his line for effect, it was not exactly fiction, either. Summer storms could be bad, and he did not want to hang around long enough to find out how bad this one intended to be. "Watch it – there's a snake!" he said pushing her to one side. The snake was total invention. Sarah did not know that. There was nothing invented about her scream; she had been saving it for the rapist, but the snake got there first. If the flash flood had impressed her, the snake more than convinced her that perhaps the tow might not be such a bad thing after all.

"I'll get the rope," was all she said.

"Good girl. Keys?" he demanded, holding out his hand as she meekly dropped them into his palm still shaking from shock.

The Indian was totally unconcerned about what had just happened. She had escaped being bitten by a poisonous rattle snake by a mere inch or so, and he wasn't in the least bit bothered! What's more, he walked off and left her! A surge of anger flushed Sarah`s face at such indifference, and she had to struggle to contain her irritation even though the snake could not have been his fault. She glanced around nervously, then decided it might be best to follow him – or safer, anyway – so hurried to catch up.

The light inside the van was reassuring and as her eyes readjusted, she found herself staring at the back of the stranger's head for the second time. This time he was bent over the contents of the toolbox hidden in the floor. Now would be a good time to cosh him with something and then escape in his car, just like they did in old films. She was actually looking around for her torch when she realised the enormity of what she was contemplating. "Stop it!" she hissed at her reflection in the darkened window. "You are becoming hysterical again! How can you possibly think about coshing anyone without being certain they mean to harm you?" The thought that it might be too late before she was certain was difficult to dismiss, but she managed it.

When her would-be assassin straightened up holding up a length of new tow rope, he was unprepared for the sight of a wild-eyed woman staring at him clutching her throat. She dropped her hand quickly, hoping he had not recognised the significance then blushed an even deeper shade of red as she diverted the offending hand to her hair in an attempt to give it some legitimate task to perform. The Indian stood and stared back.

If Elinor had been here, Sarah knew she would have used this whole disaster to her advantage, made a joke out of it, and no doubt pronounced the Indian "fit" or "dishy" or some other equally appalling word. It was bad enough that she should know what Elinor would have thought, but it was worse that she thought it herself. She had never intended to stare; she had sort of accidentally noticed that he was about six foot tall with rather nice, dark hair and eyes that had a way of looking right through her. Okay, he was handsome, -well, almost perfect. Like most Californians he had a nice tan. Unlike any Californians she had met to date, he wore evening dress – well, an evening shirt minus the tie, and the trousers minus the jacket – with an easy panache. It was a cavalier outfit for a cavalry man except he was an Indian, and instead of a shiny sword he had only the Rolex watch, which she was still holding. She hastily recalled herself, coughed politely, and handed back his weapon as if it were programmed to explode any minute.

The Indian had no such reservations. He was used to checking out enemy territory, and he had every intention of using this opportunity to check out his would-be seducer thoroughly. He replaced his watch slowly, doing exactly that.

The subject of his assessment could only squirm uncomfortably under such a penetrating gaze. There was no need for him to do that. No respectable person would be so rude! He made her feel like a small child who had been caught playing in the mud when she had been told not to. Now she was mortified as well as scared!

By the time she joined the Indian outside, he had reversed his car back to the front of the camper, and although it was very dark, she could now tell that it was some sort of sports model – not at all what she had in mind for a breakdown truck.

"Do you know what you are doing?" she enquired, trying hard not to let it sound patronising. She knew she had failed by the look he gave her, but he had to be very ignorant about such things because she felt sure he would never consider using such a vehicle to tow a camper if he did know what he was doing. Even she knew high-performance sports cars were not intended for such tasks, so she felt obliged to try again. "It's not exactly a pickup truck, is it?"

Rick finished fastening the rope to his car and then stood up and rubbed his hands. "No, it's a Ferrari," he said smoothly. "I'm real glad you noticed the difference. The salesman assured me people would." She had the grace to blush. The last time she had failed to recognise a very fast and expensive car, the boys' witticisms had been kinder.

"I wish it had been the truck," she muttered under her breath. It had been meant for her ears only, but she had forgotten about Indian powers of hearing.

"Gee, I'm sorry! This will just have to do. I didn't know I would be picking anyone up tonight!" Her embarrassment turned to anger and humiliation in equal measures. He softened his tone and offered something inane, but she knew instinctively that his first comment had been the true one, and it had been meant to hurt her. He explained "It's only a couple of miles to the approach road, and then it's all downhill from there, so I daresay I only need get you started." She did not understand that, either, but she nodded, refusing to get more upset by things she could not understand, and having pointed out his folly twice and being rewarded with derision both times, she felt under no further obligation. He continued, "I'll get you to safety up at the house. You can call your repair truck out from there. Okay?" He looked at her for confirmation, but that wasn't forthcoming. She was actually reconsidering his whole solution when he added irritably, "Unless of course you would rather I abandon you and call out the local breakdown when I get home? Come on; make up your mind, lady. This storm isn't going to wait for you, and neither am I! Which is it to be?"

"Are you sure you don't mind?" This was the nearest she could trust her voice to asking, "Why are you doing this?"

His answer was equally oblique. "I daresay Molly can find you a bed for the night somewhere, if you need one."

Why would she need a bed? She already had a bed. She could stay in the camper very comfortably, thank-you-very-much, but she had no time to protest as he hauled her from the van steps just as she registered he had a wife! The blessed Molly! Her alarm receded. Prayers of gratitude for Molly were felt, if not uttered. Well, they were mixed prayers of thanks and pity, but then, some women were saints, and this Molly must surely be one!

Molly's husband more or less manhandled her across to the Ferrari. Worse still, he banged her head against the door column as he pushed her inside. "Ouch!" she complained, rubbing her head. "That hurt!" Knowledge of Molly's existence had given her courage to say this, and so she said it quite deliberately because she wanted him to recognise that she was not Molly, and her injury was entirely his fault. It was meant to provoke an apology. It was impossible to say whether he comprehended that, but she got no apology, so she rubbed her head again. It had been a sharp blow, and it had made her feel quite sick. She forgot all about the apology as her eyes took in the phone in front of her.

He did notice that. "Go ahead, pick it up," he ordered shirtily. Just for that reason she shook her head. "Pick it up," he said again. She obeyed, half expecting the thing to explode in her hand, but it was dead. His frown was replaced by an ugly sort of smirk. "Dead, just like your camper. You and I seem to be having a lot of problems tonight, don't we?" He did not wait for an answer but instead squatted down beside her and asked sharply, "Can you drive a car with manual transmission?"

What the heck was manual transmission? She was about to admit defeat when it dawned on her what he meant mere seconds before she made a fool of herself yet again. "Of course I can," she sniffed in a manner not dissimilar to some of his comments. "Just show me the controls." Her second phrase had less certainty than the first because she had noticed with some dismay a bewildering array of controls on the dash that in no way resembled those on her mini. He ran through them all briefly and finished with a distinctly unfunny joke about the clutch and the brake pedal, which she ignored. Humour like that was on a par with the third-year boys.

"I am going to get behind the van, so when I shout, 'Now!' I want you to accelerate gently. That means—"

"I know what gently means," she protested. "I do understand English."

Less than five minutes later the van was back on the hard road surface. All it had needed was a simple combination of strength and know-how, and though she possessed neither, the Indian obviously possessed both. That was doubly annoying. Compared with all her unsuccessful pushing, grunting, and groaning, this obnoxious man had accomplished with ease what she had failed to do with enormous effort. "Good girl," he said, handing her out of his car. "Well done!"

"Don't patronise me!" she hissed, still shell shocked from the bump.

He was about to respond in kind but then decided against it. She missed that because her attention was still not all it should be, though she did register him telling her to get back in the van. He did not wait for this instruction to be carried out either and more or less dragged her back to the camper in much the same fashion as he had pushed her to the car, so she stopped moving at all, which only made matters worse. Her mouth was open and ready to say, "Stop ordering me around," when he bundled her hostage fashion inside.

"Just get in," he said, impatiently slamming the door behind her. "We have no time for arguments. Give me a minute while I wash my hands; I don't want oil all over my car. You do have water, I presume?"

She directed him to the back of the van, and he climbed in through the side door. He might not be the mass murderer she had first imagined, but he still made her feel nervous, so she opened the driver's door again, just in case she needed to make that quick getaway. She continued to watch his every move through the mirror until he got out. This whole episode was so surreal, that when he poked his head round her open door, she was already primed to scream. Fortunately shock robbed her of the necessary volume.

"Take it easy. I'll signal good and early so you know what I'm about to do. *Do not* run into the back of me!" he emphasised.

"I wouldn't dream of it," she said, pulling the door shut with a slam.

"Good! Believe me, your insurance company will not be very happy if you do, and neither will I," he added ominously. She glared back at him, but it had absolutely no effect on his manner, which was still the wrong side of civil. "Pedal on the left of the accelerator is the brake," he stated irritatingly. "Make sure you use it." The only thing that prevented her from being sarcastic back was the knowledge that he was helping her, so she smiled as sweetly as she could through gritted teeth.

True to his word, the Indian signalled long and hard before moving off, and Sarah released her handbrake to the accompaniment of a few choice Shakespearian sayings, but then she had to concentrate hard to steer straight while keeping her left foot poised above the brake, as per his instructions. Sure enough, the road was all downhill, just as he had promised, so she began to be a little more understanding of why he had warned her so forcibly about the brake. Only a little understanding, though, because the delicious thought that it would be quite easy for her foot to slip presented the sort of temptation she could only just resist. This man was helping her, and here she was thinking about "accidentally" bumping him. What was wrong with her?

A couple of minutes later the rain started for real, and then, even with wipers working at full speed, she had to strain to see the tail lights of the car in front. Being towed in even started to seem like a good thing; consequently all remaining thoughts of bumping him were banished as the downpour helped promote him from renegade to something approaching hero in a matter of minutes.

She could not recall Elinor having said anything about California being subject to monsoons, but then, she had not been listening to much of what Elinor had said about anything. This deluge seemed to fit the sketchy knowledge she had of monsoons. Whether it was or it wasn't, it took them the best part of twenty minutes to reach that approach road she had whizzed past almost four hours earlier. It had not warranted a second thought then, but now she wondered where it might be leading them. Less than five minutes later, her new hero signalled to turn left, and gates swung open before them.

It was a long drive for a private house she thought, but because it was pitch-black and the storm was raging all around her, it was not possible to discern much about where it was taking them. She guessed it was about half a mile before he indicated he was stopping. A big black building lay right ahead of them and while he was getting soaked freeing his car, she sat staring vacantly at this edifice. It was in total darkness. A threatening presence. So much for Molly! Either she was not home, or maybe she did not exist. Anxiety started to get the better of her again. The clock on the dash flashed 1.45 AM. Of course, if Molly had any sense at all, she would be in bed, not waiting up for her extremely rude husband.

Relief was temporary. A second later a flood of light almost blinded her. It took a moment to realise the source was a garage door being raised. Seconds later a soaking figure was banging frantically on the van door. She opened it reluctantly. "Come on, are you deaf? Let's get up to the house."

She stared in disbelief. No way, she thought. He opened the door wider, pushed her along the seat and slid himself in next to her. It was cramped, he was wet, and so was she now. After taking in her stony, resolute face, he grinned. "No one is going to come out tonight in this except emergency services, and as you are no longer an emergency, you may as well have a decent bed. I daresay Molly can find you one somewhere."

"I have a perfectly adequate bed here, thank you." Molly need not bother, she thought.

"You can sleep with all this din?" he asked, pointing to the roof which was literally shaking under the violence of the rain.

"Of course."

His shrug seemed to indicate acceptance. "Well, at least have the benefit of hot and cold water, then. You look as though you might need it."

Even after what she had endured, such an outright insult shocked her, but she held her cool and managed to answer primly, "I have that, too. Thank you."

"You sure?" he asked, shaking his head. "I think you are almost out, but I am not wasting any more time arguing with you. I need to get out of these clothes."

Sarah did not reply but swung round to check out her water situation almost before he had climbed out of the van. The trickle of water was conclusive. No water meant no drinking, no washing facilities, and no toilet! Without thinking she opened the door and yelled into the rain. "Wait! I will have to get some things together."

He stopped and ran back. "You are joking me!" he declared as he grabbed her arm to pull her out, but this time she held fast to the door frame. "Leave 'em. Come on, I am already soaked. Someone can come and get what you need later."

It seemed more than a bit stupid that someone should have to get wet later when it would take her only a minute to throw some things in a bag now. Besides, who was someone? If it was her, she would much rather get wet once than twice, and if it was someone else, then she wasn't sure that she liked the idea of a perfect stranger going through her things. She was about to say all this when his grip on her arm tightened, and he pulled her down the steps, banging the door shut after her.

"Wait, I have to lock it, at least," she shouted through the noise of the rain.

He grabbed the keys from her hand and locked it while she watched. "Now come on!" he ordered. This time she obeyed and ran silently behind him. "Satisfied?" he asked as he shook the water from his hair after they had reached the shelter of the garage. "Even if we should get unwanted guests tonight, I know of no sane car thief who will persist in trying to take a locked camper when there is an unlocked Ferrari in an unlocked garage." She nodded miserably because she was not prepared to offer further explanations right now. "Come on," he said forgetting that debate to concentrate on more important current issues. "Let's get out of these things before we both get pneumonia." She followed him in silence through the garage till they emerged at the far side under a covered walkway, which led to a door in a huge black building. The garage had been bigger than her house, so the size of this new building was not that big a shock, except its door was bolted against them, and knocking and banging brought absolutely no response. Molly must be a deep sleeper. His cursing was not Shakespeare, but luckily for him all of it was lost in the storm, so he escaped reprimand. Eventually he decided that there was no chance of them getting in, and he yelled, "Can you run?" Had she not she just proved that? The thought of getting in out of this rain would ensure it. Without warning he grabbed her hand and dragged her away from the small amount of shelter offered by the canopy and out into the teeming rain again. She would have complained at his lack of manners if she had not stumbled immediately over a boulder protruding onto the path, and because it was his hand that saved her, it warranted just enough gratitude for her to swallow the rebuke. Trying to keep upright in this lashing rain denied her the power to complain anyway, because it was difficult enough to breathe.

Sarah had never experienced rain like this in her entire life; it hit her bare arms and legs like tiny bullets wounding her flesh, causing her to blink continuously as her eyes struggled to cope. The house seemed the size of a football pitch, but they did eventually arrive breathless and dripping wet under its front porch and while the Indian fumbled with keys, she leant forward resting her hands on her knees, desperate to get her breath back and stop her teeth from chattering. It was even darker here and he was cursing the lack of light as he tried several keys at the lock without success. She waited, cold, silent, and shivering, and although this porch now afforded a little shelter from the rain, she shared his impatience to get inside and get dry.

While he continued to struggle with the door, she made herself look for some means of identifying this unexpected sanctuary. There was no name or number on the door. She noted that the four windows that opened onto the porch were all shuttered from the inside, and no light shone through the cracks in their boards. There was only blackness. Were they shuttered or just plain boarded up? Had he brought her to an abandoned house? That possibility made her shiver some more. She looked around for potential means of escape but only noticed the debris littering the terrace and the flooded and bedraggled potted palms and flowers on the lawns; they were all of them stranded in this storm. This house must have been very attractive once with a rather nice Mediterranean influence. Was it Spanish? The Spaniards had owned California; she had learned that only this week and was pleased it had proved useful so soon. She wondered how many such houses there were in these parts, and whether it would be sufficient to trace this place from if she needed to. She had seen a picture of a similar house recently on an advert for Mexico in the Los Angeles travel agency where she had changed some money. She remembered staring at it while waiting to be served. A most alarming thought presented itself for consideration. Could this be Mexico? Could she have wandered so far off course that she had actually strayed across the border?

Finally the Indian found the right key, flung open one of the doors, and pushed her inside with as little ceremony as he had dragged her round the outside. She stumbled over the threshold, leaving him to catch her a second time, and though she could hear herself saying, "Thank you," she really meant, that was your fault – again! But this was sanctuary for now, and so she overlooked everything else in favour of shelter.

Chapter Thirteen

It had to be the commotion they made getting into the house, not his yelling for Molly at maximum decibels that brought that lady scurrying in to the hall, because she was there almost before he had finished uttering the first syllable of her name. "Oh, it is only you," she complained with some relief as she surrendered a large rolling pin onto a nearby table, trying to make it look as though it were the sort of accessory she carried regularly at this time in the morning. "I heard some noise at the back, and I thought it must be you or Mr Perry," she explained, tidying her hair in attempt to divert attention from her offensive weapon. "But then it went all quiet again, and no one rang, so I was getting a bit worried. Everyone knows you can't be too careful these days. There are some weird folks out there." An observation that caused Sarah to turn away to hide a smirk. "So how come you didn't ring the bell?" Molly demanded, unwilling to let go of the irritation she still nursed.

"Because I didn't know *you* would still be here," came the equally irritable reply.

"We're all still here because of this storm," Molly said in a slightly less acid tone, not that anxious to inflame the situation further. "Well, I am. Everybody else has been out since six when we got the imminent warning. I have been on my own since then, but it's why I figured you wouldn't be back tonight. Last time Mr Perry called, he said they were on their way to the station, but that was more than two hours ago, long before the storm got started properly. How come no one ever considers the folk left at home worrying? Do you reckon they will be okay?" The Indian shrugged to shake off the rain, but Molly mistook it as her answer. "So everything will be okay?"

"I didn't say that. Storm hasn't hit yet, but it's moving fast. Perry has enough sense to call if he gets into difficulty. Don't fret."

"And everything else?"

"Least of my problems," he replied. Molly scrutinised him closely, not sure how that could be. "Can't do anything about a storm," he explained bluntly, "except clear up the mess when it's over. If they have been out there since six, they should be back soon. I suppose we had better wait up to hear the news."

Molly's eyes swivelled like searchlights to where the other half of this "we" stood dripping quietly. It seemed the height of ingratitude to do anything as messy as drip in this perfect place, but there was absolutely nothing Sarah could do to prevent it. Worse still, the cold, wet, weight of her shorts and shirt made it certain that her little puddle would continue to grow unless someone did something about it quickly. She squeezed a glimmer of a smile for Molly's benefit but her effort was rewarded with a stare fierce enough to frighten most sensible folk. That made the puddle even more alarming. How she could have ended up in this crazy predicament with its uncanny similarity to Alice in Wonderland when she had been under Indian attack a short while ago was way beyond her. From Peter Pan to Alice in one move, she thought grimly. Even Ali would be impressed! Could Alice even be considered an improvement on Peter Pan? She had never featured in a fairy-story before, but if this was one, Wonderland was as good a title as any; on the other hand, she had to admit the duchess didn't usually figure this early.

It had taken less than a minute for Sarah to realise this was no ordinary house, and less than two to realise that no ordinary family lived here, but weird as it was, she reckoned this place suited these individuals down to the ground! Both of them were only just the right side of spooky! And Alice had nothing to offer that could improve her image of either of them or their house. Elinor had never actually said that America didn't have stately homes, so she knew she must have presumed that, but this house had to be a near relative because it was very old, and if it had started out as slightly scary because of the storm, those thoughts about the darker side of Alice had only added to the effect of the giant shadows sprawling across the light from the door Molly had come through. It was not a comfortable combination. Perhaps that's why the smell of flowers and beeswax made her think of a funeral parlour. She had grown up in a house smelling of exactly the same things, and though they had always seemed synonymous with comfort and love there, here they definitely seemed tokens of the macabre, if not the trade of the undertaker. She gulped audibly.

Molly switched on a nearby lamp. The better to see her by? To measure her up? The light did little to settle her nerves, but at least the ghouls shrank back into furniture as the creepily perfect order of the place became clearer.

Museum was the unkind if slightly less worrying alternative to funeral parlour. But neither was inhabited by living souls.

Up to now she had been paying little attention to the conversation between the Indian and Molly, but she gathered enough of her wits together to force some because they might be saying something about her. She was still dripping wet and in danger of catching pneumonia, and her sneezing loudly several times underlined that point, but neither of them seemed bothered by it, so, she gazed longingly at the stone fireplace and prayed for some spontaneous combustion. The fire basket remained as it was, full of unlit candles. This house, despite all its obvious attractions, was cold and miserable and more intimidating than any funeral parlour or museum.

Something else that was strange: the number of doors. This was not so much a hall, more a concourse. More of Alice? That was amusing for a few minutes, but it became a little more unnerving when she realised that on each side of the doors nearest to her were matching carved tables. The similarities were beginning to be more than creepy. They were frightening! Fortunately there were no small bottles marked "Drink Me" on either, or she might have fled, wet or not, storm or not. The lamp Molly had switched on had a mirror behind it, and that provided her with an image of a pitiful, bedraggled creature that looked as if it had walked straight out of the sea. It took a minute to register that the creature was her because to "slightly grubby," she had now added "dripping wet" and the combination was not flattering. The real Alice could not have felt or looked this bad at her nine foot worst! "I am not here," she muttered. "This is all a bad dream! I will wake up in a minute." She was willing that to happen when the sneezing began again: one, two, three times, and then a machine gun volley followed.

The others turned to look at her as if they had just realised she was there, but she carried on sneezing and shivering so uncontrollably that the Indian finally remembered about this other disaster awaiting his attention. Sarah was pretty sanguine by now, she knew that she needed to get out of her wet clothes right now – and preferably into a hot bath and then a warm bed – and she had every hope of escaping pneumonia if that could happen. Perhaps this Molly person would recognise that, even if the Indian didn't, so she sniffled apologetically and turned her soggy smile on Molly again, abandoning all speculation about who she was, in favour of getting her help.

Neither lady realised it, but they had both been struggling with essentially the same problem. Sarah's hopes of Molly being the Indian's squaw had been flattened the moment Molly had walked in clutching that rolling pin: she was much too old. Molly was at least in her late fifties, whereas he was probably about her age. A younger husband, maybe? No, there was more than just years between these two. He had style; she simply had the attitude of one who was impervious to the idea of it, let alone the practice. He was in charge, whereas she was clearly suffering -almost in silence. One didn't even need to be observant to work out the likelihood of this being man and wife was about the same as aliens choosing tonight to take over the planet. Could be his mother? That idea did not last long, either; it was flattened by his very next words. "Okay, forget about everything else for now. You see to her, and I will sort myself out. Oh, and rustle us up something to eat afterwards? Hot would be good. You hungry?" he asked Sarah as he strode past her towards stairs. No one – not even a rude, bad-tempered Indian – addressed his mother in such a way. There was no opportunity to answer his question, but apparently he did not require one. "Well," he chivvied Molly- whoever-she-was, "go on. Go run her a bath before she gets pneumonia or floods the place." He had noticed after all.

Molly disappeared up the stairs, but not before she had fired off the sort of withering look that adequately conveyed all the things she was not able to say to this visitor. Their eyes met for only a fraction of a second before she flashed her displeasure by glancing down at Sarah`s little puddle. There were no mice swimming in there yet, and Sarah was still the same size, but she must have fallen down a weird sort of rabbit hole to have ended up in this madhouse. That look had left her in no doubt at all: she was not welcome here.

The Indian announced, "Come down when you have changed. Molly will have fixed us something to eat by then."

"Please don't go to any trouble for me. I am fine. I am just tired."

"Eat first." It was not an invitation.

There was absolutely nothing she could do about him being bad tempered with Molly but being bad tempered with her was a different thing entirely. She had inconvenienced him, true, but she hadn't asked to be towed here, and she was not one to be so easily intimidated. She enquired, "Do you always sound so easy going?" in what she hoped would be an easy, informal manner, but her growing dislike of him had made it sound more like sarcasm.

The Indian merely looked her up and down and smiled the sort of smile that Elinor reserved for unfortunate delinquents with double detention – the ones she was about to terrorise.

Sarah was about to say something more when Molly chose that moment to reappear at the head of the stairs. It was impossible not to feel this woman's presence, so she looked up, drawn to the impassive figure with pursed lips and fierce scowl. "Off with her head" was the dialogue that should have accompanied that glare from this perfect duchess in this mad adventure, but failing that, she reckoned that stare could reasonably fit into any dark novel needing a thunderous presence to terrorise innocents – a Bronte romance perhaps, or even a Mrs Danvers. Eureka! Puzzle solved! Molly was a housekeeper! Correction: Molly was housekeeper to the Indians in these parts. Could Indians afford housekeepers? That led her through a whole train of more exotic theories, starting with the queen and ending with the thought that maybe he was foreign royalty in exile. And Molly? She would be the faithful old family retainer minding her master. Or maybe she was minder for something more sinister! Maybe he was a lunatic, the mad son of a wealthy family, a drug baron, or a Dracula. The lightning flashed right on cue followed by the thunder crashing closer than ever. This last allegation had not been meant seriously, but she shuddered all the same and hoped that it would be mistaken for the fact that she was still wet through and probably running a temperature by now. That would explain her ramblings, anyway!

With a great deal of effort she dismissed all her more macabre theories by accepting that being well read might not be the best preparation for some things. Even bears, snakes, and the odd mountain lion had begun to seem mild by comparison with some of her more bizarre theories about this house and its residents.

"If you would like to come up, miss, I have a bath ready for you." It was a hard, cold invitation without the least degree of warmth, but Sarah managed to smile graciously at the older woman on the grounds that she would probably not be too welcoming herself at this time in the morning. At least now that she had solved the mystery of who Molly was, she would get to keep her head!

"Well?" the Indian said, watching her carefully, "Are you not going to sample what I have to offer?" This proposition alarmed her a little, so she looked across at him to see if she could identify why that should be; but he just shrugged. "Water's getting cold," he said as he dropped her keys carelessly on the table at the foot of the stairs before gesturing for her to lead the way. She obliged because she was too tired to think of a reason not to; any reason she could think of would probably only invite more flippant remarks, and she would not give him that satisfaction. He was too sarcastic by far. Maybe no one had ever told him sarcasm was the lowest form of wit. And she was not the one to do it right now. She might do it later, if he continued. Part of this delayed bravado was down to her vulnerability. It was not unlike the sort a fly in a spider's web might feel. Alice of course was of no use at all on this matter as she had not encountered spiders. Perhaps she would have been safer out in the van after all.

The Indian watched her silently until she had climbed almost halfway up his stairs, and then he said, "For someone who has just been rescued from a fate worse than death, it seems like you aren't that grateful."

Sarah could no sooner allow him to believe that than the real Alice could have resisted the white rabbit's provocations, her manners were too well programmed, so, even though her spirit counselled her to remain silent, indignation took over. "On the contrary, I am *very* grateful," she said, smiling sweetly and forcing such politeness that it provoked a laugh as he followed her.

"We shall see," he said glibly as he reached her side. That was an odd thing to say, but then, some Americans were odd, and he fitted that category perfectly. At the top of the stairs he remembered something else. "Oh, Molly, I guess if you can fix our guest up with whatever she needs for the night, then you can stay dry. Otherwise it's a trip out to her camper front of the garage. Keys are on the hall table."

For once Molly had nothing to say, so she led the way along the landing in silence with her charge trailing behind her leaving only a thin, silvery, wet line in her wake. Thankfully they were heading in the opposite direction to the Indian, and even though she was being spared further difficult communication with him or his housekeeper, Sarah's gratitude was limited because her head ached and she felt sick. Was this how pneumonia got started?

At the far end of the landing, a massive window soared up into the roof timbers. It wasn't usually thought of as terrifying, but the fierceness of the storm, and particularly the lightning that regularly tore across its blackness, fully qualified it as such tonight. A particularly vivid streak smashed against its panes, lighting up the entire landing for a second. Its nearness left both ladies shaken. No wonder Molly had been nervous on her own. It seemed a good time for Sarah to remind herself how fortunate she was to be in out of it; perhaps the van was not such a good idea on a night like this after all. With that admission she neatly disarmed all her remaining reservations about her host, his mental state or his marital status; his home's secrets or his housekeeper's manner by focusing on her more pressing need for a bath and some sleep.

Molly ushered her into the sort of room she had seen only in expensive magazines in doctor's waiting rooms or hairdressers. It warranted genuine admiration. The older woman sniffed dismissively; her thoughts were very different to those of her charge. This girl was just another trickster, all innocence and devotion on the surface, but she was just like all the others, out for what she could get, any way she could get it. Molly didn't waste much time over it; her employer obviously wanted her here, whatever her motives, or otherwise she would never have got past the gate. Molly had never bothered to examine whether pleasantness was expected of her in such situations; she simply did as she was told, and given that her manner was always just the right side of civil, no one had ever complained – but then, no one had ever dared to suggest she could be more welcoming to a female guest either -whoever she was. Until they did, they would all get the same treatment, and that was just sufferance.

The room which had earned such spontaneous approval was decorated in the most delicate shades of ivory and peach, and everything in it -from the exquisite silk-covered armchairs by the window to the rare Chinese silk panels adorning the walls, spoke money very loudly - if with some taste. Its newest guest stopped by a little table that held a bowl of such perfectly colour-matched orchids and lilies, she had to check that they were real.

"Bathroom is through there, miss. I have run a bath for you." Molly was never impressed by any display at all, so she was turning back the bed as she pointed her charge to the open door. No soaking wet refugee would ever need a second invitation. Molly's voice made this one's jump as she had followed her through. "Tell me what you need for morning, miss, and I will get it for you."

Sarah looked around at her, decided against protest, and listed the things she would need. She resisted the urge to apologise. Somehow or other she didn't think that apologies or explanations would soften this woman's hostility and so she made do with a simple thank–you, which Molly acknowledged with another sniff.

"Well, if you have all you need for now, I will leave you to clean up. By the time you're finished, I will have something ready to eat, so just come down." Two minutes later she knocked and popped her head back round the door. She was about to utter her one and only almost civil sentence. "Clean forgot. I've put you some pyjamas out in the dressing room. Everything else you need is in here. Use whatever you want. I will have your things for you in the morning. Is that okay?"

"I need my toilet bag for my toothbrush …"

"New toothbrush and all you need is there," Molly said, indicating an open vanity unit. "Like I said, use whatever. I am sure we have most things you could want," she added, unable to resist some sarcasm. Sarah thanked the woman, wondering if her sarcasm was because she had had a bad day as well, or whether it was a household habit. "That's okay, then?" Duchess Danvers sniffed as she was about to leave.

"Except …"

Molly turned back. "Except what?"

Did she sniff all the time? "Well, it seems a bit improper running around in …" She was about to say "in someone else's house" or "in someone else's pyjamas", when she caught Molly's eye. The hostile look made her reconsider. "Please don't bother with food for me; I am not hungry. I think I will go straight to bed after I have had a bath. Would you give my apologies to …" Heck, she didn't even know the Indian's name! Her cover-up was impressive, with hardly a second's hesitation, she added, "Downstairs. Please say I don't want to eat and have gone straight to bed."

Molly stared at her. "I think you had better deliver that sort of message yourself," she said coldly without any hesitation.

"I have no clothes," Sarah pointed out nervously.

"So? That's current practice, ain't it?" This conversation was getting more difficult to understand by the minute; one of them might have no idea what the other meant, but the other one knew exactly what she meant. Molly nodded and turned to leave, but she sensed that she might have overstepped the mark for once, and so she neatly covered her tracks by adding a little more amenably, "There are robes in the dressing room as well. Like I said, just help yourself, make yourself at home - use whatever you want." The older woman's face had softened for only a second before she remembered herself, sniffed again, and added, "If that's all, I'll leave you to clean up, miss. Come down when you are ready."

Sarah decided that before she applied the relevant dormouse reality check, she would put this crazy illusion to some good use and take a bath. "Might even get to wake up clean," she promised herself fancifully. This bathroom was just waiting to be used, and there seemed no point in letting it go to waste. It was every hedonist's idea of total pleasure, a narcissist's paradise, and to someone whose single understanding of the word "therapy" was a bath, this was nothing short of heaven – an ivory marble and suede heaven, at that! She touched the walls gingerly to make sure they really were suede, and then she shook her head in utter disbelief when her fingers confirmed what her eyes told her. Suede walls in a bathroom! Suede walls anywhere was beyond her. *All* of it was beyond her! It dazzled and beguiled her so much that a full five minutes after Molly had left, she was still stood gawping and dripping. Eventually another violent sneezing spell reminded her it might be better to admire these surroundings from the comfort of the spectacular circular bath if she wanted to stave off that dose of pneumonia.

The bath might not have been big enough to cope with an entire rugby team, but it erred on the side of the grossly indulgent for one person, and Sarah was anxious not to get oil on it or on the stack of cream towels waiting by its side so she looked around for something to clean off her oil slicks before she surrendered herself to its charms. The vanity unit turned out to contain a small shop's worth of creams and potions lined up in neat rows like soldiers awaiting inspection. She surveyed their ranks with deep mistrust. Indians on the frontiers of civilisation never possessed such things – well, not in any of the books she had read or the films her mother had seen. Maybe Indian wives did. That intrigued her, but dire necessity had to overcome any impropriety in this instance though she still took a little cleanser from what she hoped was the least expensive pot, and apologised to its absent owner as she scrubbed her face clean. She removed her sodden clothes with some difficulty and deposited them in the second basin. Not much else to be done with them for now, maybe she could wash them through tomorrow. All preparations completed, she approached the bubbling perfumed water rather like a small child at a fairground approaches a strange ride: a little apprehensive at first but sure that the experience will turn out to be enjoyable in the end. She settled back to enjoy it. Any remaining misgivings about the house and its occupants melted along with the dirt as the water massaged her tired, frozen, aching limbs back to life. That done, she lay back to survey the rest of this watery paradise.

It was the towels that held her spellbound. Dozens of them, all perfectly colour matched and beautifully arranged on subtly lit glass shelving – the complete opposite of the soggy, mismatched items usually found adorning her bathroom floor. But then, all of this was beyond her experience. Only anxiety about incurring more of Molly's displeasure eventually forced her to abandon the bath and then she discovered the towels felt as wonderful as they looked. This time it was easier to persuade herself that she could use some moisturiser without feeling too guilty though she was still debating the issue of ownership as she went in search of the dressing room.

The second door in the bathroom led into a long, narrow room lined with panels of mirrored glass. Another Alice site? A dressing table and stool stood in front of French windows at this end, and a screen and an elegantly upholstered day bed at the other end were the only items of furniture. The clothes draped over the screen and the bed provided eye-catching splashes of colour. There was twenty feet of mirrors between her and them. She crossed it as if it was booby trapped, the ripple of anxious replicas accompanying her. When she picked up the first item of clothing, the same mirrors multiplied her moment of utter disbelief followed by perplexity. When she dropped the third item in shock, they caught that, too. She spun around, panicked by her lack of understanding, but there was no one there except her own dizzying reflections, images of some woman she hardly recognised. "Fish out of water I maybe," she explained to the images, "but these are definitely *not* pyjamas!" This last pair was made of the softest honey-coloured satin with shoestring straps that crossed over low at the back; the next was sheer coffee lace, and the third was black chiffon with a decorative ostrich feather trim. She could no sooner imagine what it might be like trying to sleep with ostrich feathers tickling your nose than she could imagine why anyone might want to. Every single garment was the same: all of them delicate, fragile concoctions in sumptuous fabrics embellished with beading or embroidery, feathers, or diamante. They were all beautiful, but they were hardly Marks and Spencer! Maybe she was simply not meant to sleep in these things. What else would one do in pyjamas? She was currently outdoing even Ali's most persistent curiosity, but whatever else it was one did in such clothing, one did not need a degree in textiles to know that they were high fashion, and probably very expensive. That added weight to the investigation about ownership.

When she had exhausted herself with trying to solve what could not be solved, she sorted through the dozen or so garments again, trying to find the nearest match to her idea of what pyjamas were meant to be: modest and functional. Modesty and utility had clearly not been part of the owner's specification, and when she did find some that approached her idea of propriety, they didn't fit. There was no way she could fasten the jacket. The label made her feel quite faint – they were size four! Who on earth was size four? Not even Alice! Her pulse was only restored to something like normal when she remembered American sizes were different than British. Still, size four! Just saying it gave her a complex.

Her second choice fitted better, and she breathed a sigh of relief; these were size eight. "I am size eight," she purred with a superior smile to the nearest reflection, omitting to disclose she meant she was American size eight; nevertheless, the words held their own intrinsic magic. "Size eight! Wowee. Elinor, eat your heart out," she chortled as she acknowledged the slightly shocking but nevertheless pleasurable shiver of delight as she shimmied and twirled. She brought herself rapidly to heel as she realised they were transparent, so she discarded them without a second thought.

The next was another pair of size four – in fact, there were several pairs of each size between four and ten. Nothing strange about that; her own wardrobe had everything in it from a twelve to a sixteen. "People lose weight," she pointed out, trying on another pair of size eight. "And then they put it back on again," she added miserably when these proved to be too small. She studied her reflection in the mirror. "They lose height, too?" This pair finished way above her ankles. It took a whole minute to come up with an answer for that. "Maybe he's a dress designer." That seemed plausible enough when one might have pneumonia. "Or a lingerie salesman?" That elicited a chuckle. The dress designer theory seemed more likely; he didn't appear to have the right personality for the latter profession.

Choosing between the third pair of size eight and a pair of size ten was hard. Size ten won in spite of obvious size eight satisfaction, because the ten was more akin to M&S. She twirled around again to check this choice for drawbacks; but there were none. The long, slim pants and long-sleeved, fitted jacket, covered her nicely. The top even had tiny jet buttons all the way up to its mandarin collar. She fastened every single one. She could actually admire these pyjamas, and they felt like nothing else she had ever worn. The label said pure silk. Teacher's pay did not extend to such sybaritic delights. Pity.

A quick glance at her watch dispelled all such decadent longings. It was later than she thought, but Molly had mentioned robes, and right now she was only to be satisfied with matching perfection. Such demanding needs had taken less than an hour to develop, and though she could not claim she needed a dressing gown for warmth, she reckoned a robe would make her feel more properly dressed. They had to be somewhere in here. Behind these mirrors? The nearest one moved under the slightest pressure to reveal a wardrobe stacked with more nightwear, including several robes. That designer theory was gaining credibility quickly. It was easy to spot her robe amongst this collection; it was the only green one, and it coordinated with her pyjamas exactly. Matching satin mules could have been made for her. She twirled, silently admiring her new appearance, and suddenly she was imbued with a desire to be different. She removed the band restraining her hair.

A familiar blue canvas holdall sat on a towel inside the bedroom. It was very wet. A small stab of something like pain robbed her of her smile and replaced it with a frown. "Oh good," she told herself briskly, trying hard not to wish its contents were as wet. They were bone dry. Sense told her she ought to change right now, and caution told her she must, but sheer feminine vanity of the sort she would have denied possessing a few hours ago pointed out that she might never see clothes such as these again, let alone get a chance of wearing them. Besides, she was late enough already. The mental struggle lasted all of three seconds: feminine vanity won. She replaced her holdall on the towel so as not to mark the carpet, and patted it kindly for compensation. Right on cue, the lightning flashed, and the lighting failed, plunging the entire room into darkness. A strangled scream escaped her lips, and it took a minute for her to recover. Her heart was still pounding wildly as her head pointed out this would be retribution for her choice. Controlling such thoughts was difficult in the dark, so she groped her way to the bedroom door to admit light from the landing, but that was out as well. What was happening here? Being a mother and a teacher only allowed her a minor panic before she rallied her wits. There had to be a proper reason for this, not a silly, over-reactionary one. The storm must have put the lights out. She wasn't sure if that was possible, but it sounded less esoteric than the alternatives, so she grasped at it thankfully. All of the recent flashes of lightning and rolls of thunder had shown the storm was moving closer, and right now it sounded as if they were on top of the house, so she half expected to be hit by something any second. There was absolutely no comparison between American thunder and lightning and the English version. Maybe they were all going to die in this storm! Lack of sleep and unfamiliar surroundings might be making her more melodramatic than usual, but her trembling was definitely for real. Hadn't Catherine Morland just got ready for bed when the lights went out at Northanger Abbey during a storm? Had she panicked? No, she had just got into bed. Sarah couldn't for the life of her recall what happened next, or why it had happened, so there was no way she was about to try her solution right now! "Stop this at once," she ordered. "It is just the storm! But better to know what the rest of this house is up to and better to be downstairs," she concluded cheerfully, forcibly dismissing all thoughts of deliberate sabotage and murderous intent as she placated herself with, "And I can't see to change now." The perfect justification for her choice.

She went back into the room to find her spectacles, thinking they might help her better negotiate her way downstairs. The fact she only wore them for reading and looking suitably authoritative in class did not matter right now. Edging her way along the corridor wall as carefully as any blind man would was necessary to avoid falling, but it also meant no one could get behind her either. She eventually reached the hall.

"Hi there."

Her hand went to her mouth automatically. This scream escaped without restraint.

"So you didn't drown!" the renegade said, uncovering his ears as she recovered her composure.

"No, but I just nearly died of a heart attack," she pointed out faintly, her heart still testifying to that fact.

"I thought perhaps you already had. Could have sworn I heard a scream when the lights went out. I came up half expecting to find a body."

She didn't reply, partly because she didn't know how much to admit to, but mostly because she was irritated by his manner. She tried to look as though she had nothing at all to do with any scream he might have heard, so she walked smartly across the hall towards the door he indicated. There was a soft light coming from inside.

"Candles," he pointed out, answering her unasked question. "I figure you have worked out the electricity is down. Phone's down, too, but don't panic. We have emergency power, the men will have the lights working in no time, and the phone company will have us back on as soon as the storm's over. But for now, it looks as though your luck is in – you're stranded for real."

She overlooked the bit about luck; she even dismissed the "for real" bit because she was too busy regretting that she had not used the phone before she had taken her bath. But however hard she tried, she could not overlook this word "stranded," or the sudden desperate waves of anxiety which flooded her mind and body as it finally dawned on her that she was totally alone with these weird people, and they were all of them cut off from the rest of the world.

While she was evaluating this catastrophe, the Indian designer had been on critic duty, making a note of what she was wearing. Eventually she noticed he was now dressed all in black, Dracula fashion, so the simple act of him walking past her took all the confidence she could muster. Dracula smiled, exposing perfect white teeth. Whoever she was, she had amazed him twice already, but now at least she resembled a human being again, so it might be interesting finding out more about her. Sarah was almost thinking something similar. The only things she knew with any certainty so far were: Molly was not an Indian squaw, this was not Molly's house, it was Dracula's fort, and she was Dracula's guest. What on earth am I doing in this madhouse with these mad people, was a recurring, if pretty irrelevant, question because she still didn't have an answer for it. Elinor would not believe any of this. Come to think of it, she would! Hadn't Elinor been prophesying something like this the day she broke her leg? Sarah sighed. Better not tell Elinor about any of it. It would only give her grounds for saying, "I told you so," and the only thing worse than getting in a mess was someone keen on rubbing it in.

However much unlike Elinor she reckoned she was, Sarah had not missed that Dracula looked different in his black shirt and jeans than Len would have done in similar attire. Len would have simply looked dressed, like all the other men she knew, but this man was different than all of them. She was trying to decide what she meant by that without reference to scalps or fangs when she realised it was an Elinor-type observation, so she thrust it away quickly and turned her attention to the room instead; house surveys were safer.

This room was predictably large and beautifully furnished; "simply stunning" could get quite boring, and even Ali's "awesome" and "ace" appeared to have met their match. It was light and warm and inviting despite the lateness of the hour and the drop in temperature caused by the storm, so it was more than welcome and almost felt normal. The stone fireplace in here was filled with dancing flames and its warmth and light was framed by banks of huge candles in man size iron candlesticks on either side of its hearth. Strange – she didn't think Dracula could stand the light. Ha- ha! Regular lightning flashes reminded her that the candles were there due to necessity, and that the lamps that normally lit the room did not stand idle by choice. Until this very moment she had never ever considered electricity to be a blessing; it was too much tied up with the horrendous winter bills that she always struggled to pay. Right now she looked at the lamps and wished them lit. Maybe if she remembered this next time she got a large bill, she would not moan so much. Others would have noticed that this was an incredibly romantic setting, but ten years of worrying about big bills was too stiff a competition for romance.

Rick crossed the room to the farthest window and started closing the shutters, battening down his castle against the storm. There were four large French windows along the length of the room, so his task took him a while. Sarah watched in silence. The shutters might be shutting out the storm, but they were also providing an impossible barrier to escape.

"Can I ask you something?"

"Sure, ask away."

"Are we in California?"

Rick turned to look at his strange guest, unable to hide his amusement. "Where do you think you are? Transylvania?" he jested.

"No, of course not," she protested a little too hastily, unsure how he could know what she had been thinking. "I mean, are we still in California, because for all I know we could be in Mexico, and it's good to know where you are." She realised too late it was almost as bad as admitting to Transylvania, and certainly as bad as, if not worse than, the garage blunder.

"Well, it is California. I am sorry about the storm, but I have no control over the weather, just like I have no control over the border. That's miles away."

She nodded and started to fiddle with the cord trim along the back of the sofa she was stood behind. It afforded a substantial barricade; and as she had every intention of staying on this spot, fiddling provided some focus for her nerves and a release for her anxiety.

Rick completed his task and then walked back into the middle of the room and pointed to the sofa she was defending. "Aren't you going to sit on it?" he asked as he flopped down on the one opposite. "People usually do." She nodded reluctantly and surrendered her barricade. "So what makes you think you might be in Mexico?" he asked.

There was no way she was going to admit again that she was so utterly lost that she didn`t know where she was. Instead she replied, "This house is Spanish, isn't it? And the Spaniards owned Mexico?" This was that piece of useful information coming in handy for a second time. She thought it sounded reasonably intelligent.

"They owned California, too," he pointed out with some equanimity. "But yeah, the house has Spanish roots, though it's not as old as it looks. It's not real adobe, if that's what you mean." It wasn't, but she tried to look as though it might have been. "You need to go to San Diego for that. There are some adobe mansions there from the early eighteen hundreds."

"This is very beautiful, anyway," she offered hopefully, much as if his explanation was meaningful. She could only think of a line in a song that mentioned adobe, but she had no other inkling of what it might be.

"I'm glad you approve."

She blushed again. This man had the ability to make her feel like a gauche schoolgirl, but she was unable to respond to this last comment with any confidence, and so she didn't risk saying anything at all and sat staring at her feet instead.

"I was beginning to think you had drowned until I heard you scream," he said, changing the subject completely. She was not listening; daydreaming was no way to make oneself appear sensible. "I said, I was beginning to think that you had drowned."

"Oh, no. I was just enjoying your bath. I'm sorry if I took too long."

He was amused by that. Ladies that lay in wait for him for hours were usually more impatient to claim what they wanted, but novelty was always refreshing, and she would pass the time till Perry got back. "Well, all the time you have taken has improved you."

The shock this comment caused was obvious. Sarah could not recall what she might have said or done that would warrant him being so rude, but she had no doubt he had said it deliberately. She half wanted to retaliate in kind but stopped herself just in time. "No reason to stoop to his level," she muttered heroically. "Rise above it, breathe deeply! Count to ten!"

The offender missed this measured response because he had picked up the phone to ask where his food was, only to be reminded the phone was dead. He cursed, walked to the door, and yelled for Molly. When she didn't appear in five seconds, he yelled a second time. Obviously he had never had a mother who taught him not to shout unless the house was on fire!

When Molly did appear, he asked about news ahead of the food, making it clear he expected his guest to keep him company until there was some of both, so Sarah decided to take the bull by the horns and play assertive, or whatever it was that women were supposed to be these days. Be a bit braver, at least. She started well enough as Molly left. First thing she needed to know was his name; it would not do to keep referring to him as Dracula – or Indian dress designer for that matter. "I am sorry, I am forgetting my manners. I don't think I thanked you properly for rescuing me. I know it didn't seem like it at the time, but I am very grateful. How do you do? My name is Sarah Chadwick." It was a little speech delivered with perfect Sunday school propriety, just as she had been taught at the age of six, and she finished it by offering her hand, fully expecting him to shake it and introduce himself in return.

He merely looked at the hand and smiled indulgently. "Sarah, eh?" And that was it.

She waited a moment hoping he would remember it was now his turn and that she needed his name, but she waited in vain. No name was forthcoming. It eventually occurred to her that maybe he had already told her his name, and if he had, and she had missed it; and there was a good chance that could have happened in one of her daydreaming moments. He might not see the need to tell it me again, so I can either sit here wondering about it, or I can ask him. Either way, he will probably think me nuts! Nothing to lose, then. "I am sorry; I don't think I caught yours."

If she had been more observant right then she might have caught the look of total surprise which flashed across his face in response to this question. By the time she did look his way, his face betrayed nothing more than what she thought was amusement. Consternation replaced all her good intentions because of that. There was absolutely nothing funny about this situation, and he had no right to think that there was! "You are ...?" she prompted, raising the teacher eyebrow.

"I am ...? Sorry, I guess I didn't realise." He paused and then simply said, "You can call me Rick."

Just Rick? Not even Rick Dracula or Chief Rick, Apache Indian? Just Rick. Paranoia insisted he must have a reason for not introducing himself properly, so bloodsucking vampires got another look in as visions of hostages, murderers, rapists, and kidnappers returned as large as ever.

She even gave consideration to how many rich murderers there might be in this part of California. Common sense tried telling her this man had a lot to lose by getting involved in such a heinous crime, but its voice was outdone by the competition. Maybe all this wealth comes from crime? That was a disturbing thought. Even if she disallowed murder; things like drugs or vice were hardly friendly. Stop it! Enough, she threatened herself. You are getting hysterical again!

While these deliberations about the nature of his citizenship had been underway, Rick had been pouring drinks. When he handed her a full glass, it seemed a simple thing to him. It was not steaming or exuding strange smells, but it might as well have been the way she sniffed at it. "What is it?" she asked hesitantly, sniffing the honey-coloured liquid like she were a drugs hound searching out illicit substances.

"Brandy and hot water. It's good for shock," he promised. "Drink it. It will do you good."

She had absolutely no intention of following his advice. Brandy makes people drunk! And I don't want it to do me any good, she thought petulantly, even if his motive is helpful. I do not have to drink stuff I don't like! She applauded these brave thoughts. Her actions were less laudable: she hid it round the corner of the sofa.

Rick missed that manoeuvre because he was busy with pouring himself a drink. If he did notice her glass had disappeared, he didn't mention it as he settled down to enjoy his drink and his strange guest. In the middle of a period of mutual contemplation while they were both waiting for Molly to return with food, the lights snapped back on just as suddenly as they had gone off. "Looks like we have some light on the situation at last," he observed. "Now we can see what we are doing." He had ignored the fact that the lamps generated only about the same amount of light as the candles, in favour of his sarcasm.

Sarah answered civilly enough. "So we can." It was an exchange that achieved nothing and satisfied no one.

At length she tried to stimulate conversation by telling him about the breakdown. "And of all the places to break down, I have to pick the worst possible place at the worst possible time. You won't believe how relieved I was when I heard your car."

He didn't say anything just continued to give her the same lazy smile. She tried once more without any more success and then gave up. He said nothing to fill the gap, so there was silence. Natural conversation seemed beyond them and she was relieved when Molly reappeared with food. It was set up in silence, until Molly announced as she withdrew, "Mr Perry just sent Harv to tell me they have finished up at the station. They are on their way back, and he's coming to see you. Harv didn't say how long that would be. If you are waiting up, can I go?"

"Sure. Thanks for hanging around so long."

So he could do polite. Molly only sniffed and nodded to him. "Goodnight, then," she said before adding, "Goodnight, Miss," as an afterthought.

Sarah was not hungry, but she ate because it was a way of passing time that saved her from making conversation, and that gave her time to think of ways out of the disturbing new fears circulating in her head. How could Molly go anywhere in this storm, and why would she want to? Only one solution seemed reasonable: he was planning to harm her. Stupidity was no longer optional! She was saved from hysteria by one single, rational thought: How can he possibly harm me when Molly knows I am here, and this Perry character could arrive any minute? The word 'accomplices' was not a great thought to have at such a time. The only thing she was one hundred per cent certain of was that she wished with all her being that this particular member of the American population had been fat, fifty, balding, and married, preferably with a wife in attendance and a house full of children as well. That way he would have been more like those very nice, normal, pleasant, helpful American men that she had met at every campsite – the ones who had helped her to empty her tank and refill her water countless times. Every one of them had been a gentleman, and not one of them had had a mysterious agenda she could not understand. The fact that none of them had ever done it at three in the morning slipped past her. If Chief Rick Dracula had been more like one of them, it would have been easier to be friendly with him. She half suspected that all her attempts at civility were being misconstrued, but as nothing else was functioning properly, she took scant notice of this premonition. She could only hope that the wife and children were asleep and would show up in the morning.

One of the reasons she wanted Mrs Dracula to be real was that even from her limited experience, she knew enough to know that good-looking men inevitably thought all women fancied them, even if one only asked them the time of day, and good-looking, intelligent men were the worst of all. How do you know he is intelligent, she asked herself. That was a dumb question. Apart from the fact that rescuers probably did not come much better looking than this one except in novels and movies, he had a noticeably witty intelligence. He was probably everything most women could ever want in a rescuer, but that only meant he was most certainly all she did *not* want! Okay, she admitted candidly, so he is clever and quite handsome. So what? It`s not important. What is important is finding out more about him. What would Elinor tell me to do? This last thought was followed by rapid repentance. She had enough problems without thinking what Elinor's advice might be; it made her shudder.

"You still cold?" he asked.

"I'm sorry?" she said, emptying her mouth of ham by swallowing it too quickly and nearly choking. "Did you say something?"

"I asked if you were still cold. You are shivering."

She said not and then went back to chewing and thinking – except Elinor's advice kept popping into her head. Who said it was only men that made sexist statements? Elinor was finally over-ruled. One thing remained clear: she had to attempt the impossible and be friendly without being too friendly. Surely, somebody somewhere had written a book on how to deal with situations as ridiculous as this. If not, someone should because she needed a copy. "That was delicious. You should have eaten." Fortunately for her he, didn't ask what she had eaten, because she would not have known, but he said he wasn't hungry. Okay, so you're not hungry, but we have progress: you answered me civilly.

It was not destined to last. A moment later when she refused the cigarette he offered, he complained, "You don`t smoke, and you don't drink." He glanced right at the glass hidden by the sofa. "So what *do* you do?"

She knew she was missing something here, but she chose to ignore his question because she thought there was nothing more annoying than someone missing something clever a person has said, and judging by the smirk on his face, he clearly thought his last comment was a gem. She had no doubt that he would be unable to resist returning to it again. She would act dumb for now. "Do you live here alone?" This was her new brave, assertive attitude. It was called, be nosy, ask for what you want to know, and hang being polite. But even this was a compromise because she really wanted to ask if she could expect the appearance of a wife at breakfast, but she had chickened out at the last minute.

"Except for Molly and Chas."

Who the heck was Chas? Hope flattened, she tried to sound as normal as possible despite growing alarm at her predicament. How was she supposed to have known that Molly was not his wife? Only the constant, noisy battery of rain and wind on the windows, as well as the thunder crashing overhead, gave evidence in mitigation of her stupidity. Even thoughts of what might have happened if she hadn't accepted his assistance didn't help much. Drowning in a mudslide seemed a better alternative. She knew the snakes were real, so the mountain lions probably were as well, but all of them put together could not appease the irritating little voice that said, it would have been safer to have asked the dumb, stupid question than get stuck in this situation. The rain and the bears and the snakes had won over her common sense out there; the possibility that other things could still be winning over her common sense in here did not even occur to her. No, she was definitely better off inside out of that storm. Another course of mental callisthenics completed, she smiled nervously and said, "I am very grateful to you for offering me a place to stay tonight."

"So you have said already."

There it was again. This time she knew for certain there was something she was missing. His words amounted to an insult, though she was still in no position to identify why.

Well, I am grateful, she thought. So what! Perhaps it's a crime to admit to gratitude around here. Assertiveness had not been able to make her feel better but it was about to make her sound stupid as she said, "Molly didn't seem all that disturbed when we arrived. I am sure I would have been horrified at folks being dumped on me at that time in the morning. Well, I would have been bad tempered, at least." That appeared to be received with as much good humour as it had been delivered, and she hoped that the smile beginning to cross his face was the start of some success, so she rushed to pursue her supposed advantage. "Unless, of course, she is used to it?" His smile disappeared and his eyebrow arched in anticipation. "Are you one of those people who collects strays?" she queried, completely oblivious to the response this was generating. "My neighbour Jen collects stray cats. Every time she goes out, one follows her home. My mother and I collect awkward friends," she added limply, suddenly aware of how silly all this sounded.

His reply was not the caustic statement she was expecting – or at least the first part wasn't. "I try my best not to pick up strays," he said gently before adding, "but then, we don't get many stranded out here in the middle of nowhere."

Ouch! Silence again. She needed to sort out what it was she was missing, but she couldn't. So, if he wanted to sit there in judgement on her, she would just have to let him. She could not understand him. She might be his guest, but it was not up to her to mend his manners or save the day.

Rick checked his watch several times before he asked, "So, how do you reckon we should pass the time?" Instead of giving her time to answer, he added, "What game shall we play?"

She took the first half of his remark to be a comment about the severity of the storm, and she answered the second part as evenly as she could without being flippant. "I am too tired for games." They then managed a reasonable conversation for all of five minutes before he asked how long she had been in California, and that naturally led on to why she was in America in the first place.

"So have you done what you came to do?" he asked slyly.

No good pretending she knew why that was, so she answered absently, "Mm, most of it."

"What have you missed? Has the rest lived up to expectation?"

"I don't know on both counts. I have never been here before so I know very little other than New York is not the capital." Elinor's jest did not find an appreciative audience here, either, so she hurriedly continued. "But I have loved all of it. Elinor might not forgive me if I told you more," she pointed out confidentially

"Why is that?" he asked, completely forgetting that this was not what he had meant at all.

"Long story."

"Looks like we have plenty of time," he said with a yawn before refilling his glass and offering her another drink.

"Would you have any water without the brandy?" He handed her a glass of tonic water, and she sipped it after sniffing it. She nodded her approval. "Elinor is my best friend, and this trip was her idea. My not wanting to come was just a minor detail. She was quite certain this was an experience that I could not miss. She was absolutely right for once: I have loved every minute – well, perhaps with the exception of the last few hours. Oops, sorry, I didn't mean right now – I meant before, when I was broken down, before you came along." Embarrassment only added to her confusion and made the explanation worse than the original error.

"Of course. So where is this Elinor character now?"

She recited the story of the broken leg. "It happened the day before we were due to fly out. Leg and ankle actually"

"How convenient."

"Don't you mean inconvenient?"

"Do I? Oh sure. Interesting story, anyway," he remarked dryly. "I did wonder why you were all alone. Women don't usually go off around strange countries by themselves, unless.."

"Unless what?"

"Unless there is a good reason, like you say. So what do you and this Elinor character do back in England?" His tone, along with the memory of Elinor's comment about people's thoughts about two women friends, was enough to make her colour with embarrassment.

"We teach," she said firmly. That was evidently highly amusing, so to deep embarrassment she now added indignation. "Is that funny?" she asked, standing as carefully on her dignity as Molly had done on hers earlier. He denied it of course, but the sarcasm in his voice contradicted his words, and she was left nursing the impression that his humour was not meant kindly.

"Dare I ask what you teach?" he said.

"I teach English."

"And Elinor?"

"She teaches geography," she offered defensively. What she had wanted to say was, "Please talk naturally like other human beings – not like a one-man inquisition. "North America is Elinor's pet subject; she is an expert on it, and she wanted to write a travel book about it." She almost added, "Anything else?" but restrained herself in the nick of time.

"We can't write our own travel books?"

"I didn't say that."

"No, I know. So why not cancel when Elinor broke her leg? Unless you are writing the book instead of her?"

"No, of course not! I couldn't. Most everything I know about America, I have learned since I have been here." She thought better of repeating the New York pun or the line about Mexico and the Spaniards. Instead she explained humbly, "I am just a traveller in a strange country."

"Coming alone was kinda brave then, wasn't it? Or should that be kinda stupid?" he asked impertinently.

"I know that now," she admitted humbly, "but I didn't know it when I had to make the decision. It was one of those spur-of-the-moment things. If Elinor had broken her leg a week before, I might have had second thoughts. As it was, I had no time for second thoughts – I had to be on that plane. Besides, if I was really honest with you, I would admit that I couldn't afford to risk losing my money if we had cancelled. This holiday has cost a lot!" Her last words, although offered simply enough and without any trace of irony, would not have been said at all if she had felt more kindly disposed towards him. She realised only too well that what she had said had been said with the intention of making him feel uncomfortable in the midst of all his luxury. She never knew whether she had succeeded, but she did experience instant regret the moment the words left her mouth. Less than two hours in his house, and she had already been reminded of her shortcomings on several occasions. Now she had to add regret to that list, because the urge to try and inflict embarrassment upon this man was not acceptable, whoever he was. He had been good enough to shelter her, and all she was offering in return was spite. Penitence made her try extra hard to soften her next words. "Besides which, the girls were already at my mother's, so I had nothing to stay home for." It had never occurred to her that this revelation might be just that. But it was.

"You are married?" His remark was a combination statement and question that contained neither accusation nor presumption, just acceptance.

"Not exactly."

"You live with someone?" Same tone.

"No, of course not!" Definitely not the same tone.

"Well, how can you be 'not exactly' married? Either you are or you're not. Which is it?" He had finally dropped indifference in favour of impatience.

"I am divorced," she said quietly. It was still an effort to admit it. It was stupid and entirely without logic, but try as she might, there was no getting away from the fact that she hated admitting it.

"I see," he said casually, returning to indifference.

Such bland statements were usually guaranteed to make her see red, but tonight she was on the defensive and she was getting tired of this sparring, so it didn't seem to matter that much. It wasn't as if she even liked this man or cared what he thought, so his silly opinions and lack of sensitivity mattered even less. She doubted he could understand any of it, even if she took the trouble to explain, and because she was not about to do that, he would have stay ignorant. All his money and affluence would prevent him from understanding anything she might have to say about being divorced. All she would accomplish would be to expose her wounds for him to laugh at, and she had no intention of doing that. She had provided him with enough amusement for one night.

"The girls are staying at my mother's for the summer," she said, picking up on her previous topic. "She has been promising to have them stay for ages, so when I got the chance of coming here, they didn't take much persuading." She looked at him and half smiled. "Well they needed none, actually. My mother is their most favourite person on the entire planet, me included. But that's only because she indulges them and spoils them, and I am an old ogre by comparison. I guess all grandmothers are the same, aren't they?"

She accepted this might sound like she was digging for more information instead of the innocent comment she had meant it to be so while she was still deliberating whether attempts to explain herself would make matters better or worse he interrupted her to ask if she wanted another drink. She declined but watched him refill his glass for what seemed like the umpteenth time. You drink too much, she registered silently. It is not good for you. There had been a whiff of alcohol on his breath when they had first met, and he had downed at least three or four more since then. The fact that he still appeared sober and articulate was not admissible when she was prosecuting counsel, judge, and jury.

"How long did you say you had been here for?" he asked.

"This is my third week," she said quietly; adding mentally, and if you hadn't drank so much, you might have remembered that from the last time I told you.

"And are you enjoying it?"

"Mm, it's fantastic." And I have told you that before. "This country is so big that it seems impossible that it should all be one country. Then again, I suppose Americans think England can't be so small until they've seen it for themselves. Have you?"

He nodded. "I know what you mean."

Whether that remark referred to England, America, or both was not clear, so she ignored the ambivalence and recommitted to being rash and brave enough to say what she meant instead of continuing with this stupid two-level conversation where she said the polite bits to him and saved the truth for her head. "Do you ever answer a question clearly?" she asked, looking him squarely in the eye and daring him to answer her truthfully. It was a brave gesture that took him a little by surprise, but he stared right back.

"Not if I can help it," he admitted with a quirky grin. "I am trying to make it a lifetime habit never to answer any questions at all."

"Oh? Why is that?" It died on her lips as she saw the impact it had.

There was an awkward silence, and then finally a challenge. "Why should I?"

A deep breath helped her say, "Because it is difficult talking to you?" He didn't respond so she prompted more gently, "Now it's your turn to tell me you don't understand that, and that's how conversations work." She silently thanked Jane Austen for the inspiration.

"Because it's automatic." That was it. Nothing else, just more silence.

Because it doesn't make sense might be more truthful, she thought, though she didn't say that either. Instead she said, "So, three hundred miles a day might not look that much on paper." If there was no sense to be had from her previous line of inquiry, then she could talk about other things just as easily. "That might not be much to an American, but let me tell you, it's a great deal to an English person. We are only used to travelling a hundred miles to go on holiday!" If that was a joke, she had messed up the punch line, because he did not laugh. "So when I started covering that sort of distance nearly every day, it didn't take long to realise that it would have been better to have had two drivers," she concluded with a sigh.

"So how many miles have you done?" he asked lazily, already as bored with the subject as he was with her, because he glanced at his watch for the third or fourth time in less than a minute.

"About four thousand, I reckon, maybe a bit more. I haven't kept count." If he had been bored, this answer dispelled it. He sat up straight and asked if she were joking him. "No. Should I be?" she asked, a trifle more offended by his tone than by his look. "I started in New York." He laughed out loud at that, but the information causing him this degree of amusement was not meant to be funny. "So is it the first time it's ever been done?" she asked crossly.

"No, of course not," he admitted.

"So what's so funny about me doing it, then?" she demanded.

He shook his head. "You need to ask? Well, apart from there being a very real chance of you being mugged or raped or even murdered, how about all that driving!" The feat seemed beyond his powers of comprehension, and he alternated between hitting his head with his hand and shaking it in dismay. "You are one crazy woman!"

Sarah overlooked the crazy bit because she had heard nothing past the reference to rapists and murderers. That had been enough to cause a spontaneous blush to spread across her face, and though she momentarily considered telling him of her own concerns on the matter, she dismissed that idea on the grounds that he might not see the funny side of it when he knew who she had cast as the villain. Besides, he still might be one.

"What on earth made you do it?" he asked.

She repeated his question complete with the same derision before answering it in the same manner. "I have done it because we planned it that way. The van was in New York, and so it seemed sensible enough to start there. And now I am going to finish in Sacramento because my friend lives there, and Dave, her husband, is going to sell it for me."

"You own it!"

"Yes. Well, no, not exactly."

"What sort of an answer is that?"

"Elinor owns it. Oh, it's a long story."

"Obviously you specialise in them," he said with some degree of humour. "So that's why you didn't want to leave it?"

She nodded. "I couldn't, even if it meant sinking with it."

"You are unbelievable, do you know that? Totally unbelievable." She had no way of knowing he meant it literally, and there was no way she was going to guess it while he continued to play the game as he saw it. "So what made the two of you arrange this kamikaze driving course in the first place?"

"I told you – Elinor."

"...Wanted to write a book. So why not fly?"

"Because all you can see from a plane is a few clouds, and I don't much care for flying." Was she under any obligation to reveal all her weaknesses to anybody who cared to ask?

"And does this Elinor have a lot of these bright ideas? Do you always do what she wants you to do?" Before she could have a chance to answer, he added, "she sounds like a pain in the butt to me. No doubt she is one of these crazy 'women can do anything' people."

She was tempted to laugh at such a disturbingly accurate picture of Elinor, but she stifled it. Still, she was curious to know how he had drawn such an accurate picture from so little information. Only a sense of loyalty to her friend stopped her from asking. "So what is wrong with that?" she asked curiously.

"Don't tell me you are one as well. Gee, that's an incredible mix."

Her determination to stay calm and to resist all provocation failed at that. "Listen," she said coldly, "I am trying my best to be polite, but you are making it very difficult for me." She paused and wondered if she dared say what she wanted, and then she threw caution to the wind. "You are very rude as well as patronising. I daresay you might even have been called a chauvinist before now." This was greeted with a bellow of laughter.

"Don't tell me you won't say 'chauvinist pig' because you don't swear, either!"

"That's right," she said between clenched teeth. "But I could make an exception for you!"

When the chauvinist animal finally recovered from his laughter, he looked across at his adversary, who was sat as primly as any schoolmarm could – a proper cover for her offended dignity. It made him grin as he asked, "Tell me, are all English women so dotty?"

"Depends what you mean by dotty," she countered in a perfectly even tone of voice that belied the complexity of her thoughts.

"Well, there isn't much that's dottier than New York to Sacramento on your own in a camper. And by the way, just one small point: you were heading in the wrong direction for Sacramento."

She knew that and wasted no time telling him so. "I missed the turning a few miles back; that's why I wasn't sure if this was California or Mexico. I was trying to cut across country to pick up the highway which leads back to the interstate."

"That's a pretty obscure route."

"Well, I know that now, and I would never have found it by myself. An old man gave me the directions."

"You seem to make a habit of getting yourself in some pretty alarming situations, don't you?"

"I don't think that there is anything alarming about asking directions. I got lost – so what? I stopped to ask the way. I do speak the language, you know."

Rick shook his head in dismay. "I think you are missing the point here. You could have been in real trouble back there." He seriously doubted the story about the old man – in fact he didn't believe a single word she had said, but he did want her to understand how serious her predicament had been. If he had stayed over at Jon's, she could have had all sorts of problems out there in this storm, and no one else would have rescued her. She might even have been killed. That was a high price to pay for anything – even him! He hoped to shock her sufficiently to make her think of easier ways to waylay people in future. He didn't think for one minute he would dissuade her altogether; these women never stopped altogether because they collected stars like Apaches used to collect scalps. It was a lifetime obsession. She had been lucky tonight. She had got inside his house, and that was some luck, but it had only happened because of the storm. Any other time, he would have left her in exactly the same place he had found her.

Sarah was trying to recover her composure because she could see little sense in continuing to argue, and she realised what he was saying about her breakdown was true: coming here alone had exposed her to unnecessary danger. She had the grace to shudder when she thought about what might have happened if he hadn't come along when he did. Nevertheless, she had already said thank you twice. Maybe his ego just needed a re-run of the "thank you for saving me" routine.

He finally said, "Who cares – you carry on doing what you want. If you end up dead somewhere, it won't be my fault." That earned her biggest sigh of relief yet.

Chapter Fourteen

Chas Sampson was sprawled out across a chair in the kitchen of their small apartment when he heard his wife come in. He had arrived home less than ten minutes before her, but instead of changing from his wet working clothes, he had simply dropped his dripping waterproofs into the bath and sat down to light his pipe, hoping for a peaceful smoke before she showed up. The door banging like that meant it was not to be. He knew that slam and what would follow, just as he knew that their small hall where she would hang her coat would not delay her long before she came hurrying through into the kitchen. Then there would be an almighty row if she caught him smoking in her kitchen.

These days she was forever on at him to give up smoking, and he knew that tonight would be no exception, storm or no storm. She had been able to ban him from smoking in the big house because their employer had announced he intended giving up smoking, damn him. That was bad enough. She had then decided he could give up his pipe altogether if he had a bit of encouragement. Banning it in their apartment was her idea of a bit of encouragement. He sighed but banged out the pipe all the same. If her mood improved some, he might get a smoke before bed, though pigs probably had more chance of flying tonight. It had been a lousy day, what with the storm and all, and now to cap it off, no bedtime smoke. Some days were just made for suffering.

Chas was a pragmatist, the sort of guy who normally chose to avoid head-on confrontations with his wife over religion, politics, and her philosophies; and because he was creative, he more often than not managed his nightly smoke without her knowing, but there were times when even creativity was stretched to its limits. On these occasions he would sneak outside on the pretext of checking something or other before bed. He wouldn't do that tonight, not even for a smoke.

This apartment was part of the big house even though Molly treated it as separate. It was why she insisted on wearing a coat for work, and why she always walked round the outside of the house to get there and back. Maintaining her independence, she called it. Chas used a different name, but it was something he had stopped trying to figure out a long time ago:

that was what Molly thought, so that was what Molly did, and it was easier all round to just accept it. He reckoned anyone with any sense would have used the internal door on a night like tonight, but he knew without checking that she would have braved the storm to walk round as usual. Old Nick himself wouldn't have stopped her maintaining that independence! It was a fact like Monday following Sunday, and a great big storm wouldn't have changed it.

Chas gathered the pages of his newspaper together and removed his feet from the other chair at the table, making sure to remove the tell-tale dirt marks from the seat with his shirt sleeve at the same time. Forget the smoke, he told himself. From the way she had slammed that door, he could tell she was none too pleased, and when she was none too pleased, life was easier for all if folks were obliging enough to humour her for the short while it took for one of her famous miffs to wear itself out. When provoked in such a mood, she was more likely to sting than an angry bee. Heck no, why should he forget his smoke? No smoking was *her* rule, not his. Folks could get the better of bees!

Molly buzzed into the kitchen, muttering under her breath about the state the world was coming to while trying to dry her hair. She was into tidying up mode before she could discard the towel she was using on her hair, so it partially blocked her vision. She stopped dead in her tracks when she caught sight of Chas filling the kettle. "What are you doing here? I didn't expect you back yet," she declared suspiciously.

"Mr Perry said to come home; we've done all we can. Everything's mostly inside anyhow. He's goin' up to the house to see Mr Rick, and then he's staying over with the horses. I said I'd join him, but he said to come home – no sense two of us losing sleep. He'll call me if he needs me."

"You are wet," she said, sniffing dismissively as she swept his newspaper off the table and took the kettle from him.

"No, I'm not," he said, retiring to his seat and retrieving his paper. "But the bathroom is." A disclosure he qualified with his next words, "'Cos it's raining wet water, if you ain't noticed." There was no reply. He couldn't tell whether that was because she hadn't heard, or because she had chosen to ignore him. It didn't make much difference either way, so he contented himself with a more amiable inquiry. "You all finished, too?"

Molly nodded and went on complaining mostly to herself, but occasionally she drew him into her argument. "I have never known a day like it. I'm done in, but I daresay you could use some supper seeing as how you missed dinner. Ham and beans okay?" she asked, not expecting any argument. Then she continued to mutter to herself while she organised it. Most of the mutterings were about the events of the night, and that and the non-stop activity conveyed a fair imitation of an angry bee. When the buzzing stopped, she asked pointedly, "So what happened with the electrics?"

Chas turned in his chair to look at the familiar back bent over their worktop. So that was the reason for her bad temper. "Dunno, generator needed some attention, I reckon," he said.

"Gee, I didn't realise that!" his wife exclaimed as she banged the bread board down on the table in front of him. "I nearly cut my thumb off when the lights went out!" She held up a bandaged finger to prove her point.

Chas tutted to show sympathy, but shook his head. "Storm ain't my fault," he protested.

"Maybe not, but the generator is. Will it hold out till morning?"

"Might do, might not do."

"What sort of an answer is that?" she demanded impatiently.

"Same sorts I gave Mr Perry."

Molly stopped doing what she was doing and glared at him. "Hmph! Neglect!" Then she slammed the coffee pot down onto the table with such force that it caused the hot brown liquid to spill out of the spout. Chas avoided being scalded because he moved in time. He understood only too well that beekeeper`s lives sometimes depended on them having the sort of instinct about their bees that they tell immediately when something is wrong. That didn't necessarily mean they had to stay clear – just be properly covered up.

"I see we have some new company," he observed calmly as he poured himself a mug of the steaming liquid before sitting back with the air of a man interested in passing the time of day. To the uninitiated, what he had said must have seemed like the height of lunacy – a bit like pinching honey from an angry queen, because Molly started to buzz around in all directions almost before he had finished saying it. The fridge door was slammed shut twice in less than ten seconds, then she banged the bread board down again with even greater ferocity before knocking over a chair as she pushed past it. By raising the subject of the house guest, Chas was hoping for three things: one, she would release all the feelings she might have on the subject, because she would definitely have some, and that would save her endless brooding and taking her bad temper out on him for days. Two, by releasing this pressure, he hoped to divert her attention so that he could smoke his pipe in peace. Three, and most important of all, he might save closer scrutiny into exactly who had been at fault over the generator. He had just worked a long, hard day too; and whatever Molly thought, she did not hold exclusive rights to that.

"Tell me when we *don't* have company," she snorted, completely missing the fact he had lit the banned pipe. "I sure do not know what this world is coming to! Well, this part of it, anyway."

Chas nodded his agreement, wisely judging that now that he had lit this particular little fire, the best thing to do was let it burn; perhaps he'd fan it a little now and then; but otherwise he'd be as agreeable as he could, and say as little as possible to attract her attention. That way he might avoid becoming a target for any of her more stinging comments, and maybe he could enjoy a whole smoke in peace while Molly, bless her soul, talked out the fire in her belly, thus harmlessly dissipating her wrath. Come to think of it, there was something about bees and smoke screens, if he could only remember what …

Molly Sampson had been raised by strict parents in a devoutly Christian home, and she still practised that faith just as carefully as when she had been small. It was the measure for her existence, so she sometimes had a good deal of trouble justifying her job in the light of her beliefs. The only reason she agreed to stay on in the job was that she hoped and prayed that one day her employer would see the error of his ways and mend them. Apart from that, she was genuinely fond of him, and even she had to admit that but for that one big glaring fault, he was a generous and mostly considerate employer -very nearly a gentleman.

Chas did not share Molly's religious beliefs or her views on their employer, but he did understand the complexity of her feelings about both, because he had many years' stored experience of the verbal manifestations of her most complicated theories concerning them. He knew very well that the original battle facing his wife when Rick Masters had bought Box Meadows five years ago could still flare up at any time; all it needed was fuel, and as there was always plenty of that, life was never peaceful for long. For the first year or so after Masters had bought the place, she had been set on them leaving almost every other day. It usually wasn't quite that bad these days, but Chas had been mightily relieved all the same when she had alighted on a partial resolution for her big problem. She had decided that her employer's women friends were to blame for his immoral lifestyle and that he was merely a pawn. It was not known whether the man concerned would have been pleased or flattered with this theory, but it served Molly's purpose well enough because it made him an object to be pitied and helped, instead of damned and abandoned. Chas generally went along with it because it meant he got some peace, even if it never lasted long.

"I mean," she said, fetching his favourite sauce to the table, "who can blame him when all these women keep flinging themselves at him?" It was much the same tone as Sarah would have used for rapists and murderers. "Him being a movie star, I suppose it's bound to happen."

"Money helps as well," Chas added, not being able to resist stoking the fire he had laid so carefully.

Molly turned to peer at him from her place at the sink. "What do you mean by that?"

"Just agreeing with what you said about women flinging themselves at Mr Rick, and pointin' out that him being so stinkin' rich must help. What do you reckon he's worth? Five million? Fifteen? Fifty? Gee, I bet it's fifty at least. That's a helluva lot of attraction." Molly glared at him, trying to establish if he was serious, but he ignored her scrutiny. "Being rich attracts women" he promised, nodding his head.

"The wrong sort of women!" Molly explained with a sniff, turning her attention back to her rapidly filling sink before it overflowed.

"Real disadvantage, that," Chas said sympathetically. She thought he meant the sink, so she nodded. But that wasn't what he meant, as his next words proved. "The wrong sort of women are always so darned pretty," he said ruefully before adding quickly, "Mind you he don't always look that rich, so maybe you're right: maybe it's the movie star they're after. And I suppose once you've passed your first million bucks, it don't make that much difference how many you're worth."

Molly shook her head. "Like I was saying before you interrupted, when these women fling themselves at him, like this one has, who can blame him for taking what's on offer?"

Chas could have said, "You can," but it was too great a price to pay for one moment of truth. He could recall having once suggested that the solution to this problem might be to recruit only monks for movie stars, but Molly had failed to see any humour in that then, and there was even less reason why she would see any now, so he let the opportunity pass. Last time she had merely reproved him for not listening, as well as being irreverent. Given the mood she was in tonight, anything could happen!

"This one's English or something," she explained, wrestling with the can of beans. "Speaks real fancy, anyhow." There was a short silence until the beans had completed the transfer from can to pan, and then she continued, "Though she ain't the usual sort." While the beans warmed, she attempted to qualify her last statement. "Though there's so many of them, I'm sure I don't know what 'usual' is anymore!" This gave her licence to grumble on in a similar vein for the rest of the time it took to serve up supper.

Chas mostly ignored her, throwing in the occasional "Mm" or "Sure thing" to make her think he was paying attention. He was really only concerned with smoking his pipe in peace.

Finally as she sat down to eat, she meant to close the subject by admitting, "At least there's a grain of decency in her," as she remembered Sarah's comments about the pyjamas, and though her sense of justice demanded she acknowledge that, her patience was clearly tried by the fact that she then had to explain the entire bedroom saga to Chas so that he could understand what she was going on about.

"An' what does all that signify?" he asked, showing a spark of what might be deemed as interest. Molly sniffed and shrugged her shoulders. It was unthinkable that she would admit she didn't know; the sniff and the shrug were the nearest he would ever get to such an admission, and he knew that. "So what did you say to her?" he persisted.

"What could I say? It was hardly my place to be saying decent folks don't act like this, now was it? Talk sense. Decent folks – well, decent women – don't spend the night with Rick Masters, do they?" She sighed heavily. "Though I didn't tell her that, either, much as I might have wanted to. Maybe one day I will," she warned ominously.

Chas nodded indulgently but didn't take up this challenge either. "So what about this grain of decency?" he asked, patting her hand.

"Maybe I am mistaken," she confessed snappily "It's been a long day, and I'm tired. Maybe I'm going soft in the head and making excuses for her. She's probably just like all the rest of them, out for what she can get and not minding what she has to do to get it. And if she's not, what is she doing here, eh? You tell me that."

Chas shook his head; he didn't know the answer to her question any more than she did, but it was certainly novel to hear his wife admitting even a little uncertainty. Her opinions were always black or white – grey did not exist.

As usual she answered her own question, though this time with another. "There is only one reason why he brings these actresses and what have you home with him, ain't there?" That was thought provoking, and though Chas scratched his head to show he was obeying orders and thinking about it, Molly hit his arm with her fork the instant she could tell those thoughts were not without attraction. "Rick's a fool sometimes," she hissed.

"Mr. Rick, you mean," he corrected. "He is our employer, not just some nodding acquaintance." Molly looked at him but said nothing, sensing there was to be no argument about this. That was unfortunate for Chas because while her tongue was silent, her brain registered the fact that he was smoking in her kitchen, and he was supposed to have given it up. Fortunately for him, he had been equally observant and had banged his pipe out before she could chastise him. This action on its own might not have been enough to save him from the sting in her tongue, so he proceeded to pour more oil on his fire so that the flare-up would divert any further repercussions. "Mind you," he said reflectively, "it can't be all fun and games being rich and famous. It must have some drawbacks. Most things do."

As expected, his wife dismissed this idea immediately. "For a grown man, Chas Sampson, you talk some real garbage!" This time she put down the fork that she had been waving in her hand for several minutes – the one that had not yet got as far as her mouth – and shook her head and while wagging her finger exclaimed, "I'll tell you this much! My legs and feet are killing me! Now that's what I call a drawback: being on your feet all day from six o'clock every morning. I can't say as how I ever saw him get home at the end of a day with swollen ankles and legs ready to collapse. You tell me when you last saw him worn out with work."

"Right now" would not have gone down well at all, so Chas edited his answer carefully. "Maybe not like you, but being a movie star has to have some disadvantages, 'cause I ain't ever heard of a job that's not got any."

"Such as?" she demanded irritably as the first mouthful of beans finally connected with her mouth.

"Well, for instance, all the money he has to earn."

"You're a fool," she exploded, almost choking as she sprayed beans across the kitchen. "And an old fool at that!" she added waspishly, clearing her mouth as she collected the scattered vegetables.

"Well, how about all that weight he had to lose for that film last year? He looked ill then."

"I *am* ill, all the time," she pointed out with feeling.

"And what about the other year when that thing fell on him, and he fractured his shoulder? Or when that snake bit him? I reckon those are disadvantages. Besides, I've heard him moan that they can sit around for hours on location just waiting for the weather to change. It must get mighty boring. You couldn't stand it, anyhow."

"Maybe not," she admitted grudgingly.

"Well, that's what I'm getting at, woman: them's hardships."

"My feet still think they're hard done to," she pointed out sulkily.

Chas realised that he was not going to get the last word, so he let the subject drop and got on with his supper. After all, supper was only hot for a short time, while the subject of their employer had been hot conversation for the last five years, and he had little doubt that it would remain so for the next five years as well. He had managed most of his smoke in peace, so he could afford to let Molly have the last word for now - food was more important.

The Sampson's problems with Rick Masters had started well before he signed the sale documents. They had been part of the estate for over thirty years by then, and as they had felt as much at home there as either of its previous owners, a newcomer third owner, was never going to find acceptance easily. Masters might own it now, but they knew every inch of the place better than him; they were the fixtures, and he was merely an inconvenience: they were here three hundred and sixty five days a year, whereas he was hardly here at all. He had been responsible for moving them from their apartment over the stables into this new self-contained apartment in the west wing of the big house but he had done that for his benefit rather than theirs. Remote places were more secure with on-site custodians. But it had suited them, too. If there had been a catch to their improved living conditions, it was two years of living with builders and their mess, but that had passed, and they were now as settled in the big house as its owner.

Chas had been raised most of his life right here on the estate, and though he had left it as a young man in the mid-forties, he had returned as a young married man in the fifties and never left again. In the few short years between leaving and returning, he had learned that the rest of the world had little to offer that could compare with here. When he left, he had been only months off seventeen and all fired up, looking forward to the excitement of being called up to this war everyone was always talking about – and then they had called it off! At the time Los Angeles had seemed the next best exciting thing a young man could do when there was no longer a war to look forward to, and his body was still itching to find some of that "young man's action" that was so severely limited in these parts.

Los Angeles had been exciting, all right: he had met Molly. They had been married for a couple of years by the time they returned to the estate to nurse his ill father. It was supposed to have been a temporary thing but it had lasted thirty-five years to date. Chas's father had helped them get their first positions up at the big house, Molly starting as an assistant to the cook, and Chas as the second chauffeur. By the time the old man had died, they were settled. There had been a lot of changes over the years since, not least of which was their increasing importance in a diminishing household. That post-war household had dwindled from seventeen staff to just them and a part-time gardener by the time Rick Masters took over. Things had got a bit better since then, but they both knew the place would never have as many staff as it had in the past. It was a different world, and their boss seemed to like it that way.

The first time the estate had changed hands way back in 1965, they had been devastated. Box Meadows had been in that family for only thirty odd years, and though it had passed from father to son, before that it had belonged to the same old Spanish family for nearly a hundred years. The Da Santis were aristocratic émigrés and they had built the original house in the eighteen hundreds. Rick had omitted to tell Sarah that some of Box was almost as old as the mansions in San Diego, but it was part of the reason why Molly and Chas had been truly shocked by its sale: they believed, as did countless others, that old estates like Box Meadows were not built up to be sold like common houses; they were built up with pride and they were meant to be passed on with respect from father to son - thus preserving more than one set of self-interests. People had no right to be selling history and Box was the history of these parts. They had survived that sale, but fifteen years down the line, the unthinkable happened a second time. Not only did an estate like Box Meadows go up for sale in this changing world, but it went up for sale twice in less than a generation.

This second time had been far more serious than the first because of the insatiable thirst for land in southern California. Land had always been valuable of course, but now it was more valuable than ever because it was wanted for development. Real estate, they called it! That meant no fruit, just more people. More people meant more homes, and huge swathes of good citrus fruit-producing land had already been swallowed up like that, so the sale of a rundown estate like Box could be expected to attract a lot of attention. This time there had been a lot more people worried than just Molly and Chas.

Until that point no one had ever tried to put a figure on the amount of money it might take to put a place like Box back on its feet. Now they had to and it was staggering! All the interested local parties were soon put off by the amount of dollars needed, and after that the whispers about developers grew almost as fast as the size of the bank balance needed to float the place. Neglect by rich, indifferent owners had left them and many others vulnerable, and that had put their homes and their livelihoods at risk a second time. Molly had never forgotten that, or forgiven it. She had never been able to tolerate any form of neglect ever since without remembering what had almost happened to them as a result of wilful neglect. That had been the reason Chas had diverted the conversation from the subject of the generator. He knew there would be no mercy.

The period of time when they had really thought Box would be sold for its development potential was when Molly had first started commenting upon her lack of understanding of this different world. How any sane person could want to do that to here, of all places? Anyone in their right mind could see that it was a crime. Box was good growing land and always had been. The Da Santis had been one of the first growers with which Eliza Tibbets had shared those first cuttings. Why should that change now? The phrase Molly had started using then to express her confusion had stuck, and she had never stopped using it since: "I just don't know what this world is coming to," had become synonymous with Molly and anything she didn't understand, or approve of.

Eighteen months of widespread worry and anxiety had understandably turned to general euphoria when a buyer had been found who was not a developer. This unknown deliverer was going to save them all and so was the subject of much general rejoicing, but in Molly's case her rejoicing was short lived when she discovered that their deliverer was none other than a movie star! It was ironic really: the expanding film industry had swallowed up thousands of acres of fruit-growing land over the last thirty years for its ever growing needs, but now it was providing Box with a saviour. Molly did not see it quite like that. She was unable to decide whether a movie star was better or worse than a developer. It wasn't that she had anything personal against this Rick Masters character; she didn't know much about him. She simply knew of his sort, and movie stars were all the same. In defence of this attitude, she had the evidence of her sister's neighbour's cousin's lad, who had worked for a pool-cleaning company in Beverley Hills. He visited the homes of some of these movie stars, so he knew all about them. What he said about the goings-on up there was enough to make your hair fall out.

Chas had been unable to refute Molly's allegations because he didn't know much about movie stars either, so he had finally persuaded her to give this new arrangement a try for that very reason. Everything they knew was based on gossip and speculation and therefore they could be leaving their home for no good reason at all, because the only evidence they had was hearsay. Even if the stories about Beverley Hills were true, Beverley Hills was a long way from Box, and if Rick Masters was in as much demand as folks said he was, he probably wouldn't live out here anyway. Box was as far away from Hollywood in lifestyle as it was in miles. Even if this sale went through, Masters would only be buying it as an investment. Movie stars did that – Chas knew that much. He reckoned Masters might only visit once or twice a year and then not stop for more than a day or two. He might not even bother them at all. Chas had been almost as sure of this as Molly was that Bacchanalia was about to arrive the minute the contract was signed.

When the fateful day arrived and no truckloads of half-naked women arrived by dinner time, Chas felt sufficiently justified to point out that the day had been no different than any other day during the last thirty years. "See?" he said confidently. "All pointless speculation." The fact that builders arrived within a week, and within three months a Mr Darren had assumed control, seemed to confirm his theories. Mr Darren had then moved them into the newly constructed apartment in the big house and that had been acceptable to both of them. They knew Mr Darren was not the real owner and his name was not as important as that name on the deeds, but the way he gave orders about everything was very reassuring and seemed to substantiate Chas's theory about them being museum curators. Better still, this Mr Darren lived in a separate house on the estate with one wife, three children, and a dog. Even Molly could find nothing wrong with a job as a museum curator, with a happily married man for a boss who lived in a separate house. It was all she could ever have wished for, and with a little careful coaching, Chas had been able to plant these ideas so naturally in her head that she had almost started to like the idea of being a museum curator … when the note had arrived to say that their real boss would be home the following week. The devil had been on location. Four months' work had gone down the pan in the two minutes it took for Molly to read that note! All the horror stories were swiftly resurrected, and nothing Chas could say made one iota of difference. Sodom and Gomorrah loomed as large as ever.

No one would ever have guessed from the amount of friction this one little note caused that this would be their very first contact with this loathsome being, but the sale contract and their continuing conditions of employment had all been dealt with by his personal assistant and lawyers, and everything since by the very bossy Mr Darren. Molly's misgivings multiplied almost by the hour; and as a result Chas's common sense was impotent by comparison; his only real defence being, "Thirty years is a lot to give up for what a sister's neighbour's cousin's lad says about goings on hundreds of miles away!"

It was clear to everyone from Rick Masters' very first day at Box that he intended living there as often as work permitted. Box was no investment property – and Molly had crossed herself just thinking about all the things that would inevitably follow. The fact that she had been manoeuvred into promising Chas she would stay for three months whatever happened didn't help one bit. How could she explain to her friends why she was now the housekeeper in New Babylon? How could she stay treasurer of the town's Moral Reform League when she was living in the same house as … words failed her, and that did not happen very often! She had begun to amass evidence supporting the folly of her promise even before her new employer had properly unpacked.

At dinner that very first evening, Masters had informed her that his partner would be home in two weeks so he wanted the stables apartment redecorated before then, because they would be moving out there for the time being while the rest of the house was renovated. Even the impending invasion of more builders was overshadowed by this more pressing concern, and when Molly had inquired politely why his wife had not come with him now, he had merely laughed. His reply had been no laughing matter. After wiping his mouth on his napkin, completely unaware of the controversy he was about to unleash, Masters had simply said, "Molly, Danni is not my wife – and don't you go giving her any ideas on that score, either." The sister's neighbour's cousin's lad had been right! Chas had been wrong – and he had got her involved in all this! She would never be able to hold her head up in town again.

No one could claim that Rick Masters led the life of a saint, but even the Moral Reform League representative was relieved to find that it was not exactly the permanent round of orgies she had been expecting, and because no one had demanded she resign as the league's treasurer, she had eventually calmed down. It never occurred to her that everyone else might be so thankful that Box had been saved that they were prepared to overlook everything else, or that the league was mostly financed by the big players in town and so was sort of dependent upon the very people who would have had to finance a new packing station if the one at Box had closed.

After the initial shock of the live-in lover wore off, the rest of Rick Masters' lifestyle turned out to be something of an anti-climax: there were not many visitors, even fewer parties, and absolutely no orgies. He was away a lot, for months on end sometimes, and Danni, his girlfriend, always went with him if she wasn't working somewhere different. At such times the estate reverted back to how it always had been, and they became the happy museum curators again for a while. These were the best times: peace reigned because Molly got her own way. The worst times were always when their boss was home alone. He was generally bad tempered and impatient, and that made Molly the same. She had even found herself half wishing on more than one of these occasions that Danni would come home and stay home like a good wife should, before she had realised her error and repented of it. Apart from that, Rick and his girl were like any other couple that regularly saw each other once or twice a month, and it was only a matter of a year or so before most folks had lost all interest in their affairs.

Molly had made her next stand for independence when Rick had moved back into the big house after two years of difficult renovations. The Moral Reform League might not be asking for her resignation, but nothing would induce her to live in the same house as refugees from Sodom and Gomorrah. Chas had been equally opposed to them leaving, and so pretty spectacular rows had become a fairly regular feature of their lives too. After one of these rows, Molly had put on her coat and walked around the house before work to cool off, inadvertently hitting on her means of resolution whereby she could claim to live in a separate house: the internal door was never to be used again by anyone. It was her price for staying, and so it was a price Chas had to pay.

Meanwhile, Rick and his partner, oblivious to all the chaos they were causing, ate together, swam together, and argued a lot, just like everyone else. Admittedly the real difference between their rows and everyone else's was a pretty spectacular one. When he slammed doors on his way out after one of their blazing rows, he would drive off at speed to return with a pair of diamond earrings hidden in the flowers, or a designer gown as a make-up present. But even practiced gossips could only get mileage out of these things for so long. Molly remained tight-lipped about all of it. Her objections never fed local gossip and were kept personal. It had taken a long while to win her over, but eventually Sodom and Gomorrah, and then Babylon, had been confined back to Bible conversations, and life had more or less had returned to normal. That was, if one could ever describe life in a house filled with two temperamental actors, a guardian of public morality, a conciliation expert, not to mention a small resident army of builders and decorators, as normal.

After five years Masters had redeemed himself somewhat, retaining only one really serious fault in his housekeeper's opinion, but it was the one that always cooled her very real affection for him, because it was still the same fault. It was still female. He might find it difficult to live with one, but he could not live *without* one, either, and because there had never been any shortage of applicants in the last five years, there had never been any lasting peace. Molly had found out from experience that when one went, he was more bad tempered than ever. Then a new one would come along and things would calm down for a while. At such times, Sodom and Gomorrah got regular reviews. He might have had only two long-term lovers in the last five years, but there had been a couple of others that had lasted some months… and then there had been the one-night visitors. Molly despised these most. There was always a chance he might marry one of the others, so they were tolerated slightly better. Her comments on finding that some of them did not want to marry him, were not repeatable, but other things did have a stronger pull for some of them: a movie contract, or even one of his friends with a regular movie star lifestyle. Molly had soon learned that fame and fortune were not related to fidelity; the only place they lived together was in the dictionary where they both started with F – but then, so did fickle. It gave credence to her really useful theory.

The latest of Rick's lovers had moved out a few months before he had started work on his last movie. She had been back several times to pick up belongings, and things had even seemed quite amicable between them at first, just as they did between him and most of his other ex`s. That had not lasted this time, but Molly did not know why that was; there were some things even she didn't get to know. Most of his women did stay friends and some came back for dinner occasionally. It was when they stayed the night that Molly got almost as upset as she did at the one-nighters, and then what upset her had a knock-on effect on everyone she came into contact with -except of course the one man who was responsible. It was the most common reason for her favourite saying being aired nowadays; except nowadays when she asked, "What on earth is this world coming to?" she didn't really expect an answer.

Chas had been less dogmatic about everything right from the beginning, and tonight was no different. "So tell me what is the difference between him making love to one upstairs overnight, and him making love to one downstairs in an afternoon?" Molly huffed and puffed some but essentially she was cornered by this question; she didn't know what the difference was, but to admit it was unthinkable. Chas's little victory backfired on him within minutes.

"Well, seein' as how you know so much, you tell me why the same thing happens to him time after time?" It was a mystery to her, so she had no doubt that Chas would not know the answer. It wasn't that her boss was mean or violent or foul mouthed, though some of his girlfriends had been all three. Well, maybe he *was* a bit bad tempered and selfish at times, and he drank too much, but she thought he deserved more than what he got.

"Perhaps he don't want more," Chas suggested.

Molly could see no sense in that at all. "That's a dumb statement!" she said, not expecting there to be any answer to that either.

Chas was unwilling to chance upsetting his wife forever by suggesting that marriage might not be all that attractive to their employer because it did have some serious drawbacks, so he merely shrugged and contented himself with saying, "Well, maybe it's not what he's after – marriage, I mean." It was what the women were after that worried Molly. "Listen, honey," Chas said, wrapping his arms around his wife's comfortable waistline and chucking her affectionately under the chin. "S'long as they've got two yards of leg, look as sleek as racehorses, and are as obligin' as a hack, I don't reckon it matters much what they're after – he can afford it. Come on, let's me and you call it a day."

Chapter Fifteen

It was well past three in the morning, and there was still a light in the living room. That meant two things at least: the generator was still working, and someone was still up. It was debateable whether either of the people concerned would be able to recall anything of what was being said in the morning, but at least the long-awaited Mr Perry had arrived, and one of them was sober enough to figure out that his arrival must surely mean her ordeal was nearly over. Rick returned from this meeting as Sarah`s eyes were fluttering shut for the umpteenth time and her chin was tapping rhythmically on her chest, indicating sleep was only seconds away. Instead of excusing her as she had expected, he poured her another drink and started his interrogation all over again.

Sleep had been kept at bay until now with the aid of the adrenalin surge from the night's excitement, but now that had been resolved, its nemesis had crept on steadily and since she had eaten and was warm and dry again even insecurity was unable to hold it back any longer. It pounced from the recesses of her sleep-deprived mind like one of the wild animals of her imagination. She fought it valiantly, but an act of will was no longer sufficient, so her body was going through its ritual of shutting down even though her mind was decreeing stay alert as he handed her the drink. The gibberish that came out of her mouth was testimony to this struggle, and if most of it was incomprehensible, all of it was evidence that she had been up since four thirty the previous morning; and that was almost a full twenty four hours and a whole lifetime of experience ago. The Chadwick psyche was not used to such endurance tests.

Her host did not share her problem so he did not allow for hers. If anything he seemed livelier now than when they had first met. This rather supported her Dracula theory, but fortunately for him, she was too tired to contemplate taking the prescribed remedial action. For some bizarre, but unknown reason, he just kept repeating the same questions over and over again. It seemed odd behaviour even for an intoxicated Indian vampire. His interrogation had only one objective: a different set of answers than the ones he had already been given because they did not make any sense to him – that is, they didn't match his theory. This woman had spun him an incredible tale even for a would-be seducer. "So what age do you teach?" he demanded impatiently as he forced another drink upon her in an attempt to focus her mind.

By now his detainee was finding it difficult enough to focus her eyes and marshal her thoughts, let alone her speech, but she managed it well enough to ask almost assertively, "What is so interesting about teaching?" It produced not a glimmer of anything remotely like repentance, so she conceded and gave him the information he wanted.

"And what exactly do you teach? And don't just say English – you've already told me that."

"Grammar, literature, everything! It depends on the age of the class. Last year I read Shakespeare, George Eliot, Chaucer, and the Metaphysical poets with the A-level students, and Datership Wown and Sust Jo stories with the eleven-year-olds, and everything in between with the others. Like I said, everything – Austen, Bronte, Chaucer, Dickens, Weats, and Yordsworth. You name it, if it's English and any good, I will have taught it at some time or other." She thought that had to be the definitive answer, even if some of the details were a little odd.

"And do you enjoy teaching?"

"Yes, of course I do! Well, on the whole I do. I wouldn't do it otherwise, would I?" Confusion was getting the better of her.

"Wouldn't you? You are lucky, then."

"I am?" she queried, trying unsuccessfully to stifle a yawn. Or should that be, am I?

"Well, it's either that or you take an exceptionally naive view of life."

She managed to look interested at that, although it was an effort.

"I do? I mean, I am?" No, it was I do. Heck, did it matter? "Maybe it's time I went to bed," she said, yawning again, "while I am still making some sense. Please excuse me. It really is very late, and I must go before I fall down. The storm seems to be passing now, though to tell you the truth I could probably sleep through a hurricane right at this minute."

He acted as if he had never heard her request. "But then, perhaps you have never been in the unfortunate position of having to work at a job you hate. Otherwise you would realise that it's not always possible to do something just because you like doing it. Some people have to work at jobs they hate all their lives just to pay the rent." Even though she was exhausted, it was not difficult to understand that this remark had not been meant kindly, but she was too tired to bother asking why, and she thought he was probably too drunk to know why anyway, so she ignored it. He continued. "Teachers live in ivory towers playing meaningless memory games with well-behaved cardboard kids, while the rest live out lives that you know nothing of and care even less about! Kids are rotting all around you, but let's applaud the academic and disown the rest! That's a fair definition of teacher in a western education system, wouldn't you say?"

Tired or not, it was one insult too many. The hairs on her neck fairly bristled. That insult had been as effective as any red rag in front of a bull. Like all bulls, she responded true to type. "With respect, you are entitled to your opinion, of course – but it is only your opinion. You may have had a bad experience with a teacher, which may or may not excuse your assumptions, but please do not brand all of us with the same brush. There is room for some flexibility here," she promised. She was quite pleased with that. She had defended herself and her profession on a contentious issue without giving offence. Bolstered by that, she chanced more. "Strange as it may seem to you, *I* do not live in an ivory tower, and I do know about real lives and real choices because I do care." Of course, she had to go on to prove her point. For someone who had been tired to the point of exhaustion only two minutes earlier, she was suddenly acquitting herself with some degree of animation again.

The debate took some strange turns after that, and neither of them followed it fully, or somebody would have realised that neither of them was making much sense. Sarah brought it to a close as she stood and proclaimed, "Well whatever *you* say, I don't see any great tragedy in being a teacher! But then, I don't see there is any great tragedy in being a shop assistant or anything else, for that matter, if it makes you happy and it's what you want to do! I promise you there are people who love being shop assistants. That shocks you, doesn't it?" she needled, more disconcerted by his raised eyebrow than any verbal criticism. He was not equally needled by hers and so he said nothing. "And I applaud them," she emphasised, angling again for some response. "There are millions of jobs and millions of people, and we are not all the same, so some people's dream job would naturally bore me to tears or scare me witless, and that doesn't mean I am being snobbish, though I do admit it makes me sound almost as patronising as you! You see, I do not think being a shop assistant or a factory worker is any less important than being a teacher or a rocket scientist: I understand our society needs everyone, and so I try to educate everyone who comes my way the best I can, the factory workers and the socket rientists. Rocket workers, I mean. They science in factories, anyway, don't they?" she added querulously in case he had forgotten.

A moment passed, filled only with another superb series of yawns and further reflection on both sides. Neither of them remembered how they had got to this point, but it was a point too close to the teacher's heart for her to let it pass even if she was heading for that shut down. This meant more to her than her rational thinking being a bit slower than usual. She wasn't sure that she had explained herself well, or accurately, so she tried again. "I simply meant to say I am a great believer in the principle of being what you want to be," she said, purposefully before allowing another yawn to escape unhindered. Hang being polite – maybe it would help him to understand how truly exhausted she was. She spoiled the effect by adding after the sixth, or seventh yawn, "I have no doubt you disagree."

"Considering you have invented your own argument and fought both sides of it, I daresay we can say you have won it without fear of disagreement, but if you want to tell me *clearly* what you are going on about, *I might* tell you whether I agree with you."

She blushed furiously, and though she knew she should have resisted the lure, she couldn't. Her professional reputation seemed at stake here, but she stood up just to show him she was serious about leaving as well. She was also hoping standing up might improve the flow of blood to whatever it was that controlled brain-to-mouth communication. "It really is no big deal," she yawned. "Some people who moan about their lot sometimes do little to change it. I like my students because I believe in them – *all of them*, not just the academics. I believe in all of them!" The repetition and emphasis was in case he had missed it the first time round. "I believe everyone has the power to change anything they don't like." She thought for a moment and then added, "Nearly all of my students come from disadvantaged backgrounds, some worse than others. I try to show them that this is not a life sentence, because they can change their future if they really want to. Ability to change is not connected with academic ability, or even wealth and privilege." That last part had been added exclusively for his benefit. "I don't just teach useless facts and figures. Studying English gives people an opportunity to stand back and evaluate their lives against others, and then hopefully they are able to make better choices. All my pupils will end up being just who they want to be, just like you and me. That's what I have to help them to understand! And I need to do that now while they are young, because choices add up just like sums." If she hadn't been quite so tired, she might have been as impressed with this last line as he was, but she misread his look and missed her ace. "And I can tell from the look on your face that you disagree with that, too! But I really am too tired for any more discussions. It's half past three, and I have been up since half past four yesterday, or today – no, yesterday, so you will just have to forgive me." She ruined the effect of this by sitting down again. "Why do I keep thinking you are deliberately looking for an argument? Why do I think that? Forget it; I am too tired for the explanation." She rose unsteadily to her feet and glared at him, daring him to disagree. He said nothing, but now that irritation had had its say, honesty demanded she acknowledge the truth. "But I suppose if you want a totally honest answer to your question, then no, I don't enjoy teaching all the time. There are days when I don't enjoy it at all, because there are some things I have to do that I hate doing. But then, you show me anyone who is being honest that can say their job is any different. I reckon every job has its boring bits and its stressful, rather-not-do chores. Maybe happiness is being able to cope with the bad as well as the good." She ended her monologue with, "Now, I wish you good night."

The happiness bit had not been meant as a lure; it had tripped neatly off her tongue with hardly any thought at all. She was en route to the door, congratulating herself on her escape, when the question to end it was hurled at her back. "What's happiness got to do with it?" he asked.

She turned around slowly and looked at him sceptically through boggle eyes before she pulled enough functioning from somewhere to articulate slowly, "Happiness has got to do with everything, hasn't it?"

It was no longer exactly clear which of them was the drunk. The hollowness of his laugh should have been the giveaway – except it was drowned in his next drink. When he had downed it all, he said steadily, "I'd say happiness has got precious little to do with anything, but then, I am a realist."

"Sounds more like a pessimist to me," she replied without hesitation.

"Well, it would to a pie-in-the-sky optimist."

Perhaps it was the rudeness of his last comment, or the fact that she was drunk tired and he was just plain drunk, but what had started out as a conversation an hour or so ago had become this strange cross between a slanging match and a hangover from the Spanish Inquisition. She could no sooner leave it like this than she could resist putting Elinor straight. "I suppose I *am* an optimist. So what?"

"So not many people are, *in my opinion.*" He wasn't talking sense, she wasn't thinking sense, and both of them should have had more sense. Neither of them noticed.

"Not many people are what? Optimists, or happy?"

"Both."

"That's your opinion again. I disagree. I know lots of happy people, and all of them are optimists."

"You do? Who?"

"Well, there's me, and ..."

The list suddenly appeared exclusive. His look annoyed her as much as it had done before, but her mind remained a complete blank, and she could offer no further evidence, not a single sensible piece of evidence in defence of her stand. No names came to her rescue.

He waited, leaning forward in his seat with an air of exaggerated expectation, while she struggled to search her memory banks for the names of some of the numerous happy optimists of her acquaintance. "How many?" he finally queried annoyingly.

"Well, I am one," she repeated defiantly.

"I think we've already established that."

"Oh! And my mother is, and the girls are. Well, I hope they are."

"And?"

She shrugged. "I am too tired to think right now. Ask me tomorrow when I have had some sleep." She turned away again.

"Hang on a minute! You were the one that said there were loads."

She turned back wearily and sat down cautiously on the edge of the nearest sofa. Then she watched suspiciously as he walked across to join her. She rather wished he had stayed where he was. "Then I suppose that just proves the world is a fairly mixed up place right now," she conceded, moving steadily down its length, away from him.

He shook his head and slid down after her. "Maybe *you* are the one that's mixed up. Happiness has got nothing to do with anything! The ablest take what they want, and the rest have to make do with what's left. That's all there is to it. Which are you?"

It would not have been a simple question for her at the best of times, but right now it was unfathomable, so she bit her lip and frowned at him, trying to decipher what he meant and what she was.

"I mean," he said, taking hold of her hand, "do you take what you want, or do you spend your life daydreaming about something while others help themselves to it?" Whether or not he meant what she now thought he did, this was a bit too near to home for comfort.

"Don't be stupid," she spluttered, completely forgetting where she was or that he could have no way of knowing about the daydream department. Besides which, she was his guest, and people were supposed to be polite to guests. Guests were also supposed to be polite back. After acknowledging her part, she apologised, hoping he would follow her lead. Maybe he was too drunk to understand that, and so she tried to explain herself in a nicer way, but she only succeeded in making it worse. "What is wrong with being an optimist?" she finished limply. It sounded tired and defeated, like she was.

"On this particular occasion, nothing at all," he said, grabbing hold of her hand and patting it, before holding onto it. She looked up at him from under a thunderous brow. "Hey, I didn't mean to ruffle your feathers. Calm down."

She nodded, though she had no intention of doing any such thing. Stay alert, was her (almost) modus operandi, and so she tried to get up because this seemed an appropriate point to make that exit before either of them could say or do something to upset the other again. Besides that, she didn't like him touching her, and she reckoned he must let go of her if she got up. He didn't, but short of asking him to let go of her hand, there was very little she could do except hope he got the message from her black looks. She was berating herself for this sudden lack of courage when it dawned on her he was not going to release her unless she *did* ask. She shuddered. Elinor would not have got herself into such a mess! For the first time ever, she wished she really did possess some of Elinor's skills. Wishing did not make them available so she had to rehearse asking for her hand back.

He asked if she was still angry in such a conciliatory manner that she forgot about rehearsal and replied, "No, of course not. Why should I be angry?" She was about to add the bit about releasing her hand, when he interrupted.

"Well, relax then."

Relax? That was the last thing she was thinking of, but the instruction surprised her so much that she didn't notice him let go of her hand, though she did notice him lean across and remove her glasses as he tried to push her backwards on the sofa. His murmured cliché about rosy lenses achieved nothing at all. It was wasted on her. She coughed and blushed and struggled upright. "They are light sensitive, not rose-coloured," she pointed out primly while trying to retrieve them. "I only wore them to save me from falling down the stairs when the lights went out." This protest was ignored as he consigned the glasses to a table behind them and pushed her back more firmly this time. Then he leant across and kissed her before she could stop him.

She couldn't move, but her mind was doing some pretty advanced acrobatics. Panic, anger, and chaos tumbled for supremacy; none of them achieved it. Fear joined in and won hands down. *He was that rapist after all!* Her brain flashed some now blatantly obvious warning signals that she had previously ignored. How stupid could she be? Anger fired the desire to fight back – she was not going to allow this to happen to her! Quite how she would prevent it was not that clear, but she knew enough to know that rehearsals would not help. She had to do something, and she had to do that something right *now*! A monumental surge of strength came from somewhere, and she pushed him hard. There was only a split second before her hand made contact with his face as she scrambled up from beneath him. "You flatter yourself if you presume I wished that to happen! Now, if you don't mind ..." She attempted to rise, but he grabbed her wrist tight. For the millionth time that night, she panicked. It was an effort to speak because her throat had gone quite tight, and the lump in it made it even more difficult to get the words out; any second now she knew that the tears would come or that she would pass out. Tears were preferable. This was some awful nightmare. "I am sorry for slapping your face, but I really didn't want you to ... to do that, and ..." Her voice trailed away miserably, as she added, "And if I gave you the impression that I did, then I am sorry." After the tumultuous events of the last twenty-four hours, she was too tired and overwhelmed to be either sane or sensible, and he was still too plain drunk. She reconsidered the wisdom of screaming and wondered whether Molly would come to her aid or just ignore her cries. Instead of saving her, a loud scream might even push him over the edge, and he might strangle her to silence her.

The instant he let go, she moved away. "Tell me one thing. What the hell are you doing here, then?" he asked.

The question was no longer lost on her. Reality dawned with blinding clarity like the light on the road to Damascus, and though she didn't understand the why any more than she had before, she did finally understand the what. Her brain raced back over the entire night's conversation, picking up on all the double meanings and sarcastic one-liners she had missed – or worse, ignored. Her face registered only blank confusion. "You rescued me, remember?" Even she had to admit that it sounded incredibly naive now. Colour flushed her face. She got even hotter as she reluctantly allowed that the inevitable result of naivety meeting insobriety was always going to be disaster. Why had she not understood that before now? Why had she not known that two one-track minds – with different destinations – getting their lines crossed would result in catastrophe? Metaphors danced in her head like whirling dervishes, mixing themselves with abandon, but however many times and in however many ways she asked herself the question, there was never any sensible answer, so she blushed an even deeper shade of scarlet from shame. At least he was drunk; that rather excused him. She was sober, and a fat lot of use it had done her!

"I am sorry," she mumbled rather incoherently, much as if she had been the drunk. "I mistook you for someone who had gone out of his way to help someone else in difficulty. Perhaps I was unduly dumb," she finished meekly, unable to look at him and choosing instead to gaze at the floor. That was unfortunate, because she could not avoid noticing the silk slippers and the rest. Vanity had never been dealt such a crushing blow. Another thousand awkward questions queued in her head. All of them unanswerable. "I am sorry. Forgive me. Perhaps it would be better if I left." She turned towards the door. "I need to get my things and then I will sleep in the van. You know I can't move it until I get help when the phone is repaired."

Rick had sat through this entire disjointed explanation, nursing his cheek. The shock of that slap had stunned him. "Suit yourself. If that's what you want to do, go ahead. I wouldn't recommend it, but suit yourself." She was already at the door when he yelled after her. "There is a lock on your door! And I am not so stupid to ask for two of these." He rubbed his cheek gently, bravado being completely overcome by shock. "You are safer inside," he promised, before ruining it by adding sarcastically, "I can be a gentleman!"

The line from Lear about "the prince of darkness is a gentleman" seemed appropriate, but she wisely decided against quoting it or commenting on the value of his word. However, she did stop mid-flight. That was unexpected but gratifying. What was even less expected and definitely less gratifying was the sight of huge tears. He hated tears. It didn't concern him for one moment that he might have caused them, though he did give a brief consideration to her fanciful story about being a teacher on holiday and getting stranded. It was brief because his mind had powerful reasons not to believe it. He was not a stranger, and she had admitted tampering with the van. Enough said. He dismissed any intentions of apologies. Get real, he told himself. She's clever and she is playing games. He simply wasn't sure what this particular game was. Maybe she was a weirdo! She could be dangerous.

Neither of them spoke for a minute. Finally he said, "Go to bed." It was a direct order, but it replaced the need for further thinking or talking, and as she was too tired and too upset to argue any longer, she nodded and left without saying another word.

Chapter Sixteen

Rick stopped at the head of the stairs. The door to the guest room was just visible from here. It looked shut. He stared at it for a minute, fully expecting it to open any second, but it stayed shut. That door was always open to him. His room was the opposite way but if he walked towards the guest room it would surely get that result. She would hear him and open the door. It proved impossible to make enough noise without abandoning the carpet in favour of the wooden floor because old houses had thick walls, and thick walls meant good sound insulation, so in the end he did exactly that, striding around furniture and deliberately banging his feet down hard on the floorboards. Fortunately for him, there was no audience to witness it. The door stayed shut. He stamped as loud as he could outside the guest room door, but it stayed shut, and no one came out to inquire what all the noise was about. No one even called out to make sure he was okay! Obviously he hadn't made enough noise. Maybe she was deaf. He made more. The same result. Maybe she was *very* deaf. He banged a lamp down as hard as he dared, but that didn't produce any result other than an annoying scratch on a table. A sneaky itch to try the door handle hijacked all his more rational thought processes. He satisfied himself that he was only contemplating it because he wanted to find out whether she had believed him when he had said he would not try again – or whether she had still locked the door. That justified him in trying it, except he couldn't do that without reneging on his previous promise, so he walked away muttering. A few yards down the hall, he turned back. He had to know. Promise or not, he had to know, because if it was open, Cosi could stand.

A single sober thought stopped him as he reached for the handle: if the door was locked and she saw the handle move, would this crazy woman understand his reason? That tiny part of him that was sober said she would not. He withdrew a second time, only for his head to remonstrate. Come on, this is just a pick-up! He had never had to work this hard for anyone.

Sarah was sat bolt upright in bed. The noise on her landing had seen to that, but now it had all gone quiet again, and like Molly she was trying hard to persuade herself that she had imagined the whole thing. She focused on her breathing, but remained alert for the sound she really did not want to hear – the one she must hear if she was to stay safe. Such vigilance did nothing for the oxygen levels in her blood, and although her door was securely locked, the slightest sound was able to raise her anxiety to panic level until she remembered that this was an old house and old houses made strange noises. It could turn out to be a very long night if she jumped at every creak. After all that had happened downstairs, she couldn't really understand what had possessed her to come up here in the first place, but it was too late now for such regrets. She jumped nervously as several rapid lightning flashes reminded her that she was probably much safer behind a heavy, locked wooden door in a solid house than in any flimsy van, but it failed to reassure her for long. Even this amazing bed, which was totally wonderful after three weeks in the less than luxurious skybunk, could not persuade her to relax. Paranoia would have its victim.

She had been sitting upright in this manner for at least ten minutes before she finally relaxed. Then, rather red faced, she exhaled slowly, letting go of her dread at the same time. The absence of further noises allowed her to do that. Unless he was waiting outside – a thought that, once thought, proved impossible to un-think. In the end she slid out of bed and tiptoed to the door, just to reassure herself one last time before she went to sleep.

She was stopped by one singularly awful thought. What if he is there? What could she say to justify such strange behaviour? There could be no possible explanation for him being there, of course, but what rational reasons could she offer for tiptoeing around his house at the dead of night? Checking doors? Sleep walking? It would only prove beyond a shadow of doubt that she was mad, or well on the way. "Sarah Chadwick, stop this now!" she remonstrated. "This is stupid. Go back to bed. You are safe in here. He would need a battering ram to get through this door. One kiss, and you imagine you are holed up with the Boston Strangler."

For once she took this advice without question and crept back to her bed, relinquishing her exhausted body into its wonderful embrace. Some minutes later as she was beginning to drift towards sleep, she heard a comforting thud down the hall. "See?" she told herself, snuggling down further between the cool linen sheets. "It's the strangler's night off!" She didn't have time to consider her dark humour further as exhaustion claimed her, and she drifted into a deep if not altogether peaceful sleep.

The would-be strangler surveyed himself in his bathroom mirror. She had amused him at first, but now she alarmed him. Could he be losing his touch with women? No, that wasn't it. What about his sex appeal, then? That neither. *Freedom* magazine readers had recently voted him the man they would most like to spend the night with, and that by a huge majority. He switched out the light. Perhaps she had simply changed her mind. He kept coming back to that, however unlikely it sounded. He yawned, climbed into bed, switched off the bedside light, and thumped his pillow. If it wasn't any of those things, he couldn't come up with any other answer, so he cursed some more, pummelled his pillow into the sort of obeisance his brain could not achieve, and flung himself down into its softness, hoping for sleep. As he drifted towards sleep, he said to himself, "What's your problem? It's just another woman."

Chapter Seventeen

Rick Masters was not a natural lark. The fact that his profession demanded early starts had been a big disadvantage at the beginning of his career; his well-established night owl habits had seen to that. And even though he was now an old hand, it still wasn't exactly pain-free, but it was more manageable. Over the years people in general, and directors in particular, had tried to show him that early starts were not arbitrary decisions taken just to annoy him; they were real operational needs. He might have started to practice the habits of a lark from compulsion, but those original misgivings had taken a long while to die. He must have tried most of ways known to man's ingenuity, before he had given up - suffering did not suit him. None of his ways had succeeded, not even when he had joked God would have made him able to crow if he'd wanted him up so early. This view had not excited much sympathy among the crew who had been there long before him. One guy was cocky enough to point out, "So what makes him think he don't crow?"

He had finally settled for a practical solution to his problem: sticking to the early riser routine even when he was not working. It had eased the pain some. His trainer called it self-discipline; it still felt more like masochism. Whatever it was, it did not come easy, though it had eventually converted him from being a lunchtime riser suffering more or less permanently to his present status as a pretend lark. Occasionally he broke the habit, but never for more than a day or two: the transformation had been too hard won.

The morning after the storm was no exception. The day before had started with a banging headache, and though he knew that was only partly because he had stayed in bed too late, he had no intention of repeating it this morning, so despite the fact that he had drank too much again last night and had been in bed only since four this morning, he dragged himself out of bed shortly after eight and went outside to the pool.

It was already warm enough for the sun to be sending up steam from the saturated ground. He did notice that as he rolled the pool cover back, but nothing else. Twenty or thirty swift lengths should do the trick and purge the physical and mental debris of the previous night. That habit had become master, and though the water would need to work its magic before he would be in any fit state to notice anything else about the day, including the substantial damage from last night's storm, he knew he would soon feel better.

Rick was too absorbed in his rejuvenation task to notice when he had company join him. His houseguest had lain awake since a little after seven, and because she could no sooner induce sleep than her host could command his late starts, she had dozed lightly until shortly after eight. There was no point in staying in bed if she could not sleep; she would only end up with a banging headache, and she had a big enough headache to deal with as it was. She propped open the bedroom door to listen for signs of life as she dressed, and when she heard some banging downstairs, she persuaded herself it would be the housekeeper, so she threw all her belongings into her bag and hurried down.

The scene of last night's little drama was empty; its doors flung wide open. Two empty glasses on a table were all that testified to what had happened. She shuddered as the more embarrassing details came flooding back in glorious Technicolor. "Yes, well, we all make mistakes," she muttered primly, easily exonerating herself of any blame while hoping that the real culprit was unconscious somewhere with sufficient alcohol poisoning to knock him out all day. After all he had drunk last night he should not see daylight for a whole week. Maybe his name really *was* Rick Dracula! That amused her more than it should, and she closed the doors carefully, fully satisfied with this ludicrous theory, blissfully unaware she had given no consideration to the difficulties that might prevent her from getting anywhere either.

The house looked and felt somewhat different in daylight, and though she did concede that it was rather beautiful and not at all scary like she had thought last night, she still considered there were too many doors. The banging had stopped long before she had got downstairs and there were no signs of any life anywhere – but then, Dracula's house would be deserted during daylight! Vampire residence or not, she headed straight towards the first sound she heard. Dracula's minder, the housekeeper from hell, was just visible through some French windows. A second later the lady herself came in.

"Morning, Miss," Molly said, sniffing in a most disagreeable manner that revealed her top teeth. Sarah noted there was no sign of any fangs. "Breakfast is outside when you are ready," she announced gesturing in the general direction of this offer before disappearing with a final sniff. She left Sarah struggling to pluck up enough courage to venture out to see if Master Dracula had found a way to survive in sunlight. If he had, this might not be an easy encounter. Two things consoled her: this could hardly be tougher than facing Michael Davies, and she would be out of here by lunchtime today, so it didn't matter how difficult it was, or how stupid she appeared. She took a deep breath and marched out much the same as she might march into her five alpha class.

The vampire was hauling himself from the water as he caught sight of his strange guest hovering nervously on the far side of his pool; her arms folded primly like some parent about to scold a naughty child. He had no way of knowing that she was visualising herself confronting Michael Davies. She had no way of knowing he had completely forgotten all about her. Each stared at the other. He appeared a little taken aback and she coughed and blushed.

He recovered quickest. "Morning. Did you sleep well?"

Sarah blinked hard and stared harder. How could he possibly look so ... well, fit, and with not even a hint of a hangover? All the alcohol he had consumed last night should have sent him straight to the bottom of that pool. Vampire powers, undoubtedly, she decided. She tried not to notice anything else, or investigate that "fit" conclusion further, and if he could act as if nothing had happened, so could she. Incredulity was more than happy to be ousted by thankfulness on this occasion. A slightly puzzled smile accompanied her reply but pleasant was infinitely better than rude, and polite would be a novelty for both of them.

Dracula continued to defend his side of the pool while he dried his hair, totally unfazed by the sunlight. Another good theory down the drain! "Come on over. I take it you do eat breakfast?" He had done well to manage one comment without sarcasm, and this one had not been as bitter as some of last night's examples. It had almost sounded like real humour. "Help yourself," he said as he headed towards the house. "Back in a minute. I didn't expect you up yet."

She echoed that sentiment, and while she sat down as instructed, she was much too stressed to do anything as bold as help herself; simply thinking about food made her feel ill. The Chadwick stomach was not in great shape this morning. He drank, and *she* got the bad stomach – how fair was that?

When Dracula returned, she followed him to the breakfast table with less nervousness than she might have expected, though she took only water, a little yoghurt, and some fresh fruit in the hope that these would be kind to her delicate constitution. While she was doing this she kept one eye fixed firmly on him as if he might pounce on her any second, and the other on her bowl, anxious to avoiding spilling yoghurt down her front. Oblivious to this scrutiny, he poured himself some juice, filled a bowl with prunes, and took a couple of slices of dry toast. Strange diet for a vampire, she thought. Perhaps it was a cure for hangovers.

"Did you sleep well?" he asked again as he sat down, his first such inquiry already forgotten.

Her reply was a polite version of the truth. It was also much too prim for it to appear natural, but it was the best she could manage without mentioning the things that she had no intention of mentioning. It would have to do.

They ate in silence for a while until he enquired, "You like peanut butter?"

"Mm. Though I don't believe I have ever had it for breakfast."

"Live dangerously, then," he said, pushing it across to her. "It's good for you, packed with protein and iron. Great for the blood."

She nodded again and tried to smile but failed miserably. She had almost abandoned her Dracula theory until that blood reference. The realisation that she was in danger of losing her rationality again over this one little comment restored some semblance of normal functioning, but she had to get out of here quickly! This had to be the most bizarre conversation she had ever had with anyone, Michael Davies, Elinor and the entire fifth included. In fact this must surely equal Alice's experience at a certain tea party. Had the Mad Hatter been quite this mad? Or this dangerous, her head chimed in.

She produced the by now crumpled card from her pocket and asked very politely if she could use the phone to summon help. "Then I can get out of your way," she added as inducement. "Los Angeles is the nearest depot, so I suppose the sooner I ring, the sooner they will get here. It could take quite a while, I suppose," she added forlornly, as if recognising this truth for the very first time.

"Could take even longer for you to get to them," he pointed out casually, pouring them coffee. "Phone's still down, but don't panic. Molly says the engineers have been working on it since dawn, so I suppose we might get service sometime today."

"Sometime today?" Hysteria could show in people's voices.

"Hopefully." So could indifference.

"Oh."

They returned to eating, and silence descended again. She was busy calculating what time the phone line would need to be mended by if she was to get a mechanic out here from Los Angeles, have the van mended, and be out of here before nightfall. His thoughts were a little more mundane: they concerned only peanut butter. Right now his day looked a lot more promising than hers. He was on safe ground, whereas her usual optimism could not summon enough enthusiasm this morning to even manage a hopeful rating because her memory kept reminding her what a mess optimism had landed her in yesterday. When she did raise her eyes from her plate, he was engrossed in considering whether to have peanut butter on a second slice of toast.

There had to be some other way of contacting Los Angeles. He might have one of those mobile phone things. She wasn't knowledgeable enough to know if they would they work out here, and she did not want to show her ignorance by asking, but desperation was about to make her abandon pride and risk it.

Molly came out again. "Mail's got through," she said, handing her employer a pile of letters. "Jesse says the highway is flooded north of here. We have some damage I believe. Trees are down, and all sorts of stuff blocking the road, but here to Wilson is sort of okay – well, passable with a truck."

"Any news about the phones?" Sarah asked eagerly.

Molly shook her head. "Maybe later, if we're lucky." Then she went back to informing her boss of the devastation caused by the storm. Most of Wilson had no power, and worse still, folks in the south of town were evacuated because of flooding. "Jesse says we only caught the edge of it. We were lucky this time"

Sarah disagreed. It did not feel anything like being lucky! But maybe none of them had ever been in any danger at all. Dracula seemed nonplussed by the news and was already sorting through his mail before Molly had finished.

"Looks like you are here for the day then," he said as Molly left, although really he was more interested in the contents of his post, than her. "I can't entertain you – I have some business to attend to."

"That's okay, I don't need entertaining," she said miserably. "I need to see to the van." Another awkward silence. "I am really sorry I can't get out of your way," she promised. Then she remembered her previous inspiration. "You wouldn't have such a thing as a mobile phone, would you?"

That grabbed his attention and he looked up with no small degree of interest. "Sorry, you are talking to the one person in California who voted against them." She could hardly manage a smile at that, however funny he thought it was. "Don't even know if we have cover, but I'll check with Perry. If he has one, I'll bring it back at lunchtime."

Perry rose to undisputed number one in her popularity chart, but how she could survive a whole day here remained a big problem. A bigger problem still, even with Perry's phone, -she had to accept she could be stranded for another night.

Molly came out again as she was berating her misfortune. "Chas just rang. Phones are back on," she said as she cleared away the dishes, not recognising the enormity of the information she had imparted with such brevity.

Sarah looked up at the sky and gave silent thanks. "Perhaps I could be the first to ring out?"

Rick nodded to a phone on the table behind her. After misdialling twice, she realised her error and applied the required area code. It was embarrassing, and she was beginning to wish she had asked for somewhere different to make the call. Her third attempt was rewarded with a ringing tone. Relief proved to be a little premature because the camper company were even slower in answering, so she drummed her fingers impatiently. "Come on," she urged under her breath. "Pick up!"

After what seemed an age, someone answered. "Good morning, Davison's Private and Commercial Sales and Hire Centre. Tammy speaking. How may I help you?"

"Oh, good morning. Repairs department, please."

"You mean the garage?" the pleasant drawl inquired.

"Yes, whoever is responsible for mending broken-down campers."

"Campers as in people?" It was Saturday, and the strangest of requests always happened on Saturdays, but the drawl had asked this in a voice bereft of any hint of mockery.

Sarah did not answer in the same way. "No, of course not campers as in people! Campers as in motor homes, or whatever it is you call them out here. You know, caravans with wheels and an engine." Whoever had said American was the same language as English had obviously never had a broken-down camper.

"Oh, I know!" the drawl said with some enthusiasm. "You have one of our vehicles, and it's not running right?"

"Right!"

"Then it is the garage you need."

"Except it's not one of yours, exactly. It's mine – well, it's a friends, but I bought it in New York from your branch there, and the man said that any of your centres would honour the guarantee. Does it make a difference?" She realised too late that it did, and she should have kept quiet about the complications until she had sorted out the action. It seemed quite impossible to explain to the receptionist why she was ringing Los Angeles when she had bought the vehicle in New York, and she got so frustrated in the attempt that she was at the point of asking if no one in America ever broke down out of their own state. She restrained herself – just. "Put me through to the garage, please, and I will sort it out with them."

"Not today you won't."

"Why not?" She was beginning to get a tiny bit frazzled.

"Because they are shut."

"Shut! What do you mean they are shut?"

"I mean they are shut, as in they are not open," the drawl responded in a bemused voice. She wondered if all English people were so strange.

By now Dracula was listening with increasing glee to one side of the conversation. Things were looking a whole lot better to him. Sarah noted that and wanted to say something to wipe the smile off his face, but she was denied the opportunity by Molly reappearing to collect the rest of their dishes, and of course she worked slower than ever the instant she sensed that there might be something going on here that she knew nothing about.

"What do you need my name for? Oh, yes, I see. It's Chadwick. Yes, Chadwick." She spelled it out slowly. "Mrs Sarah Chadwick."

The clatter of clearing pots stopped precisely at the second Molly's ears registered her title. The sudden lack of activity alerted her boss who signalled for her to go and leave the rest of the things until later. In the face of such a direct command, there was very little Molly could do.

Sarah was still struggling with the girl on the phone. "How can they be shut? It says here twenty-four-hour service cover."

"They can, because they are! Nothing you or I can do about that until Monday."

"You mean they are shut till Monday?" That was worse than saying Armageddon was tomorrow.

"That's the general idea, honey."

"What would happen if I had hired it?"

"Ah, that's a different thing entirely. I would call out an independent mechanic for you, but standard owner guarantees do not cover that. You need extra coverage," she explained apologetically, "and you don't appear to have that."

They had failed to consider that – correction, *she* had failed to consider that. "You are not joking me, are you?" she asked stupidly out of sheer desperation. The drawl wasn't. "I have a vehicle from your New York branch that has a guarantee that says seven days per week, twenty-four-hour recovery service. It says nothing about that being only hired vehicles, so what am I going to do until Monday? I am broken down right now!" If stamping her feet would have made her point any better, she would have done it.

"Oh, recovery isn't a problem," the drawl explained.

"It isn't? Then why are we having this conversation?"

"Because you said you needed to speak to the garage," the drawl pointed out with the patience of a saint, "and you can't do that until Monday."

Sarah sighed. This conversation was becoming more farcical by the second. "I know what I asked for, so what is the problem?"

The drawl elaborated on the choices she could offer. She could send a truck to bring Sarah back to Los Angeles and the garage would start repairs Monday. Or, she could call a truck to take her to a local garage today. Either way involved expense.

"How much will each cost me?" Sarah enquired dubiously, anxious about both. As expected there was no good news about either.

Although Rick could only hear one side of this conversation, he could tell from the tone of her voice that his guest was far from happy.

"No," she said firmly after one suggestion, "that is definitely not an option!" A longer silence followed before her explanation. "Because this is a private house! I was given a lift here last night; otherwise I would have been stuck in that storm." Second big mistake, now she had to relay information about the state of the local roads. This time there was a longer silence because she didn't exactly know where she was. She hardly wanted to give the girl at the other end of the phone any more evidence she was speaking to an idiot, but there was only one unpalatable way to avoid it: ask Dracula. It was rather like swallowing cod liver oil as a child, but she took a deep breath and did just that. As expected, it earned gleeful derision as he supplied the missing information, adding, "California, United States, Planet Earth," at the end. She relayed the information minus the sarcasm. The silence at the other end of the line told her that it was not good.

"Well, if I were you I would ask if I could leave your *vehicle* there, and then you can get a cab to the nearest motel. Even if I could get a truck out to you today, there's no guarantee it would make it back to this Wilson place, and this way I have time to work on getting permission to get a mechanic out to you first thing Monday morning, as a special concession. How's that?" The drawl sounded genuinely pleased with herself.

Sarah was less so. "Can I ring you back in five minutes?"

She didn't think for one minute that there would be a problem about leaving the van. She simply didn't want to ask for the favour, but she accepted that she had no alternative, and so she replaced the receiver and considered how she could manage it with the least embarrassment. Dracula's presence prevented her from giving way to the almost overwhelming urge to have a good scream on a par with top note of Ali's tantrum scale. This was the most fed up she had been since leaving home! Last night she had been scared, but this was plain exasperation. Elinor had been right: it had been a crazy and dangerous thing to do, and all those household chores that she had so cheerfully abandoned to come here queued up to underline that point. Nothing to do now though, except to ask for the favour.

The explanation of her situation and the options available to her were as awful as she had expected because she had to expose herself to more of his sarcastic comments, but for some reason, although Dracula was obviously highly amused, he spared her the sarcasm. Things had turned out much better than he had expected. Less than an hour ago, he had been feeling uncomfortable because of last night's little episode, but now things were much more even handed, he was even a little sympathetic.

"Here," he said, passing her a handkerchief, "have a blow!" In return for this solicitude, he got a fierce stare, but she took the hankie. Though she resisted his invitation, she proceeded to twist its fold in her hands as he continued to be painfully helpful. "Why not get a local firm out, an independent?"

The smallest of sighs preceded her mumbled confession. "I would rather not. I have no idea how much it would cost to put right. Davison's will cover it under the terms of the guarantee, even if it means I have to wait until Monday."

Fortunately he said, "I understand," before she had to admit that she would not be able to afford expensive repairs, and that two nights in a motel might be cheaper and within her budget.

"So stay here, I am not going to throw you out," he said. He was about to add "because of last night" but decided it might be prudent to let the matter rest. Besides being so generous in spite of last night's events made him feel quite the regular hero, and he completely forgot for a moment why he had stopped to help her, or what he had thought of her explanation. "That way you will be on hand to keep an eye on Elinor's property, make sure no enterprising car thieves spirit it away before Monday." He liked that nice touch of humour and was so busy applauding his altruism that he almost missed her reply.

"Thank you for the offer, but I couldn't." He didn't even try to disguise his amazement as he enquired why that was; after all, one night was a one-in-a-million offer according to the entire circulation of *Freedom* magazine, and here she was turning down an entire weekend! He mistook the silence for reconsideration, and so before she could say otherwise, he announced, "Problem solved. You stay here till Monday."

"I don't know … I don't think …"

"Then don't. I'll go tell Molly you are staying. Call them back," he ordered, dialling the number from the card on the table. "Go on then, tell them it's sorted."

"Are you sure?" she asked anxiously, waiting for the number to connect. She felt sure he must want to be rid of her as much as she wanted to be rid of him, but he dismissed her question, and so she had to accept his offer at face value, or else be downright rude. As a well-brought-up girl (most of the time), the latter option was difficult, especially now she was nearly functioning normally again. She had left him room to withdraw his offer, and he hadn't. Besides, truthfully it was even a bit of a relief to know that she did not need to start moving all her things to a strange motel. The downside of this arrangement was that she had to stay here for forty-eight more hours! That seemed akin to a life sentence right now, but the last few days had taken such a toll, that sheer weariness meant she overlooked all objections. All she really wanted to do was get to Shelagh's as soon as possible, and right now this seemed the easiest, most straightforward way to do that. However, she did promise herself she would never be adventurous again.

She had no idea how someone she had written off as nothing more than a sex-obsessed, egotistical clothes dummy with a much-nourished, but fragile ego, could be so magnanimous, especially after the treatment she had handed out last night – a reaction that seemed a mite hysterical right now. Maybe I was wrong about you, she admitted grudgingly. And after all, you did rescue me! Taken together these two facts seemed sufficient justification for shelving those remaining doubts.

Rick wasn't quite sure why he had made his offer, but he didn't bother with an inquiry. "No point messing about looking for a decent motel. The best is across a road that's blocked, and the nearest is nothing special. We have one big advantage over both of them: we are free!"

Colour rushed back into her cheeks. If she hadn't been so keen on inflicting her poverty on him last night, he wouldn't have been able to fling it back at her now with such perfect timing.

"Well, if you are sure. I can't pretend I'm not grateful, especially …" She paused, took a deep breath, and said it, "Especially after last night." There, it had been said, and she felt lighter; it had been there since she had woken up, nagging at her like an invisible thorn, embedding itself deeper every moment that it wasn't pulled out. "So, I would like to apologise," she continued hurriedly without spelling out what it was she was apologising for. She meant it: she was sorry for her part in last night's debacle, whatever that was, and she did her best to convey that without looking or feeling too foolish. It was no easy task, even for one who had been brought up to understand that it rarely mattered who was most at fault in an argument; one made a move to restore peace. Her mother had called it forgiveness. It was something she was struggling to teach the girls, especially Ali. This time it had taken every last bit of her resolve to practise it herself. Rick looked directly at her and smiled benignly. If she had been expecting him to reciprocate, which was usually how it went according to her mother, then she was to be disappointed yet again. But then, she already knew apologies didn't exactly trip lightly from his lips. Maybe he needed the lesson as much as Ali. "So, if you are sure about me staying till Monday, I am asking you, can we start again?"

He nodded slowly. "Sure," he said at length. The deliberation perturbed her a little.

"Friends?" she asked lightly, holding out her hand, hoping that it clarified her intentions.

"Friends," he echoed solemnly, taking her hand and shaking it without releasing it.

This time she withdrew it quickly. This was how last night's little affair had got started, and she was not about to make the same mistake twice. She was sure he had done it intentionally, but he said nothing other than inform her he would go tell Molly she was staying.

Another of her mother's lessons obligated her to offer a proper thank-you, but she didn't quite know how to say that sensibly without appearing silly or sentimental, so she reached out to catch his arm as he passed, simply to stop him leaving until she had found the right words. The gesture was spontaneous, the sort of touch a small child might employ to get the attention of a busy adult, but it grabbed his attention in a completely different way, and he turned around and stared at her. Her blush told him she understood the question his eyes asked, because she withdrew her hand fast. She cleared her throat and pushed back her hair in the hope that it would cool her down and help her regain her composure, then she tried again. This time her voice came out as that tinny little croak, and so she abandoned trying to be sensible and just croaked. "Thank you. You are very kind." This attempt was only slightly better than the last one, but she let it be. She could hardly stay here for two whole days offering two or three attempts at saying anything before she could make herself understood. Why not, she asked herself. I do that at home! And I certainly do it at school, and I have been in both a lot longer than two days! That made her present difficulty sound more reasonable, though she realised that whatever she did at home, or at school, and for whatever reason she did it, it was nothing like here. She coloured up again as she registered the amusement on his face. Obviously she had said something wrong yet again, so she ended her awkward pause by adding lightly, "Even though you try your best not to show it," in a spirited attempt to regain that composure.

He nodded indulgently. "I'll go sort Molly out."

She leaned back in her chair and let out a sigh of relief which Len would have been proud of. Two days here was not going to be without its problems; she had just aged ten years in the last half hour! There was only one consolation: she didn't have to spend all the time in Dracula's company. In fact, the less time she spent in his company, the better.

Molly received the news that their house guest was staying quite calmly. She had been expecting it. She had never had any doubt that the weekend would turn into six months, and she clucked with some satisfaction at

269

being proved right yet again. "I don't know what on earth this world is coming to," she warned the kitchen door as he closed it behind him, but whatever it was it was coming to, *they* would not be here to witness it, and she went from kitchen to terrace pronouncing biblical wrath while struggling to resolve her own.

Sarah missed Molly as she came back from the terrace through the dining room to the hall. She was not as fortunate in avoiding Molly's boss: he was in the hall. She smiled awkwardly because she was still smarting from her recent embarrassment outside, but she was anxious to get over it and announced that she was going to spend the rest of the morning sorting out the camper and bringing what she needed up to the house, so he had no need to worry about her being a nuisance or needing company. He was free to carry on with whatever he had planned without feeling in the least bit obliged to look after her or involve her in any way.

As a speech it sounded like mitigation in a murder trial, but he nodded and left her to answer a call in a nearby room. "I'll see you at lunch, then?"

She watched until the door closed behind him, and then she borrowed another of Len's sighs. She needed to develop a strategy for talking to this man that didn't need a sigh of relief at the end of it! Could that be the reason Len always sighed when he had been talking to her? It was not yet ten o'clock, and it had already become a very trying day. Yesterday had been trying, but then she had been thoroughly exhausted and dripping wet, so that rather excused it. This morning, this side of breakfast, things didn't seem that much better except that she was dry. Levity apart, she realised she needed to keep a grip on her imagination; this was America, and Americans operated from a different set of rules to English folk in England! Yesterday was a bad dream and was better forgotten. Act normal, was her new instruction.

She had made it as far as the stairs before she remembered about lunch. There was no way of knowing what time that would be if she didn't ask him, or go find Molly. The first option was bad, the second was worse, but how long she could hang around for without it going down as more eccentric behaviour was debateable. She needed a legitimate task with which to occupy herself. Several paintings were worth admiring but she abandoned them so that no one could think she was eying them up as potential swag. The fireplace seemed safer; no chance of removing that. Its crest and motto were beyond her because they were in Spanish, but she studied them anyway. No one would know she didn`t understand Spanish. Half an hour later she abandoned the fireplace for the large-winged armchair by its side and earlier professions already forgotten, started imagining the people who might once have lived here using the portraits on the walls as models. There was absolutely nothing to say that they had ever been connected with the house of course, but then again, there was nothing to say they *hadn't*, and this enjoyable pastime provided ample material for a lively mind to manufacture all sorts of scenarios. Certainly this house must always have been owned by someone very rich, and its present owner came in that category. Maybe very few things had changed round here over the years; the house had simply collected people and their stories.

"I am a very strange story," she confided to it humorously. "I bet you have never had a broken-down motor home refugee before." The possibility that she might be something new was strangely satisfying.

When she had exhausted all the nearby material and there was still no sign of Dracula, she decided to leave a note apologising for the lunch mistake in advance, so she headed to the stairs with the notepad off the hall table, with the express intention of writing one, but she was soon sliding back into her history game because it was easier than composing her note. There were several paintings of ladies in Spanish dress on the stairs. She imagined them sweeping down these stairs, checking their appearances in the great mirror at the bottom; maybe they'd had to interrupt busy men, even write notes. Men had been busy throughout the ages and Spanish ones would be no different. She had arrived at this apparently unconnected conclusion through examining a nearby life-sized portrait of a man dressed in formal Spanish attire. A strange feeling took hold of her as she crossed the hall to stand before him. She turned around quickly, but there was no one there. *Creepy.* Thoughts of Dracula and ghouls returned.

"Don Phillippe Miguel Alonzo Escallido Da Santi," she read quietly, and then she announced, "a fine figure of a man" out loud, to banish the feeling he had caused. He looked very stern; she put that down to him probably being used to having his own way and being too busy to stand around all day for artists. The dog lying at his feet liked him anyhow because it gazed up adoringly. She pondered his potential connection to this house but had to admit he could just be a part of a colour scheme. "See?" she said, addressing his imperious gaze. "Maybe you only got wall space because you wore the right colour jacket." She had no way of knowing if any of her theories were correct, but she continued observing his aristocratic face and arrogant bearing for several minutes, trying to trace a resemblance to the present owner. She was still contemplating this possibility when she turned to find her host watching her with the same look. He could indeed be Ricardo Da Santi III, or IV. Anything had to be better than Rick Dracula the renegade Indian. "I am sorry, I forgot what time you said lunch was," she said quickly.

"Will one o'clock do?"

"Yes, of course, whatever time you normally eat. Please don't put yourself out on my account."

"Like I said I have some business to see to, so see you at one then,"

She nodded, then he turned and left without saying another word. She watched him go then advised Don Phillippe confidentially, "He looks just like you! Bit scary really! But at least your dog liked you! He doesn`t even have a dog! He has business to see to and I need to find something to do before I go completely crazy."

The camper was exactly the same as she had left it, except for the small hand towel tossed casually on the sink – evidence of the first of last night's visitors. She folded it neatly and dropped it into the linen bin. Molly had left no trace of her visit; all cupboards and drawers were closed and nothing was out of place. That seemed creepier for some reason, but the contents of the small ice box needed sorting, and so she set about doing that refusing to think of more difficult things. When she finished, she tidied the whole van twice even though it didn't need doing once, and then when nothing could be made any tidier, she packed a few clothes into a holdall, but even that was a task that refused to be stretched out to more than ten minutes in spite of her devoting such care to folding each garment that parachute packers would have been impressed. She stuffed a well-thumbed copy of *Much Ado about Nothing* into a spare pocket and then replaced it with *King Lear*; the first book being relegated back to the table because she needed to finish Lear first, and then she could read *Much Ado* for pleasure. Work always came first. Last of all she grabbed her two smart outfits on the pretext that she would probably need to wear something other than jeans in two days here, and then left the van before she could ask herself why. She checked her watch: ten forty five precisely. What on earth was she going to do for the rest of the morning? Go for a walk, perhaps, and pick up *Much Ado* on the way back -kill some more time.

"Hi there, you need a hand with all that?" A rather battered-looking cowboy figure caught up with her. She answered with some uncertainty, not really sure whom she was addressing. Could this be the much-mentioned but never seen Mr Perry? "Chas Sampson, Miss," he said raising his hat. "Wanna give me those heavy bags?"

It was the sort of offer that he did not need to make twice. She dropped both bags gratefully and held out her hand along with her greeting. Chas Sampson stared at the outstretched hand. "My hands ain't so clean, Miss," he said, holding them up for inspection. Sarah nodded and continued to hold out her hand until he recovered himself enough to wipe his hands on his jeans and reward her with a firm handshake. "Mighty pleased to know you too, Miss," he said with a grin. "These to go up to the house?"

She nodded and fell in beside him and they walked a few yards in silence.

"It's gonna be another scorcher," her new acquaintance mused. "Good job after that storm. We need some hot sun to dry everything out."

"I thought that was usual around here?" Sarah asked.

"Sure is," he remarked evenly as he changed the heaviest bag from one hand to the other, "but it always helps to make conversation with the English, talking about the weather, don't it?"

She laughed with delight. "You recognise my accent," she observed happily, "and you must know us, because otherwise how would you know that the weather is a national pastime?"

"My granddaddy was Welsh. Does that count?"

"Of course."

"And my grandmother, who was from Texas, always used to say that never a day would pass without old Jack – that was his name – moaning about the weather. It didn't matter what it was like, he would always have a good moan; it was either too hot or too cold, too dry or too wet, or too something. He was a grand old man, though. I have real fond memories of him."

Sarah smiled. "That's nice. I never knew my grandparents; my parents were older when they had me, and my grandparents were already long dead by the time I was old enough to remember anything. But your picture of Jack sounds wonderful, and the weather bit is a fairly accurate picture of all of us, I am afraid. If we didn't have the weather to talk about, I daresay we might be a nation of mutes."

Chas looked at her and then scratched his head. "That bad, eh?"

"Worse," she admitted solemnly but with a twinkle in her eye that showed she was only half serious. "It's discussed at cricket matches and tennis matches with all the gravity of international affairs. It's prayed about fervently by mothers of small children in the summer holidays. It's even permitted to speak to complete strangers on trains as long as you are discussing the weather. Yes, I'm afraid it's that bad. You could never know living here just how serious the weather is to us – you see, we get a lot of it."

He laughed out loud at that, and she laughed along with him. They were chatting like old friends by the time he dropped her bags inside the bedroom door. It was reassuring to have found someone who welcomed her without word games or stern judgements; the past three weeks had been a bit short on conversation most of the time, and she was like a traveller arriving at an oasis, desperate for refreshment.

Chas doffed his hat and nodded in response to her thanks for his help. As he turned to leave, she remembered about the walk. He scratched his head; it was a favourite gesture of his, and though it generally it meant little, this time it signified sheer amazement. "There's plenty to do, but there ain't anywhere to walk to. We are twenty miles from the nearest town of sorts, and I daresay the roads between here and there are a bit of a mess this morning. Might even be dangerous what with mud slides, fallen trees, and all."

Sarah nodded. "Of course. I forgot about that. Thank you. I will be fine; I can always read. I just thought it might be nice to get out and get some exercise."

"There's a pool," her adviser offered apologetically, "and a tennis court. That should be dried out by lunchtime. There's even a gym somewhere, though you will have to ask Molly where. Think it's down there somewhere." He nodded in the opposite direction.

She could hardly say she wanted to get away from the house and his boss for a few hours and so the gym might not be that good an idea. Chas nodded and closed the door after him, and then a moment later he returned. She opened it cautiously.

"There is another way to see round here," he said pensively. "If you can ride?"

"You have horses?" she asked.

"Best in the county."

Her heart skipped a beat as she asked tremulously, "And you think it would be okay for me to ride one?"

Chas looked only a little puzzled by that. "Sure thing. Tell you what, if you can hang on for half an hour or so while I finish a job, I'll come with you, show you around. Might be as well – what with the storm and all, we don't want you getting yourself in any trouble, do we? That's if you don't mind some company?"

Her brief blush at the mention of getting in trouble was replaced by a wide grin. "I would love some company, but I don't want to get you in any trouble, or take you away from your work."

"Heck, no. I ride the horses out every day. You will be doing me a favour."

"Well in that case, if you are absolutely sure that it's no trouble."

Chas looked at her real strange from under his hat. He wondered why it being a trouble was suddenly a problem. Mr Rick's girlfriends were never bothered about how much trouble they caused a body, so why she should be different was worthy of his deepest thought. He remembered Molly had asked much the same question last night. He didn't have an answer for it, either, but he did agree to meet her in half an hour. "Stables are behind the garage block," he told her. She was about to disappear back inside her room when he turned back a second time. This time he looked distinctly uncomfortable. "Don't want to give offence, Miss, but how well can you ride? I don't want to be putting you on anything you can't handle," he explained apologetically

"Like a cowboy, Chas," she said with a grin, slapping her thigh. "Well, almost like one!"

Chapter Eighteen

It took Sarah less than five minutes to unpack and hang all of her belongings in the first of the dozen or so wardrobes in the dressing room. Two pairs of jeans, one pair of shorts, one dress, and one suit could not take any longer however many times she rearranged them, and two pairs of shoes were always going to look forlorn beside the tiny pile of T-shirts. These wardrobes had been built to accommodate more clothes and shoes than she would likely possess in her entire lifetime. She didn't need to be a maths genius to work out how many clothes would be needed to fill them, though how any one person could justify owning so much, let alone wearing so much, was beyond her.

Her initial disappointment on finding that this wardrobe was empty intensified as she furtively peered inside all the rest and found they were all the same. Not so much as a hankie in any of them, except for the very last one, and she knew what was in there. "How very odd," she announced as she examined the interiors all over again, much as if they might reveal secret contents the second time around. If there were any such tricks to be performed, she lacked the necessary ability because they all remained resolutely empty. "Very curious," she muttered, unaware she was beginning to sound like Alice, but then, even the real Alice would have been hard pressed to come up with an answer for her next question. "So how come number twelve has contents?" What it lacked as a question was an answer, but as speculation it was without limit, and she was still giving it her full attention when she remembered Chas and her ride. She shelved her mystery by deciding it was probably normal practice in big houses to keep a supply of clothing for guests, and this must be a guest room. After all, she could hardly call herself an expert on the domestic habits of the very rich. "Perhaps you are just too plain nosy!" she told herself.

Outside afforded alternative food for thought. She had already acknowledged that her first impression of the inside was wildly inaccurate, and she took a minute to reassess the outside now that the storm had passed. Long white walls and sweeping arches sheltered beneath a pink tiled roof that swooped low in places as it covered some odd protuberance like a mother hen sheltering all its young under her generous wing. It hardly supported the abandoned theory of last night. Quite the contrary: this house had such a reassuring, organic charm that whatever its genesis, it seemed laughable that only last night it had terrified her.

She followed the same path around its perimeter that they had taken last night, but even though she had ran it then, when she reached the corner she was amazed to find a wing stretching back almost as far again. That was why it had felt like running round a football pitch. It was the size of one. The path meandered by some tall windows hidden beneath an arched terrace, on top of which a full-length window was flung open onto a balcony – the perfect setting for a well-known scene if one transposed Verona for wherever it was she was in California.

She had started to conjure up her players when she was rudely interrupted by a conversation coming from inside the open window. It was not Juliet. It sounded rather like the housekeeper talking, but it was the reference to a breakdown that fixed her attention more. Molly was evidently telling someone about last night's events! Romeo and Juliet lost out to the immediate and quite tantalising thought that Molly's listener might be none other than the mad wife of Mr Rick Rochester, locked up and cared for by the housekeeper from hell. That would solve all the mysteries in one fell swoop! It would be a natural part of the housekeeper's role to keep her mistress informed of the goings-on in her house, and that would explain why Molly had been so unwelcoming last night and why her host needed a housekeeper at all. Mrs Danvers had been spot on! Well, if one allowed her to stray from du Maurier to Bronte with alacrity. Why not? Attractive though this theory was, she eventually dismissed it as too melodramatic for a Shakespeare fan, even if it was fine for a Bronte follower, but as she had no pretences to the latter she settled for trying to establish where the window room might be located inside the house so that she could check it out later if she failed to get more information from Chas.

The horses were housed in stalls in long white buildings either side of an immaculate yard; buildings that were reminiscent of the main house. That produced a genuine smile as Sarah opened the gate to the yard. She was more than ready to be impressed by any property where the horses got the same quality accommodation as the humans, so Rick Dracula–Da Santi–Rochester, part-time Indian scout, part time dress designer, earned himself his second tick of the day. The yard's residents were just nosy enough to snort or push their heads at her as she walked past them; of course it was necessary to stop and meet each one in turn.

"You're early," Chas pointed out when she found him outside the tack room adjusting stirrups. Without looking up from his task, he explained, "We are not quite ready for you yet."

"Couldn't wait. I hope you don't mind?"

"Heck no. I said half an hour because then everything would be just ready. You'll have to wait a minute while I finish; Anatu is having some fun with me."

"Can I help?"

Chas shook his head. He was used to working in a world where everything was always wanted immediately, if not five minutes ago, and where people – especially women – did not like being kept waiting for anything. "Naw, I'm nearly done. Come on over and meet Anatu. Ain't she a beaut? She's gentle as a lamb usually! Got the nicest temperament that I've ever come across in a horse, or a human for that matter. She's having some fun with me this morning, but she's a real lady, aren't you?" The horse whinnied, and they both laughed. "She knows it, like most other beautiful women. But she likes you telling her just the same."

Sarah nodded, "I had no idea that when you said horses, there would be so many. Do you ride them all?"

This was a leading question, a bit like asking a golfer does he putt. It gave Chas an opportunity to explain about his job, and the business with Mr Perry who bought the horses as yearlings and then schooled them before selling them on. "All good horseflesh, but these are playthings for rich folks, and that's where they will be going soon."

"Anatu will be sold?"

"Oh no, not her. She's one of the fixtures – she belongs here," he explained warmly, "just in case anyone wants to ride. Not that they ever do." He shook his head. "When I was a young man, these stables were full of real horses, working horses. But times change, so I suppose it's better they're filled with horses for folks that've got nothing better to do than prance around all day. It's better than the stalls standing empty."

A sharp, painful memory escaped confinement. Chas's words and sentiment had summoned her father's presence. He noticed the change in her expression and asked, "You okay?"

"Just a bit of dust in my eye."

"Well, as I was saying, Mr Perry schools 'em, and then they're sold. Between you and me, I think it was the promise of the capital for buying horses that really brought him here. You met Mr Perry?" She shook her head. "You will. Mighty clever guy. Not much goes on round that here he don't have a hand in. He knows everything there is to know about running a place like this, and he's good at his job – unlike some I could mention but won't. Anyways, he's the best I've ever seen with horses, and I've seen some good 'uns in my time. S'ppose you could call him a natural. Know what I mean? Now, try this hat; we don't want you falling off and me getting in hot water with Mr Rick, do we?"

"It is okay, isn't it? You taking me out for a ride? I don't want you getting in trouble because of me."

"The only way I'd get in trouble is if I let you ride without a hat, and you fell off and got hurt," he pointed out with some energy. "I exercise all of the horses every day – well, me and my lads do. You will be doing us a big favour by helping out. Nobody except us rides every day; Mr Rick ain't here that much, and Mr Perry is too darned busy to ride for pleasure, so it's down to me and Steve and Andy, my stable lads."

If that was a chore, it had to be one of the best she had ever heard. As Chas chatted on about each of the horses, she couldn't help recalling last night's conversation about happiness. Such a pity she had not known about Chas and this Mr Perry then. Both of them were right here under his nose, and they both shared her dad's passion – *her* passion at one time. She knew that people with this passion were always happy when they were occupied with it! It was intriguing to know there might be other men like her father; he had been the most truly happy and contented human being she had ever known, and the fact that Chas and Mr Perry shared his love of horses more or less implied they must share his general state of happiness. She was about to check that out when she stopped herself. Why was it so important she was right about this?

"Something wrong?" Chas asked as he noticed her open mouth. He was leading out a liver chestnut gelding with white socks and blaze so she confined her comment to that because this animal was just as handsome as Anatu, and it was easy for her to excuse her strange manner with a platitude. A single thought spoiled her act: if she could find two happy people within hours of being here, how come their employer had missed them? She didn't have time to ponder it any further because Chas was talking to her about his new horse.

"This here is Tiamat," he said, running his hand down the horse's neck. "We'll take him out because he gets along with Anatu, and he's young enough to keep up with her – she's a mighty fast lady."

Sarah took the bridle from Chas and slipped it over the horse's head, but saddened by its fate in the economics he had described. That sadness was alleviated a minute later as Chas filled her in on some unexpected details. "Tiamat's another fixture, him and Anatu. And that little bay at the far end there, that's Ishtar. Then there's a big black guy called Marduk."

She nodded approvingly. "Someone has had a classical education," she muttered.

"Aye, they're classics all right," Chas agreed. "Best horses for miles."

It was pretty clear Chas intended her to ride Tiamat, and it seemed downright ungrateful to argue, but the opportunity to ride an animal like Anatu would probably never happen again, and so she overcame her sense of impropriety and asked if it would be okay to swap. Chas was dubious. "She's a lady with a mighty powerful stride, Miss. Better be safe. Take Tiamat." Her willing acceptance of his decision unnerved him because he was not used to it happening: Molly never did, and Sherri, Rick's last lover, would have argued with the devil himself to get her own way – she frequently had, in fact. "Rather be on Anatu, wouldn`t you?" Chas said indulgently, still troubled by the acquiescence. Her face lit up. "Go on, then. I'm a sucker for a pretty face."

"Thank you! And if I fall off, it's all my own fault," she said.

This was more familiar territory; he was used to women getting their own way, and so he said no more as he gave her a leg up onto Anatu`s back. "Be careful, though!"

"Chas, it's my middle name," she promised him confidently. He shook his head. Mr Rick always went for high-spirited women, and she followed suit on that.

They walked out of the yard slowly, the music of clip clop ringing in their ears. For Chas this was simply routine. For Sarah it was nostalgia, exhilaration, and a joy like nothing else could deliver; with the warmth of Anatu beneath her - it was like coming home. That hit her hard. It had never dawned on her before how long she had been away, but the whole of her life in between seemed like she had been in exile. Unaware of his companion's emotions Chas set off at an easy pace once they had cleared the yard. She followed him, allowing action to replace emotion. The ground was soft and the going was very heavy because of yesterday's storm, but within minutes they were kicking up significant mud because the horses were just as eager to go as their riders and Sarah soon found enough confidence to give Anatu her head. She was glowing from exertion by the time they stopped at the edge of endless orange groves fifteen minutes later. Chas and Tiamat were still way behind, so she removed her hat and leant forward down the length of the horse's sweating neck. "Steady on, girl. I'm not as fit as you," she said softly as Anatu shook her head and snorted. "And neither is Chas and your friend Tiamat, so I'm sorry, but we will have to wait for them. You may know where you are going, but I don't, and I cannot get lost again, not even for you! But that was truly amazing. Ace, even," she confided with a chuckle.

Chas shouted as he pulled up beside her. "We couldn't keep up with the pair of you."

"Tomorrow you will! But that was worth every ache and pain imaginable!"

They were ambling along in the sunshine, their conversation focusing very much on horses and riding when Sarah confessed, "I was going to conquer the world with Lady, my last horse. When you are sixteen, dreams come as big as you can make them."

"So what changed 'em?"

The most practised eyebrow in North London raised itself in a silent question. "You are a very astute man, Mr Sampson."

This time it was his turn to laugh. "Who, me? Naw, I'm not! Let's just say I've had plenty of practice at listening to ladies and working out what they really mean to say, but don't."

"That's astute, isn't it?"

"So, you and Lady? Listen, tell me – I'm a nosy old man."

"Nothing monumental. I just grew up. Well, actually it ended when I went to university. It seemed like there were more important things than going home every weekend to compete in shows." She shook her head sadly before adding more brightly, "Besides which, it needs more than weekend riding if you are going to be really good. Might have been better if I had stuck with the horses and going home," she admitted, forcing a grin that only her voice betrayed.

"Sounds like regrets to me," Chas offered gently.

"Maybe."

He wasn't fazed by her favourite non-answer, so he shook his head and wiped his sweating brow with the sleeve of his shirt. "Don't waste your time on regrets," he advised. "All the regrets in the world can't change a thing. Can give you ulcers, make you ill, and send you mad, but they can't change a thing. My granddaddy Jack had a favourite saying and used to tell it to me regularly. Wanna hear it?"

"Why not!"

"'Chas,' he used to say, 'don't you ever go wasting your life on regret. It's the most expensive thing in the world because it robs the future. Sort it out or leave it behind you.' Ain't that profound?"

"He would have got on well with my mother; she talks like that."

"I does it all the time myself, nowadays," Chas said clearing his throat. He did wonder what the heck he was doing, prattling on about things as if she was just anybody. "Well, I'm beginning to," he said apologetically. "I think they call it the voice of experience, or something like that. It's supposed to be one of the advantages of getting old, so I guess I qualify."

They had covered a good few miles so even though Sarah felt a bit stiff she knew enough to know that the real aches would not set in until much later, so she was happy to ignore them for now and continue ambling along, discussing this and that with Chas, enjoying the movement of bump and roll as the horses picked their way over the uneven ground. In one reckless moment she recited part of a poem she had read last term with the fifth – the one that talked about Islands of Joy. "And this qualifies!" she announced at the end of it. "Sun, blue sky, warm breeze, wide open spaces, the smell of newly washed earth, and the perfume of drying fruit trees –all in good company and on a great horse. What more could anyone want?"

Chas nodded. He wasn't sure whether that signalled she had had enough, or what. "You want to go back then, or would you like to see the packing station while we are out here? It's not much further now," he suggested rather hopefully. She agreed easily, and they picked up speed again and then slowed to a walk as they crossed a small footpath onto a road surface.

"Civilisation!" she groaned. "I had almost forgotten about it. Such a pity we have to come back."

Even though Chas knew her last remark hadn't required an answer, he couldn't resist commenting on the onslaught of that civilisation on his beloved fruit industry. This was passion for him. "People think movie stars and real estate and gold made California. They didn't. It was fruit that made here! Fruit, you hear! But California is getting so dammed full of movie stars and movie people, I daresay the fruit will go altogether before long so the land can be used to house them all. Bah!" He stopped himself short, recollecting he wasn't talking to one of his friends here, or even Molly. "Of course, we all hope that Mr Rick will never sell out," he added hastily, trying to explain himself. "Folks have got used to him." His companion was too preoccupied with taking in the packing station to notice what he had said, and he was not about to repeat it, or elaborate on it, so he breathed a sigh of relief. She had lulled him into making that big error.

Chas fastened the horses to a convenient post in the corner of the yard, and then threw himself into giving her his VIP tour; it was safer than conversation. He did this with so much knowledge and pride that it could have been his own place he was describing. "Over here," he began, pointing the way, "is the grading shed, and over there is the packing department. This here is quality testing, and that block over there is the offices. So if we start here and follow the fruit through, we will finish over there."

This pleasant enough prospect was rudely interrupted by a vehicle screeching to a halt at the opposite end of the yard. It was the car from last night: the Ferrari pick-up truck. Sarah had the grace to blush as the real owner and another man about the same age got out.

Automatically she backed up behind Chas, hoping to avoid being seen. The two men were engaged in earnest conversation, so it seemed quite likely she would get her wish, but then Chas shouted to them just as they were about to disappear into a building at the other end of the yard. "The other guy's Mr Perry," Chas informed her seriously as the pair walked over to join them. That helped some, so she concentrated so hard on this paragon of horse management that she completely missed the look of amazement on his boss's face. Chas did not miss it – or the quizzical expression fired his way.

"Mornin' to you, Mr Rick, Mr Perry," Chas said amiably. "I have been showing your young lady round the estate, so as we were passing I called in to tell Pete about the damage to the number one line before he starts it up again. I didn't know whether Mr Perry would get a chance to see him today, what with the storm an' him supposedly goin' off on holiday."

Sarah could hear the men talking, but she didn't register any of it; Chas's huge gaffe mortified her and all she wanted to do was to correct his appalling error, but she could see no way of doing that without embarrassing Chas and possibly making the whole thing infinitely worse. How he could be thinking that was beyond her! His boss didn't look irritated, so she hoped he hadn't noticed. That seemed unlikely, but she was almost sure he would have said something if he had. As he was not showing the slightest signs of having taken any offence, she tried to do the same. After enquiring whether she was enjoying herself, he nodded farewell and walked off with his Mr Perry in tow. They disappeared into one of the nearby buildings, leaving Chas to mutter something indecipherable and Sarah to roll her eyes heavenwards. The encounter had robbed both of them of their relaxed frame of mind.

"You wanted to see someone?" she reminded Chas thoughtfully, but wishing she could ask if they could leave.

It took only a few minutes for Chas and his man to locate the nature of the damage, so they were on their way back to the yard and their tour when Rick and Mr Perry emerged from an opposite door. Perfectly awful timing – no possibility of missing them! The men shook hands and parted company. Perry nodded at them, but Rick walked across looking as if he had every intention of joining them. Sarah forced her face to smile. "See you at lunch," was all he said as he walked past them on his way to his car. A few seconds later a cloud of dust and the lingering sounds of his engine were all that was left to testify of his presence.

She waved her hand to dispel the dust cloud. "Does he always do that?" she asked, realising too late that it could sound less than polite.

Chas answered her openly, forgetting for the second time who he thought she was, and who it was they were discussing. "Oh yeah, he likes to create a stir does Mr Rick." It was the slip of a moment and he checked himself so quickly that he had changed the subject before she had time to ask what that meant.

With business completed, Chas was eager to resume showing her the rest of the station, explaining the various processes and introducing her to any of the workers whom he deemed sufficiently civilised not to ask embarrassing, nosy questions. This naturally excluded most of the women. Chas was a very popular guy, and whether or not they stopped, most people called out a greeting to him. Sarah wasn't quite so sure what these people thought about her because she seemed to excite a mixed reception. Despite Chas's best efforts at keeping her away from nosy women, one of them managed to ask if she were staying up at the house. Her nod was met by such an immediate and frank visual appraisal from all the women on the line that Chas hurriedly whisked her away her to meet Pat, the station's oldest employee and quite possibly the only woman on the site who he reckoned wouldn't want to ask too many of them nosy questions. What was it about women and questions? They were never satisfied until they knew the ins and outs of a body's business.

Pat Trotter had worked on this station for almost forty years and was still going strong at sixty-eight. Her only concession to age was the tall stool she leaned on for part of the day. She motioned for Sarah to come and sit beside her on the pile of boxes as she continued inspecting her line. It was fascinating to watch.

"What are you looking for?" her visitor asked at last.

"Faults," Pat said with a grin, exposing a large gap in her teeth. "Same as the rest of the world."

Sarah smiled at that. She had not expected to find philosophy on a production line. The old woman leaned over the line, picked up a lemon, and held it out to her new trainee. "See? Just a tiny flaw right now, but if I let it pass, by the time its shipped it will be rotten, so it has to go now, before it spoils a whole lot more as well."

"But how did you spot that? It's such a tiny mark! You must have very good eyesight."

"That, and experience and practice. I know what I'm looking for, that's all," she said not entirely modestly. Pat was a good fruit packer and she knew it. "Best packer on this station, anyway, whatever some of the young 'uns might tell you."

"You make it sound so easy."

"It should be after forty years – well, forty years next month."

Sarah did not reply as she was marvelling how one woman could spend a lifetime watching fruit pass by. It humbled her. For once she was completely at a loss for words. Finally after a few more minutes' silent observation, she ventured, "Pat, can I ask you something?"

"Sure, honey, ask away."

"It's something personal."

Pat looked at her. "That's okay. Daresay it's not as personal as most of us would like to ask you, given the chance."

Sarah smiled. She didn't know what that meant, but it seemed harmless. "It's just, well … have you been happy here all these years?"

It must have been funny because Pat laughed outright, a loud unforgiving bellow. Then she looked at her guest and shook her head, "You have a lot to learn. Happy? What's happy got to do with it? What's happy got to do with anything? I had six kids to feed! My old man's a drunk, and this job has kept a roof over our heads and food in our bellies.

When the kids left, I had nothing else to do so I kept on coming. Pity I wasn't as good at sorting men as I am lemons," she cackled. "Life might have been a lot different." She continued to take out suspect fruit but said nothing more, leaving Sarah to wish she hadn't asked. "Why do you want to know, anyway?" Pat finally enquired as she handed Sarah another lemon to inspect.

"Something I'm trying to sort out," she confessed, wondering how to explain it without introducing the subject of her host. She was saved from that by Chas coming to collect her, but when she got up to go, she was disturbed to find that Pat was weighing her up in the same frank manner the others had. *Serves you right*, she thought, wondering what it was about her that could make others stare so curiously.

Pat grinned her usual toothy grin, grabbed hold of Sarah's arm, and whispered confidentially, "Listen, honey, there's only one thing a woman needs to sort out, and that's the right guy. All fruit goes off eventually. Get my drift?" Sarah didn't, but Chas excused them before Pat could say any more, and so she couldn't ask what that meant either.

It was ten to one by the time they were walking the horses back under the gatehouse clock. They had ridden most of the way back in silence; Sarah thinking about Pat, and Chas trying to remember all he had to tell Molly. For once he reckoned he might have the edge on the day's news. He might even go up to the house to share some of it over lunch, sort of whet her appetite. If he didn't exactly rejoice at the idea of teasing Molly with his new insider information, it came pretty close. Sarah slid from her mount and handed him the reins, apologising for having to leave so hurriedly. "If I don't go right now, I will be late for lunch," she said, conveying by her tone and facial expression that it was not something she wanted to risk happening. "But I will come back after lunch and help out, if I may?"

"You come back whenever you want Miss, but forget helping – I wouldn't think of it. Go on, you go get your lunch before I have Molly after me."

She nodded and smiled gratefully. He clearly knew about the stern looks as well. She had opened her mouth ready to ask about Molly but decided against it and closed it again. She had asked enough difficult questions for one day. Halfway to the door she relented, "Chas, do you know Molly well?"

"Should do. I've been married to her for more than thirty-eight years."

"Oh!" It was not an adequate word, but it conveyed some of the relief she felt.

"You're welcome anytime, Miss." Strange conversation, he thought scratching his head.

Sarah scowled. "I thought we had sorted this out," she remonstrated. "I told you that if I call you Chas, you must call me Sarah."

"So you did, I'm sorry, Miss – I mean, Miss Sarah." She wagged her finger at him in her best school teacher manner, but he replied, "Real hard to teach an old dog new tricks! And didn't I hear you say something about being late for lunch?"

She waited while he led Anatu back into her stall. "Chas, there is something else …" He looked up from his task of sorting the tack. "This morning you called me Mr Rick's young lady. But I'm not." She knew from the flustered look on Chas's face that her intention to put him straight had been thwarted by her own sensitivities. Her words had tumbled out in an off-hand manner that smacked of rebuke.

His reply conveyed that he understood that. "Anything you say, Miss."

Her second attempt was hardly better than the first. "I don't mean to offend you, or be offhand, or anything like that, but I am not his young lady or anything like it. And I don't know why you think I am. We hardly know each other."

Now she had Chas's undivided attention! Though she did realise that she did not have to explain herself to this man, it mattered to her what he thought of her, so, she had to take this opportunity to put him straight, and difficult though it was to convey the real history of her relationship with his boss without embarrassment, she was determined to give it a try. He got the whole story about the camper and the storm and the rescue, all casting his employer in the role of Good Samaritan. Naturally, there was no reference to the events of early this morning.

"So you see, I am just a passing ship – well a passing motor home – and nothing else. I'm here until Monday and then I'm gone for good."

Chas scratched his head, as much in amazement at the thought of Rick Masters in the role of Good Samaritan as the thought of her going to the trouble of explaining it all to him. Most women he knew would be only too delighted to have their names linked with Rick Masters, true or not. He was still perplexed why she should be any different, but he nodded. "I see," he said slowly, because he couldn't think of anything else.

On impulse Sarah laid a hand on his arm. "So you see I have had some pretty major problems recently, and if anyone ever needed cheering up this morning, it was me. I really needed someone to talk to, to listen to me, to let me have a moan. You have done all that. Thank you! If I don't see you again before I leave, you take care, eh? No regrets!" Then she ran off, anxious to make up lost time.

"You, too!" he shouted after her, but she was already at the gatehouse and out of hearing. "Well, I'll be darned," he announced to Tiamat. "What will Molly make of that?"

Chapter Nineteen

It was almost one thirty when Sarah ran downstairs. She started to offer apologies from halfway up when she saw Dracula striding through the hall looking like he was a man on his way to a fight. Although her apologies were brushed aside, his tone betrayed his truer feelings. "Forget it," he snapped. "Let's eat – I am busy." Then he frogmarched her into lunch in much the same manner a busy parent would a small child who was too intent on playing.

Molly served them in silence with not so much as a sniff marring her performance. That could have been because they were late and her food was spoiling, or maybe it was because of her "other things." Whichever it was that was uppermost in her head meant she did not notice their silence at first. Having spent all morning nursing the breakfast disclosures, discussing the implications with herself as she completed her work, Molly had yet to decide whether announcing she was going, or simply going, was her best option. This was her only ace, so it had to be played exactly right if it was to cause maximum inconvenience to that famous scheduling presence that sat sulking as she served him his spoiled lunch.

The diners were no more communicative with each other than they were with her. Sarah was deliberating whether she should tolerate such rudeness when she was a guest; 'nice' Rick having been consigned back to being Rick Dracula again and Rick was still too plain bad tempered to contribute anything at all. Eventually Molly picked up on this delicate atmosphere and surmised that right now might be exactly the right moment for her bombshell – so she surprised herself by leaving without dropping it.

When Rick's bad temper had subsided a little, he enquired about the morning's activities in what could have passed for a civil manner. His guest overlooked the brusqueness of his manner and answered with her usual enthusiasm, more than willing to end the awful atmosphere by telling him all about her ride if he would give her the slightest sign of encouragement. No such encouragement was forthcoming, but neither was disapproval, so indignation got the better of her, and he got the works whether he wanted it or not. She narrated the whole morning's adventures featuring Chas, stables, Anatu and her ride, in the minutest detail she could recall.

By the time she got to the packing station episode, he had looked up from his lunch on at least three separate occasions, smiled once, and been almost diverted by her delight twice. Then he remembered that this was all a setup, she had an agenda…okay he didn`t exactly know what that was yet for sure, but it sorted out his reaction pretty fast. He might have believed the stuff about the ride was for real, except for that. The smirk that curled the corner of his mouth only persuaded the storyteller that she had said something he thought was funny. She had not meant to be funny and so she swallowed the rest of what she was about to say. He had a bad habit of flattening people when they were only trying to be polite, but in clear defiance of his sneer, she confessed, "It was amazing! Thank you. I don't have adequate words to describe it, except … it was a bit like coming home when you have been away for a very long time." She had never intended to share that with him, and she knew the instant she did that it was a mistake. She had done it because she needed to prove to herself that he didn't intimidate her, and she had not reckoned on there being any other interpretation for her explanation, but after having given so much away, she continued bravely. "It was definitely balm for a beleaguered soul anyhow." She tried to ignore his disbelieving eyebrow. Why had she never realised how extremely irritating that could be? She finally decided to shut up. The vampire put his fork down and leant back in his chair, the better to intimidate her, but this time she didn't blush or stammer, and she met his gaze for a full three seconds before looking away. "All that space and freedom to lose yourself in – I envy you that," she added forlornly. If it sounded a mite melodramatic, she didn't care one bit. "It's the thing I miss most living in the city: no solitude." His gaze locked on hers again, but this time she blushed and looked away quickly, picking up the coffee pot to offer him another drink, quite forgetting she was neither his hostess nor his mother.

He accepted the offer and sat mulling over her comment with his coffee. He was used to people wanting a share of what he had to offer. It was the first time anyone had ever wanted to share the space or the solitude though.

Sarah had lost interest in the salad dish she was eating a long time ago, but she revived it now and chased a piece of wayward lettuce around her plate with the determination of a bounty hunter. After cornering the reluctant leaf, she was faced with the difficult decision of either letting it go and repeating the chase, or turning it in and eating it. She wasn't particularly hungry, but she did check to see that she was not being watched before she dared think about freeing the prisoner. Rick appeared occupied with his own lunch and as he was completely oblivious to her scrutiny she reprieved the lettuce leaf and put her sudden lack of appetite down to stress, concluding she was simply not meant to hobnob with the super-rich. That pleased her at least.

Other things didn't please her quite as much. His silences were top of that list, closely followed by his questions, so even though she had been more than willing to volunteer information not ten minutes ago, she resorted to evasion when he eventually asked what she had thought of the station. It had to be another trick question. Elinor might be good at answering trick questions, but she wasn't. A few minutes later, resolutions forgotten, she slipped back into enthusiastic mode again.

"The next time I buy oranges, I shall know how they got into the shop. I never thought about it before."

"Chas gave you the full tour, then?"

"I hope you don't mind? Blame me if you do – he was just being polite because I was interested."

They were both quiet for a moment until she remembered to ask about the storm damage. It seemed the polite thing to do. He replied that it had not been as bad as he expected, and then there was silence again. Neither of them were going to win any awards for conversationalist of the year. Back to chasing lettuce.

"What does Chas include on this famous tour?" he asked after an eternity of the sounds of cutlery and very little else.

"You never took it?" she asked, finally swallowing the ill-fated green with a gulp.

"I don't reckon I did."

"Then you should. It's great! Like trips to the chocolate factory at junior school," she joked and attempted to laugh, but she gave up the effort as she met only a serious gaze. "I might use it with my younger classes when I get back."

"How?"

"Essay material. 'My life as an orange' – or better still, 'How the lemon got in lemonade'."

He actually managed a nearly-normal-sounding laugh at that, and she joined in more from relief than anything else. Whatever Elinor might say about laughter, it felt better than gloomy silence.

"So go on then, tell me about the rest of this tour."

She recognised that she could be walking into the same trap here but she dismissed any reservations on the grounds that it was too late in the day to start being laid-back and sophisticated. What the heck – "In for a penny," as her mother would say. She did try to be a little more restrained, but she still spoke fluently about the rest of the morning's delights.

Rick listened attentively; unconsciously watching for her face to light up again as she remembered some little gem and forgot about being careful. "So what did you like best?"

"The smell of all that fruit as it is being washed," she said without hesitation.

"Me, too."

The practised eyebrow shot up effortlessly. "Really?" She had not meant to sound so surprised.

"Yes, really. Do you reckon it's allowed for us to agree?"

"Of course it is," she protested, colouring furiously. "I didn't mean to, you know ..." There was another awkward silence until she remembered her previous promise not to be so easily intimidated, then she cleared her throat and added, "And I met Pat as well," reverting back to her previous topic as a way out of her present predicament.

It took him a second to catch up with her train of thought. "Pat who?"

"I don't know. The Pat who has worked at the station for forty years next month."

He nodded, but she guessed he didn't know who she was talking about. That was sad. A woman gave forty years of her life to her job, and her employer didn't even know her name? His loss, she thought dismissively, but she was angry all the same. "Anyway, tell me why all your horses are gods?" she asked innocently; trying to change the subject as much for her sake as his.

"Only four are. I don't know what the rest are called; they come and go all the time."

Like Pat, she thought, though she didn't say anything.

"The guy I bought the place from was an archaeologist and the horses belonged to him. The names are Babylonian gods, I think. The whole family was a pretty weird bunch, into digging up bones and things."

She did have the grace to bow her head as he answered, because she had only asked the question expecting to somehow be able to score over him by exposing his ignorance. Rick watched her face as he disarmed that intent -it provided more amusement for him. She didn't share the emotion. He was not one to be kind to fish on hooks so he added provocatively, "So knowledge of obscure civilisations is a required part of teaching English literature these days?"

"No," she admitted miserably, "though I doubt the Babylonians would be impressed with being called obscure."

He ignored the detour and kept to the point. "How does an English teacher get to know about such things then?"

"Archaeology has always fascinated me."

He recognised the emotion if not the subject. "You don't seem the type for being stuck down a hole digging up old bones."

Despite herself, Sarah laughed; genuinely amused by this idea. "That's a serious bit of type-casting, isn't it?" It didn't get the response she expected, only another of those awkward, penetrating stares. It reminded her of some of last night's strange looks, and that was reason enough for her to change the subject yet again. She kept her enthusiasm firmly in check and returned to talking about the land and from there to fruit growing in California, and then to farming in England. From there it was but a short step to discussing the two countries in general and then the vast differences between them, and almost without noticing it they had progressed through geography to culture until inevitably William got his mention, and then her enthusiasm returned for real.

"So is he your favourite author?" As if he had not already guessed that.

She nodded vigorously, swallowing the last mouthful of her dessert so quickly that she nearly choked on it in her haste to answer. "Shakespeare is more than a favourite – he is one of my life's passions!"

He wanted to ask what the others were but contented himself with asking why that was. "How come you feel like that about a guy who has been dead four hundred years?"

"Three hundred sixty nine actually," she corrected primly. "And I feel like that because he is unique -a genius. Shakespeare says the things we all want to, but he says them better. He makes me laugh, cry, shiver with horror, feel pity or contempt -and he can do all that in a few short lines."

"I get your drift! If this guy were alive, I'd say you were in love with him."

"Maybe I am. I am in love with his talent anyway. I am his number-one fan and I spend my life trying to get others to feel the same." She finished this rather hesitantly because she had noticed that strange look returning again. She was no nearer to understanding its meaning now than she had been before, so she ignored it once again and settled for it being the end of lunch and they had managed a reasonable conversation for all of twenty minutes – that had to count as some sort of progress.

Rick had the last word. "Can't imagine you down on the farm. Teaching – well, lecturing – is definitely more your style."

She responded in kind. "Likewise! You hardly seem to have the right image for the cowboy farmer." She had not thought it through sufficiently; so even though she knew what she had intended to say, it had come out differently and she winced as he grinned and shook his head at her.

"No cows, just oranges."

She tried to rescue herself one more time. "Pity that. I used to be quite good with Dad's."

"So you could see yourself here, if I had some?" he asked.

"Tell me something. Why do you always answer every question with another one? Do you always have to have the last word on everything?"

He met her gaze without effort and held it. "Usually," he replied in that intensely annoying way of his. "Although with an English teacher with Shakespeare for back-up, I daresay I can't expect that to last." He picked up his reading glasses to imitate her, and it was difficult not to laugh.

"I hope I don't ever look like that!" she exclaimed indignantly as she excused herself from the table, secretly congratulating herself on surviving lunch and holding her own – finally. And okay, she had been impressed by his general knowledge and surprised by his intelligence, but none of that warranted a total re-evaluation of his very doubtful character; a little amendment, maybe. She was almost at the door before she remembered about Shelagh. No doubt explaining all of it would take time, so she sat down to do it. "When I don't turn up by dinner time, she is going to start mobilising the FBI, unless I have called her. Would you mind? I will pay for the call, of course."

Her offer of payment was dismissed, he even sounded a bit irritated by it, but this time she didn't back down. He was having none of it and said, "Phone calls are nothing. Phone home. Phone England, whatever – but stop asking."

The combination of gratitude for this, and guilt for some of her previous judgements, made her confess, "Do you know something? I think I might have misjudged you a bit." His amusement renewed her original embarrassment, and though half of her wanted to be open and honest, the other half advised restraint. The reluctant half won, and it made her backtrack. "I did say a bit," she stressed.

"Okay, I reckon I'm asking for trouble here, but what the hell, let's live dangerously. How did you misjudge me *a bit*?"

"I guess I am shocked to find that you are really a nice person after all," she confessed, omitting any further reference to last night's events in the interest of continuing amicable international relations. His look of horror was a front for the laugh that followed it. This was the second time today she had told him he was a nice guy, and by now he was quite prepared to believe it.

Halfway to the door she remembered about the tennis. This time she was expecting her politeness to be brushed aside, and he didn't disappoint her. "Listen, as long as you are here, just treat the place as your own and use whatever you like – horses, phones, pool, court, gym. Whatever you want, but please … stop asking!" She was half way through the door when he shouted after her, "You want a game, then?"

"What?"

"Do you want a game of tennis?"

"With you?"

"Well, I wasn't thinking of sending for John McEnroe."

"I only meant to bash away at your service machine. I noticed it this morning when we rode past."

"Is that a yes or a no? I have never known anyone do so much explaining when asked a simple question! Do you do it with everybody, or is this a privilege you reserve especially for me? Do you want a game or not?"

"If you are really sure you want to," she said seriously. "Not just being polite." Okay, that was unlikely. "Thank you."

"Go make your call and be back in half an hour – no, make that an hour. That'll give us time to digest lunch and you time to finish your call. Is that long enough?"

"Of course it is." How long did he think she talked on the phone?

She watched him head towards the kitchen and then she ran across the hall and up the stairs two at a time, anxious to gain sanctuary. Lunch had been no less trying than breakfast.

After the problems with the morning call, she dialled Shelagh's number very carefully. This time she connected successfully the first time. A very young child with its mouth full greeted her. "Hi, we are home. Who do you want to speak to?" The receptionist passed on her answer in typical juvenile fashion. "Mom, it's for you! Don't know who it is, but she sounds *weird!*" She missed the next bit because it had to compete against a background of shrieks and shouts of "Mom, I need you, quick!" This was much more familiar territory than tennis courts and private swimming pools, lovely though they were.

Once greetings had been exchanged, the inevitable enquiries began. "Please don't tell me you are at the other end of the block, because I shall scream. My house is a *mess!* The kids are having a whale of a time, as you can probably hear. I made the mistake of saying Mickey could have a few friends over for his birthday, and now my house has more kids than a downtown McDonald's – there are bodies everywhere, and most of them are still wet. Agh! Go dry yourself properly before you come in here." This was definitely more like home even if they did have the swimming pool. "You know how it is," Shelagh continued. "They bring the three friends home with them, and then everybody else's kid just happens to pick today to call. My house has been spotless for the last two days, just waiting to impress you, and now that it is in a complete mess and looks like Water World, you are about to arrive!" Sarah`s explanation didn't help Shelagh any. "You're lost," she shrieked. "I knew Dave should have met you somewhere."

"Calm down, I'm not lost." Well, that was true now. "But I do have a problem."

"Only one? Gee, you're lucky! Swap."

Sarah had to laugh. "I'd swap you this one any time, but you wouldn't want it. I have had a spot of bother with the camper."

"You have had an accident!" her friend shrieked an octave higher.

"No, I didn't say that! Calm down, I am fine, honestly. I just have a breakdown, and my only real problem is I can't get it fixed until Monday."

All the implications of this mishap were examined in depth, including the inevitable delay, but eventually assurances were accepted, and Shelagh reluctantly agreed there seemed no need to send Dave out to rescue her. The conversation seemed to be drawing to a natural conclusion when Shelagh remembered something relevant. "Hey I still don't know where you are! Tell me exactly where you are. I hope you are not stranded in the middle of nowhere!"

"I am fine."

"What does that mean?"

"It means I am fine. I am not stranded in the middle of nowhere." The general location was described confidently enough – well, as well as she could remember it from this morning's call to the garage - embroidery only replacing fact in a few strategic places.

"What on earth are you doing out there? Hey, didn't that storm hit down there? It looked real bad. Were you in that?"

Explaining all this had not been on Sarah's list of things to do, but she had no alternative now, so she had to take the time to explain why it was she was where she was. "Have you ever read Alice in Wonderland?" Shelagh said she had. "Well, that's a bit what the last twenty-four hours have felt like. I turned this corner and found myself in Wonderland -this weird place with even weirder people. Everything and almost everyone is quite mad."

"You are in Hollywood!"

"No, of course I'm not. I told you where I am."

"I know what you told me, but you just described Hollywood. I'm beginning to worry again."

"Well don't, because I am fine – honestly. It isn't Hollywood, just 'Orangewood', and I exaggerate. The people are just a tiny bit weird." This naturally prompted more questions and more speculation. "I promise you I am safe; someone towed me in."

"Who did? Where to? This Wilson place?"

"No, not exactly."

"Sarah Chadwick, there is something you are not telling me here, isn't there?" Shelagh usually employed this tone with her kids.

"Only because I don't want you to worry, and I know you will if I tell you."

"That's it – I am sending Dave down there right now! I have a map in front of me. Hang on while I find this Wilson place."

"Shelagh, listen to me! Please don't do that. I will be so embarrassed, and Dave has already done so much. Promise me you won't send him, and I will tell you the rest."

"Everything?"

And with that Sarah recounted the rest of the rescue saga right up to being towed in. This was where fiction was allowed to soften fact more than a little.

"Let me get this straight. This man towed you back to his house because it was the nearest place? And you only just made it ahead of the storm?"

Sarah agreed that was so. "And I am only here now because of the breakdown. I was really lucky last night; apparently the road isn't used much, and it's flooded today. I could have been in real trouble if he hadn't come along, but he did, and so I am fine. I don't think I have ever been so grateful to see another human being."

"So who is this guardian angel?" Shelagh asked, thoroughly intrigued by now.

"His name is Rick. He grows oranges. I think he must be pretty rich even by your standards. You'd be impressed. Well, maybe not," she said, remembering that Shelagh had just mentioned they had a pool as well, and she hadn't yet seen the Phillipson's house. Any reference to the other events of last night, including Dracula and all her dress designer theories were omitted for obvious reasons.

"Guess you were lucky he came along, then. What did his wife say when he rolled home with you in tow at that hour?"

Now she had to lie, or admit to the truth. It was difficult to fudge this. "I don't think he has one," she said glibly, hoping the noise at the other end of the line would be great enough to mask what she was saying.

"Millionaires usually do," Shelagh observed dryly. "Californian ones always do – usually several!" There was no answer. "Well, his mother, then?" Still no answer. "So I take it he is no youth? Is he seventy? Are you sure that you are okay? I mean, all alone in a strange house with a weird guy you know nothing about. I hate to say this of the state I live in, but it's true, so why not: California has more than its fair share of oddball characters, and some pretty weird things can happen without you wanting them to."

"I did not say he was a weirdo."

"Yes, you did."

"Well, maybe my sort of weirdo isn't the same as yours, and I'm not alone with him, either. He has a housekeeper and her husband living here."

"I would have preferred him to have had a wife! Please let me ring Dave and have him come get you. Leave the van, one of his drivers can pick it up next week when it has been repaired."

"No, please don't! You promised me, remember? I only have tomorrow, and the repair man is coming first thing Monday. I will be with you Tuesday at the very latest. Besides, it might take until Monday for the road to clear."

"Ring me every day, then?"

"I can't do that! This isn't my phone, and I have been on here much longer than I intended to now. How expensive is this call? I will ring you Monday as soon as I am on my way, promise."

"Okay, but you'd better give me the full address and phone number. Then I will know where to send the homicide squad when you don't show up Tuesday!"

Sarah could not laugh too loudly at this anxiety without deriding her own, but Shelagh forgot about her noncompliance when she shouted excitedly, "Hey, I just found this Wilson place on the map. It's right near to where my Aunt Nora lives. I bet it's not fifty miles to her house."

"That's 'right near'?"

"Sure it is. Hey, you could go see her tomorrow because it's not down that road you said was flooded; it's in the opposite direction. She would be thrilled to have you visit! I have told her all about you. Please go!"

Although this seemed to present exactly the opportunity Sarah had been wanting not that long ago, she answered hesitantly. "Is it not a bit cheeky, just dumping myself on their doorstep?"

"Thought that's what you have done with this orange grower guy, and my Aunt Nora is not as much a stranger as he is. Besides, I will feel a lot happier if I know you where you are. This may sound ridiculous," she admitted slowly, "but while you are in this country, I feel kinda responsible for you."

This time Sarah did laugh out loud. "Shelagh Phillipson, I am an adult! But thank you for the thought. If it will make you happier, I will go see your aunt tomorrow – providing I can get through."

"Great! Hang on; I will get her address for you. I can never remember it properly." Shelagh returned with the details and dictated them very carefully. "It's straight down that highway, away from Wilson. Ask your millionaire guy; he should be able to give you better directions than I can, but be warned: they live in a real way out spot. You will have to ask when you get into town. Billington is only a small place, and everyone there knows them. Daniel was the local mortician!"

The whole thing seemed settled until Sarah recalled one small but rather important detail: "I can't go," she wailed. "I have no transport!"

"Ask your millionaire to lend you a car."

"Will you stop referring to him as my millionaire?"

"Sorry! Why can't you ask him? If he is as rich as you say he is he might even give you the chauffeur to go with it! Now *that* would really impress

Nora." This advice went unheeded, but Sarah could not help chuckling as Shelagh went on to describe various other ways of getting to her aunt's – a list that sounded alarmingly similar to Elinor's ways of getting across America. "Alternatively, I suppose you could take a cab, but I think my first suggestion is the one with the most merit, because it's free and doesn't involve physical effort of any sort, except talking, and you used to be pretty good at that. Use your charms on him -ask!"

"I am not sure which charms you supposed me to have, but if I ever did have any, which I doubt, you need to know I don't have them now. I wouldn't know where to start."

Shelagh's reply sounded amazingly like one of Elinor's homilies.

"I hope no one is listening to this call."

"Serves 'em right if they are! Folk who listen in to other people's conversations rarely hear any good about themselves. Listen, I'll ring Nora and tell her to expect you, and then you won't even be dropping in unannounced. How about it? She'll love it. She'll love you, I promise. You must have us sussed by now; we just love to entertain our quaint little cousins from across the pond." Quaint seemed an improvement on odd, so Sarah concurred without any further discussion, though a taxi seemed the better way to get to Billington, even if it was expensive. "Oh just one other thing," Shelagh cautioned. "They go to church!" She conveyed this information in tones not unlike those used by spies for disclosing national secrets. "Do not laugh! I am telling you this is real serious stuff. Ritual every Sunday! I mean it! They are the sweetest, loveliest people on the planet, but everyone has their faults; and this is theirs. If you can't get there before ten, I'd leave it till after lunch. I'd leave it till after lunch anyway, but I'll leave that for you to decide whether or not you want to suffer. Hell, I suppose I shouldn't say that, either – maybe you like to go to church, too!"

Rick was sat in the hall reading some papers as his opposition skipped down the stairs. He glanced at his watch: two minutes late. She missed the time check as her attention was fixed on the selection of racquets on offer. He coughed, and after a not so slight gesture at his watch, led the way outside; his immaculate whites providing an interesting contrast to her more bohemian attire of denim shorts and T-shirt. Okay, so he looked fit in the normal sense of the word, but that was when it dawned on her that she could be taking on more than she could handle here. It prompted her to enquire innocently, "Do you play often?"

McEnroe's stand-in turned round, looked at her, and grinned. That annoyed her for all sorts of reasons, not the least because it confused her. What came next confused her even more. "There's more than one answer to that," he pointed out facetiously. She blinked and then blushed furiously as recognition dawned – yet another innocent attempt at conversation thwarted.

"Tennis, I mean," she said firmly. It was not funny.

"Not much. I don't get much time these days. Why, do you?"

"Recently I have," she confessed, though she added hurriedly, "but I'm not that good because I haven't played for years until this year, so please don't be disappointed if I don't play a good game."

"So what made you start playing again?"

"I needed the exercise! Sitting in a classroom all day is not exactly strenuous, but it is stressful. Stress and lack of exercise is not a good combination for anyone. I could hardly run for the bus when my car was in the garage. I can't say that I'm super fit yet, but I am less stressed, and that has to be a good thing, doesn't it?" This summary clearly excluded the last twenty-four hours.

By the time they reached the court, they had discussed the merits of keeping fit and the various means of achieving that with all the seriousness of professional trainers. For a farmer he seems very knowledgeable about things that farmers generally know little of and care about even less, she thought. Her dad had never had time for anything other than farming and his family, but after adjusting the net position, this farmer retired to the base line and knocked the ball down to her with some speed and skill. He won the toss, too.

"You were saying about stress?"

She had to think for a minute what it was she had been saying, and while she was thinking, he served. She ran to hit it, but it came at her with such unexpected speed that her arm recoiled from the force, and the ball bounced off at an unexpected angle. It only just remained in play. She had never played against a man before. It did not take long for her to register the difference, so she was pleased that she had been able to return his serve at least once.

"I said, tennis is very therapeutic because it gets rid of all my tension and frustrations safely," she said, stretching, but missing his return. "Fifteen love," she called cheerfully as she waited for his next serve. She missed that, too. "Thirty love." There was slightly less cheerfulness in her voice. This could turn out to be a walkover. She returned the third serve easily, it was almost *too* easy after the others, which made her think it had been made deliberately so. That was even more annoying – being patronised always was. "Besides which, hitting a tennis ball is infinitely better than hitting your children or murdering your pupils," she added, finishing her remarks between exertions.

It did not require any effort for him to return her shots, so before she knew it the ball was whistling back over the net and dropping unexpectedly short. She realised that too late, and it was forty love. This was humiliating.

"I don't believe you would do either," her partner shouted as he served a fault. He tried again and this time it landed safely, but she was able to return it accurately. It bounced just out of his reach.

"Forty fifteen," she said, trying not to sound too smug. Winning Wimbledon could not have been more important than that point. "Why not?" she asked, waiting confidently now to receive his next serve. Rick stretched back his arm and hit a ball that whistled over the net and bounced low, landing inches behind her with sufficient spin that made it difficult to get at or control. The racquet reached the ball, but the ball bounced off at a strange angle, and this time it went out.

"Well, I reckon you wouldn't do either on principle," he said with a grin, knocking the balls across to her for her service. "First game to me." She laughed but easily curtailed it to concentrate on placing her serve to his backhand. "Minx," he said, retrieving the ball.

"Fifteen love. Well, as you seem intent on getting mileage out of my principles, perhaps I should do the same with yours." This time it was his turn to laugh, and he did so as if the idea appealed to him.

"Nice return," he observed, "but you won't score many points from my principles – I don't have any."

Her next serve wasn't quite so accurate, so he reached it, but his return still wasn't as powerful as from his forehand. She had found his weakness. "On the contrary," she puffed. "I have observed a few admirable qualities in you." Then they battled silently for the point, which she eventually took.

"Stop changing the subject. I believe the issue was your principles, though I must admit you have me intrigued," he teased as she pocketed the balls for her next service. "So go on – tell me what you think are my virtuous principles."

"Thirty love," she reminded him before adding, "Virtuous might be a bit strong." She had been more intent on getting her line in than placing her serve, so it hit the net. She tried again, and this time it whistled past him on his backhand to land three inches from the line. He missed it. She could hardly wait to declare forty love, but she did until she had said, "I didn't say virtuous! Let's just say that I have seen some admirable qualities in you, though I can't tell whether they are principles you live by – not enough evidence for that. But that is forty love, I think." She emphasised her victory with only the slightest hint of smugness.

She held the rest of her game, much to her delight, and started the next eager to win more, but it was not to be. He won all the rest. As they were changing ends at the end of the first set, he handed her a drink and asked, "So are you going to tell me what these admirable qualities are?" She was not prepared for disclosure so tried evasion. "Well, I am not about to beg," he added. "Know what I reckon your strongest principle is? Never give an inch or lose an argument when you can find an answer." He then proceeded to emphasise his point by serving two aces in succession.

"What gives you that idea?" she queried, trying not to be bothered by his perception as she straightened up after missing the second of these blasts. The nonchalance appeared natural, nevertheless he grinned widely as he swung back his racquet to deliver the third ace.

"It's not an idea. It's a fact, and I have enough evidence to support it. It's what you might call a much-observed fact."

After this, conversation lapsed in favour of concentrating on the game. It followed a predictable pattern: she would fight to save her service; two she held, the rest she lost. She would fight even harder to break his, but she never did; she was lucky most games to win a point. Not only was he faster and stronger, but he had just scored an important psychological point: she did not like to lose. She had spent a huge chunk of her life sparring with awkward pupils and Elinor, and it had never been a secret before, so why it should annoy her so much now that he had discovered it was beyond her. She added it to the growing list of things for which she did not need a reason. Her greatest asset was her intelligence, but he had just put that out of play. Less than fifteen minutes later he declared, "Game, set, and match to me, I believe." He had won in straight sets, 6-1, 6-2. His opponent experienced a mighty unpleasant, unexpected surge of anger for letting him win so easily. He was always going to win – she knew that, and she wasn't annoyed at that. It was the manner of her losing that irritated her. Still, she managed a passable smile and accepted his mock bow as he escorted her from the court carrying all their gear.

Annoyance did wonders for her bravery, consequently before they had gone very far, she had managed to steer the conversation around to transport. It did cause her a moment's concern that she should be able to manipulate things so easily, but it was only a moment. And it was easily cast aside. Were these the skills Shelagh meant? "Would you happen to know the number of the nearest cab service?"

"Why?"

"Because I need a cab!" She almost spoiled it by asking him if he was always so nosy, but she bit her tongue and resisted, smiling as sincerely as she could manage in the circumstances.

"Where do you want to go?" he asked patiently.

"How do you know I want to go anywhere?"

"Because that's usually the reason people want a cab," he pointed out with thinly disguised sarcasm.

"Taneela Park, Billington. Do you know it? I think it is about fifty miles from here."

"Never heard of it, but I know Billington. There's nothing there of any interest."

Right now she was back to having two sets of answers: one was what she would have liked to have said but didn't, and the second the afterthought, which was usually nothing like the first but was generally more polite. This was no exception. That's what you think, was the reply she thought of first. "Shelagh's Aunt Nora," was the eventual answer she gave him. His blank expression told her that he had already forgotten who Shelagh was so there was little chance he would understand who her Aunt Nora was. She supplied the missing information along with the explanation. "And Nora lives in Billington. Shelagh thought it would be nice for me to call tomorrow and say hello. It'd give me something to do, provided I can get there. That's why I need a bus or a cab."

"No buses here this isn't London," he snapped grumpily, shocking her by the abrupt change in his manner. "And cabs are not reliable. Besides, there's not many of them in Wilson. Better take one of the cars in the garage – but not the Ferrari!" he warned. "I daresay Chas might even drive you if you ask him, but if he's not around you'll just have to find it yourself with a map – although maybe not if past performance is anything to go by. Better leave a time for us to call out the rescue squad if you don't come back." She knew she had asked for that, telling him how many times she had been lost. Nevertheless, it still earned him a derisory glare, before they lapsed back into silence.

Rick had never worked out to his total satisfaction what percentage of his unwanted guest's story was true, and what percentage was fiction. His opinion had been changing pretty rapidly. Right now he was more confused than ever. How she could want to spend Sunday with somebody's Aunt Nora when she could spend it with him, was beyond him. No magazine poll had ever asked that question, and there was no way of finding out the answer without him asking. There was no chance he was going to do that, so he had to remain sceptical. Asking would be exactly what she wanted.

Sarah was silent because instead of feeling pleased at the success of her mission, she felt only guilt – until something far more important dawned on her. *If Chas is around?* That distracted her from the burning ethical issue to the infinitely more important, practical one. If Chas wasn't around, would Molly be? And if neither of them were, that would mean she was alone with Rick Dracula Da Santi Rochester, or whoever he was! She tried not to panic. "You said if Chas is around?" she asked more calmly than she felt.

"It's their day off, but they rarely go anywhere. I'm sure he'll be happy to oblige you. Remind me to ask him when we have had a drink. Come on." He was already way ahead of her by now, so she was left to trail behind him wondering how she could get herself out of this predicament. Even more reason to go to Billington!

Chapter Twenty

The door that had been bolted against them last night was wide open. It led through a passage into a huge grey and lemon kitchen flooded with sunlight. Sarah facetiously dismissed it as yet more precincts of Wonderland, but her brief moment of wonder was not missed. Its owner made a point of asking if she approved of it as he searched an outsize refrigerator in search of the orange juice she had requested. The style critic floundered for a moment: she realised that she would have to come clean and admit admiration, or lie. The first option was unpalatable, the second unthinkable. She tried humour instead. "Who wouldn't? It's a bit intimidating for someone used to a ten-foot galley kitchen, but it's very desirable all the same. Swap."

"Well, it doesn't look like we have any juice, but there are oranges, so we could squeeze our own, I suppose." He was easily deterred, though she could hardly believe that there was no juice in a fridge that was big enough to cater for the QE2 on a short journey. He was listing the alternatives when he hit gold and produced the required carton with such a flourish that she was justified in thinking he was expecting applause. *Good boy,* she thought, mentally administering the pat. Even Ali did not demand this much support.

They sat at opposite ends of a small table, predator and prey, temporary truce. Both were silent and apparently concentrating on their drink. Both were wondering what came next. By the time they had finished, he was sprawled out on his chair while she was still sat stiffly upright in hers.

"Molly doesn't like the colour," he informed her casually.

It had all the innocence of general conversation, but she knew it wasn't; she doubted if anyone had ever had an innocent conversation in this house. Her next thought that the housekeeper from hell could hardly be expected to like a sunshine kitchen was never uttered because however delightful the kitchen might be to look at, she had to concede it might not be that delightful to keep clean. It would never cope with chocolate fingers! She tried to express this sentiment with some tact, but it only earned her a blank stare. Wrong move! She backtracked and added thoughtfully, with only a frisson of mockery, "Then again, there are no children here, so I suppose it

306

doesn't matter how difficult it is to keep clean as long as you are not partial to chocolate biscuits." Humour failed to impress him, so she corrected herself properly. "Forget about the swap. I will stick with my own – it is chocolate finger proof. But yours is truly awesome!" It was the second time she'd used that word today. "Maybe I could even get enthusiastic about cooking, if I had one like it. Well, make that occasionally enthusiastic." She might as well have said she didn't like breathing. Explaining her theories about food fuel and time economics took some time. "Am I boring you?" she asked curiously.

"No, not at all," he said, stifling a yawn.

"Then that strange look on your face means that you think I am some sort of a nutcase?"

"I didn't say that, either."

"You didn't need to," she pointed out truthfully, ignoring the Cheshire Cat grin that contradicted his words and confirmed hers.

Glamorous women had fallen over themselves to cook for him in this kitchen, yet here was this mousy little schoolteacher dismissing her biggest chance yet – with sarcasm! "Well, I guess I will have to make us dinner then, or we could starve," he said wearily. As expected she protested that was not what she had meant, or said. In the end after some debate, they compromised: they would do it together. This agreement provided her with a legitimate opportunity to ask questions about Molly's sudden absence. "Don't fret! We only have to do this once. They are back for dinner tomorrow, and they are staying right here, so you won't even need to be alone with me," he said, moving his chair closer to hers, and prompting her to move hers away swiftly. "So, if I promise there will be no repeat of last night, can we call a truce? I am tired of your weird word games."

"That's fine by me," she assured him calmly; mentally making a note to say what she meant in the future. He had this uncanny knack of seeing through subterfuge even when she tried to be clever and disguise it. Not knowing what else to do, she excused herself to go write letters to her mother and the girls, emphasising, "I daresay it will keep me busy for the rest of the afternoon."

It had been agreed that they would eat at six thirty, but her assurances that she would be on time to help prepare this meal amused him. "We'll see," was all he said.

As she had committed herself to the letter writing, she sat down on her bed to do exactly that. Both letters were filled with lengthy, detailed descriptions of all sorts of minor things that had happened recently. Neither version contained a single word about the momentous events of the last twenty-four hours. She sealed both envelopes carefully, fully aware of the cover up she had manufactured. It bothered her. She hadn`t exactly told lies, just not told the whole truth. Good job it wasn`t in a witness box. She stretched out on the bed to try to justify herself some more. They would only worry if they knew the whole truth. She realised it would be a mistake to lie down, but lethargy made her disregard all of her half-hearted rebukes and she made herself comfortable while trying to make some sort amends for her sins by recording the last twenty-four hours truthfully, exactly as it had happened, in her journal. The pen continued moving for a short while after her brain had retired, its graceful squiggles embellishing her usually neat handwriting in a fashion reminiscent of a two-year-old's efforts at copying.

She awoke clutching her head though it was her heart that was racing. She looked around. No card guards, no mad duchess screaming, "Off with her head," no chocolate fingerprints on kitchen cupboards, and no white rabbits in dinner jackets dangling a gold Rolex in front of her nose berating her poor timekeeping. It had all been a bad dream. This place was getting to her!

She had showered and was fastening the buttons down the back of her only dress when she remembered Elinor's acid comment mocking this very dress. "An Alice in Wonderland frock for big girls who should know better." Elinor had hated it, of course, and she had made it very clear why that was. "Not enough on show to attract even Len!" But despite Elinor`s derision it had been her favourite thing to wear until right this very minute. She had been joking when she had said this place was like Wonderland. Becoming Alice had not been intended as part of it! It was not funny! A Shakespearian heroine should not end up in a children's story – least of all a nightmare version of a children's story! Julie had always been a little afraid of the book, and now she understood why. It did have some dark moments. Worse still, other parallels now danced beguilingly in her head. So was the dream a warning? Could she end up losing her head if she didn't wake up? Her entire existence had become so muddled these last twenty-four hours that she was in no state to decide. She did decide to change the dress, or at least she had until the school teacher in her intervened with a timely, no-nonsense reprimand, so she obediently refastened it and twirled silently in front of the mirror, contemplating her decision. Surely this could not warrant the same result as last night's choice. It was definitely not sexy. It was rather demure, exactly the same as it had always been, but did it look … well, better than usual? Did *she* look better than usual? She left the dressing room resolutely refusing to consider why it mattered how she looked.

"Pity we didn't have odds on you being on time," Rick said as she entered the kitchen. Her excuses were lame. "I was beginning to think you had gone to sleep rather than risk my cooking."

She did not want to give him an opportunity to back her into another corner so she admitted to the sleep but confined her explanation to it being the effect of too much strenuous exercise, before she concluded cheerfully, "Now, what can I do to help?"

He turned and whistled softly. "Your being here does that."

Sarah was no more used to male compliments than she was to talking with rabbits, so she flushed deep crimson: there was none of this in the original version of Alice. "You are flirting with me," she scolded, sounding more like the duchess than Alice, but in spite of her stern voice she was a little unnerved to find that her stomach was performing its own unbidden response.

"Is that a crime too? Flirting with you?"

"Yes. You promised not to!"

He said something about her being the strangest woman he had ever met, but it wasn't clear whether that was meant as an insult or a compliment, so she didn't reply and remained worried.

"Why be afraid of a simple compliment?" he asked.

"I am not afraid! I just don't like flattery."

For some reason not entirely clear to himself, he chose not to compound her embarrassment. "Then why are you afraid of me?"

"I am not afraid of you either," she responded too quickly. "I am thirty-five. Why should I be afraid of you?"

He had no inkling of the possibility of people losing their heads, or rapists, or murderers for that matter, so he answered back with the only line he could think of. "But, you are."

She didn't answer at all this time; because she didn't know how to. She shook her head vigorously. "I am not afraid of you," she repeated adamantly. "Why should I be?" Was this the third or fourth untruth today?

"You sure?"

"Positive!" The fifth passed without the slightest hesitation. Remnants of conscience made her qualify it. "Okay, I am a bit wary. But that's not called being afraid – it's called being sensible."

"How come?"

"What? How come it's called being sensible?" She did her best to explain tactfully about being a woman alone, and that sometimes meant that people got the wrong idea about one's intentions. He didn't disagree, which was a nice surprise. "You seem to have a fair understanding of what I mean," she concluded cruelly.

"Would I be one of them?" he asked, the humour in his eyes mocking his offended tone.

She answered as straight as she could. "You would know that better than I. Anyway, as I was saying, I try to avoid getting into difficult situations – besides which, flattery makes me feel uncomfortable."

"Except it wasn't flattery," he said seriously. "It was a simple and truthful compliment. There *is* a difference, you know."

Rather than prolong this distasteful discussion, she smiled and turned the conversation back to more prosaic matters. "I thought this was supposed to be a joint effort. I have done nothing yet. Where is the salad? I will sort that." Amazingly, he let her off the hook, and she was grateful for that. He shrugged and returned to cooking his steaks so there was silence for a few minutes apart from the noise of chopping and the hiss from the steaks under the grill. Eventually he pointed out that had he cooked the steaks for six thirty, they would have been cinders by now. It was a generous attempt to return the conversation to safer ground, and she grabbed at it, muttering another equally banal comment about not being habitually late. "My best excuse is to blame your bathroom." He grinned his Cheshire Cat grin, but she missed that because she had her back to him.

"Gee, I'm glad something in this house throws you!" he observed comically.

She blushed, but he missed that and only heard the fierce denial. "It doesn't throw me!" she said emphatically, totally missing the humour.

"No?"

"No! I just like it, that's all."

"Same thing. You're admitting to liking something very sensual."

"No, I am not!" She sighed. "I just like being clean! Change the subject."

"Okay. Did your divorce really hurt you that much?"

"That's not the sort of subject I had in mind," she said equally bluntly. He didn't fight back. That was unnerving, but she had forgotten he was a tennis player and knew how to place drop shots. It helped that she didn't have to look at him and so she talked directly to the lettuce. "But if you must know, of course it did. Don't all divorces?"

Because she had answered at all, he ignored her request for the change of subject. "Nope, don't reckon they do. Round here people collect 'em like trophies!"

"I don't live round here," she pointed out politely, "and I wouldn't want to collect any more. It's not a trophy – it's a scar." It was the sort of statement destined to kill any conversation stone dead, and for a few minutes all communication was confined to the absolutely essential. Sarah would have been happy to have kept it like that all evening.

Eventually he did slide in another comment. She ignored that by reminding him that he should baste the steaks as he turned them, which gave him grounds to observe, "So you can cook, then. He didn't divorce you because you starved him. Sorry – take no notice of me. Some of my jokes are not funny." But he wasn't that sorry because a minute later he threw in another comment in much the same vein. "So if you fed him, what did he go short of?" She didn't answer that, either. "Sorry, I know how bruising divorce can be, and new wounds open up easily. Hey, I am sorry."

The shock of finding he could make a genuine apology was at least equal to the discomfort his last comment had caused. She snapped, "Forget it," without much consideration, but then she ruined it by asking, "What makes you think it's a new wound?"

"Because it still hurts."

"So does it have to be recent to still hurt?"

He turned to look at her, but her back was bent over the worktop as she administered to the lettuce. "People usually recover fairly quickly," he ventured. It was the way she acknowledged his explanation that made him realise that hers wasn't recent at all. "So how long ago was it?"

"Long enough," she said soberly, sweeping all the ingredients from her board into a bowl.

"Except it's never long enough?"

She turned to face him, the dressing she had been mixing for the salad still in her hand. "No, it's never long enough," she admitted, meeting his gaze before turning away to hastily administer her dressing to the salad like a priest administering absolution. "I hope you like a lot of vinegar in your dressing; my hand slipped."

"Hey, I shouldn't have asked that, either. Sorry."

"So why did you?"

"Comparing notes."

"You are divorced?" She had tried to make it sound natural. She had failed because she was thinking, why am I not in the least surprised by that?

"Years ago. Lot of water under my bridge since then. Steaks are ready."

They carried the steaks and overdressed salad to the table like sacrificial objects in solemn processional silence. She was considering whether this last piece of information should be seen as progress or warning, and he was wondering why he was telling her stuff which was common knowledge. All his exes had known he had been married; all the women he had ever met had known. They had all known his territory. But what if she didn't want what all the others had? There was only one other reason he could think of: she was a journalist! That was worse than the devil himself; even overly persistent fans were minor irritations compared to some of the things journalists got up to. He returned to his silent sulks, leaving her free to speculate on the more difficult aspects of their communication.

"Our experiences might be different, but maybe the hurt's the same," she offered finally in a heroic attempt to restart some sort of conversation.

He grunted. "Tell me what happened, and we'll see."

"Twelve months of blindness followed by five years of hell."

He almost smiled at that. "Sounds familiar, so maybe it's the experiences that are the same, and the hurt that's different."

She shook her head and clarified as best she could. "It didn't start out like that. It started out ..."

"With moonlight and roses?" he proposed.

"Something like that. Certainly high hopes and, dare I admit, optimism."

"So what changed?"

She had absolutely no desire to give him any details, and so she merely said, "It just did, and that changed me." He repeated her last words as a question, so she went for damage limitation and closure. "I think anyone who says that divorce didn't change them is a liar or a fool."

It didn't sound like closure. If she had been trying to provoke a reaction, it did seem a good place to start. He half choked on his wine, but he recovered enough to say, "That's strong stuff." It wasn't that clear whether he meant the wine or the comment.

She went for the latter. "Well, divorce is such a huge thing that it has to affect people."

"Isn't that just your experience?" he asked more gently. "Your hurt? Some people might not care."

She shook her head vigorously this time. "I can't believe that. They may not care but it still hurts. That's non-negotiable. Maybe it hurts some more than others, and maybe it hurts in different ways, like you say, but it always hurts." She was thinking about Elinor but did not say anything except, "And it's the hurt that changes people, though I take what you say about degree, because it obviously didn't hurt you enough to stop you from trying to seduce women." She had not intended it as a rebuke, merely humour, but Elinor was right, she wasn't sophisticated enough to get the tease right, and it seemed clear he hadn't taken it the way she had intended, so she added the apology out of habit.

"I suppose I asked for it," he admitted with a smile and an amazing amount of good grace considering the insult she had just handed out.

"I am sorry," she repeated. "That was insensitive of me."

"If it's okay for me to be insensitive, I daresay it's okay for you, too."

She smiled slightly at that and caught his eye before looking away quickly. "I know I'm right about me," she conceded. "Divorce altered me. Maybe you are right about the rest, I am just being presumptuous."

"I expected a better fight than that."

"What is there to fight over, except scraps?"

After a few minutes of general conversation, he returned to the subject of divorce. The directness of his questions unnerved her, because she still had no wish to tell him anything at all. "It's personal," she said finally, paying very careful attention to her steak as she said it.

"No therapy?"

She laughed easily at his dramatics and agreed. "No therapy. Unless you count two six-month-old babies and plenty of hard work as therapy."

"Not what I meant," he pointed out. "I didn't think anyone got through divorce without therapy these days. Out here they don't. Most are stuck in it for life."

"And you?"

"I escaped. Couldn't afford it at the time," he said blithely. That was food for thought. She wanted to know more, but he offered nothing.

"Correct me if I am wrong," he said slowly, "because mental arithmetic was never my strong point, but you told me the girls are ten now?"

"I did? When?"

"Last night. And if they were six-month-old babies when this divorce happened, it must be more than nine years ago. You have been divorced that long, and it still hurts!"

"There is a time limit to regret and pain?" she shot back.

"No, of course not."

"That's okay, then."

"Most people have got over it by ten years. You know, the forgive and forget thing," he suggested.

"I didn't say I hadn't forgiven, did I?"

"No."

"Then please don't presume," she said primly. She reached for the water to pour another glass and added, "I forgave Tony years ago. It's forgiving *myself* that is more difficult."

"Why is that?"

"Lots of reasons. I don't think I want to discuss any of them right now."

"Is that why you are so hostile?"

Sometimes in conversations, people ask a question that is so unexpected that it is able to get behind even the best defences. This question did that to hers. "What do you mean, hostile? I am not hostile! Am I?"

He put his fork down and studied her with a mixture of curiosity and wonder. "You say the strangest things," he admitted, "and you ask the strangest most unbelievable questions."

"Why do you say that? I don't understand you."

"Well, that makes two of us!" he acknowledged, returning to his dinner. "Steak okay?"

"Yes, it's excellent, thank you."

"More the butcher than the chef," he said, raising his glass.

For a second she wondered what to do or say, and then she returned his toast. "To modesty, then?" she asked impishly. "See? Even you have some!"

This time he laughed outright, and she relaxed a little, hoping that this might lead to a change of subject and get them back to discussing safer things like farming or the weather.

It was not to be. "So what makes you different?"

"Different? Different to what?" she asked. That was definitely hysteria.

"Other women."

"Am I?" she said, struggling to control her emotions. Up to now Elinor had been the only person who had said this to her face.

"I would say so – put money on it."

"Oh!"

"You don't sound pleased about that," he noted. She was only used to Elinor telling her she was different when it was never meant as any sort of compliment, so it was beyond her current capacity to think there might be more than one explanation. He continued. "Okay, what's different about you since your divorce, then?"

Her sigh of relief was followed by a nervous smile; if that was all he had meant it was fine, and she quite forgot that she had told him not five minutes before that she did not want to discuss any of it. "Well for a start, I think I am kinder." She reconsidered that upon seeing his grin reappear. "Though you might not think so after some of the things I have said to you," she added quickly. "But I promise you my whole attitude to life has changed. I try to be kinder to myself, too, though I suppose all the years of being on my own has toughened me up, made me a bit pig-headed and stubborn …"

"No!" he said in mock dismay.

"Is it a disappointment to find out I know my failings? Or that you are not the first person to notice them? In fact most of the men I know think exactly the same – and some of the women, too," she admitted wryly. "Elinor says I am too bossy for the men and not organised enough for the women – loser all round. Although I promise you I am a coper, one of life's natural survivors. I'm a bit battered and bruised, but I'm a survivor all the same."

"An optimistic survivor at that!"

"Most of the time," she acknowledged, smiling naturally for the first time.

"So how come you never remarried? Most people do."

"Don't know," she said, losing her smile instantly, "but I have probably been on my own too long now to swallow silly attentions from shallow men, so maybe I never will. That's not men's fault, it's mine." Rick said nothing, but as she did not clarify whom she had been referring to as shallow men, he was less than satisfied. To end it all she declared in quotation mode, "So, '*What's gone and what's past help, should be past grief!*' That's from *A Winter's Tale*," she informed him primly. It explained nothing but it tidied up a difficult conversation that had become far too personal and maudlin for her liking.

They finished dinner discussing the sort of things that she wished they had kept to from the beginning. She wanted to know more about the history of this part of California, and once she had got him started, he turned out to be an interesting and knowledgeable raconteur. He was able to make her laugh, then shiver with horror, or shed a tear at some of his more tragic tales – and all within the space of half an hour. Without realising it, she relaxed and sat with both elbows on the table, chin cupped in hands, listening intently. The instant he stopped, she corrected herself and stood up, anxious to hide her gaffe by gathering the dishes together. She did admit, "That is so fascinating. I shall see it with different eyes now. Thank you."

"My pleasure," he said smoothly.

A little before eight he led the way back into the living room where last night's little drama had taken place. She had been dreading this moment all day. It seemed likely that she would have to spend at least a couple more hours in tortuous interrogation before she could escape to her room – a predicament that clearly called for her Michael Davies No 1 strategy: keep him busy. If she could achieve that, she felt reasonably sure she could avoid a repeat of last night's little disaster, even if he forgot his promises. Teaching Michael Davies for the last year had to have had some benefit other than suffering for suffering's sake. This might be it! She might even give thanks for him if this worked. But even if every single one of her Michael Davies' tactics failed, she still had her five alpha experiences on which to fall back! Something from all that carefully garnered experience must work here: juvenile male egos always conformed to expectation sooner or later.

Sarah had no need to look any farther than a corner of the living room to find her desired occupation. A chess board had its own spot, and she concluded from this that he must play and dismissing any reservations about the wisdom of challenging someone whose ability was completely unknown, she offered up a silent prayer and issued her invitation. He accepted enthusiastically; extending a warning that this was something at which he was really good, so she should be prepared to lose.

"I think I can take that risk," she conceded more calmly than she felt. "My dad taught me to play, and he was good, but I beat him occasionally. So what happens if I beat you?" she asked carefully, checking her pieces and flashing him a wide grin as she realised the idea of doing just that was not without attraction.

"We'll see," was all he said as he fixed them drinks. All previous concerns about him drinking too much were now outvoted by one single new observation: if he wanted to get drunk and lose, it was not her fault. The phone rang while he was searching for tonic water.

"Get that will you? It will be Chas about tomorrow."

It was not Chas. It was a woman. A woman who announced herself in such a way that it seemed impossible not to conclude this was his girlfriend, or his lover even. Sarah answered her carefully, well aware that he might have a lot of explaining to do, and she reckoned he could do that with less embarrassment all round if he was alone. It was the perfect opportunity for escape.

"Don't go," he said as he took the phone from her, adding. "This will only take a minute, and then I will annihilate you. Set the board up." His other conversation was equally adamant, and it left plenty of room for speculation. "That's fine," he said dismissively, "but right now is not the time for us to be discussing this. Paula, listen to me …" The tirade of abuse was audible, and he held the receiver away from his ear while he regained control. A few seconds later he said peremptorily, "Paula, I am going. I will ring you next week. Yes, I promise." Without waiting for any further discussion, he put down the phone.

"Sorry, I couldn't help but overhear some of that," Sarah said. "I hope I wasn't the cause of it." He looked at her for explanation. "I mean, she wasn't…upset because of me answering the phone, was she?"

He shook his head. "No, forget it. It's nothing to do with you. Come on, let's play."

They picked for play, and she lost again. She knew from the tennis match he would never be gentleman enough to give way. Right again. She'd had a suspicion it might not be that easy playing against him, but as she was now more concerned with wondering about his relationship with the woman on the phone than considering her game plan, it was more difficult than she had expected. At the centre of her curiosity was the simple fact that she knew very little about him – well, except his name was Rick -he drove like a maniac, wore a Rolex watch, lived in this wonderful but mad house, grew oranges, wasn't married, had been divorced, was an authority on Californian history, swam like a fish, and looked as good in tennis whites as he did in a dinner suit. Oh, and he could still be related to vampires but probably wasn't a rapist – and hopefully he played chess a lot less effectively than tennis. The rest of him was fertile ground for a lively imagination, and hers qualified on that score. As he was magnificently reluctant to talk about himself there must remain ample scope for conjecture -unless she asked, and as she had absolutely no intention of doing that, curiosity would have to remain unsatisfied. Besides, she told herself firmly, what would you do if you found out something you would rather not know? Such as ...? Those original thoughts of villainy were no longer quite as permissible because he was a nice man – well, nicer than she had thought.

Because of her lack of concentration more than her lack of skill, her opponent won as easily as he had said he would, and she was left smarting with embarrassment, berating herself for losing within half an hour. An absolute beginner could have done as well! Of course, he had to point out that he had warned her how good he was. It was more than sufficient to make her abandon about any ideas for a rematch. Time to change tactics! On to the second Michael Davies strategy: praise. This was more difficult than number one because the praise had to be truthful if it was to work, and apart from him being kind and generous, which she considered she had already overdone, she knew very little about him, except of course the things she would rather forget.

"I love this painting," she said, alighting on a potential subject. "I can almost feel the heat. Did you have it commissioned?"

"Suppose so. I did it."

Sarah experienced a shock not unlike finding out that Michael Davies could make a bookcase. Her response was similar also. "Really?"

"No need to sound so disbelieving! Art is not the exclusive property of the penniless soul, you know. I paint for pleasure, a bit like you and your sketching, or perhaps it's more like you and your tennis: it's emotional release. Portrait is my strong point, but the house is okay. I painted it the first summer I was here. I was still in love with it then." Before she could pursue that, he added, "If you're interested, I will show you my studio sometime, but not now because I can tell what you are thinking. But while you are doing nothing else, I have just had a great idea ..."

"You have?" Shock was outranked by sarcasm, but then, Michael Davies had never offered to solve her problems. His American counterpart nodded and produced a sketch pad and pencils from behind a nearby sofa. "A premeditated great idea, perhaps?"

"And yours wasn't?" he countered. She looked at him with a little more respect after that. So they had both spent some time thinking about acceptable ways of passing the evening. Could that be counted as progress, or was this just another game? Her Michael Davies experience did try to warn her it might be, but before she could answer or object, he had positioned her on a nearby chair and instructed, "You can keep your clothes on, but sit still and look this way."

Small talk was difficult, so she sat quietly and thought. After twenty minutes she complained that her neck was beginning to ache. "Price of being a muse," he said without sympathy. "I thought you would understand that– the guy provides the means and the woman the inspiration."

There were several witty answers to this; she ignored all of them in favour of a humourless rebuke. "I hope you are not suggesting that we are living together!"

"Would I dare?" he challenged. "But this way, you sitting for me for half an hour can be payment for me rescuing you and keeping life and limb together until the cavalry gets here Monday. This way, you don't owe me a thing. Seems a pretty good deal to me."

"You do have a slight tendency to over dramatise things," she said much as if she were addressing the real Michael Davies. All the same, she carefully avoided mentioning Indians or vampires, or anything remotely like them.

He raised his eyebrow again in exactly the same way she was used to doing and carried on drawing. "Me, over dramatise? No way! Am I the one who quotes Shakespeare at the drop of a hat?"

"You noticed?"

"Some. I've probably missed loads."

"You haven't said anything."

"Is that a required part of the game?"

She laughed suspiciously. "No, of course not – and it's not a game. I thought you were drawing."

"Is that permission?"

Her nod was pending thinking of a better answer. It came eventually. "I don't suppose it would matter that much if it wasn't permission, would it? I think you are used to getting your own way – *too* used, perhaps?" The little caveat had been added quite deliberately to tease him and to divert him from pursuing the Shakespeare enquiry. She was finding the whole conversation strangely difficult.

Fortunately, he swallowed her bait and answered simply. "Yep, I know I do."

Half an hour stretched into forty minutes and her back was really beginning to feel the strain when she complained again. Sitting in the same position for so long was not easy. The loud groans were supposed to make him aware that she had sat for well over the agreed time.

"Don't move!" It was another of those blatant commands, but he realised he had been corrected about this before, so he tempered his imperative with a half-hearted, "Please!" It made her smile all the same. At least he was trying. "Five more minutes," he pleaded, throwing in one of his best smiles for good measure.

When he signalled that he was finished, she ignored her aches and pains and stretched out quickly as she crossed the room to inspect his work. In her haste to see what he had produced she even forgot that she was supposedly committed to preserving the maximum distance between them at all times. What she saw amazed her. "Oh!"

"Don't sound so surprised!" He obviously did not share her difficulty. "Or did you think I was lying when I said that I had painted the house? You did, didn't you?"

She coloured slightly. It would be too awful to admit to that, even if she had thought it only briefly, or that it had found some willingness to be accepted. She was anxious to avoid the entire subject, so she laughed and exclaimed, "You flatter me too much, though!"

"On the contrary, you underestimate yourself. You have beautiful eyes."

"There you go again," she warned, shaking her head to show disapproval, though she didn't qualify that until she had retreated to a safe distance, then she declared. "Sir," and facing him, she placed her hands on her hips and raising her practiced eyebrow, bowed briefly and proclaimed, "*'tis my occupation to be plain.'*"

"Okay," he said with a sigh. "I guess that's another bit, so go on, tell me where it's from. I can see you want to."

Her laugh was sheer delight. No one had ever asked to be told where a quote came from before – they usually didn't want to know, even when she told them.

"I said something funny?" he asked.

"No," she said, recovering herself. "Just that you read me like a book." That was a slip.

"Not difficult," he pointed out. "You are a volume of Shakespeare."

"Ouch – that's a bit cruel, isn't it?"

"Is it? I would have thought that would be one bit of flattery you might like."

His ability with the quick rejoinder was quite inspirational. It dazzled her. She smiled slowly. Elinor meet your match, she thought. He was certainly too clever for her. No, he wasn't – what was she thinking of? "It's from King Lear," she said thoughtfully, trying to get back to stuff she could handle.

"Do you know every line of every play that this guy wrote?"

In spite of her decision to play serious, she clapped her hands and laughed delightedly. "Oh joy, how I wish I did! But no, I'm afraid I don't," she sighed. "I cannot claim such skill, much as I might like to."

"Well, it sure as hell seems like it," he said, watching the smile dance in her eyes. He wondered what else he could say that would make it dance again.

"If you really want to know," she said as seriously as if she were about to confess some dreadful secret, "I only know a few of his plays really well: the ones that come up on the exam papers year after year."

He nodded. "And the rest?"

"The odd throwaway line that appeals to me."

"Which is *Lear*?" he asked.

"Middle ground."

"Which means?"

"Not known well enough for me to quote huge chunks at you."

"That's a relief."

Without thinking she laughed again and then corrected him. "You didn't let me finish! *Lear* is on next year's syllabus, so I am reading it right now. By this time next year I will be able to quote chapter and verse at …" She stopped.

If he had followed her train of thought he gave no intimation of it except to say, "So, what do I need to be worried about right now? You know the huge chunks?"

As he had asked this seriously, she replied in the same vein. "*Hamlet* and *Twelfth Night,* I reckon – they were this year's A-level texts. Bits of them are still creeping into my everyday conversation without me noticing."

"I have noticed," he replied heavily.

"You have?"

"Probably missed some, like I said, but yeah, I have noticed. And the O-level crowd, what did they study?" She did not answer immediately, prompting further enquiry. "O-level students don't do Shakespeare?"

"Yes, of course they do, but how do you know about O-levels?"

"There's a lot of things I know about. Well, what did they do?"

"*Romeo and Juliet.*"

He laughed. "You want to rehearse that now?"

She wanted to laugh too, but felt too embarrassed until she remembered that the other O-level book had been *Much Ado About Nothing*, so she told him that instead and added innocently, "I suggest that says it all."

"Well, I suggest," he said, repeating her words with exactly the same emphasis, "To do or not to do might be the new question, whether tis nobler of this host to suffer the quotes and misquotes of an outrageous house guest, or to take earplugs against a torrent of Shakespeare, and by so plugging, silence her."

"Ah, but the gentleman doth protest too much, methinks. You never said you knew *Hamlet.*"

"You never asked. Anyway, I don't know him; we are nodding acquaintances, not bosom buddies like you and him."

"Did I tell you the other O-level play was *Much Ado About Nothing*?" she checked hastily, trying to win back some ground.

"You did, but remind me again, no point in two of us wondering what the hell is going on."

"Be serious," she reproved, not really sure what he meant.

"When I was, you took offence. Me saying you had beautiful eyes was serious."

"Just a pity about the rest of me," she quipped unceremoniously.

"'Tis your occupation to be plain, you said, not your nature." There he was again: instant wit, instant line.

She looked up at him and almost smiled. It could not hide her confusion. How come she could not access her usual facility with words right now? How come the space between her ears was filled with scrambled eggs? There was certainly nothing remotely cerebral going on in there, so it was better to stick to the boring lines than trying to be clever and failing. "Thank you, but please stop teasing me."

"I am not teasing you – I am serious."

"Seriously what, though?" she jested. "Short sighted?"

Rick *was* short sighted, and he wondered how she knew that if she really was unaware of who he was. She had to know! So, he had to ask his million-dollar question – the one that might give him the answer to who she was. "Tell me one thing, and preferably without William getting a say: why wouldn't you let me kiss you last night?"

Sarah walked further away. "Not that again!" She had to be on her guard, so she measured her next words as carefully as she had her strides. "You promised me no repeat of last night, so let's just forget it. Please!"

"I never mentioned not asking about it."

"Semantics!" she muttered. "And well you know it."

"That's good, coming from you!"

"I didn't want you to kiss me. That's all."

"Gee, I would never have guessed that! Come on, don't treat me like an absolute imbecile," he said, rubbing his cheek to show he still remembered the explanation in question.

"I don't see why I should answer such a personal question from a total stranger."

"Quite right, I agree," he said thoughtfully. "Though you can hardly call me a total stranger now. I rescued you from an early grave, remember? Then I lent you my bath and clean clothes? And now I am asking politely. Besides, even conversations with relative strangers have to get beyond asking about the weather at some point."

There was a heavy silence. She tried to stare him down, but he only shook his head and smiled that annoying grin, the one that more or less called 'check.' This had to be another variation in that elaborate game of cat and mouse chess, and if he was the cat, there were no prizes for guessing who the mouse was. Keep your distance seemed fairly reasonable advice for any mouse – and as important, stay alert and ignore tempting bits of cheese!

"Well?" he said after a couple of minutes' silence.

"Well what?"

"Well, aren`t you going to tell me?"

This time her sigh was as heartfelt as it was impatient. "Do you never give up?"

"Not till I get what I want. Better tell me, and then we can talk about something else." The cat called check again.

Sarah bit her lip, and then against all her better judgement she started to do exactly what she had cautioned herself against. "Well, if you must know, I don't go around kissing even *relatively* strange men. It is as simple as that." Her words had come tumbling out in a garbled, embarrassed rush, and she knew they offered little defence, so she tried to close the whole discussion quickly. "So now can we change the subject?"

He did appear to think about her request for a brief moment. "Okay… But before we do … I'm not even a relative stranger now. We have exchanged stories about our divorces so we must be at least friendly acquaintances and you slept in my bed, remember. Kiss me now!" Check -a crystal-clear declaration of intent. Face it, or give in!

She shook her head. There was nothing else she could do, she felt unable to trust her voice to say anything else without it betraying her vulnerability. She wished that she had listened to her own advice and never embarked on this, or that she could think of the witty answer right now to end it – the one that would inevitably pop into her head in three or four hours when she no longer needed it. Wishing did not make a scrap of difference, she was too stressed to think of anything remotely adequate. Even William abandoned her in her moment of greatest need.

"Then there is another reason," he said.

The constant bombardment was weakening her resolve and it showed in her snappy reply. "You are playing games with me again," she said, hoping that a reprimand would save her and divert the conversation.

He didn't flinch and instead looked her straight in the eye. "Am I?"

She knew the effect such a look could have on a pupil. This one did the same to her. Thankfully, William rushed to the rescue this time. "Yes! *'You would play upon me, you would seem to know my stops; you would pluck at the very heart of my mystery; you would sound me from my lowest note to the top of my compass.'*"

"Yes, I would," he said soberly, ignoring the quote. "If you would let me."

She had not been at this point for so many years that she had no idea how to handle it, and so she tried deflection once more. "*'Do you think I am easier to be played on than a pipe? Call me what instrument you will, though you can fret me, you cannot play upon me.'*"

"Will saves the day," he quipped. "That *Hamlet* or *Twelfth Night*?"

"*Hamlet*," she said quietly.

"Well, neither Hamlet nor anyone else Will can come up with is going to put me off, and I am not playing games – or at least no more than you with him. But forget last night, I want to know why you won't let me kiss you now."

"No!" she said vehemently, "That is my reason. You are just playing with words!"

"I am playing with words? Gee, that's precious!"

"You know very well what I mean. You might be 'known' to me now, but I hardly consider twenty-four hours' acquaintance to pass for intimacy. You see, as far as wanting you to kiss me is concerned, I don't want you to kiss me ever! I can't think why you would want to, anyway. I don't think we know each other, or even like each other enough for a kiss like last night." Like most other bombs, this one exploded causing devastation and shock.

"You are joking me," he said finally.

"You wanted to know? Now you do, so let's change the subject. How about another game of chess?" Even annihilation at chess beat this sort of exposure.

"Not so fast." He followed her across to the chess table and grabbed hold of her arm to stop her from rearranging the pieces. This time her eyes flashed from his face back to her wrist. This time her message was loud and clear, so he released her. He asked slyly, "So, what if I asked you to come to bed with me then, let me make love to you right now?"

She knew it was deliberate provocation, but it still worked, and she was unable to stem the immediate rush of colour to her cheeks. She struggled to control her emotions as she said icily, "Seeing as how I don't even want you to kiss me, I would have thought that any reasonably intelligent human being would be able to work out that there is absolutely no chance of me agreeing to that. But then, maybe I forget who I am talking to here." The urge to insult him had been too great to resist. It was her last defence before emotion took over. "But if you do need it spelling out, let me do that for you: I am sorry, but that's just not a part of who I am."

He had tricked her into disclosure. Any thoughts she might have had about him not noticing that, lasted precisely two seconds. He got straight to the point. "So, you are one of those battling spinsters, last of the honourable virgins. Sorry, should that be divorced virgins. Is there such a thing?"

"You can be the most appalling bore at times. You obviously have a one-track mind – dirt track!" She realised as she said it that it was a pitiful response, but she couldn't think of anything better, so it would have to do. Emotion had got the better of her intellect once again. "But you are quite right in your quaint assessment if you finally understand that I have personal standards. And by the way, I am not the only one, or the last! And your opinion doesn't say much in favour of you or your friends."

Laughter was never going to heal this breach, but when he had controlled his sufficiently, he said quite seriously, "I have never understood people like you. What on earth makes you think that there is any need for anything other than enjoyment? No, don't tell me – I can guess." He went on to answer his own question before she had a chance to reply for herself. "You will only go to bed with someone you love, right? Tell you what: pretend you love me, and that should solve both our problems. I promise you it will be more than worth your while, although I suppose after nine years, *anybody* should!"

"You are in danger of getting a slap for the other cheek as well," she warned, unable to think of anything else to say that could possibly ventilate her anger. Emotion made her give away even more with her very next breath. "And I wouldn't even go to bed with someone I loved if I wasn't married to them!" She regretted this more than any previous indiscretion, because she knew instinctively that it was the last thing she should have said.

Rick stood and stared, and then he whistled long and slow. "Wow, I take back what I said about Shakespeare being four hundred years too old for you. You are stuck in the middle ages yourself. Incredible, unreal! What is the point of this?" he asked, thoroughly amazed.

"The point of what?"

"The point of all these principles or standards or whatever you call them, apart from frustration of course! No wonder you need tennis!" His remark amused him but left her unmoved. "The rest of the world is happy doing its own thing, and here you are, one voice in the middle of what was the place called? Sodom and Gomorrah? Have you never heard of the sexual revolution? Even nice girls do it nowadays," he promised as he stretched forward to grab her hand to stop her from leaving. "It's not a sin anymore!" he shouted after her as evaded his grasp and walked past him.

At the door she turned and glared back at him, daring him to listen. She had given all her secrets away, and now it was either concede defeat, or stand and defend. She had nothing to lose now, but it had been so long since she had defended her beliefs with anyone other than Elinor that she did not have time to consider whether she could still do it, before she replied acidly, "I am not only person in the world to profess such beliefs.

Okay, I grant you that I might be in a minority these days. But truth is not dependent upon numbers or a popular vote you know. And a sin it most certainly is, whether you or anyone else tells me otherwise." She stared hard at him to reinforce what she considered to be her ace. "'*Who buys a minutes mirth to wail a week? Or sells eternity to get a toy? For one sweet grape who will the vine destroy?*'" Michael Davies tactics might have failed her, but William had not deserted her completely.

The opposition shook his head in complete disbelief, and then he walked off to the other end of his living room, silent. She stayed put, also silent. It was not a comfortable silence, definitely more like the quiet which precedes a storm, than the peace that follows it. "Is it a sin because God says so?" he asked finally. That might have sounded like light-hearted provocation had he not refilled his glass and raised it to her in a mocking salute. What followed showed he had been deadly serious. "The evidence of your friend is inadmissible because I believe he also professed the opposite opinion in other places, though I am not smart enough to be able to quote them at the drop of the hat."

"Well, you seem to know more than one reason," she replied scathingly, deliberately ignoring the Shakespeare argument, which she did not feel up to facing right now. She might have been better taking it.

"You are too much! This is the twentieth century, and nearly the *end* of the twentieth century at that."

"I fail to see what that has got to do with anything!"

"Well, maybe it was okay for people to go around believing in a God prescribing rules for their behaviour when they didn't even understand the natural forces of physics. Life must have been pretty difficult back then, and I suppose believing in God was a sort of primitive insurance policy. A 'do this, don't do that' sort of God must have been quite useful in keeping the peasants under control."

"That's sheer speculation!"

"Well, one thing's for sure, there is absolutely no logic in it. Face it: God is a control mechanism, and that's all he has ever been."

"For an intelligent man, you talk some rubbish."

He might have wanted to pursue that she thought him intelligent, but he didn't, because there was something more important at stake. "So I take it you subscribe to this myth then?"

Sarah shook her head, "I am not sure what I believe about God," she explained wearily, "though I am sure that you are wrong about why some people believe." She hoped this would be sufficient to deflect him from the more personal angle.

"Because you want there to be," he said simply.

"This is getting tedious. Let's change the subject. No – I am going to bed."

"Wait a minute! Why is it always 'let's change the subject' or 'I am going to bed' whenever it gets difficult for you? Let's not change the subject! Don't go to bed! Let's stay with this! Everybody needs something to live for, so what should be more natural than people choosing to follow this being who takes care of everything? I think I might have bought it then as well. But we don't need God and his sins today. He has outlived his usefulness, and we know better."

"We do?" God's defence might have been appointed without much consultation, but as she appeared to be it, she allowed her voice to rise to reflect what she hoped was profound disagreement verging on disgust. "I wasn't aware that science – which is what I presume you are referring to – has all the answers, or has ever claimed to be anywhere near to disproving the existence of God." She dropped her voice, realising that she was sounding more like a defence barrister than the real thing. However, she couldn't resist adding, "What little I do know persuades me that a lot of truly great scientists have been just as convinced of the existence of a Creator, as other lesser folk. His rules have seemed okay to them, sins included."

"Seems like you know a great deal about something you profess to know nothing about."

She shook her head more vigorously and admitted, "No, I don't. But I am open minded, and I am interested and I want to understand, so I will always listen to anyone who will talk to me about what they believe. Anyway, if we have no need of God today, then how come He's still around?"

"That's another of your curious questions," he pointed out, sitting down with another drink. "Habit! Have you never seen people coming out of church on Sunday? It's all habit and hats, and that's all it is."

Whether or not she liked him, she had to admit he had a neat way of putting things that hijacked her admiration: "all habit and hats" was simply the latest evidence of that skill. Her response was mixed because her feelings were the same; half of her wanted to applaud, and the other half to chastise. The applause half would have laughed at his use of language if the disapproving half had not intervened. "How long is it since you went to church then?" He confessed it was some years.

"Well, whether you believe in God or not, there is enough evidence that extramarital sex is a sin – or call it socially disadvantageous, economically imprudent, or just plain stupid, if you can accept that better. Sin seems to cover it all pretty well, though." She reflected on that for a second and could not resist adding what had just occurred to her. "Come to think of it, isn't that a great reason for believing in your mythical being? *He* knew enough to get it right from the beginning! Maybe He was never interested in spoiling people's pleasure. Maybe He knows the inevitable result of immorality, and all He ever wanted was for us was to get it right and be happy!"

"You are seriously weird."

"Maybe, maybe not."

"Will you stop saying that!" he scolded.

"Sorry. Either way, there are lots of people who feel unable to run their lives without having some form of moral standards. What is 'weird' is your senseless suggestion that the rest of the world is quite happy 'doing it', as you say. Dare I mention AIDS? I could rest my case there, but if you want more evidence, take a close look around you. Adultery rocks marriages, breaks homes, shatters lives, and causes poverty and misery for the innocent. Immorality destroys childhood at a swipe. It causes nothing but pain – you know that thing we were talking about before dinner! But let's forget about adultery. Sleeping around spreads diseases and distress that causes heartache, misery, and emotional instability, besides making children think they are old enough to tell the difference between love and lust when they can hardly spell them, let alone understand either." She drew breath, but it could not stop her – this man had crossed the threshold into one of the passions of her life, and she was about to launch into a full-blown lecture on it. Five alpha could have warned him. "And if you think that 'the sins of the fathers' is no more than a quaint expression of that make-believe God of yours, then I suggest that you get yourself away from all this protective padding." She waved her arms around. "And look at the *real* results of all the senseless immorality there is out there in the *real* world." She deliberately emphasised the word real both times. She hardly stopped to draw breath and continued before he could comment. "Then you go look in the poorest inner-city schools at the kids whose divorced and single mothers live on the breadline. Do you know what their home lives are about? Books and aspiration are often alien things only encountered on that strange planet called school. Some of these kids don't know where their next meal is coming from."

"That's an insult to divorced mothers," he said warmly.

"No it's not! It's a cry for help! I work in such a school, and my heart bleeds for some of the kids I teach. And before you say it, I know that I have contributed to those statistics. Do you think I am proud of that? Well, I am not! But I do realise how fortunate I am. I have a good education and so I can earn a reasonable living. Many of the women with kids at my school have no such advantage."

"Isn't that the fault of the education system then, not public morality?"

"No! I have a reasonably good job and so I get by, but for every me there must be thousands more, less fortunate. Education isn't to blame – it's the scapegoat! Education masks the devastation that the public acceptance of immorality has caused in my family. You still doubt me? Then go and talk to my mother who spends her life worrying about me. Go talk to my children, who don't know their own father, and then come and see me at the end of the day when I have run myself ragged trying to hold down a job, keep a home running, and be both parents." She sank into a nearby chair. "You come tell me then education saves the day! It doesn't because it can't. It helps us eat, but that's all." He had begun to think she must be through because she was quiet for a whole minute, but it was a mistake because then she added almost apologetically, "If you go into any big town or city to the poorest areas and look on the street corners, I guarantee that you will find gangs of children, and some of them are not much older than my girls. They should all be home; instead, they are out looking for adventure, kicks, and eventually for sex or drugs, or both. That is how it works these days, is it not?" She shook her head wearily. "They must all have been in school at some time; maybe some of them still are. So how come education isn't saving them? Just what chance do they have? Who helps them see the risks they are taking with their lives? No one! Well, unless you count teachers and our so-called sex education in schools! But what about life preparation?" she asked forlornly. "Worst of all, you look at the fourteen-year-olds who become child mothers and are then deserted by the equally childish, equally incapable fathers. These girls are left to struggle to bring up another generation of deprived, poverty-stricken children, and I don't just mean no money. Some of these kids think good parenting is about providing Nike trainers for two-year–olds, and we let them go on thinking that. Do they not matter? Should we not be held responsible as a society because we see such things as acceptable?

Last night you asked me if I enjoyed teaching, and I told you I did. That's true, but there is one bit I hate. Do you know what it is? How could you? Well, let me educate you! Are you ready for this? It is the inevitable recognition, every time I get a new class, of the girls who will be pregnant by the end of it. I try to stop myself doing it, but sometimes it is so blatantly obvious that there is no escape from it, and worst of all is the feeling of utter helplessness to do anything to prevent it. Education gets blamed, of course, but education has little to do with it. It never stood a chance – the damage has already been done. And I have to watch that happening, year after year and in life after life, because despite my best efforts, it happens to someone in at least one of my classes every year. This year I taught two sisters in different years. Both are clever. The oldest is plain awkward and a complete pain, but she has plans to go to college and make something of her life. I *hope* she succeeds. The youngest is fifteen in September and she left school in July four months pregnant. No qualifications, no ambition except a council flat, no future. Nothing anyone at school could have taught her would have made one iota of difference. And I mean nothing, Shakespeare included. Do you know how that feels to watch, or be part of? Do you hell as like! And I doubt you care."

The anger that had flared so rapidly passed just as quickly. "I am sorry, I should not have sworn at you. I hate it, but it's no excuse for swearing. Can't you see what I am getting it?" Rick looked at her blankly, still wondering what she meant by the apology and trying in vain to identify any swearing. She attempted reconciliation. "Perhaps it's different in America," she said morosely, "but back in England the numbers of girls who live to get pregnant, get a council flat, that gets them away from home, is a national disgrace. They see it as a career choice! It would be funny if it wasn't so pathetic. And before you say it, I know that immorality is not the only cause of such poverty or heartbreak, but it is a cause that hides itself well, and it colours despair darker with every generation enmeshed in its clutches. This isn't freedom – it's slavery!"

Whether Rick agreed or not, he withheld the sarcastic comment he was about to make. His silence gave her confidence to finish the lecture.

"Perhaps you can tell me how I can teach these children the self-respect that really frees them, the sort that helps them to make something of their lives, and then their children's lives. Can you tell me how I do that when most of the adults around them have abdicated any sense of moral responsibility and are doing the exact opposite? You tell me how I stand a chance against that." She didn't notice that she didn't actually give him a chance to tell her how, but after all, this was her lecture. "I'll tell you how. The only way I know how, by being true to who I am, by living by my standards. I don't influence all of them, but occasionally I win one here and one there. That's how I do my bit: I change the world for one or two at a time. So go on, laugh if you want to. I reserve the right to think, do, and say as I believe."

Even as she finished saying it, she remembered about the gossip about her and Len last Christmas – the gossip that she had done nothing about and she had let die a natural death because it was easier and didn't involve her in declaring things she knew others would find strange. Right now she felt more than a bit ashamed of that, and somehow or other she had to find a way to admit to it before he started to think she was some sort of superhero. "Have you ever heard of a man called Robert Letchworth?" she asked.

"No, is he another schoolteacher?"

She shook her head. "He was American, but I don't know what he did. I had never heard of him until I saw a sign about him in a park in New York State. The Indians knew him as 'the man who always did right'. Isn't that wonderful?" He looked amused, but she overlooked that. "If you could choose what you would have people say of you, I can think of nothing better. But I don't want you to think I am a relative of his, because I'm not. I am a bit of a coward, really; I don't always do everything I should. I compromise sometimes – though not on my personal standards," she explained hurriedly in case he mistook her meaning, "but in defending them – you know, 'the anything for a quiet life, let someone else lead the revolution,' attitude." For appeasement she added, "You wouldn't have got such a lecture if you hadn't provoked me so much." As an apology it fell rather short, but she didn't think he deserved one anyway. As explanation it sounded just about right.

"It was very good," Rick said indulgently. "You should have been a social worker or a politician. Well, maybe not a politician. But if I remember right, we were talking about us, and I don't see what any of that has to do with us."

"A typically selfish reply!" She stopped herself short and smiled. "There I go again. Sorry! Please understand that I only get so fired up because it matters so much. At least you are honest, and that does not deserve my judgement." A second later she added, "Surely you must see it would be necessary to say; well, okay, you can be immoral if you can afford the consequences. Social and moral behaviour just doesn't work like that. I don't suppose your immorality would ever affect you unless you were unfortunate enough to pick up some nasty bug. It is quite disgusting, but some don't recognise rich people are different. This HIV bug? Now, that's really immoral; it refuses to go away however much money one has!"

"I thought I'd had the lecture," he said, yawning to try to change the subject.

"This isn't a lecture, it's a plea! It can never be about just you and me. It's always about all of us, the nameless billions of people out there."

"I hadn't thought of inviting an audience."

The withering look she gave him was eloquent enough, and he got the message. "We have an audience to every action," she said. "Have you ever read John Donne? There is a piece of his that explains it better than I can. I can't quote verbatim."

"Now that is a surprise!"

She ignored his comment. "*Send not to ask for whom the bell doth toll, it tolls for thee, for each is a part of the main … every man's death diminishes me.*" She added, "I think that Donne is trying to say all individual action impacts on everyone else, and so what we do is important. We have a collective responsibility to care for each other, and that means more than just charity donations; it means that it's up to us and others like us who have the influence, or the money or the power, to at least try to reverse the damage that people like us caused in the first place."

"Hallelujah!"

"Don't patronise me! Only yesterday you said you didn't know any happy people. Now you are trying to tell me the world is happy being immoral. I suggest you sort your story out, because right now it doesn't add up."

"How do you figure that?"

"Simple! Immorality is the biggest lie of all. It promises you freedom, and all it delivers is slavery, pain, and suffering. It is wicked, and when did wickedness ever have anything to do with happiness?"

"Wicked, huh?" He repeated the word aloud at least a couple of more times before he said, "That's a word I haven't heard in a long time."

"You may not have heard it, but it doesn't stop us practising it. When I told you I was happy, I was speaking the truth. Happy doesn't mean I don't have problems, or that I live in an fairy world of constant pleasure. That's not happiness."

"It's not?"

"No, of course it's not – and stop sending me up," she declared shirtily, exasperation verging on desperation. "You must know happiness is something else. Happiness is …"

"A cartoon?"

"That neither," she said, but she did relent enough to smile a little. "I think happiness is a state of being that isn't dependent upon externals."

"No Ferraris?"

"No Ferraris."

"How about tennis courts?"

"None of them, either."

"Whirlpool bathtubs?"

She laughed and shook her head. "Not even them!"

"How about horses?"

After her comments at lunchtime, this was a particularly devious bit of questioning. She smiled genuinely as she admitted almost convincingly, "Not necessarily. I only know one thing for sure: happiness was never down to wickedness, and it never will be. But please don't think I meant the other things you mentioned are always the product of wickedness, either," she confessed hurriedly in case he had misunderstood her. "I mean that they simply can't secure happiness by themselves."

"And wickedness?"

"Never can."

"How's that?" he asked.

"I would have thought you would have had enough of my lectures by now."

"So humour me."

She knew this would be a trap, but she had already blown her cover, and there seemed little point in pulling back now. "I can't deny wickedness can bring you pleasure, comfort, luxury, money, possessions, power, and sadly even some people. But it never, ever, includes happiness because wickedness is a means, and I think happiness is a result. Wickedness cannot buy happiness however hard it tries; it is forever outside of its reach – the wrong currency. Never enough! I believe happiness is acquired with a different currency. Do you know what Eudomaides means?"

"Shakespeare again?"

"No, Socrates actually. Eudomaides means the pursuit of virtue. Socrates reckoned the path to happiness was virtue – not a lot different from Jesus or God, really. Have you ever considered how different a society we might live in if we had followed God's prescription for happiness, or even Socrates, instead of the Epicurean one?"

"Which is?"

"The pursuit of pleasure," she said mechanically. "It's the 'me, me, me' philosophy, the one that has got us where we are today. Strange that so few of us recognise it." He didn't have anything to contradict that, which in itself was remarkable, and so she continued confidently. "I know that part of the reason I am as happy as I am is the result of how I feel about myself, and that comes from what I believe, and …"

"I know – you act how you believe," he said, wearily draining his glass.

"That's right. No one makes me. Not Socrates, or even your God. I choose to act that way. Maybe it pleases God - I don't know - but I choose it, - I am responsible. So like I said, if you want to laugh, you go ahead. Just don't expect me to join you."

He didn't laugh, but he didn't have his usual witty answer either. Defiant as ever, he cautioned, "That's just your idea of what happiness is. Other people might find it by a different route."

After all the times he had outwitted her, she weighed this last statement with some legitimate hesitation, because her so far unfulfilled desire to get the better of him had so far got the better of *her*, and though she easily persuaded herself that it was because she wanted him to understand more than she wanted to win, she smiled graciously and smoothed the skirt of the Alice dress as she said a little more patiently, "The last book I read with the girls before I came over here was *Alice in Wonderland*."

That scored a ten for amazement. "You actually read something that wasn't Shakespeare!"

She ignored the jibe. "Have you read it?"

"Can't say I have. Another hole in my education."

"Well, let me remedy that. This is a story about a little girl that goes on a very strange journey to a place called Wonderland." She omitted to tell him of any similarities, except one. "She meets lots of strange characters there including a cat that grins a lot, the Cheshire cat. You would make an excellent Cheshire Cat, by the way," she said generously. "When she gets lost, she sees this cat in a tree at a crossroads and asks it which way she should go from there. The cat grins and asks where she wants to get to, and she says she doesn't know. It replies that it doesn't matter then which way she goes, because all the paths will lead somewhere. We seem to live in a society that asks the same question but expects that all the paths lead to the same place: happiness. They don't – they can't. Even the Cheshire Cat knew that. Eudomaides or pleasure, Socrates or Epicure, the path to heaven or the path to hell. It is not the same destination, so the path must be different, even if you persist in calling it the same. But I suppose if you don't know where you are going, then it doesn't matter which way you go, because all paths still lead somewhere. But I *do* know where I am heading, and I know I can't get to it by the path you suggest, or by any other path than the one which leads to it. To think otherwise is an illusion."

"I think you are the one with illusions. Reality is very different."

"The reality you talk about is not happiness. Whatever it is you have the wrong name for it. Happiness is something very different," she insisted.

"How do you know? How can you be so certain that you are right and everyone else is wrong? All the ills of society are supposed to be down to the inequality of wealth or something like that, aren't they?"

She was no longer afraid or even embarrassed. She looked him directly in the eye and exhaled noisily. He was more difficult than Michael Davies, five alpha, and Elinor all rolled into one – but this mattered. "I don't *know* in the sense you mean know, but I believe it, and I feel it. Yes, I have heard the theory you mentioned, but if that were true, all rich people would be happy, and all poor people unhappy, and that is certainly not the case, is it? It has never bothered me that I am not as rich as Croesus, but it always bothers me when I am not happy." Memories of electric bills and two teaching salaries made her qualify that. "I grant you I have occasionally thought it would be nice to have a bit more money, just enough not to have to worry about bills and such like, but I know money can't make me happy any more than, say, owning an airline would make me like flying. On the contrary, from what I see around me, more times than not lots of money seems to have the opposite effect. Pop stars and the like seem to have more problems, not fewer. I couldn't cope with all that, and I wouldn't want to."

"You wouldn't want to be seriously rich?"

"No."

"Why ever not?"

"I have this thing about it making you more accountable."

"Who to? God?"

"Maybe." She looked across at him and smiled briefly, recognising her argument had come full circle. "Maybe it's to yourself. I don't know. I have never given it much thought. I am never likely to be that rich, thankfully. If you want a serious answer, consult your heart." Speculation was self-contained, and so Sarah was not privy to the effect this declaration caused in him, so she continued unrepentantly. "You are far richer than I am ever likely to be." It was not the follow-up he had been expecting because it stopped short of that much anticipated declaration – the one he was sure she could make. Sarah looked across hoping to find some sign of acquiescence but met only vague indifference. She had picked the wrong fight with the wrong guy, and any such victory was never going to be that easy.

Rick was busy re-examining his second theory: the one about her being a journalist. Some of them held strong beliefs. The ones he usually dealt with didn't, but they were different. So what would a serious journalist want with him? Nobody had been interested in his head for a long while. "You still haven't explained why you are right and everyone else is wrong," he pointed out.

"Yes, I have," she emphasised. "Maybe not very eloquently, but I have done it the best I can, and I am not doing it again, even for you!" It was wearing stuff, and she was quite worn out with the effort she had expended so far. "It's not just me against the world, you know. There are others who think the same, so why don't you ask them or read what they have to say?"

"You counted them recently?"

"Don't believe me, then! I don't care. Check a few good history books, and you will find that as long as men have kept records, there is proof that a high moral code has helped to preserve and improve civilisation – and equally, immorality has been one of the chief reasons for its destruction: Rome, Greece, Babylon. Do you need more?" It was difficult for her to tell whether her words were having any effect. She could have been chastising Michael Davies for not doing his homework; the result was exactly the same. She announced, "I give up!" and finally accepted it was something she should have done a long while ago.

"Why? I thought you were enjoying yourself."

She had to laugh at that, simply because it was impossible not to. "Well, it's far too complicated to explain in any five-minute conversation and I suspect by that look on your face that I am wasting my breath anyway. So, I shall give up, whether you like it or not, because it's like speaking Chinese to someone who doesn't understand the language. Come back when you have a few years to spare and a more adult attitude, and I might try again."

"Ouch! That's a bit below the belt!"

The urge to insult him had been more than she could withstand. His indulgent reply meant he had won again. Her insult had lost it. She offered a practiced apology.

He said, "I still don't see what all this has to do with you and me. Don't you find me ... well, desirable?"

It was impossible not to smile at that. Her thoughts were less kind, though there was only a hint of derision in her voice when she answered whimsically, "That sounds a teeny weenie bit like fifth form vanity. Perhaps like them you need reminding that physical attractiveness has nothing to do with it – or at least it might make it more difficult, but it doesn't change anything. Just what sort of principles would they be if you dropped them for every passing attraction? Principles are principles: they are immutable and don't change whatever is involved, or whatever anyone else may think about them. What you believe in, you internalise -that's what principles are. Someone once said, 'You can't be a hurdler if you give up at the first fence.'"

"Someone other than Shakespeare?"

She nodded but turned away slightly while she blushed, and confessed. "Apart from all that, of course I find you attractive. The fact that you are a clever, manoeuvring, domineering, impatient, vain, sarcastic man may be only the tip of your attractions." It was as near to wilful flirting as anything she had said in the last dozen years or more. Intellectually he was attractive because he challenged her in a way that she enjoyed, and she felt no awkwardness about admitting that. But physically? That was something she hadn't seriously considered until that very moment, and the recognition left her flustered.

Rick brushed off the comment, though it did little to alleviate his increasing annoyance with her, or with himself for being unable to make her see things his way. "You can't tell me you haven't slept with anyone for the last ... how many years since your divorce? Nine, ten?"

This sigh was the biggest so far because it meant she had failed to close the matter. "If you already know all the answers as well as the questions, I wonder why you bother asking me. But if you are interested in my answer, then no, I have not slept with anyone since then. Did I not make it clear that principles are principles? I guess it would be easier for you if I said I have slept with dozens of people? That would make me normal, would it?" She didn't give him time to answer or protest before she added, "As far as I can see, the only advantage in my lying – besides fitting in with your expectations – would be that you wouldn't have to treat me like some sort of freak. On the other hand, maybe principles don't count for much if you don't own up and take the stick that's handed out for having them."

"You haven't felt a thing for ten years? Not even been tempted?" he asked, still stunned.

"I didn't say that." The fact he had to struggle to work out the difference made her smile. "Of course I have," she added gently.

"Then why?"

"'*Tis one thing to be tempted, Escalus, another to fall.' Measure for Measure*," she said simply, realising that if she hadn't been so frustrated by his questions, she could have pulled Shakespeare into the argument earlier. Hopefully William would have the last word.

"You are an absolute nutcase!" A comment that was neither gentle nor kind.

"I have heard that before. In fact I have heard much worse, so if you are expecting me to get upset about it, I am sorry, but I won't."

Such calm acceptance of his condemnation made him laugh at least. "How much worse?" he speculated.

"A *lot* worse," she said soberly, meeting his gaze without hesitation. "Some of it from women."

He shrugged and looked away, and by the time he looked back, she was on her way back to the door. "Okay, I am sorry. Sit down, please!"

She stopped but only so that she could think about her answer before delivering it. "I don't see the point in staying here to be endlessly insulted. Even insults lose their attraction after a while. Besides, what is the point of us arguing like this? I am going to bed, if you don't mind."

"Okay, okay, calm down. Truce? No more arguments!" She raised the sceptical eyebrow, the one that had been getting too much practice recently, but that annoyed him even more and prompted him to add, "After you tell me one last thing."

"And what might that be?"

"Am I the first guy that has tried to get you to change your mind in all that time?"

"No, you are not the first," she said seriously, but instead of telling him about any others, she cleared her throat and came back to stand behind the sofa opposite his. "Let's get one thing straight then before this so-called truce begins yet again. You seem to have this strange idea, though goodness knows where you get it from, that I am doing all this just to annoy you. This has got nothing to do with you." She stared hard at him, daring him to find any deceit in her face or disbelieve her words. "I know that I am here in your house, and I can see that that it doesn't fit very well with what I have been telling you about the standards I set myself, but please try to understand that the reason I am here is also far from normal. If this had happened to me in England, I would have coped very well. You don't believe that either, do you? My vulnerability is misleading – it's due to strange geography. I would have refused your help in England and stuck it out in the van until the storm passed, or I'd have walked to the nearest phone or something. But here? Well, there's so many things that I don't know, and perhaps I let my imagination run away with me a little," she confessed, rather shamefaced. "I was afraid of the unknown."

"Such as?"

She hesitated then offered quietly, "Wild animals?"

He looked up, immediately interested. "Wild animals, eh? What sort?"

"Grizzly bears, maybe? Mountain lions? Alligators? Snakes? I don't know – whatever was out there!"

"Grizzlies, mountain lions, alligators, and snakes, eh?" he repeated the list seriously before grinning ruined his performance. "Well, geography might be Elinor's strong point, but it's certainly not yours, is it?"

"What do you mean?"

"I mean there are no grizzly bears here. North of your friends, or Canada you might find some if you are unlucky, but not here." He deliberately kept quiet about California's black bears. It wouldn't help telling her.

"What about the rest?"

He shook his head. "Mountain lions, nope, not seen any lately. Alligators, 'fraid not."

"Snakes?" she shrieked. This much she knew for certain.

"Probably. Have to ask Chas." He also failed to tell her about the deadly varieties in California in favour of getting his line in.

"What about the one outside the van?" Even as she said it, the truth dawned. "You made it up! You made that snake up, didn't you?" She looked at him in total disgust. "I cannot believe you invented that snake!"

"I needed you to make a decision quick. The snake worked."

"You took advantage of the fact I didn't know what was out there!" she exclaimed, horrified.

"We couldn't hang around all night while you decided what to do. There was a storm heading our way, remember?"

"True. And although you were a stranger, and you could well have been a murderer or whatever" – she thoughtfully avoided the word "rapist" – "I made a quick decision and took you to be a nice man."

"Rescuing a damsel in distress? Gee, you are incredible!"

"What's wrong with that?"

"Nothing, apart from the fact that knights in shining armour are a bit thin on the ground these days. Round here they are about as plentiful as poisonous snakes."

"Then I have been lucky! You have been … well, perhaps not a perfect knight, but a passable one."

"Not by choice."

"That's as may be, but the fact still remains…"

He nodded and interrupted wearily, "Do you always talk like this. I have had enough of your lectures for one night, besides being confused as to whether I am a Cheshire cat or a knight in shining armour."

The urge to tell him he needed her lectures was not easy to resist, so she didn't, but then she relented and added, "I never meant to lecture you or sound 'holier than thou,' and I wouldn't have done either if you hadn't provoked me like you did. You like to sleep around? Go ahead, I can't stop you. You have the right to choose what you do, but so do I, and just because my opinions don't coincide with yours and I happen to be a guest in your house, does not give you the right to expect me to change mine to suit yours."

"You talk too much."

"I know. Let's leave it at that, shall we? I am tired, and it's been a very long day. I am going to bed this time. Good night."

Chapter Twenty-One

There was no sign of Chas next morning. There was only silence and a lazy beetle waddling across her path, but then, it was only five to eight. She was early for once. "Pity no one is around to witness it," she observed to the beetle. Every inch of her frame ached exquisitely. Yesterday's relentless activity was to blame of course – except riding could never be regretted whatever the price, but she did wish she had resisted the tennis. It was too late for any such wisdom, the simple act of walking would be painful for days but compared to the mechanics of sitting down that was a mere inconvenience. Sitting down ranked just below torture and would probably remain like that for the rest of the week. Thankfully, a day with two nice, sedate old people would demand nothing more energetic than breathing, so suffering some measure of discomfort to get there, was a price worth paying to get away from her bigger problem all day.

By five past eight she was wondering whether that son of a Spanish vampire had remembered to ask Chas at all. At ten past, the black Ferrari reversed smartly out of the garage and pulled up beside her. The fact that the son of a Spanish vampire was driving it multiplied her anxiety tenfold.

Rick ignored her startled rabbit look and nodded, "Morning. Hop in," much as if this was routine and he picked her up every day of the week for work or something equally mundane. For once his invitation did not produce the required action, so he leaned across the car and pushed the door open wider, explaining only a little sarcastically, "I know where you want to go, and I know which road will get you there." Before she would relent, he had to smile and urge, "Come on, my Shakespearian Alice, get in! I'll take you where you want to go."

Doubly incapacitated as she was, Sarah did her best to slide in next to him without giving any indication of the pain it was causing. That was not easy; this car had to be the lowest thing on wheels, barring homemade bogeys. Was that why he was doing it? She fastened her seat belt a little too deliberately to compensate for not challenging him. She had scarcely done it before they were away, leaving only the usual cloud of dust behind them. Neither of them had any conversation, but as this was now commonplace, instead of worrying about it, the passenger turned to admiring the scenery.

Who knows, she thought, trying to regain some perspective and her sense of humour, maybe a ride in a Ferrari will restore my credibility with the sixth! Pity the sixth in question had already left! Oh well. No doubt she could use it to impress other worldly students; after all, she now knew that a pick-up truck was not the same as a Ferrari! What could she not do with knowledge like that? Still, it was a pity about last year's class. The thought of impressing the likes of Marcie Hadley was irresistible. Eventually she abandoned the sixth and remembered to ask about Chas, but his answer didn't make much sense, so she went back to watching scenery and imagining the conversation with Miss Hadley.

Speed was an addiction the driver could not easily resist, so he hardly ever did, It was one of the few things that obliterated all his other demons because it was both challenge and therapy – a sort of exorcism by nerve. It was an addiction Sarah's nerves did not share, and had she known of his, she would not have been as calm as she was. Nevertheless, it was the reason they arrived at the Marshalls' a lot sooner than she'd expected, although after his less than polite remarks about her navigation skills, he was lucky to escape without at least one comment about his when he got lost leaving the interstate. Gratitude for the lift saved him, besides which Shelagh had not been exaggerating when she had warned that Nora's was difficult to find.

The Marshalls' house was clear out of town on a back road that had no name and only three houses, one each end and one in the middle. Their house was the farthest away from town. It was a neat, two-storey, wooden building painted grey and white with a flagpole in the front garden. Thankfully, standard American.

"It's nine now. What time do you want picking up?" Her protests were ignored. "Do you never listen? There are no buses out here – this is not London. Five do?" That meant, discussion over, bar the timing."

She realised that, gave in, and nodded as she attempted to climb out gracefully, though that meant she had to grit her teeth to prevent any indication of the pain it was causing from escaping her lips. She smiled grim thanks. A bus would have been a lot more practical right now! She was trying to stoop as best she could to confirm the arrangement and offer proper thanks, but she had scarcely stepped out of the car before he roared off, leaving her standing open mouthed by the roadside.

"Genies do that!" she declared, waving her hand to disperse the dust. "Cheshire Cats are not on record as *ever* disappearing in dust clouds!"

Nora was, in every respect, everything an Aunt Nora ought to be. Not least of her many attributes was a dignified, slow walk and the most welcoming smile on the planet. She administered her usual big hug while enquiring how her visitor had arrived. "You should have rung us. Daniel would have come over and picked you up. I can't think why Shelagh didn't think of that, but no matter – you are here now. Come on in and meet my Daniel."

Muffled grunts were the only response to her pleas to hurry. Nora answered them evenly at first, "I know, hun, but please hurry, or we are going to be late!" she pointed out picking up her hat and fixing it in place with a lethal looking hat pin. Their visitor had to apologise if she had caused these timetable problems, to avoid grinning. "Heck, no! I am sure that the good Lord will be pleased to have you worship with us, and I know Daniel will. He is the main speaker today."

Daniel Marshall came down wrestling with a wayward tie and a reluctant top button, and demanding to know what all the fuss was about because they had more than half an hour to get to church, and it was still only a twenty-minute ride away, just like last Sunday. Introductions completed, Daniel made the relevant number of checks on every door and window before Nora allowed him to shepherd both of them out to his ancient, shiny black Oldsmobile. She continued to remind him of all the things he had forgotten to check while he reversed out of the drive. He ignored all of them. Fortunately Daniel`s driving was in keeping with his appearance: sedate and calm which was not really that surprising considering his previous calling in life, so by the time they arrived at church, Sarah had recovered from her previous journey and was listening avidly as he recounted his and Nora`s history. There was plenty of it because between them they had served their small community for nearly a hundred years. She suspected some of his stories about Nora's famous apple pies were as well baked as the real thing, but they kept her entertained all the same. He followed that up by impressing her with his address in church, though it was the stories about his job that had her really captivated. He was adamant there was more to do with this ritual of dying than she had ever considered possible, prompting her to paraphrase Hamlet's speech to Horatio about heaven and hell for his benefit. According to him, dying was not the worst thing that could happen to a body. That was news in itself. It had always seemed to her to be the absolute worst thing that could happen since her dad had died, but Daniel related so many examples where death had been welcome, where it had afforded the human spirit opportunity to shine, or the gloriously awkward to take centre stage at the most critical moment, that she almost wanted to believe him, and that was a minor miracle in itself! He was a gifted, natural storyteller with the ability to observe and remember greatness in the strangest of people – the natural result of a deep respect for his fellow men.

"Have you ever read any Shakespeare, Daniel?" she asked after one particularly intriguing tale.

He laughed as he replied. "It was always too late for the '*to be, or not to be,*' by the time they met me," he said dryly. "Never had much time for reading – well, not Shakespeare at any rate."

"You should try some. He's good," she promised. "You remind me of him with some of the things you say."

"Did you hear that, Nora? I remind her of William Shakespeare." He was tickled and flattered by that. "I'm no scholar," he insisted. "I reckon the only thing Shakespeare and I have in common is age. Is he older than me?"

"Not true," she laughed. "You both see things the rest of us miss. He wrote them down – that's the only difference. I love your story about Laverne and the gravedigger! I think even Shakespeare would have approved of the way you told it. You should write it down! Write them all down. Write a whole book of them!"

"Hey, hang on a minute, let's not get carried away here. Folks don't want to be listening to my silly stories about little things when they have a lot bigger things to worry about," he protested.

Sarah shook her head and met Daniel's glance in his mirror. "Sometimes I think we get side-tracked by what we think are bigger things, and then we forget about life and death. We fool ourselves that we are here forever. I think we often fill our lives with things that are not important at all. You just restored my perspective. Thank you." Daniel didn't get a chance to ask more because she added, "Other people must forget too – I can't be the only one. Your stories have helped me, so maybe they can help others."

"I don't reckon you ever forgot," he said seriously. "But I thank you for the compliment all the same."

It was easy to decide Shelagh had been only half right about these two. True they were two seriously lovely people, but despite Nora's hat, their churchgoing clearly went much deeper than mere ritual, and Sarah was glad it did. She would be sure to tell Shelagh that. Pity Rick hadn't stayed around long enough to meet them. So, he had been wrong about habit and hats as well as happiness and she had been right again. And this time she hadn't needed to ask.

Lunch was an informal affair with no hidden agendas, not even a word game to trip over. There was talk about families and children and after that had been thoroughly exhausted, Daniel was encouraged to tell how he had met and courted Nora when she had been the minister's daughter and he had been a temporary gravedigger. "Just like Laverne and the gravedigger?" Sarah asked.

"Well, no, not exactly," he said with a grin. "Nora wanted me to go up in the world, get out of my rut – which was fairly deep, you understand. In fact I remember her saying, 'If you think I will marry you, Daniel Marshall, when you spend half your life six feet under already, you are mistaken!' I hadn't actually asked her at the time," he said comically, "though I admit I did nothing else but think about it. She was the prettiest eighteen-year-old I had ever seen. Still is." He patted her hand. "Never seen anyone who could compare with my Nora."

"Take no notice of him, Sarah. He was a charmer then and he still is. Did I tell you he was the most cock-sure gravedigger we ever had? He was full of himself and thought he was such a hit with all the girls."

"I was," he said humbly. "You just knew a good thing when you saw one."

By the time the dishwasher was being stacked, Sarah was up to date with all the Marshalls' extended family history, including their four sons, twelve grandchildren, and two great-grandchildren, as well as numerous other relations. "If we had known about your twins, you could have called in on Randy; he lives in New York, and they have new twins. Tammy, his wife, is feeling a bit low right now, and you could have given her some advice, told her it all passes, all the diapers and bottles." Randy and his wife were clearly Nora's biggest worry and Daniel's biggest frustrations, so while Sarah helped to tidy the kitchen, she tried to tell him about her mother's concerns about her.

Daniel listened but observed, "You have no husband, though, and Tammy has. That's a big difference! Randy is a good boy, and Nora needs to let them get on with their lives. We should only help out when we are needed. I wouldn't have liked it if Nora's mother had been forever staying for months on end when we were just married, but Randy is her baby – the one we didn't plan on having. He just sort of arrived. There's nearly eighteen years between him and our next boy, so it's hard for her to let go of such a special baby even when he is twenty-six."

The ladies were about to sit down with Randy's wedding photographs when the living room door burst open, and a heavily pregnant young woman almost fell into their laps. She had stumbled between Daniel and Nora several times before any of them could work out what she was saying. "She ran off. I chased her, I didn't know she was going to fall. She shouldn't have done it, should she?"

"Who ran off? Who fell? Jodie? What did she do? Where did she fall? Is anyone hurt?" The list of questions produced no answers but lots more sobbing. Nora was doing her best to coax the distraught young woman to provide the information they needed while Daniel rang to request an ambulance. Amidst the tears and hysteria, they heard one word quite distinctly: 'estate.' It meant nothing to Sarah, but it did to the others. "Call them again, honey, and get them to send another truck to the estate.

Daniel extracted his glasses from the pocket of his jacket. "Come on. Nora will stay with Dilys. Let's you and me see what we can do."

Despite the difference in their ages, speed was more of a problem for her than for him because her legs had stiffened up since this morning. They hurt more than she could ever have imagined possible, but she tried to force them to run and hopped and hobbled along, struggling to keep up with a man twice her age. The gate to the estate was predictably locked.

"It's times like these folks miss not having neighbours," Daniel puffed, eying the eight-foot-high perimeter fencing. "Can you climb that?" She shook her head. No use saying she could; she had never been any good at climbing or doing anything remotely dangerous, and today she would count herself lucky if she could walk without pain. "Me neither nowadays. One time, maybe. Just have to wait for the medics, then, and they'll climb over." She nodded her agreement, and they both leant back against the fencing, equally exhausted by their exertions and grateful for the chance to recover. "Bet you wonder what the heck is going on."

She shrugged and tried to smile. "Some of that 'life thing' and its important problems?" she asked, drawing circles in the dust with the tip of her shoe to try to relieve the agonising cramps rising in her calves.

"Disaster waiting to happen, I reckon," Daniel said sadly. "How come folks can make such a mess of things when they are only trying to do their best?"

"I don't know," she answered honestly, fully recognising the problem.

"Jodie's dad is a real nice guy just trying to do his best, and I feel real sorry for him." Her interest produced further explanation. "He brought his family to live in the house down the road about five years ago. You probably noticed there're only three houses? Well, the other end of the road is a real difficult family, so we sort of got friendly with the Platts even though they were young enough to be our kids because they needed some neighbourly help, and Nora had got involved with the wife at some club or other. Anyhow, about four years ago Shelley – that was the wife – up and left Jack for some other fella, leaving him with the little girl Jodie. She was about three or four at the time, just old enough to know her mother had gone." He paused, reflecting on what he should say next. "Difficult time for everybody." Sarah caught his eye and nodded; she could imagine the rest.

"Jack's a joiner," Daniel continued sombrely, "the best in town, though I don't suppose that matters much. What did matter was he still had to work even though – well, you know the rest, don't you? There were no relatives around, so we sort of got involved more. Nora looked after the little girl until she started school, and then after school until Jack got home at night. Our own grandchildren are all over the place, so it was nice for Nora, especially when Randy was getting married; it took her mind off other things. So, although things were sort of difficult, they were not impossible until Randy's wedding." He could see that she looked puzzled. "Jodie was a bridesmaid with our granddaughters," he explained. "She had a great time, leaving Jack free to meet ..."

"Another woman?"

"Dilys was one of the girls that worked in Tammy's office upstate. Well, the whole thing took off like a house on fire. Next thing we know, she's giving up her job and coming out here to live. They got married last Christmas. Jodie stayed with us while they went off on honeymoon."

"At Christmas?"

Daniel nodded. "I tried to explain, told him it would be trouble, but heck, the man was in love, and Dilys wasn't old enough to realise any different. I reckon she's no more than twenty-one now, and she just wanted to get married and have a romantic honeymoon. Anyway, things have just gone downhill since then, and now ... Well, I suppose you noticed Dilys is pregnant."

"Difficult not to," Sarah said, and then she stopped suddenly. Something had just occurred to her that she should have realised before. She looked around frantically. "Dilys is pregnant," she said slowly, "so she couldn't have climbed the fence, even if Jodie could." She looked around again.

"And if they were both inside?" Daniel suggested, catching her meaning.

"There must be another way in. You look on that side, and I'll look on this."

Minutes later Sarah located a sizeable tear in the fence, and with Daniel's help, she scrambled through and then held the wire back while he did the same. It was no more apparent on this side where to start looking for the missing child than it had been on the other, their search was equally fruitless, and when they returned to the gate, they were dismayed to find the medics hadn't shown up, either.

"One of us should stay here," Sarah pointed out. "Otherwise when they arrive, they may think it was a hoax and go away." Daniel was already panting heavily and leaning against a stack of wooden pallets, so she added purposefully, "You stay here so you can tell them about Jodie. I will keep looking," A siren interrupted this planning, and a paramedic jumped out almost before the vehicle had stopped. He was scrambling through the hole as Daniel filled him in on the details, leaving the driver to radio the police to find out who had keys. While all this was happening, Sarah thought she heard something, so she set off running back towards an area they had supposedly covered, with both men in hot pursuit.

"You have imagined it," Daniel puffed when they arrived there to find nothing. "No one can get down here because of the road works blocking the alley."

"Probably just a cat," the medic observed as he turned away, annoyed by the distraction. Maybe it was only a cat, but it had sounded so much like a child's cry. Then it came again, and she picked out one clear word - "Help!" It was no cat.

"Wait! She is here," she shouted, but the men had already gone. She looked around again and waited impatiently for the cry to come again to give her further direction, but there was nothing, just the wind in the alley. As she was about to turn away to find the others, she heard it a third time. That meant there was only one place the child could be: down the road works.

The excavation was much deeper than Sarah had expected so it made her feel lightheaded to peer down it. This was no simple road works as Daniel had thought; it was some sort of mine shaft or old well, and it was very deep, with the remains of ancient wooden shoring still in place around a central abyss which started some ten or twelve feet below ground level. A narrow ledge ran around the rim of the old shaft, and from there the wall of the present excavation rose up to the surface. Several large beams must have fallen from the new excavation because they were lying awkwardly across the shaft opening and in the corner directly beneath her, trapped under one of these beams was a small child.

Sarah completely forgot about her own pain as she hobbled as fast as she could to find help. The debate about how to deliver that help was short and to the point. It was focused by a flurry of mud and pebbles descending noisily down the shoring. All three adults urged the child to stay still while they figured out how to get her out, but a moment later she was struggling again, and this time the avalanche of debris was greater.

"I can't move!" the child wailed hysterically, struggling to disprove her own words.

"Don't try! Jodie, you must not try to move!" Sarah turned back to the men in desperation. "We can't wait for help to get here!" she whispered frantically. "She may have fallen by then. We need to do something now!"

Daniel had come to pretty much the same conclusion so he was starting to take his jacket off but the medic guy would have none of it and ordered him to forget whatever it was he was planning. He asked Sarah to run back to the gate and get his colleague to call for more back-up, and then both of them could come back armed with blankets. She nodded, looking from one to the other, still wondering what they intended doing. Her question produced a shocking disclosure.

"Get down there," the man said quietly as he dismantled the rope barrier and tested its strength. She looked from him to Daniel and then back again in disbelief, but the man's grim face convinced her that he was not joking. Getting Jodie out of there was not going to be as easy as she had thought. All the other questions she wanted to ask were shelved as she stood staring at him helplessly.

"Come on, lady, move! Go get help! Can you take my weight?" he asked Daniel as he fixed the rope around his waist. Sarah looked at Daniel; he was a big man, but so was the other guy, and Daniel was a lot older. She was about to ask why they couldn't wait until she could fetch the other paramedic when the heaviest shower of stones yet cascaded down the pit, providing her with the answer. Her mind froze for a fraction of a second, and then a shocking thought formed inside her head. She swallowed hard. That single thought fired with the intensity of a bullet from a high-velocity weapon was currently ricocheting around in her head, making her dizzy with its audacity. She shuddered. The afternoon heat blurred her senses and made her perspire, but it was stalking fear that made her wipe her brow and fight back a faint. "No, he can't," she answered for Daniel. "Besides that ledge is too narrow for either of you." She breathed deeply, not at all sure she could say it, let alone do it. "But you could both take my weight, and it might hold me."

The paramedic looked at her; he was used to giving orders in such situations, not taking them. "You done any climbing?" he asked hopefully.

"No."

"Caving?"

She shook her head again. "Have you?" He didn't answer as she took the rope from him. "It doesn't matter right now what I've done, does it?" she pointed out more confidently than she felt. "It's what I can do right this minute that counts, because unless someone goes down to her, she will fall before you can get her out, won't she?"

The man shrugged; he couldn't deny the possibility in her words, but he didn't want two fatalities on his hands, either. He was already shaking his head.

She continued to insist, "It must be me! You must see that. I am the lightest."

"I can't allow you to do it, though," he said firmly. "You could ..." He didn't finish because the child's struggles had dislodged one of the smaller beams propped up around the central abyss. For a moment it balanced precariously and all eyes rested on it, willing it to stay where it was, but then it toppled over slowly and gracefully and clattered down the pit till it hit water at the bottom. The stones had not been big enough to produce a clear enough sound, but now there was sufficient evidence to convince them all -there was a lot of water down there. Another effect of the beam's fall was that it galvanised Jodie into action again, and she started to struggle with ever greater urgency to free herself.

"I don't think you have a choice," Sarah said, handing the man the rope and indicating the frenzied activity going on beneath them. "I cannot watch this child die knowing that maybe we could have saved her." Her throat dried up at that point, so she nodded her encouragement to the man instead, giving no indication of the ever tightening band of steel fastening itself around her heart. "Please," she finally managed quietly, holding up the rope.

The man did not need long to check out his alternatives before he nodded reluctantly. He secured one end of the thick rope around her waist and tied the other through a nearby warehouse door handle. He nodded at her as if to reassure her that she would be okay and the door would hold her weight should she fall. Sarah nodded back before he proceeded to give her instructions on how best to descend.

She listened as intently as adrenalin would allow, and then she knelt down by the side of the pit and shouted down, "Hey, Jodie, if you stay very still, there's room for two on that ledge. I'm coming down, okay?" She tried hard to disregard the pounding inside her chest and the thought that any minute she could have a heart attack. She tried hard not to pay any attention to the light-headedness that was making her feel dizzy, or to even make allowances for the pains in her legs that until now had been so restricting. She did stop to wonder briefly about her membership in Cowards Anonymous before she edged herself backward over the abyss and felt the men take the strain of her weight. This single action was enough to get her thrown out of that exclusive club forever! The most adventurous thing she had done in her entire life up to this point had been to cross the Atlantic alone. What had Elinor said about America being dangerous? Even Elinor could not have anticipated this level of danger. Flash floods, snakes, bears, mountain lions, and alligators – and even mass murderers, vampires, and rapists – could not compete with this. A second later she was swinging free having forgotten everything the medic had said. She waited for her life to flash in front of her as she plunged to her death. She didn't; and there was no re-run of her life either; so she couldn't be drowning yet, but at the moment of complete panic, something calm inside her head cautioned her to relax, concentrate, and listen. The medic was yelling frantic instructions down to her and as she obeyed the voice and brought her mind under control, she began to register what it was the guy was saying to her. She looked upwards for reassurance and prayed very hard that they could hold her weight, that they would not let her go, that the rope was long enough and strong enough, as well as a dozen other variables that all seemed relevant. All of them were inseparably connected with one single theme: that she would not die. It was perhaps fortunate that she did not recall that only yesterday she had gone on record as not being sure of God's existence, because today she had just been very forthright in asking for His assistance.

The man was trying to instruct her how to use her legs and feet to make her swing until she could brace herself against the excavation walls. She doubted his words but short of an alternative she tried doing as he asked and it worked, she made contact with the wall, then she clung on to the rope as they lowered her gently down. She had seen people doing this on television a thousand times and had never given it a second thought; it had always looked so effortless. Now she knew it wasn't. Now she knew it was exhausting and hard work, so it seemed like they were lowering her miles, though she knew the distance to the ledge could not be more than ten or eleven feet at the most. That expected heart attack still hadn't happened, but her heart was pumping furiously, and the adrenalin coursing into her strained muscles was making her stomach churn so much that she felt physically sick. She knew it was these same things giving her the power to move in spite of the creeping mental paralysis that would have had her stop.

"You are nearly there. Another couple of feet Sarah, that's all." Daniel's voice broke the silence for the first time, and in response she stretched her legs and feet, anxious to feel earth beneath her again.

"Don't do that!" the medic yelled, but it was too late. She had already stretched a little too far so one of her shoes came off and rattled noisily against the unforgiving wooden shoring as it fell. She knew the effect must be amplified because of the confined space, but it still disturbed her, and while she tried her best to rationalise the sound, it was impossible. It didn't help that the men stopped lowering her while it fell, so she was suspended, listening to the eternity it took for the shoe to hit the bottom with a splash. There was a lot of water down there. Enough to drown in. There was a possibility the storm had hit down here and that would have added to any already there. She kicked the other shoe off and listened as it followed the same noisy path. "Okay," she shouted up in a strangled voice that sounded strangely like cheerfulness, but was actually hysteria, "let's do this the native way! How much farther?"

"Ten inches, a foot maybe, but don't stretch! Wait for it!"

This time she listened, and within seconds her feet were touching something cold and solid. Horizontal cold, solid but wet. Still it was much better than vertical cold, solid and wet. She celebrated by breathing, and then as if remembering a debt, she raised her eyes heavenwards and offered thanks.

"What was that?" the men asked as they peered down anxiously.

"I just said thank you, but don't let me go," she added hastily in case they had any such ideas. She paid proper attention to her new instructions as she prepared to turn around. She needed to be facing into the central shaft so she could kneel down besides Jodie. If the first bit had been scary, this bit defied description because it required her to let go of the rope. And though she knew holding on to it was purely psychological, letting go was sobering stuff. It forced her to acknowledge something she had chosen not to think about for the last ten minutes: that she was totally reliant on the strength and security of that knot around her waist to keep her alive. She steadied herself against the muddy wall while she gathered the courage to launch into this manoeuvre. First she repeated her little prayer, and then scarcely allowing another thought to intrude, she let go and swung around. She had been safe on the ledge, but now she was back out there, suspended in space as her foot slipped through the mud pulled by the weight of her awkwardly centred body weight. This time she didn't panic. She remembered the drill so grabbing a tight hold of the rope she used her body weight to swing herself so her feet could make contact with the ledge again. She was only inches away from it, but she still had to swing and struggle with all her might to get back onto it. Contact with the wall of the excavation came with a sickening thud; her thigh catching on a hefty piece of iron piping protruding from the shoring before she could complete the manoeuvre successfully. She sank carefully onto her knees, exhaling like one of Len's tired balloons.

"Nothing will ever intimidate me again!" she promised herself heroically, fully aware that although she was now crouched on that frail-looking, narrow, muddy ledge surrounding the pit`s gaping black mouth, it was still ready to receive her should she do anything foolish. All her usual fears were trivial in comparison to this. Even her constant obsession with creepy things didn't warrant a second thought right now because this ledge was solid terra-somewhat-firma than the vertical wall, and nothing else mattered for now.

"Miss Platt, I presume?" she croaked in the only voice she could summon. Jodie did not recognise the reference or that it was an attempt at levity, and merely burst into tears again. "Hey, what's all this? I do my very best Tarzan impression for you, and all I get is tears? Shush, come on now."

"Okay, lady, you are doing just great. Have a breather and then see if you can find a way for us to haul you both out of there," the medic instructed. She shouted her understanding and was about to start work on this task when she remembered about the rope. "Don't worry, we have you. You won't fall!"

Jodie started to cry again at the mention of falling, and although Sarah tried her best to comfort her as she carried out the required evaluation, she wasn't entirely successful because she was hampered by her own doubts on the matter.

Jodie Platt was small for her age. Daniel had said she was nearly eight, but she looked more like six. She was a skinny little thing dressed in what must have once been a pretty pink T-shirt with a cartoon figure on the front. It now resembled an oil rag. Her denim shorts and trainers were both covered in thick black mud. Only the fear in her eyes could outdo the mud. Sarah could only hope that her own fear was not as transparent. She muttered some assurances she didn't fully believe as she stretched out to check the child's injuries.

"My legs won't move! I can't move this piece of wood – it's too heavy!"

"That's why I am here, to see how we can move it. Now, tell me where you hurt most," she said softly, stroking the child's hair to comfort her. The girl pointed to her thigh, where an ugly shard of bone broke through her skin and then she touched her chest. "You sure? Those two places hurt most?" Jodie nodded. It was no use wishing she had come down on the other side of the child; she would have to do the best she could from here. There was nothing she could do about the leg injury from here, but maybe she could support the chest injury a little. "Can you move your arms, pet?" Jodie lifted both to show how little. Sarah took hold of the nearest hand as it fell and held onto it while she completed the rest of her examination. The last thing she enquired about was the beam. Jodie confirmed her lower legs didn't hurt as much as the other things; the beam had fallen after her, and it was a great big heavy thing. There was some reluctance to speculate on the degree of injuries something that big could cause hitting something so small. Better to concentrate on her task

"How you doing, lady? Can you get a harness around her?" the medic shouted. Sarah glanced up, suddenly remembering it wasn't enough simply to gather this information. She had to get it back to the men at the top, and right now she didn't have a clue how she could do that without distressing the child even further. There was now no doubt the little girl was seriously injured besides being in shock and absolutely terrified. That made two of them for the terrified bit, but Sarah tried to forget that, and ignore her thigh which was throbbing ferociously now. She yelled back to the men, doing her best to convey some of that cheerful optimism. "It would help if you could get a pen and paper down here so we can play noughts and crosses or something: you know, pass the time till you get us out." Daniel's response was understandably puzzled, but the medic understood perfectly.

"Sure thing," he yelled back, "I'll go phone the chief to get more people out here, and I'll bring back the blankets and your paper. Back in a flash. Stay where you are, girls."

The man had a deplorable sense of humour.

Fortunately Sarah had no time to think about whom he had left in charge of the rope as she was busy comforting Jodie, and when the man returned with the blankets, she was too busy organising the blankets to remember to chastise him. As she slid the last blankets beneath herself and another around her shoulders, she did think about it briefly but it no longer seemed to matter. It was cold down here, but she was still safe. She scribbled her report, underlining the difficulties they faced in getting them out. She was asking Jodie if she wanted to play noughts and crosses when the medic called down, "Hey lady, can you move the beam?"

Damn, she had forgotten about that. "No," she said lightly, watching Jodie's face for signs of more distress. "Don't think so because I can't reach it from here and it's heavy, so maybe some lifting gear." She suggested brightly, hoping that the man would also understand this mixed message as he had the last one.

Not so. "What if I dropped on the other side? Could I move it then?"

She inched her way along the ledge until she was sat with Jodie's head right against her thigh, and she could look down into the child's face. She was still holding onto one of her hands, but she stroked Jodie's face with the other as she shouted back, "No, please don't try! You would need to throw the beam clear with some force." She closed her eyes as the picture flashed momentarily in her head. "It could bring us with it," she declared, swallowing hard to prevent herself from panicking.

"Okay, leave it. We've sent for keys, and we will get some gear out here that can do the job. You'll be okay for a while?"

"Yes, we are fine!" It was far from bona fide truth, but almost anything was better than the thought of him swinging down here like some comic book hero. She had no wish to die just yet. "See?" she said reassuringly to her comrade in the mud. "We will be out of here in no time!"

Jodie only looked more distressed than ever. "Who are you? You speak funny," she said suspiciously, and employing the usual candour of an eight-year-old, confessed, "I don't know you." The explanation necessarily involved holidays and England, where she was sure she sounded quite normal, and today's visit to the Marshall's house. It was received with equal measures of doubt and disbelief. "You have come *here* on holiday?" Sarah nodded. Jodie looked at her with renewed scepticism. "So where do you live in England?" she asked suspiciously, checking to see that she could provide an answer. The answer transformed her scepticism. "Gee! Do you know the Queen?" she asked, elevating her strange rescuer to something approaching celebrity status with this one piece of information.

"We are not on speaking terms," Sarah laughed, but upon seeing Jodie's face fall she added, "but I have seen her lots of times. I suppose I live quite close to Buckingham Palace."

"You do?" By now the child seemed quite prepared to be amiable and impressed in equal measures. "Gee, that's great! Fancy living near a real queen." Barely a second later she returned to her former interrogation. "You said you were on holiday?"

"And I didn't expect to be spending it crawling around muddy holes, but that's life, I suppose, full of ups and downs. Oops! Sorry!" Jodie attempted a smile as Sarah clamped a hand across her mouth in mock horror at her blunder; but that little smile inspired sufficient confidence in the rescuer that she could find ways to build on this, that she was hardly prepared for the serious observation that followed.

"You have torn your skirt, you are full of mud, and you're bleeding real bad. Look!"

Sarah glanced down at her thigh as instructed. A pool of bright red blood was mixing with mud with sickening effect. She could hardly say it matched the girl's leg, so she confined her comment to, "Oh, so I am," and wiped the blood away. "It's just a scratch, nothing much. I daresay we both look a bit of a mess," she confessed, trying hard to stem the sizeable flow of new blood already appearing. She had to resort to tearing a piece off her skirt and tying it tight round her leg as a tourniquet before the flow would be stemmed.

The child watched quietly and then pointed out with impeccable logic, "If I were on holiday, I think I'd rather have gone to Disney."

"Well, me, too." Sarah giggled before remembering Ali's constant check on the itinerary, and so she confessed, "except I had orders not to, so I came here instead to get covered in mud. Much more fun!"

Clearly that seemed beyond the boundaries of rational behaviour to Jodie. "We are a real mess," she warned, looking first at herself and then at Sarah's mud-splattered skirt and legs. "I'm real sorry about your skirt; it was real pretty, and now it's ruined. It's all my fault. If you hadn't come down here, you wouldn't have cut your leg."

"Hey, I told you it doesn't matter. The skirt is not important, and my leg will mend, but as for us? Well, you are right about one thing: we certainly wouldn't win many beauty competitions right now." She had offered this in tandem with stroking the child's face and smoothing her hair out of her eyes. "I daresay we might do quite well in a Miss Mudpack competition." It won another faint smile.

One clever comment did not necessarily mean there was a stream of them to follow, and this one was followed by a complete blank, so Sarah looked around her, seeking inspiration for conversation. There was nothing except this deep, dark hole descending into the bowels of the earth, and here they were, perched like ornaments on a shelf.

"I do hope," she said reflectively, "that you didn't fall down here chasing a white rabbit!"

Jodie looked up with the sort of puzzled expression she normally reserved for adults who said totally stupid things, and this adult definitely qualified on that score. "What white rabbit?" she queried. "I never saw any white rabbit."

"You didn't? Oh, I thought ... Well no, perhaps not." Sarah sighed resignedly, which had exactly the effect she had hoped for.

"What do you mean," Jodie pleaded, "What white rabbit?"

"Have you never heard of Alice in Wonderland?"

"No! Who is she?"

Sarah smiled and rubbed Jodie's nose with her finger. She thought, it's me, but she said, "And here's me thinking you were trying to be like Alice. Would you like to know about her? We have some time." Jodie thought about it for a second, before nodding. "Well, Alice was a little girl who went on a great adventure to a strange place called Wonderland, and her adventure started when she fell down a long, dark hole while she was chasing after a white rabbit."

Jodie had no difficulty in seeing the similarities, because in the very next breath she declared, "This isn't Wonderland – it's frightening, and I don't like it. I want to get out now."

"I know," Sarah said softly. "I am sure Alice felt like that at times. Shall I finish the story?" She waited expectantly for permission. It took several seconds of deep thinking before Jodie turned her head away and mumbled her agreement, much as if she didn't care either way. Reluctant endorsement was enough for Sarah to launch into the rest of the story with energy. Jodie even managed a passable smile as Sarah imitated a very realistic rabbit, twitches and all, saying, "I'm late, I'm late."

"Alice's hole must have been a lot nicer than this," Jodie pointed out soberly, weighing up their frightening surroundings. The story had not delivered one shred of comfort.

"Maybe. But can you see why I thought we were like Alice. We are even sat on a shelf on the way down."

"And I don't want to go any further down," Jodie observed vehemently, checking to see that there was no misunderstanding about this.

"Of course you don't, and we won't. Alice is just a story, but perhaps it would be better if we talked about something else right now?"

"No, go on. What happened next? Did Alice ever get out of Wonderland?"

"Oh, yes, of course she did."

"Are we going to get out of here?" Two big brown eyes were filled with tears, and they emphasised the awful reality of her question.

It was difficult for Sarah to hold her own in check, but she wiped away the biggest, juiciest tear wobbling on the edge of the youngster's cheek and composed herself before she answered stoutly, "You bet!" It was an American expression she had heard so many times these last few weeks, and she had delivered it now with as much vigour as any she had heard. "Of course we are going to get out! You heard the paramedic: they have gone for some lifting gear to move this beam, and then we will be out in no time, you'll see. I am a fully paid-up member of Cowards Anonymous and there is no way I would have come down here if I had thought for one minute that I wasn't going to get out again," she added confidentially, "Besides, we have to get out of here or else my girls will be very cross. Can you imagine how embarrassing it would be, having to tell everyone you lost your mum down a big muddy hole in California, with not a white rabbit in sight?"

Jodie smiled tiredly. "I suppose we will get out, if you say so."

Sarah kissed her finger tips and applied the kiss to Jodie's brow. "I promise they will get us out," she said softly, hoping her smile adequately concealed her own uncertainties on the matter.

"How old are they?"

"I'm sorry?" Sarah looked puzzled. "How old are who? The medics? I don't know."

"No! Your girls. You said 'my girls'," Jodie explained patiently. "You have children?"

"Oh yes. Alison and Julie are ten and three-quarters."

"One of them is ten, and the other is three-quarters?"

"Goodness me, no. Both of them are ten and three-quarters?" An explanation that was received with wonder.

"Gee, that's real neat. I don't know any real twins. Randy has new twins, but I haven't met them. Do they look the same?" Sarah recounted some funny stories about their identical looks and then as she didn't need much encouragement, she told more because talking about her girls was about as easy as talking about Shakespeare in an English class. "That's real cool!" Jodie said enthusiastically. "You got any more?"

"What, stories or children?"

"Both!" Her laughter was heartfelt.

Sarah was relieved that she had finally found a subject able to distract Jodie from her pain and their dangerous situation. "No more children," she confessed, but upon seeing Jodie's face fall, she added, "But lots more stories." And she told every single story she could remember, including repeating the doubles mix-up game in several versions.

As with all storytellers, she eventually ran out of material, and it was then that she offered a challenge. "Hey! I bet you have some funny stories of your own. How about you tell me some of yours?"

The immediate change in Jodie's manner told her she had said the wrong thing yet again. "No stories. No other children."

"Oh, I see. But you don't need other children for funny stories. You can be funny all by yourself," Sarah pointed out gently. Again it produced no response. "Well, even if you have no funny stories, you and I have something else in common."

"We do? What?" Jodie asked.

"We are both only children," she said carefully, anxious not to let Jodie see that she had noticed her rebuff. "I watch the girls together, and although they fight sometimes, I know they have great fun as well. It is more difficult to do that on your own, isn't it? Do you get lonely? I used to sometimes," she confided casually, not sure where that came from or what she had meant by it, least of all where it was leading.

"I don't!" That was a quick flash of anger.

"I had a pony, and I used to talk to it a lot, but it wasn't the same. Horses can't talk back like brothers and sisters."

Jodie looked up into her face with a grim look of determination, "I never get lonely," she repeated harshly and then she relented a little. "Well, I never used to," she admitted wistfully.

"So what changed that?" It was an innocent question on the surface, but it masked the sort of tactics that grown-ups often employ to find out what they already know.

"Dad married Dilys," the child snarled from behind clenched teeth.

"Oh, I see." Sarah nodded. "That would make a big difference, of course."

"You can say that again!"

"That would make a big difference, of course."

This time Jodie's response was a big sigh, conveying how completely mystified she was by her audience, but then she almost laughed when she recognised what was happening, though she did manage to hold it under control. "It doesn't mean that!" she explained patiently.

"Doesn't it?" Sarah said, scratching her head rather like Oliver Hardy might. "You can say that again – doesn't mean you can say it again? Words usually mean what they say, but these words don't?"

Despite all her efforts, Jodie was almost smiling by now. "No. It just means that you are right!" she said, blinking her eyes to dispel the tears.

"Oh, I see! Well, thank you for the explanation. So what did you mean? What was I right about?"

Jodie stopped smiling and looked away to hide the fact that tears were about to win out again. It was as impossible to miss this as it had been to overlook her previous hostility. When she turned back to Sarah, her little face was pinched and her voice brittle with raw emotion. "Everything changed when Dad married Dilys," she said peevishly.

"That is the problem?"

"Yes!" Then feeling that some explanation must be called for, she added. "I was running away from her when I fell. I bet she's real mad with me, isn't she?" Extreme anxiety replaced hostility for a while. It didn`t last. All Sarah`s attempts to persuade Jodie that this was not the case were destined to fail miserably. Jodie insisted, "She doesn't care about me. She is having a baby, and then they won't me want me at all. She's not my mom, and …" Her voice trailed away as shouting gave way to the inevitable tears.

"She hates me, and I hate her," she spluttered, before giving in to fresh floods of grief.

Sarah tried to placate herself with the thought that maybe all this pain and anguish was better coming out than staying bottled up. It was a nice, convenient excuse and she wished she could believe it, but she knew Jodie needed as little distress as possible down here, she had blundered badly. One thing seemed absolutely certain: Daniel had been right about this new marriage, it was no 'happy ever after,' fairy-tale. It was too late to worry about what had already been said; all she could do now was try to calm the child again; the rest would have to wait for others to deal with later. Her immediate job was to try to keep Jodie still until they could get her out of here and nothing else.

When Jodie's tears finally subsided, they talked about school and what she liked doing at home. Everything appeared to be going well until it came to talking about her friend Cory. He and his family lived in the third house way down the other end of the road. "They are on holiday right now. I wanted to go with them, but Dilys wouldn't let me. She doesn't like me going there. I hate her." It was beginning to look as if it was impossible to discuss anything without Dilys cropping up. Sarah sighed and brushed her hand along Jodie's cheek, not really sure what else to say or do. The child interpreted her sigh as sympathy, so she admitted, "I bet she won't let me go there at all now, because she'll blame Cory even more. This has nothing to do with him, but she won't believe that!"

"I'm sure that Dilys doesn't hate you or Cory," Sarah offered spontaneously. Realisation coming too late to prevent her from being sucked into what she had just decided to stay out of.

"She does, too!" There was no room for doubt here. "I knew you would be on her side – grown-ups always stick together," Jodie added bitterly as she withdrew her hand. All of Sarah's attempts to reconnect with it were unsuccessful because Jodie folded both hands across her little chest and hid them in her arm pits, ignoring the pain it caused.

"Jodie, you are wrong, pet. I am not on her side. I am not on anyone's side. I am a complete stranger – I don't know anything about you, so why would I take sides?"

"Because you're a grown-up!" That seemed fairly conclusive and not open to negotiation, so the pariah sat silently for a few minutes until the securely guarded hands were released from their confinement. Sarah hoped that it was a signal that the pique had subsided, so she chanced observing, "Grown-ups don't always stick together, you know."

Jodie mumbled something which Sarah didn't catch but which sounded like another attack on Dilys, so she ignored it. That earned her a perfectly enunciated repetition. "I *said*, you don't know what she's like!" That much was true. "And I do! And I know she hates me!" It was said with just as much venom as the first time. "And you haven't seen them kissing." It wasn't immediately clear what this had to do with anything until the desperately sad little voice added, "I just wish she would go away and leave us alone. We were okay before she came to live with us. We didn't shout at each other then."

Daylight was beginning to dawn. "So is that why you hate her? Because you and your dad shout at each other now?"

"That, and because she hates me ... and because she wants my dad."

"I'm not with you."

"She hates me being around because I make them argue. I've heard them."

"Oh, I see," Sarah said sympathetically, deploying a standard fail-safe comment because understanding had yet to illuminate the remaining shadows of her ignorance. "But I don't suppose you do that on purpose, do you?" It was a question posed with exactly the right balance of presumption and hope.

Jodie looked away and didn't answer. "I'm scared of what will happen when we do get out," she confessed, eager to change the subject.

There seemed little point in pursuing things Jodie found difficult to discuss, so Sarah simply followed her lead. "How come?" she asked, thinking quite the opposite should be true. It was impossible to miss the sadness in this child's face, or the fact that she looked up with even more tears in her eyes.

"Because this time Dad will be mad at me as well," she sobbed.

"Now why would you think that?"

The shudders and sniffing that had so recently replaced the sobbing seemed as if they would have to give way to fresh tears; Sarah reached out to wipe the puffy eyes and runny nose in an attempt to help compose the child so that she could talk instead of sob. This time solicitude helped ease the spasm of distress, only for it to generate a confession. "Because I kicked her." It was almost a whisper. "I kicked her in the stomach."

"Not deliberately?"

Jodie nodded her head, unable to answer any other way. "I wanted to hurt her," she admitted. "I shouldn't have done it, should I? I've killed it!"

Sarah's reply was gentle but firm. "No, you should not have kicked Dilys in the tummy, sweetheart – that was very wrong. Let's hope the baby will be fine. Babies are very resilient, you know."

"They are?"

"Sure they are."

Jodie was quiet for a whole moment while she considered this new information, and then she asked ponderously, "What's resilient?" It had been asked with such charm that it was impossible for Sarah not to smile, after which she apologised and explained resilient in words of one syllable. The mystery explained, the sinner checked out her understanding. "So it might not be dead?"

"Both Dilys and her baby seemed fine when I left them."

"You've seen them?"

"Who do you think told us you were here?"

"I hope," Jodie whispered, and then she stopped. Further enquiry produced the solemn declaration. "I hope that the baby's okay. I hate Dilys, but it's not the baby's fault, is it?"

"No, it's not the baby's fault."

"They won't send me to prison if it's okay, will they?" This plea was uttered without an ounce of guile, and it awakened Sarah to yet another dimension to this problem.

"Jodie, precious, they won't send you to prison whatever happens. Whatever made you think that?"

"Cory said …"

"Jodie, listen to me. Children of eight are not put in prison, okay?"

"You sure?"

"Yes, I am sure," she said, bending forward to kiss her forehead. No wonder this child's distress had been so great, if she had been imagining being sent to prison. "Better?"

A nod and a weak smile seemed to convey that she was, but then the tears won out again, and Sarah had to try once again to get the girl to understand that Dilys was hurting, too. Accepting information about escaping a prison sentence was one thing, but it did not mean that Jodie was ready to accept anything else.

"It's true. They would be better off without me. Daddy tells her he loves her more than anything else," Jodie spat between her tears. "So they must be better off without me. She will be glad I have fallen down here."

A stab of something familiar – the acute pain of rejection – pierced Sarah's heart, replenishing her sympathy for the little mite who was struggling to understand emotions well beyond her years. Miraculously, instructions came into her head. "Not possible sweetheart," she assured the child tenderly. "Your daddy sounds just like my daddy –and though he loved my Mum, he always loved me as well. I never doubted that. You shouldn`t either." Her certainty eased the child`s immediate pain, and Sarah prayed that they had finally said enough for now. Surely the full extent of her pain must finally have been aired now. Sarah hoped that the remaining tears would drain Jodie's distress so that she could achieve some semblance of peace. Even eight-year-old heartbreak could not last forever. Finally the girl lay still. "Better?" Sarah asked. This time the child just nodded; she had no words left. For a few precious minutes there was perfect stillness except for Jodie`s constant shivering, so Sarah took the blanket from around her own shoulders and wrapped it as firmly as she dared around the tiny, trembling frame. "There, you should be as snug as a bug in a rug now. A cooked bug, at that! Three blankets and baking foil!"

Jodie lay totally exhausted by Sarah`s side, but then calmness brought another difficulty. It started to look as if she might drift into unconsciousness, so it became necessary to try to introduce a fresh subject of conversation – preferably one with no emotional content. Sarah thought she had succeeded until Jodie asked quietly, "Were you really telling me the truth when you said Dilys didn't hate me? You weren't just making it up?"

The simple explanation of how that could be did not appear to be at all successful, so in desperation Sarah asked, "When did your dad and Dilys get married?" She knew the answer of course, but she needed to check something out. Pain expressed itself in the child's voice as she recited the details. "I see," Sarah said. There it was again: platitudes! This child needed reassurance, not platitudes! Apparently there had been no relatives able to have her, and the real mother had not been mentioned, so Sarah was unwilling to follow that lead. "But Nora and Daniel are nice. And they really like you. Was Christmas fun?"

"What do you think?"

"Have you told your dad and Dilys about this, explained how you feel?"

"Cory said parents don't listen when there are two of them."

"That's just not true, sweetheart," she said, thinking that she was already beginning to agree with Dilys about this Cory character, until a long forgotten memory dusted itself off and presented its evidence band box fresh, reminding her just how easy it had been at more than twice Jodie's age to be influenced by the wrong people because they seemed to care and there didn't seem to be anyone else to talk to. "Please talk to them about this, Jodie. Grown-up people get confused as well." Everyone had clearly forgotten to tell her that. "Maybe your Dad and Dilys are as confused as you are right now."

"How come?"

"Well, let me see!" Sarah put her finger to her cheek and thought hard. Her words had tripped out lightly, but now she needed to be able to justify them. "Maybe Dilys is confused because even though she loves your dad and he loves her, being married is still very new and strange. Maybe she feels confused because *she* is the new one in your house, not you. It has always been your home, but it hasn't always been hers, has it? Being new at anything is always confusing. Remember your first day at school?" From the gruesome face staring up into hers, it wasn't that hard to figure what that had been like. "See what I mean? We all think, 'Can I cope? Will I be okay? Will this work out?' These are always very important questions, and they always deserve answers."

"They do?"

"Sure they do." Sarah felt she had to risk losing the ground she had gained with Jodie, possibly alienating her altogether by trying to present Dilys' possible point of view, but she had no alternative to offer. "I can try to explain so that you understand what I mean. Would you like that?" Jodie considered this proposition as carefully as any politician studied the opposition before she agreed. "Good. It's half the battle, wanting to understand something. I know quite a lot about this thing called change, so if I explain it to you so that you can understand it, will that be good? Are you are sitting quite comfortably, then I will begin," she joked, but the meaning was lost on Jodie. Wrong country, wrong generation. "Yes, well, change is something that happens to all of us for all of our lives. Most of the time it is so slow that we don't really notice it happening at all, but it is still there. Every day we change a little bit. That is usually okay, we can deal with slow change. It's when things start to change too quickly, or too

366

many things change all at once, that we start to think, 'If only I could stop this. If only I could stay where I am, I will be safe.'"

"You mean like me and my dad? I want that to stay the same."

"That sounds about right. We can never stop change, Jodie – it's a part of our lives. We grow older every year; that's change. Imagine never having birthdays! Imagine being four forever."

Jodie laughed. "No school ever!" she trilled, obviously more than a little taken with the idea.

"Some days that might seem quite nice, but imagine never riding a two-wheel bike, or learning to play basketball properly, or learning to drive a car, or buying high-heeled shoes, or wearing pink lipstick."

"Okay!" It was not clear what had changed Jodie's mind, but the list had obviously been wide enough to appeal to something in her, because the acceptance had been unhesitating.

"So right now you are a little girl with lots of fun things to do, but the years will pass, and then you will become a teenager. Then you'll be a young woman who goes on dates, and then maybe you'll be a wife and a mother. Lots of other things will come your way as you change – you won't stay a little girl forever. You will change. Your dad is only doing the same thing, sweetheart, and so is Dilys. So am I and Nora and Daniel, and everyone else. Life is all about change. Change is not your enemy. It can be your best friend, and it will bring lots of different things to you."

"But that scares me!" Jodie said.

"I know, and it's not difficult to feel that way. Grown-ups feel that way too, sometimes."

"They do?"

"Sure. People feel funny things when they are faced with lots of change. Sometimes we look for someone to blame because we think that will help get rid of some of our fear. It doesn't of course – we just think that. That's why I don't think you really hate Dilys," she added significantly. "Though I do think that maybe you feel that way because you think she is the reason your life has changed so much, and right now you can't see anything good about the changes. Right?" Sarah couldn't tell this time whether she had hit the proverbial nail on the head. "Do you understand what I mean by emotions, Jodie?" she asked. She took the almost imperceptible movement of her head to be a yes. "If Dilys was a neighbour or a friend's mum, would you hate her?"

"I don't know," Jodie confessed sullenly, too confused by what that meant to understand what it would feel like.

Sarah was struggling to find alternative ways to explain her knowledge when their attention was diverted by someone shouting down to them. They had been so absorbed in their conversation that they had completely forgotten about the activity up at the top. Sarah looked up to see Daniel hanging over the edge,

"Lifting gear is on its way," he yelled. "Should be here inside the hour. The police had some difficulty getting hold of the right equipment with it being Sunday, but they're coming now."

"Police! Why are the police coming here?" Jodie exclaimed.

"Shh! It's okay, the police always to come to help at an accident, that's all," Sarah said, patting the child's arm for reassurance.

"Are you both okay down there?" Daniel's asked.

"We are fine," Sarah shouted back. "In need of a shower, but otherwise we are doing great."

Daniel returned twenty minutes later to inform them the gates were open and ready for the lifting gear to arrive. This time he yelled, "If you girls are okay, I'll go and tell Nora and Dilys the news. I have been hanging on until I have something positive to tell them, but I know they'll be worried by now."

"We're fine, you go ahead," Sarah shouted. She turned back to Jodie. "See? Daniel thinks Dilys will be worried about you as well. Are we both wrong? Shall we ask him to come back and tell us how Dilys is?" Jodie nodded slowly. "Okay we'd better yell then. Ready?" They both yelled Daniel's name several times before his worried face reappeared at the top of the pit. Whatever catastrophe he had been imagining, the frown on his face soon gave way to relief as they explained their request. For one awful moment before he looked down, he had imagined visions of the ledge crumbling and both of them falling to their deaths. "Sure thing. I'll be back before you can say, 'Get me out of here!'"

As he left Jodie said to Sarah, "How will they get us out? I'm frightened. Aren't you?"

"Petrified!" Sarah admitted with a grin. "I told you about my membership in Cowards Anonymous, didn't I? Well, I wasn't joking! But I am sure these men have rescued people from far worse places than a muddy little hole, so I shall just say a prayer and leave it to the experts."

"Say a prayer? Who to? God?"

Sarah had offered her words quite casually without fully realising what it was she was saying. Now she stopped and considered them, and then she remembered yesterday's awkward conversation and today's earlier plea. She offered up a silent apology. "Well, yes, to God," she said solemnly.

"Do you believe in him, too?"

Now it was Sarah's turn to nod because it took her a while longer to find her voice, but she managed it finally. "Yes, I do, Jodie," was all she could say, though she realised as she said it, it was much more than just four words – it was her first ever open acknowledgment of a fledgling faith. And it was true. She did believe now.

"Nora and Daniel do, too," Jodie chirped on, unaware of the emotions she had stirred in her companion.

"I know."

"Daniel tells me brilliant stories about Jesus, but Cory says they're not true, that miracles don't really happen." Any answer to this had to wait until the audience had regained control. "What do you think?" Jodie persisted. "Cory said Daniel's stories about Jesus are not true because miracles don't really happen." The child looked up patiently, though Sarah could still only shake her head and smile.

Eventually she rubbed Jodie's nose playfully and said, "I think Cory is wrong, Jodie. I think miracles happen all the time. I think one just happened right now."

Jodie did not pursue what that might be but simply added rather wistfully, "I wish I could do miracles."

It was sufficient to lighten the mood between them and a grin preceded Sarah's frivolous reply. "And what miracles would you do if you could? Snow in summer, I bet? Burgers and fries for every meal? Ten weeks' school holiday three times a year?"

"No. I'd make it better," came the unwavering declaration. "I'd make it all better."

That wiped the indulgent smile from Sarah's face. Who is teaching who here? she thought. "I'm sure Jesus would approve of that," she said humbly. "Maybe he would help you do that miracle if you asked him."

Jodie looked up at her and met her gaze. So much had passed between the two of them in such a short a time, but this was something new, something even more powerful than shared danger or the exchange of mere comfort. "You reckon?"

"I reckon He is still in favour of anything good, but I think He sort of assigns some of His miracles out these days." She noted Jodie's confused look and realised she had used a difficult word again. "I mean that He uses people to help Him do miracles today, because He is still very interested in all that is good."

"Oh!"

This time Sarah's reply was thoughtful and deliberate. "That's why he will help these men to get us out of here," she said with great feeling, hoping that He would hear her defence of Him and support it with the required rescue.

Without being told, Jodie guessed she was saying this as much for herself as she was for her, so she provided the comfort this time and squeezed Sarah's hand as hard as she could. "We'll be okay, Sarah," she promised, much as if she was now the adult and Sarah the child. "I know you are frightened, but I bet Daniel has said one of his prayers for us, and he says his prayers are always answered," she confided in her best grown-up voice.

Sarah gave up resisting the lump in her throat. Out of the mouths of babes, and all that.

The moment's silence while both of them reconsidered that possibility was enriched by a new sense of true companionship. "Should we say a prayer as well?" Jodie asked eventually. "We could say one together. Maybe God will listen to two of us better than one?" Sarah nodded; she was still incapable of saying anything. "What do you think?" Jodie persisted.

The adult's voice received strength from somewhere. "I think that would be fine. Would you like to say it for us?"

Jodie hesitated. "I don't know how," she confessed, and then she warmed a little to the idea and asked curiously, "How do I do it?"

"To tell you the truth, I don't know how you do it, either. The few times I have prayed, I have just talked to God just like I am talking to you, so you could try doing the same. Talk to Him like you would to anyone else. Tell Him what is bothering you and ask for the help you need, but don't forget to say thank you for listening and helping."

"We don't know if He will help us, though. I guess Daniel knows him real well," Jodie pointed out, much as if this were reason enough for their prayer to be unacceptable.

Sarah shook her head. "I don't think that matters," she said earnestly. "I don't know Him real well, Jodie, not like Daniel does, but whenever I have asked for his help, He has always given it me."

"He has? Gee!" This was an amazing revelation. "Is that all I should say, then?"

"What else should there be?" Jodie's careful consideration ran to almost a minute before she admitted she couldn't think of anything else. "Try it, then," Sarah suggested kindly.

"You won't laugh if I do it wrong?"

"I won't laugh."

Sarah wasn't sure what she had been expecting, but whatever it was, it was nothing like what happened. She was totally unprepared for the emotions that swamped her as Jodie offered their prayer. It would have been enough to see this dirty child with one hand clasped piously across her chest, her eyes shut tight, to have filled her own with tears, but it was the tiny voice full of breathless trepidation that floored her.

"Hello, God. It's me, Jodie Platt. I don't think you know me, but you know my friends, Daniel Marshall and Sarah ..."

She stopped and waited, and eventually her companion realised that this wasn't just a pause so she opened her eyes to check what was wrong. Jodie was urging her with eloquent nods. The puzzle lasted for just a second, and then it came to her. "Chadwick," she whispered.

"Sarah Chadwick. She is English. That's okay, isn't it? She is here on holiday, and that's why she is here," Jodie said confidingly. Sarah smiled and closed her eyes again to focus on the little voice with its petition. "Dear God, we both need your help real bad right now. You see, we are stuck down this hole, and it's cold and wet and real frightening, and I hurt real bad. Please get us out." She paused and then added, "I know I don't deserve it," she said tearfully. "I guess you know I kicked Dilys, but Sarah has come down here to be with me, and she is scared, too, and she is bleeding real bad." Sarah noted with a smile that the petitioner had clearly got her own favourite word, which was used quite as often as "ace" ever had been in England. "So will you please get us out for her? Thank You. I'm real sorry to have bothered you. Love, Jodie Platt." Sarah's information about the end word being "Amen" was forestalled by Jodie adding, "Oh, by the way, I nearly forgot something important. Can you make it so Dilys and the baby are okay as well? Thank You."

It may not have qualified as the greatest prayer ever offered or the most eloquent, but what it lacked in style, it more than made up for in feeling, and its power was apparent in the silence that followed because Sarah was unable to trust her voice even when Jodie enquired if she thought that had been okay. The best reply she could manage was a mechanical nod and a sniff as she struggled to control a surfeit of emotion.

"So why did you come down here, if you are so scared?" Jodie asked.

"Because I didn't want you to be alone. I could see you were in pain and were afraid."

Jodie met her gaze, and both of them smiled self-consciously. The years between them melted away. It was no longer adult and child but simply two souls at a common point in life's journey – a dangerous point – and their eyes exchanged mutual respect with tender understanding and patience. It was not without satisfaction to either.

Jodie broke the spell by grimacing in pain and turning her head away though she smiled the best she could and declared bravely, "It's okay, it only hurts real bad when I try to move."

"Then please keep still!"

Hardly a minute passed before Jodie stated, "But you don't know me," as if it fully explained her train of thought. It took a second or two for Sarah to work out that this had nothing to do with lying still; they had returned to their previous conversation. She pulled a face and enquired whether that mattered; the grossness of her facial expression making the child almost manage a laugh. "No, I guess not. I can understand you why you would do something you were frightened of, if it was for someone you loved. I would do it for my dad, and I know you would do it for Alison and Julie. But why me? You don't even know me."

Sarah had been too near to tears for too long for this not to have a profound effect, and though she tried her best to smile, it came out all crooked, and the corners of her mouth went down against her will as she struggled with the lump in her throat and the surge of emotion that threatened to overwhelm her. She tried hard to hold it back. "You are one very intelligent young lady," she croaked before she had to stop to collect herself. "And you are right, it is easier if it is someone you know and love. When I came down here, before I knew you, I was thinking about Ali and Jules, and I was hoping that someone would be there to help them if they ever needed it, even if that someone was as frightened as I am right now."

"Where are they now? Are they at home with their dad, or are they at the Marshall`s? Will I get to meet them?"

"No to all of those, I'm afraid. The girls are at my mother's for the summer."

"You came out here with their dad?" Jodie`s question held unfortunate reminders so had been asked rather shakily.

"No, I came alone sweetheart," Sarah explained kindly. "I don't have a husband. My girls have no daddy." Then she added more carefully, "A bit like you used to be with no mummy, they have just one parent to love them."

Jodie didn't actually say anything but Sarah guessed that she was thinking, I wish it was still like that.

The adult risked more juvenile tears by adding, "But now you have Dilys. You have two people to love you. I know what you are thinking, but hear me out, please. I think that Dilys really loves you, and I think I can prove it to you."

"How?" the child asked sceptically, wary of returning to such a painful subject.

"Well," Sarah announced in much the same sort of tone she would use to teach her youngest class. "Your dad loves you, doesn't he?" Jodie nodded; that proved nothing, and she made it clear that Sarah would have to try a lot harder than that. "Thought so," Sarah said, unperturbed by the disdain. "I want you to remember that. Want to know how I knew?"

"I told you."

"So you did. I'd forgotten that. Want to know how I would have known anyway?" There was no reply this time, so Sarah ignored the silence and carried on. "I know your dad loves you because you talk about him so much, and I can tell that you love him an awful lot from the way you talk about him. Love is usually a two-way thing, Jodie. You love your dad because he loves you, and he loves you because you are his child. Not all children feel that way about their parents," she added softly, "and not all parents love their children as much as your dad loves you. But I love my girls like that, and I could never, ever do anything to harm them, so I could never marry anyone who couldn't love them, too." This last sentence had been offered as a softener, but Jodie lowered her head till it rested on her chest, more than adequately conveying her deep reluctance to hear what might come next. "I think your dad feels the same," Sarah urged as she lifted the defiant chin and smiled down into the liquid pools of brown.

"But how do you know that?" the child demanded fiercely. "I told you he said he loved her more than anything."

"Jodie precious, that doesn't mean he doesn't love you, too! He still needs your love, doesn't he?" Sarah waited for the cursory nod, but it didn't come. "He still loves you, and he does still need your love," she reassured softly.

"But how do you know that?" Jodie demanded relentlessly. Words were of no use at all; she wanted hard evidence.

Sarah thought hard. "Because it's common territory," she offered hopefully.

More words, the injured party thought. They were just more words – and words she didn't understand at that.

"Can I try again?"

"If you want to." It wasn't exactly encouragement, more pained indifference reminiscent of the sort Elinor assumed when having to listen to theories on educating rebellious teenagers.

Sarah ignored the present indifference much as she did Elinor's and pressed on, going back over all her arguments, this time using very simple language. She had a little more success. At least Jodie looked as though she might be prepared to consider whether it could be true. Jack and Dilys had obviously not recognised the depth to her insecurity, so no wonder today was the result.

As Sarah sat watching the enormous struggle going on in the youngster, Jodie nodded slightly, as though it might be too painful to even hope that it might be true, and then she persisted sullenly, "They still won't want me when Dilys has this new baby!"

One battle fought and won; another yet to fight. Sarah shook her head and then nodded. "Hey, come on now, what sort of talk is that? Of course they will want you. You will be able to help Dilys with your new brother or sister. Doesn't that sound like fun?" All she got back was another fierce stare. "Besides, just because you have a new baby in the family doesn't mean that everyone else gets forgotten. You are you, and the baby is someone else. You will be loved just as much, and the baby will be loved as well, not instead of you. Do you understand?" This time Jodie shook her head and remained sullen and unconvinced. "You will always be special because you are you. This baby will not be another you; it will be a different person." There was no reaction whatsoever, so Sarah looked up, seeking inspiration from wherever there was any available, then asked with a sudden flash of insight, "Do you know Nora and Daniel's grandchildren?"

"Yes." What that had to do with anything was not clear, so it could be answered, even if in a manner that conveyed mistrust.

"How many do they have?"

"Ten, no twelve I think!" And she went on to list all their names.

"So which one do they love?"

"They love them all," she pointed out without thinking. Then she stopped and considered what she had just said.

"Of course they do. When I was quite small, like you—"

There was an immediate protest, "I'm not small."

"No of course not. I meant young. When I was quite young like you, my dad used to tell me I was a VSP. Do you know what that means?" Jodie admitted she had heard of something like that. "You've probably heard VIP. Well VSP is even better. VIP stands for very important person, but VSP stands for very special person."

"Special is better than important?"

"Special is definitely better than important. Being special means you are the only one of you there will ever be. Just think of it: you are unique!" An explanation was needed again. "You are one of a kind, an original, a special edition!"

"There's nothing special about me!"

"Of course there is. The very fact you are alive means that you are special. Like I said, you are unique. Wow!" Jodie still denied it. "Well, you might not think so, but it's true. I know there must be lots of special things about you. For instance, there must be things that you do that make you special to your dad, to Dilys, and to everyone else who knows you. Nora and Daniel think you are special," she pointed out, hoping this outsider confirmation might be sufficient to justify her words. "And so do I, and I have only known you a very short while. People who know you really well must know lots of reasons." She felt satisfied with this explanation and was about to relax when Jodie piped up with a new challenge.

"So what do you think is special about me?"

It was the million-dollar question everyone needed an answer for, and it was impossible not to want to respond to such a plaintive request positively. Whatever trouble this child had caused, past and present, she was still desperately in need of some serious attention. Maybe her methods of getting it were a bit off beam, but she was only eight. That thought prompted a change in Sarah's manner, and she adopted a new thoughtful look as she contemplated what she might have to say to address some of this need. She needed thinking time – and perhaps more of her Marcie Hadley skills rather than Michael Davies tactics.

She adopted an officious baritone boom and announced, "Silence in court! M'lord, the evidence in this case will show beyond reasonable doubt that Miss Jodie Platt is a very special person." Jodie smiled briefly but wanted to know what a M'lord was, and what it had to do with her being special. Sarah explained about English courts of law and the terms and people involved, adding that she was acting the part of a defence barrister so that she could prove her case. "And so, M'lord, the evidence will show …" She coughed and changed voices and did a fair imitation of an imperious, twittery old judge. "Yes, yes, just get on with it. Stop wasting the court's time."

Jodie giggled. "He's bossy," she said, holding her chest.

"That's the judge's job."

"Yes, but do you really think that, or are you just play acting?"

Sarah's make-believe voice was dropped instantly. "I really think that," she promised seriously. "You have been so good, and I know you must be in lots of pain. I could never be that brave. I am a—"

"Member of Cowards Anonymous," they chanted in unison.

"That's right! And besides being brave, I think you are very special because you understand a lot of difficult things when they are explained to you, and that is called being mature – I mean, being grown-up. You are very grown-up for eight."

"But how can I be special when I'm a dunce at school?" Jodie whined.

Sarah smiled. "Being special doesn't have an awful lot to do with being clever," she pointed out gently.

"It doesn't?" Now that *was* a revelation. Everything Jodie had ever done had always seemed to be connected with being clever at school – or in her case, not clever enough.

"Lots of people make the mistake of thinking that if you are not clever, then you must be a failure. Wrong!" said the school teacher marking the air with a big cross. "That is just not true! We are not all clever at school subjects like maths or English, but then, we are not all good singers, either. Do you want me to prove that?"

Jodie actually laughed at that as Sarah opened her mouth wide. "No, I believe you!" she said, shutting her eyes because she couldn't raise her hands as far as her ears without great pain.

"Then I will spare you. We can't all be top at school, but that's not all there is to life. Lots of very special people are not clever, but they are certainly remarkable, special in other ways."

"Tell me about them. Who are they? Do I know them?"

"I'm sure you must know some of them, because special people are all sorts of people. Some are famous and some are just ordinary people like you and me, but they are all living, or have lived, very special lives."

"You might be one, but I'm not. I'm a loser, and I break things," Jodie added heavily, as if this was the final definitive proof of her ineligibility for this accolade.

Sarah brushed all these objections aside and continued. "Have you ever heard of a very special lady who lives in India and cares for all the poor and sick people there? She is very famous, but she isn't famous because she is clever. She is famous because of her kindness. Isn't that something?"

"Yes! I've heard of her! She's a nun, isn't she? Her name is Sister Tessa? No …"

"Mother Theresa," they chanted together.

"Do you know who the most special person I know is?" Sarah asked gently, getting fully into her stride on this. "It's my mother. My father was very special, too, but he's dead now. My mother is still alive and I think she is the most special person I know. And guess what? She's not famous at all! And she would be the very first to tell you she's not a bit clever either; she doesn't know maths and she can't quote one line of Shakespeare."

"Who?"

"William Shakespeare."

"Who is he? Is he clever? Is he special?" Jodie asked.

"Oh yes, William Shakespeare was very special. He still is." It was inconceivable that William should not get in on such a list somewhere. "Shakespeare was a writer and an actor. He was very clever and very talented." Sarah paused for breath, recognising she was in danger of slipping into eulogy mode here and so she corrected herself. "Anyway, my mum doesn't know much about him."

"And clever people do?"

Sarah grinned and looked down into the serious little face. "Shh!" She put a finger to her lips, looked around her, and then whispered confidentially, "Sometimes people think that, but it's not always true."

"So why is your mum special?" Jodie whispered back, thinking this must be a new rule.

"Because she is wise." Sarah acknowledged openly.

"Isn't that the same as clever?"

This time it was Sarah who shook her head vigorously; this child's questions were outstripping her ability to answer them easily. "Not at all," she ventured bravely. "Some very clever people are not at all wise. Wisdom is knowing what is right and *doing* it. Being clever just means you know a bunch of facts, or you can do something well. It's not the same thing at all. I think I would much rather be wise than clever, wouldn't you? Which brings me back to what I was saying: being clever has nothing to do with being special. You can be clever and special, but you don't have to be."

"Tell me about some more special people. Are any Americans?"

Sarah laughed joyously. "Oh, of course they are, sweetheart! Millions of them are! Abraham Lincoln, George Washington ..."

"They were all clever," Jodie pointed out seriously and without any hesitation. "I know 'cause I've learned about them at school. What about American special people who aren't clever?"

This demanded some hard thinking. Sarah knew so little about America and its people, and she thought that she would fail here because she was loathe to count Daniel or Nora as not being clever; it could be misconstrued. Then just as she was about to admit defeat, she recalled the first week of her holiday here. "You ever heard of a lady called Mary Jamieson?" she asked.

"No. Is she special?"

"Oh yes, she was very special. I don't even know how clever she was, but I know she was special."

"Tell me about her, please?"

"Mary was a white woman who lived a long time ago and was captured by the Indians, so she had to live with them for many years."

"So what was special about that? I think that sounds horrible."

"It must have been very hard for her." Sarah could see that Jodie looked mystified, and so she went on to tell the story of Mary Jamieson and how she eventually married the Indian chief, settled down, and lived in the forest with the Indians. "You see, what was special about Mary wasn't the situation; maybe it happened a lot in those days. It was Mary herself who was special; it was her attitude. When she did finally get the opportunity to go back home, guess what? She chose to remain where she was. She had changed her life and made something good out of something awful. Now I call *that* special. She turned her life around. I was watching another special lady pack lemons yesterday. She had a sign on the wall that reminded me of Mary: it said, *'When life hands you lemons, don't suck 'em, make lemonade!'* Mary Jamieson did that. The lemon lady does that now."

Jodie frowned. "I don't understand."

"Well, have you ever sucked a lemon?"

Jodie nodded. "Ugh!"

"And I am certain that you have drunk lemonade."

"Gallons and gallons of it," the child said with a merry giggle.

"I bet! Which is nicest?"

"Lemonade, of course."

"But both come from lemons," Sarah said quietly. "They're the same thing, although one is bitter and the other is oh so wonderful and sweet."

Jodie sat perfectly still, digesting this piece of information by repeating it over and over again to herself softly. "*Don't suck them, make lemonade.* Does that mean that I can make something nice out of this?"

"It means exactly that. We can all go on feeling and eating bitter things, or with a little effort we can make something really great, like lemonade. It's the Mary Jamieson Principle. Special people do things like that all the time."

"So can I make something nice out of falling down here?" Jodie repeated.

"It sure do, Miss Platt!" Sarah acknowledged in her best American accent.

"But what?"

If ever there was a challenge handed out, this was it. Sarah didn't have a clue as to the answer, but she couldn't say that. "Wait and see!" she suggested. "Just be a VSP, and it will come to you, I promise. The really important thing about being a very special person is doing your best at whatever you are doing – not your second or third best, but always giving your very best effort and understanding that you mustn't give up when it gets hard. Just keep trying other ways until you get where you want to be."

"Does it always have to be my very best?" the youngster enquired timorously, already intimidated by the amount of effort this might involve.

"Absolutely," Sarah confided, putting a finger to Jodie's lips to indicate she was going to share a secret that she wasn't to tell. "Because your best is always good enough. Remember that: your best is always good enough. Then you won't be a quitter. Remember the lemons, and remember it takes time to make lemonade. Remember Mary Jamieson – it took time to turn her life around. Remember Mother Theresa and Abraham Lincoln."

"I will remember you," her student said without any hesitation. Then Jodie looked away as she added with great conviction. "I think you are special, too."

"Well, thank you," Sarah said humbly. "But remember, it has only to be your best effort. You may never be *the* best at school, but as long as it's *your* best, that's all that matters. And then when you get stuck, you can ask for help without thinking you are a dunce. Teachers are paid to help you learn you know; they are not villains, they want you to ask." Jodie snorted and shook her head in such a way that it caused Sarah to raise her eyebrow in the familiar silent reproach.

This time it had the opposite effect: it made Jodie grin. "Do that again," she pleaded. Sarah did, and while Jodie tried to copy her, she ended up laughing. "How do you do that?" she asked, trying again but ending up laughing nearly as much as before. The chest pain caused her to stop.

"Practice. Lots of it! Now, what was I saying? Oh yes, ask a teacher. Teachers aren't villains." Jodie was beginning to recognise that this woman knew many things, but she wasn't at all sure how she could possibly know that. "Where do you reckon I got so much practice?" Sarah asked humorously raising her eyebrow in a perfect arch again.

"You are a *teacher?* You're kidding me!"

"I most certainly am not!" the teacher answered in her best school ma'am voice. "Being a school teacher is no joking matter. This is serious stuff, I'll have you know." She tickled Jodie's nose until the child grinned again. When the humour had subsided, Sarah hammered home her point. "Jodie pet, everyone has talents. Being clever is only *one* talent; it's not the *only* talent. You understand the difference?" Jodie shook her head, so the teacher asked permission to share one last special person with her. Getting approval was relatively easy. She started with deep emotion. "This is about a boy who didn't think he was special either. Last year I taught a boy who was always in trouble – and I mean *big* trouble, always! No one wanted to teach him because he caused problems in all the classes. He didn't want to learn, and he did his best to stop everyone else from learning as well. He was not popular, you understand." She shook her head and raised both eyes heavenwards as she gestured. "My, was he not popular!"

Jodie copied her gesture, nodding her head just as seriously. It was a mite too close to home for comfort though. "So what happened to him?" she asked gravely.

"Well, most of the teachers tried everything they knew to help him, but nothing worked, so finally they all gave up." Jodie's face fell at that, and the almost imperceptible tremor to her lip multiplied Sarah's concern, but she continued innocently. "People started to say he should be expelled. Do you know what that means? Thrown out of school. Anyway, just before that happened, one of the teachers found out that this boy was good with his hands and that he could make the most beautiful things out of wood. He had a real talent, something that he loved to do. The teacher sent him to work at a joinery firm for a few weeks so that he could see how he might use this talent, and guess what? The boy came back a different person. He had seen where he could fit in and be ..."

"Special?" Jodie guessed.

"Oh yes, very special," Sarah acknowledged earnestly.

Michael's American counterpart nodded and then asked seriously, "What's your talent?"

The answer was accompanied by a grin. "Can I only have one?"

"I don't know. I don't have any. How many have you got?"

"Lots! Some I don't even know about yet."

"How come?"

"They're still waiting to be discovered. Isn't that exciting?"

"Are mine?" Jodie asked hopefully.

"Oh, I'm sure they are. Fields full of hidden talents, just waiting for you to find and use."

"Tell me about some of yours you know about."

"Well, let me see. I have a talent to ride."

"A bike?"

"Goodness me, no. I can only just balance on two wheels, and I am not very good at that. I fall off way too often! No, I mean I can ride a horse."

"You can ride a horse?" For Jodie, this was clearly on a par with riding a space rocket.

"Ever since I was a little girl. I lived on a farm."

"I'd like to ride a horse, but you have to be rich, and we have no money." Jodie's voice trailed away as contemplation of this economic limitation and its nefarious implications took over.

Sarah explained, "We don't all get to do the same things at the same time, sweetie, but if you really want to see what riding feels like, I'm sure you will find an opportunity sometime."

"What does it feel like?"

Sarah pulled the same odd, disconnected, simple words out of her head that she had offered Rick yesterday. "Freedom. Belonging together. Friendship. Loyalty. Adventure. All of it is absolutely wonderful – except for when you have to go pot holing the very next day."

Jodie might have been as confused as she looked by this last statement, but she only asked, "So what other talents do you have?"

After a brief moment's introspection, Sarah added feelingly, "I have a talent to be a mum."

"That's a talent?"

"One of my biggest, and certainly one of the best. I love it and it brings me great happiness. I go shopping with my girls and we choose clothes together. That's great fun – well, if you forget shopping for school uniform or Christmas presents, it is!"

"Do you ride together?"

"No, sweetheart. I can't afford for the girls to ride, either." Sarah watched the subtle alterations to Jodie's face as the child weighed this in the scale of her own experience. "But we go to the park, and we play games and ride our bikes. Well, they ride; I fall off."

"What else do you do together?"

"Let me see. We read together and do maths homework together, and we wash dishes together." The last two earned exquisitely ugly grimaces. "But then we make castles and rockets and pen trays out of the empty washing up liquid bottles. I love it, Jodie, even the maths homework and the washing up, because I love them, and I love making them happy. Mum and daughter is so very good."

"I don't know about that," the child said sadly.

"Not yet, you don't." Jodie looked up, but before she could say anything else, her mentor added significantly, "Maybe you have an opportunity to try this out as well." She did not elaborate, or say how. "Now let me see, what other talents do I have? Oh yes. I have another really special talent that I am still working on."

"What is that?"

"I'm learning to like being me!"

"I don't understand. You couldn't be anyone else, could you?"

"Not on the inside. But sometimes we don't let ourselves be who we are on the outside, because we think that people will laugh at us or make fun."

"You mean we try to fit in?"

"I mean exactly that."

"And you don't?" Jodie asked.

"Well, it's important to try to be nice to people, even when they think differently to you. But it's also important to stand up for what you believe to be right. Don't stay silent or do nothing." That comment almost exonerated the last day and a half.

"You mean like today?" Sarah had to think for a moment about what Jodie might be referring to, because it hadn't been anything she had had done today that she had been thinking about, so when she nodded hesitantly, she was still not a hundred per cent sure what Jodie meant. She was about to find out. "But this was so difficult to do. You are really special!"

"Thank you, sweetheart." At last it was clear to what Jodie was referring. "Sometimes it is difficult to be yourself, but not always, and guess what? It gets easier, and yes, it is special. Guess what else? It feels special, too. I am so happy I have met you. I think I shall award myself an ice cream when we get out of here. What do you say to ice creams all round?"

They were conferring over what flavours to combine to make the yummiest ever ice cream when Jodie suddenly dropped all pretence and admitted wistfully, "I'd like to feel special."

"Try it and see," her mentor suggested lightly. "You can feel it if you really want to; it just means you have to learn to listen to whatever is nice inside you and then do it."

Jodie nodded circumspectly. "You got any more talents?" These were the most interesting talents she had ever heard of.

"Well, I like to think I have a talent for words."

"Words! How can you have a talent for words?" This was too much. Words were dumb!

"Didn't I say that you can have a talent for almost anything? I have a talent for words – well, for using them to help people learn things. I love words, and I love using them; they are so powerful that they can make you laugh, and they can make you cry."

"That's stupid!" Jodie said disgustedly, quite sure by now that all this was being made up. "Falling makes you cry, or getting a smack. How can words make you cry?"

"How about 'I hate you'?" Sarah didn't need to say any more, but she couldn't resist. "Words can make you jealous, or angry, or any other emotion because they are so very powerful. That's why I love all of them – well, perhaps most of them. I love the happy ones the best."

"How can they make you happy?"

"I love you," she offered with real feeling, "Doesn't that make you feel happy?"

Jodie considered it and then grudgingly conceded. "Okay, it makes me feel nice inside."

"And when words are used well, they can be so very beautiful."

"How can words be beautiful? They're just words. We just say them or write them."

"Remember William Shakespeare?"

Jodie nodded. "Yeah. He's the writer that clever people know about."

"The very same. He writes beautiful words. He uses words better than anyone else I know. He says things with words that are important to me, in here." Sarah touched her heart. "And then I try to teach them to others, to share the beauty he creates."

"Shakespeare is … beautiful words?"

"Oh yes, Jodie, Shakespeare is very beautiful words."

"He's alive? You know him?"

"No. He's been dead for nearly 370 years, but I know him."

"And you love him?"

"Yes, I love his soul because his words speak to me of his soul. He paints pictures with words and helps me feel things deeply. Then he tells me about people's pains and fears, their hopes, their loves. I love his sense of humour and his faith."

"He believed in God, too?"

"Do you know, I'm not sure, but I think he did. But not just faith in God. He had faith in humanity, too." It was another difficult word, and she tried again. "Shakespeare had faith in people, Jodie. He knew we could be ugly and cruel to each other, so he used his words to show us where that leads, and to help us recognise that we can do better. He knew we could do better than that. He also wrote about how funny we can be, and how sad, and vain and meek."

"What's meek?"

"Humble, willing to learn."

"Do you think I should be meek?"

"I think it would be good for all of us to be meek, sweetheart. The world would be a much nicer place."

"Can you say some of Shakespeare's beautiful words now? I would like to hear some."

Sarah looked down into the small, deadly serious face as she brushed her fingers along Jodie's brow. She had never heard such a sincere request. "Let me see. How about this?

> 'Shall I compare thee to a summer's day,
> Thou are more lovely and more temperate,
> Rough winds do shake the darling buds of May,
> And summer's lease hath all too short a date:
> Sometimes too hot the eye of heaven shines,
> And often is his gold complexion dimm'd;
> And every fair from fair sometimes declines,
> By chance or Nature's course untrimm'd;
> But thy eternal summer shall not fade,
> Nor lose possession of that fair thou ow'st;
> Nor shall Death brag thou wandr'est in his shade,
> When in eternal lines to time thou grow'st.
> So long as men can breathe, or eyes can see,
> So long lives this, and this gives life to thee.'"

Jodie had lain quite still throughout Sarah's rendition, and it continued now that she had finished. Her breathing was quieter and there was even a faint smile on her face. She looked content. "Did you understand that?" Sarah asked.

"Not all of it, but it sounded so pretty."

"That's because it's poetry, Jodie. Sheer poetry. It is one of Shakespeare's many talents. Some of his words may sound strange to us today, but his ability with words can still touch our souls. I am so glad you felt that." After a minute's further silent contemplation, the conversation resumed at the point it had left off. This time Sarah was in tune and followed.

"Do you want to know what my talent is? I dance! And I'm going to be a ballet dancer when I grow up. I dance every day. Miss Rushton, my teacher at school, says I'm okay, and if I don't grow too tall, I might make it one day."

"See, that's brilliant. I knew you would have some talents. I bet you have lots more as well."

"You reckon?" Jodie asked hopefully.

Sarah's nod was one of the most enthusiastic she'd ever given, and she said, "So now that you know about talents and being a very special person I daresay you have all you need, except for the secret."

"The secret? What secret?"

"The secret to being the very best special person that you can be."

"What is it? Tell me, please!" The eagerness in the child's voice brought the familiar lump back to Sarah's throat.

"It is very simple, really. It's called desire," she whispered.

"Desire? What's desire?" It was hard not to miss the disappointment in the youngster's voice. Desire, whatever it might be, was a pretty lousy secret. It certainly wasn't the magic formula for which Jodie had been hoping.

"Ah, I can see that you think my secret is not very special at all." Jodie had to agree. "I forgive you. What would you have liked? A magic word, like Abracadabra or Open Sesame?" Jodie nodded again. "I thought so. Desire is more powerful than either of those things."

"It is? Gee!"

"Just because desire seems so simple, don't brush it aside. Sometimes we think that only complicated things are any good, but usually you will find it is simple things that provide the best answer. Most people walk past the answers to the problems in their lives because they can't believe that the answers can be something simple. Desire is one of the strongest forces in the universe." She repeated it very softly and slowly to emphasise her point. "That means that whatever you want, if you really want it hard enough, then you are bound to get it because you change to get it, you improve to get it, you study to get it, and you shape your life around getting it. And sooner or later, you do get it. People who tell you that it is not so are wrong; they simply desired something else more, that's all."

"So what has all that got to do with me?"

"Well, you just told me you wanted to be a ballet dancer. What are you doing about that, Miss Platt?

"I practice every day."

"Why?"

"Because that's how to do it! You have to keep practising." Jodie clearly thought that these were stupid questions; everyone knew you had to practice.

"But wouldn't you rather go out and play?"

"Sometimes." She paused then looked up. "Well, okay, most times."

"But you don't? I reckon you already know about desire, Jodie – you just didn't know what it was called, or you didn't realise you can make it work with anything."

"Anything?"

"Anything!" Here was the opportunity Sarah had been looking for, and she took it gratefully. "For instance, I was thinking that perhaps you really wanted to find out that you are still loved by your dad, and that you can still be loved by Dilys, but maybe I was wrong"

"No, you're right. But even after this?"

"Even after this. It's no good just wishing it will happen and then doing the exact opposite, so that no one gets the chance to prove it to you. You have to really desire it, and that means being big enough and brave enough to accept that sometimes we do things that don't make it easy for people to show their love for us."

"You mean like telling Dilys I hate her and kicking her?"

"That seems to fit the bill," Sarah declared with a wobbly smile. "Just remember that I didn't say it was easy, but the more you practice, the easier it becomes. Dilys may not know the secret, so it's all down to you, I reckon."

"But does it work?" Jodie asked impetuously.

"Of course it works. Would I tell you a secret that didn't work?"

"How do you know, though?"

"How do I know? I tested it out! That's how I know." The explanation covered her childhood years and wanting to be a teacher. "I didn't want anything else as much," she said clearly, a trace of nostalgia creeping into her voice as she remembered the show jumping and recognised afresh that her desire for that had not been great enough. She bent forward to whisper very confidentially, "You see, I was the world's number one duffer at maths, but I needed it to get into university, and when I kept failing my exam, I got disheartened and was just about to give up when my dad taught me about desire. I knew my Dad would not tell me a lie, so I kept on trying even when it seemed like I was getting nowhere and then guess what? A new teacher came to my school and explained things differently and that made a big difference. I made it! I passed! But I could have given up so easily if my dad hadn't taught me about desire. Desire does not make things easy, Jodie; it simply makes things possible, but that is something you must learn for yourself. You have to test it out, too. I can't describe what it feels like when you get where you want to be, except to say it feels a bit like sherbet fizz without having eaten it, or like lemonade without having drunk it. Conquering yourself always feels like that."

"I don't know what you mean."

"Try it and see, and then you will know what I mean. It makes you feel good to be you, and that's when you start to promise yourself you will always be true to who you are. When I passed my maths exam, I danced, cried, and danced some more, and kissed my dad a thousand times. Then I set to and helped a friend who was worse than me at maths. She didn't know the Secret, either, so I taught her just as my dad had taught me."

"Did she pass the exam in the end as well?"

"Of course. And guess what? I was just as pleased when she passed as when I had passed. We danced this little jig around the school hall, hugging each other, and laughing until we cried. I was so happy. I still feel like that, Jodie, every time one of my students passes an exam."

"Do you still dance?"

Sarah's grin was followed by a confession about the little song she had sung down the telephone to Elinor right after the A-level results. "I try to be a little more restrained these days – I mean grown-up – but desire is still the same. It's still at work all around each of us, all the time. You only have to know someone to see what it is that person desired most."

"How do you figure that?"

"Do you reckon Mother Theresa really wanted more than anything to be a millionaire?" Jodie shook her head. "No, of course she didn't. She wanted to help people, and that's just what she did; she found a way and the means to do what she wanted. People who desire money above everything else usually end up as millionaires, at least. Desire is such a strong force that sometimes people don't always recognise which desires are controlling their lives, but people always end up getting what they truly desire the most."

"Wow!" Jodie devoted all her attention to thinking hard about the possible implications of this for a while, and so she wasn't aware that Sarah was watching her, or that her face was betraying its thinking. "And can people change what they desire?" she asked rather nervously.

"Of course."

"What if I wanted to be good at school, and what if I wanted Dad to still love me after this?" She paused. "What if I wanted Dilys to love me after this?" Sarah had to swallow hard to force down that nuisance lump in her throat. She was still struggling to say something when Jodie added, "What if I desired to be really happy?"

"Ah, happiness," Sarah said, wiping her eyes as she dismissed the memories of the previous two days' conversations on the same subject and managed to utter somewhat wistfully, "That's what we are all looking for. But your desire has to be really strong to get it, because most of us settle for contentment." It was a confidence that seemed akin to confession without further explanation.

It fired the child's curiosity. "I don't understand. What is that difference?"

"For someone who tells me she is a dunce, I think you are asking me some very clever questions that I'm not sure that I can answer right now, but then, maybe that's as well. If your desire for real happiness is very strong, then I am sure you will keep going until you find it. The other things you wanted might come first. Maybe happiness will be the reward for desiring those good things."

"I see," Jodie said in her most grown-up voice, but Sarah could tell she couldn't see at all and was still doubtful.

"It works, I promise you. Put it to the test."

Jodie smiled at Sarah's earnest, quiet assurance and then mumbled. "I suppose I *have* been desiring to hurt Dilys, using my words to hurt her because I feel bad. Yes?"

This teacher applauded this child with as much enthusiasm as any teacher had ever shown any student. "Wow! I told you how special I thought you were," she declared triumphantly. "Now you are proving it. It takes a really big person to admit she was wrong."

"I am the smallest in my class."

"Don't you believe it! It's my bet that you are a head and shoulders above all of them as far as being grown-up goes."

"So how do I start?"

"You already have! Now all you have to do is keep going until you achieve what you want. Just try being nice to Dilys. Talk to her like you have to me."

"But she's not like you," the youngster insisted.

"No, that's true. Dilys is a lot younger and much prettier and she has no experience of eight-year-olds." She grinned at Jodie's disgruntled face. "In ten years' time when she is only nearly as old as I am now, then maybe she will be able to teach me a thing or two. I was hopeless at her age; I was still new to dealing with children too. Help her, Jodie. She's new to all this. Tell you what: try it for a month, and I guarantee that if it's not better, I'll …" She shrugged and raised her palms heavenwards. "I'll do whatever it is people promise to do when they know they won't have to do it."

Jodie attempted to laugh again, but it hurt too much now, so she looked up and said, "Sing and dance in the middle of the street again?"

"Even that! Well, is it a deal?"

"On a Saturday in a busy mall?" Jodie added.

"You drive a hard bargain. Okay, deal." Jodie looked almost happy with this arrangement, but then her face clouded over. "What is it?" Sarah asked.

"Will Dilys shop with me and do homework and read to me, like you do with Alison and Julie?"

"I don't know. Find out. If you talk to her, you will find out all these things and many more besides."

"You mean she'll be like you?"

"Maybe, maybe not."

"I just want her to be like you."

"Why?" Sarah asked.

"Because I like you. You haven't shouted at me, and you have talked to me differently. Why can't my dad have married you? I could have two big sisters then, and—"

"Hey, hang on here. I don't even know your dad. He might not even like me. I am old and grumpy, and it's Dilys he loves, sweetheart," she said as gently as she could. "But she will love you too, if you let her. I promise. Talk to her, please?"

"Okay." The reply was sullen. "But what about my dad? He still loves Dilys more than anything – I heard him say so."

So that was it! Sarah's last remarks had reminded Jodie there was more to this matter than just getting along with Dilys; it was about something else as well, something very deep and painful. "Can words do two things at the same time?" she sobbed as she choked back the tears. "Daddy's words pleased Dilys …"

"But they hurt you?" Jodie nodded, and Sarah stroked her head, "Does it still hurt?"

"When I think about it."

Sarah leant forward and brushed the child's cold cheek with her hair as she struggled to kiss her. "That feeling you have of pain is called jealousy Jodie, and it comes when we are afraid of losing something that we think someone else is taking from us." The little head went down again and stayed down as she failed to deny this. "But she hasn't Jodie. I've tried to tell you that you won't lose your dad's love, not one tiny bit of it. He still loves you exactly the same as he always has. This love he has for Dilys is different."

"You mean sex?" the sulking juvenile asked knowledgeably.

It was the adult who almost fell from the ledge with shock. Eight was young even for street-cred Californians to know of such things. It had been the last thing she had been expecting. "I beg your pardon!" she said, stumbling over her words and blushing furiously.

Jodie gazed up at her. "Sex," she repeated patiently. "My friend Cory told me about sex. He said—

"Never mind what Cory said about sex."

"It's not true? I knew it wasn't. He said ..." She launched into a full-scale, graphic account. A polite cough warned her the shock had worn off sufficiently for Sarah to take some action. Fortunately for Cory, he was not around to get what she felt he deserved.

"Jodie, listen to me," she said firmly. "Whatever Cory has said about sex, grown-up love is not just about that. It is also very special and it is so much more than just sex. I want you to remember that, because your dad now has Dilys to share this love with, and he will be happy because of it. You want him to be happy, don`t you?" A cursory nod was all the response she got, and so she reached out and planted a kiss on Jodie's forehead again. As she did so, she whispered in her ear, "I knew you would. And guess what? Because he is happy, his love for you will be better than ever."

"How come?" There was no room for equivocation here.

"Because ..." She was floundering but hoped it didn't show. "Because he has someone to help him make decisions, someone to help him care for you. This love he has for Dilys helps him do all those things, and that makes you a very lucky young lady."

This was the biggest revelation yet as far as Jodie was concerned, and it just had to be another secret because the logic of it defied her. She had considered herself many things over the last year, but lucky had definitely not been one of them!

"Yes, it does! You see, love is magic. It stretches and stretches, and the more you give away, the more you have left to give. Imagine having a bag of ten sweets, and you give five away, then, when you look inside, how many would you have left?"

"That's easy. Five," the student mathematician said smugly.

"Not with this bag, you don't! You have twenty left! Love does that: it grows and keeps on growing. Now you are very lucky because you are going to grow up in a family where there will be lots of it, and that is just about the best start in life that anyone can have."

Jodie looked at her with disbelief. Cory had never told her any of these things, and up to this moment in time, Cory had represented all to which she ever wanted to aspire. As she watched Sarah struggle to find the words which would overthrow Cory's dominance, she registered a small desire to be convinced.

Sarah pleaded, "Just because you heard your dad tell Dilys he loved her more than anything, that doesn't mean he doesn't love you as much. You are not a thing." She felt awestruck by this sudden inspiration. "You are his child, his daughter."

"But he loves her!"

"*And* you."

"Not as much!"

"Not true. Just differently," Sarah said quietly. "He didn't say more than anyone, did he? He said more than anything." She was still not sure where that had come, but she was happy to repeat it, even though she could see that Jodie was still dubious. She smiled reassuringly. "Can I try to explain this?" Permission was granted, and she launched into yet another attempt to reassure this child that her fears were just that, fears. It ended with a blunt declaration. "This love was never yours, Jodie. It is taking nothing away from you; it was never yours, and it isn't just sex, either. Talk to your dad and Dilys about all this – all of it, including Cory's theories. Ask them."

"I don't know," Jodie muttered, shaking her head. "Cory said—"

"Please, Jodie. It is important."

Although Jodie finally agreed, it was a reluctant promise, but further discussion was prevented by machinery noises and then a loud hail from above. It made them both jump. They had been so engrossed in their conversation that they had completely forgotten all about the activity at the top. They looked up together to see a strange face peering back down at them. It grinned and announced cheerfully, "Hey, you down there. You the ladies that need rescuing?"

"Yes!" they chorused in flamboyant unison.

"Then I am the guy you need. Stay put. I am going to swing my crane over to lift that beam off first, and then we will have you both out in no time. The cavalry is here, girls!"

"Getting to be a habit," Sarah muttered. "Second time in three days,"

"What's getting to be a habit?" Jodie asked.

She was saved from explanation as the crane put in its appearance and Jodie's attention was diverted to watching its complicated manoeuvring. Half an hour later she watched Jodie disappear, suspended on a stretcher with a fireman riding shotgun. The same fireman came back and helped her into a sling seat, which turned out to be nearly as bad as, if not worse than, coming down on the end of a rope. Eventually she also emerged into the bright afternoon sunlight.

The alley was no longer deserted; ambulances, police cars, and fire engines all with their emergency lights flashing were parked alongside the crane. The sheer amount of activity startled her and as she was deposited gently on the ground, a dozen or so people surged forward with microphones and cameras. A paramedic tried to push them away as he helped her towards a waiting ambulance, but he couldn't hold them back completely, so cameras flashed all around her. She automatically raised both hands in front of her face to shield herself from this barrage, but the medic's pleas to let the lady through were ignored. She spotted Daniel trying to get through to her from the back of the group, but as she tried to reach out to him, a policeman arrived, and Daniel was pushed back along with the others.

Sarah was protesting against being taken to hospital when Daniel finally got through the cordon surrounding the ambulance. "Oh Daniel, thank goodness! Come in, please tell this young man I'm fine! Well, just a little scratch, that's all," she said as the medic started to unfasten the scrap of skirt she had tied around her leg to stem the blood flow.

"This tomato sauce, then?" the guy asked sarcastically as he removed the rest of the makeshift bandage. "Grand Canyon's only a little valley too, I suppose." The evidence could hardly be denied. The bloody mess on her thigh looked worse in this clean, sterile setting than it had down the hole. Thick mud mixed with dried-on blood could never be a pretty sight, but it looked distinctly gruesome with fresh rivulets of bright new blood gushing out, mingling with the old. She had to turn her head away and breathe deeply so as not to faint as the medic started to clean it up. Gentle was not a word he understood, so she concentrated on asking for news about Jodie who had already been flown off to hospital, accompanied by her dad.

The medic interrupted her questions. "Like I said lady, this leg needs stitching. I'm taking you to the hospital."

She stared in disbelief at him and then nodded her head at Daniel, who bent forward to examine the wound. "Mm, maybe," he advised contemplatively. The paramedic looked up, piqued on hearing this second, uncalled-for opinion. Daniel was unruffled. "You had a tetanus shot?" he asked.

"Yes, before I came."

"Then I'd say a couple of them butterfly things should hold it. You got any?"

Despite all the paramedic's misgivings, Daniel managed to convince him it was the easiest thing to do in the circumstances. The lady was obviously reluctant to go to the hospital, and he was already opening the door for them to leave before the medic could change his mind.

The press menagerie were flashing away outside as the guy was warning her she was leaving against medical advice. She took one look outside then turned around and smiled at him.

"Are you leaving now as well?" she asked the weary medic, who had already started to clear his equipment.

"Looks like it, unless there is someone else to refuse treatment."

Ignoring such sarcasm was easy after the last two days, so she smiled sweetly. "Do you think you could you possibly give us a lift to the end of Daniel's street? It's not far." Seeing his reluctance to use his ambulance as a taxi she lifted one of her bare feet. "No shoes," she pointed out. "I would hate to end up at the hospital having to explain why I was out walking with no shoes on!"

Chapter Twenty-Two

The ambulance stopped out of sight of the Marshalls' house so as not to worry Nora, though Daniel fussed over her every bit as much as Nora would have done. "Shall I carry you?"

"And have me kill you? How would I explain that to Nora? 'Oops, sorry – I just gave your husband a heart attack two weeks after he retired.' I don't think so!"

"You can't be that heavy and last month I was wrestling with heavier," he pointed out bluntly, not totally convinced he was doing the gentlemanly thing even if it was what the lady wanted.

"Daniel, no! Thank you, but no thank you. I am fine. Ouch!"

"Then at least have my jacket, because you are shivering, and I am beginning to think I did the wrong thing rescuing you from that medic." He steered her to the smoothest parts of the road, clearing away potential dangers ahead of her like a soldier hunting out landmines. As he did this, he filled her in on the other development of the afternoon – the one he had chosen to keep from her while Jodie was around, the one about Dilys having been rushed to hospital minutes after they had left the house. There had been no news since. "Jodie kicked her," he said hesitantly, not at all sure how wise it was to give more bad news to someone who was already in shock.

"Yes, I know. She told me."

"Not good, in her condition." This fractured conversation reflected the fact that neither of them wanted to mention what was uppermost in their mind, so they fell silent for a while, each contemplating the other potential consequences of the afternoon's disaster. Neither version was pleasant. "Jack's a decent guy and I had hoped that this would work out for him – for all of them," Daniel said eventually.

"And Dilys? Is she a decent woman?"

Daniel turned to look directly at her, trying to figure out why she should ask that. "Yeah, she's okay. Seems nice enough, anyway." Then he added his real thoughts on the issue. "If you really want to know, I reckon Dilys is simply in way over her head. She's only a twenty-one-year-old kid herself. Eight months ago she had never been married, had never had a child or raised one. Now here she is, married to a guy of thirty-five, having his baby, and with a difficult eight-year-old to cope with as well. No small wonder they are having problems!"

"Maybe it will get better now."

"You really believe that?" His tone betrayed his feelings perfectly.

"I believe sometimes it takes a near tragedy to turn things around."

"Well let's just hope it stays at *near* tragedy, then," he said ominously.

Nora had been watching for them from inside the house and so she was at the screen door long before they reached it. Daniel and the police had kept her up to date with events, but nothing could have prepared her for the sight of her dishevelled guest, limping and shoeless in a torn skirt, literally covered from head to toe in thick black mud and blood. Nora hardly dared ask how she was. Sarah did her best to reassure her that she was all right. "Honestly I am fine. I look much worse than I feel. I might look like a street urchin but all I need is a shower and a change of clothing and then I will be good as new. But don't come near me," she added hastily, seeing Nora move to assist her, "or else you will be covered in this stuff as well. I have already ruined Daniel's jacket! If you could get me a bowl of water, I will wash my feet before I come in and then your floor won't end up the same."

Ten minutes later, as she was drying her scratched but clean feet, the urchin announced, "Do you know something Daniel? I have worn shoes all my life and that's probably why I never realised until now how important they are." She picked up the bowl of inky black sludge and grinned. "Hot water comes in the same category as shoes. Some of your choice blessings, both of them." Daniel had spoken on the importance of recognising one's blessings in his address at church. Was that only six hours ago? He nodded his understanding.

Within half an hour she had showered and was clean and dry, and almost back to normal; the second of those choice blessings having restored her frozen limbs back to pink glowing health, and except for the difficulty in keeping her injured leg dry, she would have allowed it to bless her for longer, but she gave up the struggle and sat on the side of the Marshall's bathtub wrapped in one of their pink and blue striped bath towels, surveying the neatly folded pile of clothes which Nora had left for her to try. The irony of it did not escape her. Was this just recompense, or retribution even? What followed started out as a little chuckle but soon erupted into such hearty laughter that tears ran down her face and she had to grip the bath to steady herself.

Nora was waiting outside in case Sarah should need any assistance. She could not understand for the life of her why anyone who had just endured such an ordeal should be laughing. She knocked on the door and asked anxiously, "Sarah, are you all right?" When she didn`t get an answer, she ventured solicitously, "Does everything look so awful?"

"No, Nora, the clothes are fine," Sarah shouted back, wiping away the last of her tears before picking up the top dress. There was no way to explain the situation, so she wouldn't bother trying, just as there would be no point in sorting through Nora's clothes; they would all have been made for a five foot two, size twenty woman, and as she was a five foot six, size twelve, one didn't need to be a genius to work out how that would look. She slipped on the first dress and pulled in the belt; it was shorter than she liked, and the floral pattern was not to her taste, but none of that mattered because she would change as soon as she got back to…Box! In all the furore she had completely forgotten all about Box! She had even forgotten about Rick DDSR and her lift! Her watch said four forty-five. Fifteen minutes left to tidy up and say good-bye. She gathered up the pitiful rags that used to be clothes and tied then together in a bundle, then did her best to clean the now grubby bathtub, then, tasks completed, she hobbled downstairs as fast as she could.

An awkward silence greeted her appearance. It was a giveaway: the Marshalls had been talking about her. "Can you get rid of these for me, please?" she asked pleasantly, anxious to dissipate the unease by handing over her bundle, and concluding cheerfully, "you will be pleased to know I am restored to full working order! Only one last problem to solve: shoes." A size twelve body would fit in a size twenty dress, however odd it looked, but size six feet would not fit into size four shoes, however hard she tried and however many Cinderella jokes she cracked.

Nora rose to the challenge by producing a pair of fluffy pink fur mules, which she offered as triumphantly as any fairy godmother could offer glass slippers. The fashion victim shook her head, but Nora persisted. "I realise they might not be what you would choose honey, and they are a bit small, but at least wear them for now. They will save your feet from the road." No further persuasion needed.

A persistent horn interrupted their conversation and Daniel went across to the window to check its source. "Black car? Gee, a Ferrari, ain't it?"

Nora held onto her arm. "Let Daniel go out and explain what has happened, honey. He will tell him you are not fit to travel. Stay here overnight, and Daniel will run you across in the morning.

"I'm sorry?" Sarah queried, puzzled by this sudden apprehension.

"Shelagh asked us to try to keep you here," Nora admitted, "but what with all the fuss about Jodie, we haven't had much time to talk about it, have we? She is right though: you don't know this man. Please stay here."

"I couldn't possibly do that," Sarah said quietly. "He has just driven fifty odd miles to collect me, and I couldn't be that rude. But thank you for offering. You have both been so very kind. And apart from that, I need to be there first thing in the morning to meet the repair man. I am okay Nora, honestly. Shelagh should not have worried you like this." Her own misgivings of Friday night were already forgotten.

"So what does this guy do for a living?" Daniel asked as she looked round to locate her bag.

"Grows fruit. Oranges, lemons – lots of them. Packs and ships them as well. Packs other people's too, from what I can gather."

"Must be a sizeable concern then. What's his name? I might know him. I know of a couple of growers up that way – not many that size of left."

Now she had to admit that she did not know Rick`s surname. It would never do to introduce him as Rick DDSR even if did stand for Dracula Da Santi Rochester. The Marshalls would never understand her humour. So, she would either have to lie or find a way to evade answering. She was on her way to the door when Daniel repeated his question. She tried not to hear this time either, or to notice Nora shake her head at him.

"It's Da Santi, I think," she said smoothly, selecting the name on the portrait in the hall as the only half decent option available to her. It had some legitimacy, she had considered it briefly yesterday morning when she had been stood in front of the portrait in the hall. Who was to say it wasn`t? It was grasping at Spanish straws, but they were the only ones available right at this minute. "Rick Da Santi. I suppose it could be Ricardo da Santi. Spanish, do you think?"

"Name don't ring any bells with me," Daniel said gravely.

"It might not be that. I only think it's that."

"Think?" Nora queried.

"He hasn`t told you?" Daniel queried, spurred on by his wife's animated gesturing.

"In a roundabout way, I suppose. Have I got everything?"

"Then I suggest you ask him in a non-roundabout way. Seems odd he wouldn't want you to know his name." By the time they reached the door, Nora had positioned herself across it, ready to beg one last time with Daniel nodding his agreement as he moved to assist her at the barricade. Nora promised that Daniel would go out and tell this Ricardo character, whoever he was, that she was staying. "Won't you, honey?"

Sarah moved their arms gently away from the door and shook her head. "Come out and meet him if you want to reassure yourself that I am okay, but I must go."

Rick sat in his car completely unaware of the controversy he was causing. He stayed sat in his car even when he must have been aware they were all stood on the driveway. Sarah allowed her disappointment to be replaced with crossness at his rudeness. He stayed put while she hugged the Marshalls' farewell. Glaring at him as best she could produced no action either, he remained impervious to her black looks and the evil eye. These techniques clearly did not work on him.

"Ring as soon as you get to Shelagh's?" Nora whispered.

"I will ring you tomorrow as soon as I am on my way, okay?"

Daniel took hold of her arm as if he intended to help her into the car. His real motive was a little more devious: if this character was not going to get out; then he was going to get a good look at him, just in case it was ever needed. His protégé was too busy wrestling with her own feelings to contemplate what anyone else's might be, but about a foot away from the car, she stopped suddenly. Daniel mistook her motive and thought that she must have changed her mind about going back, that's why he looked at her for verification, but she had merely bent down to empty an imaginary stone out of Nora's slippers in order to provide her with some extra thinking time for how to achieve her objective of introducing them. By the time she had emptied both slippers twice, fumbled in her bag to check that she had her house keys, car keys, and any other totally unnecessary objects she could think of, Nora had joined them on the sidewalk where they proceeded to go through the whole farewell and hugs ritual all over again. Wasting time took effort – but Rick stayed put in his car throughout it all! It may not have been obvious to the Marshalls, but Sarah's determination was keeping pace with her anger, which was escalating pretty rapidly, mostly because she had painted such a rosy picture of Rick the perfect gentleman and now here he was playing the absolute cad with consummate ease.

They were engaged on the third round of hugs when the cad finally got out of his car. Without looking at any of them, he walked the reverse way round it, avoiding them all. He held open his door; a fairly explicit signal that he didn't want to meet anyone and was impatient to be off. Sarah towed Daniel and Nora across to him.

"Rick," she said sweetly, "This is Nora Marshall and her husband, Daniel. They're my friend Shelagh's relations. Nora, Daniel, this is Rick, the man who was good enough to rescue me and shelter me from that storm."

Faced with such a situation, there was little Rick could do except accept the introduction. Nora took hold of his reluctantly proffered hand.

"Nice to meet you," she said. He muttered something before turning away quickly, but the lady was more interested in the thunderous face than in the greeting. While Rick was shaking hands with Daniel, Nora's head was working overtime. A fleeting smile at Daniel gave it away. "Of course. Ricardo…" She paused a second, and then gaining courage she laughed a little nervously before adding confidently, "Your name's not Da Santi, is it? It's Masters? You are Rick Masters?" There was no agreement, but there was no disagreement, either, so she went on to explain to Daniel excitedly, "You know honey, *the* Rick Masters!"

Daniel scratched his head, trying to place who the heck *the* Rick Masters might be. Sarah was simply bewildered so dismissed Nora's profession easily: there was no way she could she know him. Daniel finally placed the name and though he had only ever seen the guy a couple of times in films on TV and he wouldn't have associated the face in front of him with that name, he nodded his head as he recalled a rumour he had heard a few years back that he had bought a place nearby. It had seemed nothing more than a rumour at the time, and in a state preoccupied with rumour and speculation about the comings and goings of movie stars, he hadn't paid too much attention to it then, or given it a second thought since. Movie stars collectively didn't figure greatly in the scheme of things in the Marshall household; this one was no different than the others.

Sarah remained in the dark. The name meant nothing to her, but she did register Nora saying, "No wonder you would rather stay with him!" It was a sly aside, though it was her next remark that worried her more. "It's not too late to change your mind!" But the whole exchange happened so quickly that it had no chance of making sense to someone who was still in shock from the afternoon's other escapade. The fruit farmer had no way of knowing about that, but he chose to forestall the possibility of further examination of his identity by bundling his guest unceremoniously into the car and shutting the door. Nora bent down to the window as he started the engine. "Take care!" she mouthed as it roared into life. Then they were off, leaving his usual calling card behind them. It had taken Nora working out who he was for him to accept an awful fact: that billion-to-one shot had just come in, his strange houseguest really didn't know who he was. In all the scenarios he had ever considered, this one had always been the one he had rejected every time, because *everyone* knew who he was – even the old lady. But if that was so, then worse still, if the rest of Sarah's story was true – something he now had to consider possible – then he was bright enough to know that her finding out who he was, was not going to be a simple, or easy thing. Her precious principles would see to that. But anything had to be better than her finding it out right there, in the middle of the highway, in front of an audience.

Sarah had abandoned trying to fathom the little exchange because there were more important things to worry about than Nora's knowledge of the locals, though the simple act of sitting without having to concentrate on staying alive was in itself urging her towards sleep. Her eyelids were fighting a compelling urge to close before they had gone a few hundred yards, and her breathing was slowing down, lulled by the motion of the car. It enticed her to descend into a comfortable, warm blackness.

Rick breathed more easily as he observed that. He had no idea how he would impart the necessary information, because it had never happened before, but given that he had saved one nasty scene, he could probably save another – and even provide a satisfactory explanation given enough time.

The afternoon's heroine was just passing the final threshold where consciousness signs off when her mind salvaged an unasked for memory file from way back last year – one of Marcie Hadley's candidates for that genius list - Rick Masters! There was just enough mental functioning left on duty for her to be roused by that. She blinked, opened one eye in shock and then the other, and sat bolt upright. "You are *the* Rick Masters," she repeated softly, rolling Nora's words around her head and trying to hang onto what had just occurred to her.

Rick flicked her a glance but said nothing. She retrieved the memory in full, and then the awful significance of the name hit her head-on, like colliding with a fully loaded juggernaut. Rick Masters – Movie Star! Followed by all of Marcie Hadley's supporting evidence in every lurid detail. No wonder he had not wanted to be introduced. No wonder he had not told her his name. No wonder he had been so strange all weekend. As her mind rapidly scanned through a whole catalogue of "no wonders," she looked across at the stern face beside her for verification of this wild notion. His indifference confirmed it: he had been found out! "You are *that* Rick Masters, aren't you?" It wasn't exactly the same emphasis as Nora had employed, but he didn't answer this time either. "What are you doing here?" she demanded angrily.

This time he did. Same question, different emphasis. "What *am I* doing here?"

"Why aren't you in Hollywood?" she spluttered. She hadn't thought about the logic or sense in that, but the rudeness of her tone more than adequately conveyed everything that she had ever thought about certain movies, certain movie stars, and all of Hollywood. She was as certain that Hollywood should be the required residence for this distasteful breed, quite as much as Pentonville or Sing-Sing should be the expected domicile for those murderers and rapists that had figured so much in her thoughts over the last couple of days. The look he gave her said she ought to have kept that opinion to herself, but her words had been at least as stinging as that slap on Friday night. This time he recovered quicker.

"Gee, I'm sorry," he offered apologetically. "I didn't know there was a requirement I live there. I thought I could live anywhere I wanted! Well, anywhere I could afford the taxes"

She answered sheepishly, properly deflated by his sarcasm, though still trying to recant graciously without losing face. "It's just that people expect to find movie stars in Hollywood, so they aren't surprised when they do," she ended limply. She did realise her intended ending would be better left unsaid, so instead of pointing out "so they can't be anywhere else misleading people," which was probably one of the unkindest things she had ever thought, she muttered a banality, something about her not explaining herself well. It might have been noble and polite not to say what she wanted, but it also felt frustrating, and for once she was not grateful for her mother's civilising influence. Her inability to easily put aside her carefully conditioned manners to gratify passion annoyed her more at that moment than any other time she could recall, because it meant compromising truth, but this was a truth that would not be compromised, or restrained – it would be heard. In the end she had no option but to resort to William for aid in explaining her feelings because there was nothing in her mother's code of polite behaviour that prevented her quoting William when he was being blunt. "'*You told a lie, an odious lie.*'"

"Is that you or Shakespeare?" he parried casually.

"Both of us!" she snapped back.

"Then you are both wrong, because I told you nothing of the sort."

"Sin of omission!" she stated baldly. If he had been the mass murderer she had once briefly thought he was, he could not have been condemned with more disgust. "So why are you here, then?" she spat out, forgetting she had already asked this once.

He had resisted the cutting reply once, but there was nothing restraining him a second time. "I'm picking you up, remember?" he said calmly, well aware of his choice of words.

His passenger glared back and screamed, "Wishful thinking! Just wishful thinking!" Silence reigned while she tried to think of something that could adequately express her churning emotions, but she couldn't come up with anything other than, "How could you?"

"How could I what? Pick you up? Easy. I just drove over."

If he was trying to irritate her, he was doing a pretty good job, but she suspected by the mocking tone in his voice that he was more rattled than he would have her believe. His acting ability obviously left a lot to be desired. "I do not understand," she said distastefully, "how you could deliberately keep quiet and let me believe you to be just an average fruit-growing Joe Bloggs. I even told them I thought your name must be Da Santi. I told the Marshalls that! I said you were probably called Ricardo Da Santi! Do you realise what a fool you made me look?"

"Ah! That's what all this is about, is it? You looking foolish?"

"Isn't that enough?"

"Okay, if I have made you look foolish, then I apologise. As for the rest, well, I am just an average fruit-growing Joe Bloggs, and I happen to act as well. So what?"

"He happens to act as well, so what!" She had to repeat it several times, as if sufficient repetition might help her to digest it. With each repetition she tried a different emphasis. It was extremely irritating.

"That's the third time you have said it," he pointed out.

"I know, and I still can't believe it," she said, stunned by his indifference. "He happens to act as well, so what!" Even after the fourth performance, it still rattled her.

This last repetition was the straw that snapped his carefully controlled temper, and he had no polite manners to restrain him. He completely ignored the road to turn and ask tersely, "What the hell is so bad about being seen with me, anyway? I recall other women queuing up for that and thinking it a privilege." Sarcasm decorated his anger. "But then, I forget – you are not just another woman, are you?"

Angry or sarcastic – either way he didn't frighten her because she was angry, too, and she could do sarcasm as well. She declared jubilantly, "Oh, you are so right for once! And what's more, I am overjoyed that I am not just another woman. The morals of most of the women you know seem to leave a lot to be desired."

"Self-righteous prig!"

"I am not! And even if I were, your appearance this afternoon has put an end to any vestige of respectability I might have had."

"I didn't say anything."

"You didn't need to – you just had to show up! I cannot think what the Marshalls must think of me. '*Reputation, reputation, Oh, I have lost my reputation!*'"

"You are totally unreal. You are so old–fash—"

She stopped him mid-sentence. "There is absolutely no need for further insults! I have no doubt that I am old-fashioned by your standards. Guess what? Your opinion does not matter to me! And I prefer to think of myself as right-fashioned, which is somewhat different, and that is neither a sin nor a crime. I spend my life trying to counteract the influence of people like you. From what little I have heard of you, '*Thy sins not accidental but a trade!*'"

"Might know you would have to resort to your back-up." He shook his head in utter disbelief. "Poor old Hamlet."

"It's not *Hamlet*, it's *Measure for Measure* … I think."

"You mean there is something you are *not* certain about?" he retorted.

"I told you last night, *Mr Masters.*" There was no mistaking the emphasis. "My life has meaning to me, and I will have you know that it brings me happiness because of the way I live it. You are right: I do have standards, and I still try to live by them today, just as I did yesterday. If you don't have the same standards, fine, that has nothing to do with me." She paused for dramatic effect and to take a breath as well as thinking of what came next. "As long as you don't feel you have the right to make me out to be a fool, or to ruin my reputation."

"I don't like to be a bore, but didn't you just say I already did exactly that?"

She delivered her best withering look and then shook her head, mainly to stop herself from crying. Confusion and tiredness were not comfortable friends. "How do you think I feel right now?" she demanded. "I have been telling them all afternoon what a wonderful, kind person you are and what a perfect host, and then bingo – Bluebeard shows up! Do you know or care what sort of person they now probably take me for?"

"Thanks for the compliment."

Any other time she might have been impressed with the quickness of his wit. Not today. Not right now. "Your juvenile wit does not amuse me one bit!" He smirked annoyingly as she concluded miserably, "But I suppose it's no use crying about it now. It's done! *'What's gone and what's past help, should be past grief.'* And that's not Hamlet, either," she added heavily.

"Well, for once the three of us are in complete agreement," he mocked.

She looked at him stonily and then said quietly with real feeling, "Damn you!"

"Language, language! Ladies do not damn anyone, even when they are rattled."

"I am not rattled! I just don't want to play any more of your silly games. I don't even want to speak to you any longer, and I would be obliged if you wouldn't speak to me either. Leave me alone. I have said all I want to say."

The speedometer crept up towards the hundred mark and then past it. She sat rigid, trying not to notice its progress, determined that even if he went fast enough to achieve lift off, she would not speak again.

They were almost back at Box when the strange pink fluffy slippers stretched out in the front of his Ferrari, grabbed his attention. No one had ever graced any of his cars with worn pink fluffy slippers before, and then he took in her strange dress. "What the hell happened to you?"

She was tempted not to answer at all, and then she thought about telling him to mind his own business or ask in a civilised manner. Instead, it was back to the two answers: one she thought, and one she gave. "I seem to remember you reprimanding me for a milder swear word not all that long ago."

"I doubt if 'damn' could be said to be milder than 'hell', but who knows. Maybe you're an authority on that as well."

She glared at him. Elinor was more easily cowed into submission when reprimanded for swearing and she wasn't that sure what to do about anyone who wasn't.

"You still haven't told me what happened to you," he pointed out, genuinely interested, though that was unlikely to impress her. The moral minority remained silent, staring out of the window. "Okay, Miss, no more swearing. Will that do?"

His puerile sense of humour irritated her, but she did at least realise that if she were to get any peace, then she would have to tell him something, so she cleared her throat and announced without a shred of emotion, "I had an accident, I got dirty. Nora lent me some clothes. Satisfied?" The tone and content making it abundantly clear that amicable relations had not been resumed and that she did not wish to discuss it further, so they lapsed back into silence.

Chapter Twenty-Three

The rest of the journey back passed in silence. When they arrived, Sarah climbed out and marched off towards the house with the sort of determination that always signifies a fight is imminent, never over. Rick tried not to let his annoyance show quite so transparently but he did resort to kicking a nearby oil can when he thought she was out of hearing.

Unfortunately the gashed thigh, not to mention the multitude of other aches and pains she had collected, hindered Sarah's capacity for recognising the ridiculous, so the comedy rating of striding out in pink fluffy slippers at least a couple of sizes too small went unnoticed by her. It was not missed by the guy behind, who got all the laughs. Rick was unrepentant about everything, including thoroughly enjoying the amusing spectacle of the angry duck in front of him; it was even more satisfying than kicking oil cans. The duck's only reward was being met by a locked door that provided her with time for reflection.

It was not clear whether it was the wait or the reflection that took the edge off the anger she had been nursing so carefully all the way back, but instead of the acid line she had imagined herself saying, all she announced was, "I'll pack," as he produced the necessary key. For once he didn't argue, but he followed her through into the kitchen where Molly was busy working on dinner. She hardly noticed them, but Sarah was at least prudent enough not to say anything else until they reached the hall, and then she went straight to the stairs, finishing her diatribe with a distinctly theatrical flourish and a, "Right now" as her foot touched the very first tread.

"Puck and the fairies been overnight, then?" he asked.

"No," she said witheringly, "but I will be better off out there, with or without an engine!"

"Suit yourself!" he said with the sort of finality that signifies no argument, and he turned on his heel and disappeared into a nearby room slamming the door hard behind him for effect.

The duck pulled a silly face but was chastising herself for being equally childish when Molly poked her head out of the kitchen to check on the cause of the disturbance. The evidence was standing on the stairs, hands on hips, looking too close to tears for there to be any doubt. Molly decided discretion to definitely be the better part of valour for now and withdrew swiftly. She was used to these outbursts, though two days was quick, even for him. She had suspected that not everything Chas had told her about this girl was absolutely kosher, but it didn't matter much now – she was on her way out.

Slamming doors and temper tantrums might have been regular practice in this household, but Sarah was not used to such scenes any longer, except with Ali, and that was somewhat different; consequently she was almost as shocked at her own sad performance, as she was disgusted with his. "Come on, pull yourself together! What is happening to you?" she demanded mercilessly. There was no answer that could possibly satisfy her, but with the force of the slam still ringing in her ears she sank down onto the most convenient stair as the noise of cue striking balls resonated through the hall. "See, he isn't bothered, so why should you be?" She knew why. As she sat alone on the eighth stair, near to tears, she found the strength from somewhere to channel her misery into anger and spat, "Puerile exhibitionist!" at the closed door before hauling herself up to climb the rest of stairs. The move turned out to be a mite too indignant and a lot too smart for someone wearing pink fluffy slippers two sizes too small. Instead of climbing them as she had intended, she tripped over her awkwardly shod feet and slid unceremoniously down three. A last-minute lunge at the banister prevented her from sliding all the way to the bottom, but it could do nothing to preserve her dignity. She had achieved a near perfect nose-to-the-stair position for tobogganing, if one insisted on doing it backwards.

She picked herself up gingerly, rubbed her knee and nose simultaneously, and tried to placate damaged pride by pointing out that fortunately no one had been watching, and she had escaped with only a scraped knee and a burning nose. All the same, she had to admit her list of injuries was growing by the hour. Indignation had changed to humiliation somewhere between that eighth and third stair and so, weary as she was, she sank down again, right way up this time. At that precise moment she wanted nothing more than to be home. Why she had ever left it was unfathomable. The reasons that had seemed so powerful a few short months ago now appeared to be nothing more than the irrational hankerings of an overtired woman. Short of anything more tangible to blame for her stupidity, she remonstrated with her clumsy feet and the worn pink fur adorning them. "And look where following them has got you," she said bending to remove the offending articles before she could have any further mishaps. Sight of her two scarred bare feet made her recall where they had been not that long ago, and without any warning she slumped forward, put her head in her hands, and wept as waves of dizziness, nausea, and confusion swept over her in no particular order. It took a full five minutes for her to regain some sort of control, and it was only done then because she thought she heard someone coming. Humiliation could not be witnessed twice in one day. She dried her eyes on the floral skirt, scooped up the slippers, and dragged herself up the rest of the stairs. When she reached sanctuary, she flung herself down on the bed and sobbed uncontrollably. Yesterday she would have worried about the silk bedspread; today she did not give it a second thought, and if she had, she wouldn't have cared. Jodie's inexhaustible supply of woes even started to seem sensible and proportionate now. The fact that three-quarters of the known universe would have struggled to understand what all the fuss was about did not help one bit. "Elinor was right," she blubbed. "I should never have come here alone. She knew I couldn't handle this! Why didn't I listen to her?"

It was dark when she awoke. Her leg throbbed and so did her head, but then, there was hardly a part of her that was not in some sort of pain. She tossed aside the bedcover and reached across to find her travel alarm. Eight thirty – she had been asleep for more than two hours! Now she had to decide what to do. Well, not so much *what* to do but more *how* to do it. Normal functioning would only return at its own pace and could not be forced, so her head whirled around in all directions without coming to any firm conclusions. "Have a bath and then think about it again," she advised herself.

The evidence of the day's devastation stared back at her through the irritatingly well-lit bathroom mirror: puffy eyes from crying and that on top of no make-up, (if one didn't count the random dark streaks of mascara around her eyes,) together with the wild, tangled mane of hair and strange clothes, could have cast her as some frantic, deranged woman in a tragedy, or as one of the Munsters' relatives if one had a strange sense of humour and thought this was a comedy. She shook her head at the image, pushed the hair out of her eyes and concentrated on running a bath. Half an hour later, with at least three of her battered limbs feeling a little less painful, she ventured some praise for the bath. "Is that the second or third time you have saved me in the last couple of days?" Thanks to its size she had been able to position her injured leg well away from the water, and as she wiped the other leg dry, she continued to sing its praises. "I could do with you every time I have to teach five alpha," she purred. Had Alice ever spoken to a bath? She didn't need a precedent so she continued, "Could I afford you? Suppose it would have to be one of your less grand relatives, or I could get rid of my bed!" This madness helped restore her spirits before she had to attend to more serious tasks. She dressed carefully, anxious to avoid catching her throbbing thigh, then gathering all of her belongings together she crammed them without ceremony into her holdall. It was the exact opposite of the manner they had arrived in, but it matched her frame of mind. Clutching under her arm anything that would not fit into the bag, she let herself out of her room and started to tiptoe along the landing. This time she did look like a burglar, complete with all the evidence of hasty departure, and she was creeping around a house where she was a guest more as if she was after the family silver. The biggest challenge would be negotiating that front door without making any noise. The back door was nearer to the garage, but it was out of the question because Molly could still be in the kitchen, and there was no way she wanted to explain any of this to her. That only left the front door, and though she knew it squeaked very loudly and the housekeeper from hell doubled as security with ears as sensitive as any Rottweiler, it had to be done. She didn't bother to waste time thinking what she would say to Molly if she came out to ask what she was doing, or where she was going – or for that matter, why she was going. They were more questions without answers.

The front door creaked as noisily as she had expected, but she closed it gently without any sign of investigators. "Huh! You would think with all his money, he could at least manage a door that doesn't squeak." The gravel footpath was at least as noisy as the door and consequently she felt obliged to resort to tiptoe once more in an effort to avoid detection. That burglar act now lacked only the mask and the relevant dramatic musical accompaniment.

The yard was completely empty when she eventually reached it – and the camper was gone! That was enough to start a panic until she remembered Chas had pushed it inside the garage. It had seemed like a good move at the time, but now it only meant more obstacles to negotiate. She didn't dare try the big doors because she knew they illuminated the whole yard and that might be seen from the house and although she remembered telling Rick that she was coming out here, she didn't want him to know exactly when: she simply wanted to be left alone. She offered a quick prayer that the small door at the back of the garage would be unlocked, because if it wasn't, she could have a real problem, and sheepishly knocking at the front door in order to get back in did not figure in her plans at all.

Thankfully the door handle yielded easily under her grip, and she stumbled gratefully into the blackness, stopping only to catch her breath and readjust her eyes to the darkness. Warning herself to be careful she proceeded to feel her way along the wall. After what she had done this afternoon this should be easy, but it wasn't. As a result of stumbling twice in less than ten seconds, she decided that risking the light might be better than breaking a leg, and if he found out that she was here, well, that was just too bad, because once she was in the van, he could huff and puff all he wanted, she would not let him in. In a few short minutes he had changed from being Bluebeard to assuming the persona of wolf. Both roles suited him perfectly. "Tailor-made parts," she grunted. "And this little piggy isn't stupid enough to play with you anymore!" She was gloating over her little witticism as she fumbled along the wall for the switch, when without warning, or her locating it, the light snapped on. She jumped, dropped her bag with a thud, and let out a little squeal. This little piggy was easily spooked!

"Oh, it is only you," she sighed with relief, colour flooding her face as her heart stopped pounding and she shifted the large bag from off her foot.

"You were expecting someone else?"

Words had never failed her so many times in one day, but if he could be appallingly rude with such ease, then she didn't really see any reason why she should continue trying to be polite. "I wasn't expecting anyone, so putting the light on like that almost gave me a heart attack." She picked up her bag and tried to march past him. "Now, if you don't mind, I have things to do. Please go away and let me get on with them."

"Not very nice, when I just came to see why you didn't come down to dinner."

"I wasn't hungry."

"You were asleep," he corrected.

"I was asleep?" she asked staring at him thoughtfully. "If you know that, then why ask?"

Without waiting for a reply, she opened the van door and was almost inside when he pointed out circumspectly, "Cried yourself to sleep, I reckon."

"So what if I did! What is it to you? What were you doing in my room, anyway?"

"I wasn't. I didn't come in. I knocked. I only opened the door when there was no answer, I wanted to check you were okay. I saw that you were asleep so I sent up Molly."

"Oh." Another revelation she wasn't sure how to handle. "Thank you." It was painful to give even cursory thanks, so she walked into the van and tried to close the door without thinking any more about it, but he was too quick and placed his foot in the doorway, which meant she was faced with either letting him in or trying to push the door shut against him. There was no way that she was going to get involved in anything as undignified as a tussle, because besides being demeaning, there wasn't much chance that she could win such a confrontation, and as she had no intention of losing, there could be no contest. She glared balefully at him while he smiled and marched past her into the van.

It was even less possible to ignore him inside the van than it had been outside; he dominated the small interior. "Excuse me, please. I need to get into that cupboard." He moved away to allow her access, only to block her access to the next one. By the third cupboard he was getting the hang of this and moved before she could ask. As she closed it, she noticed that he'd had the effrontery to sit down and was now flicking idly through one of the Shakespeare texts that she had left on the table. It may not have been polite to snatch, but for once she made an exception and plucked the book from his hands at the same time as pointing him towards the door.

He simply picked up the other book but this time held it up out of her reach. "Ah, Julius Caesar, I feel I know you well," he said, flicking through the pages that were as amply highlighted and marked as the last text had been. "And you obviously do."

"If you don't mind I would like to get some sleep." The fact that she had only just woken up and that it couldn't have been much past nine thirty didn't bother her one bit. Right now she was not even that concerned about telling a white lie; she simply wanted him to go.

He closed the book with a sigh. "This is a pretty useless gesture, isn't it?"

"You have already said that."

He stood up as if preparing to do what she wanted him to do for once. "Well, you go ahead, then. Stay out here if you think it will preserve your precious reputation. Personally, I think it makes you look rather foolish.

But, if that's what you want to do, do it. You know your own mind. Well, you keep telling me you do."

She walked ahead of him to the door and held it open for him, an eloquent illustration of her intention that he should leave. She was determined not to respond to any more of his taunts because right now she was the one on the moral high ground and all she had to do was remain calm and unruffled. If she didn't rise to his bait, he would have to go, then she needed to get away from this place as fast as possible and forget any of it had ever happened.

They were face to face in the doorway when he observed gently, "You are a stubborn old thing, aren't you?"

She had employed exactly the same tactic on difficult-to-reach teenagers more than once, but she fell for it now because, just like them, she had been expecting harsh, sarcastic criticism and instead she had got gentleness. It tripped her up just as neatly as it did them. Her lack of response provided the opportunity he was looking for. "Isn't all this *Much Ado about Nothing?*" he asked, nodding to the book she held in her hand.

The smile happened without her permission. "Very clever."

"Not meant to be. Just tell me what the point of all this is," he asked wearily.

She said nothing, because it wasn't about a point. It was about a lot of things, and some things she didn't altogether understand herself. She was unable to answer satisfactorily and so she chose to plead whatever amendment it was that said -say nothing.

For some reason, he chose to interpret her silence as reflection upon the wisdom of her actions, so he handed her the copy of *Julius Caesar* without any further altercation. Its cover provided her with the needed inspiration and brought to mind the passage she had marked most recently – the one about honour. This was about her honour.

"'*Well, honour is the subject of my story,*'" she quoted quietly, raising her eyes to meet his. "'*I cannot tell what you and other men think of this life, but for myself …*'"

He groaned. "Okay, tell me what you mean in plain English and I will answer you."

"Honour. It's about honour," she said sulkily. "A commodity sadly lacking in these parts, it seems."

"Perhaps I was wrong not telling you who I was."

"Yes, you were!" It was neither polite nor generous to agree so readily when someone was trying to make amends, but she didn't care.

"Okay, okay, I've just said that, haven't I? I hold my hands up; I was wrong. Is that good enough?"

"Do you always have to be so sarcastic?"

"Only when it's ..." He paused, reconsidered, and then said, "Forget it! I'm sorry on both counts."

Sarah relented a little at that, mainly because she guessed it had taken a lot for him to apologise at all, and she was flattered that he had bothered. She looked up warily and then gave the briefest of smiles before insisting solemnly, "So why didn't you tell me who you were? You must have had a reason. Could it have been that you knew I wouldn't have stayed if you had?"

The smirk that curled his lip rather unattractively told her nothing, but it was sheer disbelief. "Has it never occurred to you that most women would think it reason to stay, not go?"

"More of your natural modesty, I suppose?"

"No, just fact."

"I will have to take your word for that," she droned in her most bored voice, trying to show him that she was above all this and was rather fed up with the whole thing. "Now, if have you finished ...?"

"No, I haven't! Not until you listen to me."

"I have. Maybe you're right, most women would stay. But do you know what? I don't care about them – or you." It was ruthless and final. No argument! For a second they faced each other out, and then he turned away ready to concede defeat and go.

"There is just one thing, though." What idiocy had made her say that? She had won, and now she had thrown it away again. It was too late now.

He turned back and met her gaze. "And what might that be?" he asked, not really that interested any longer.

"I would like to know why you didn't tell me, because then I could tell you what *I* would have done." It was a dismal attempt to win back that lost advantage.

"You're not going to like it," he warned.

"I can hardly say that I am wildly enthusiastic about what has happened so far, so I fail to see how I can like your reason less."

"Okay, but don't say you didn't ask for it," he said walking back into the van and sitting down. She opened her mouth to protest at that then thought better of it; better to let him have his say and go. He patted the seat beside him. "I think I would sit down if I were you."

"I will stand, thank you," she said, sniffing in her best Molly fashion and folding her arms defensively in front of her as she waited for his lame excuse.

"Suit yourself. Are you really sure that you want to hear this?"

"Of course. Why shouldn't I?"

"Okay." He grinned holding his hands palm up. "Just checking. There is a good reason, but-"

"But what? Or are you still inventing this good reason?"

"Have you ever heard of groupies, hangers-on, overly persistent fans?"

"Of course I have. Pop stars get them."

"Actors get their share as well. I have been a target at times." This was definitely modesty, though she failed to recognise it as such because she was too locked into trying to understand where all this could be leading. "Women have been known to invent the most hare-brained and dangerous schemes just to ..." He paused, checking to see if he should say the last bit because he knew that what he was about to say would upset her even more, so he backtracked. "Hey, it doesn't matter. Forget it."

"Just to what?" she demanded impatiently, tapping her foot and still not recognising where he was heading. Her intransigence pushed him into the declaration.

"Just to get into my bed." He had finally said enough.

Her first thoughts about more of his modesty were instantly dismissed by some more truly awful implications of what he had said – implications that had never occurred to her before. Dawn was finally breaking. "You thought that *I* was one of them?" she asked incredulously, her head still reeling from the shock. Then without waiting for, or expecting, an answer, she queried, "You thought *my* breakdown was a hare-brained scheme? You thought it was a fix? So everything since ..." It was just too ridiculous. He had to be joking. But if he was, he wasn't laughing. "You really thought that I was waiting for you?" He nodded, and she closed her eyes against the horror only to be confronted by an even greater one, so she opened them quickly. "And Friday night?" He nodded again, following the chain of her unspoken thoughts. She felt hot colour flood her cheeks as exaggerated but perfect pictures of that ridiculous conversation danced through her shocked mind. "How could you think that? That is absolutely awful!" She paced up and down the camper as well as she could in such a confined space. "Maybe in the first five minutes you could have been mistaken, but not after that? Surely not after that, unless … Was my behaviour really so lacking?"

"Well, I admit, I made a few wild suppositions."

"But I did come down in those dreadful pyjamas," she pointed out, completely forgetting they had been very desirable at the time or that this should be his part of the argument.

"I didn't exactly leave you with any alternative," he pointed out just as generously.

She hardly heard that because her brain was busy reviewing her memory of all those other pairs of pyjamas and how she had wondered about the variety of sizes and why so many. The answer to that particular question was now apparent. Yes, she had heard of groupies, and if his behaviour towards her was anything to go by, he probably hadn't missed a single one of them. That room! That beautiful room was his harem! Bluebeard had been spot on. Marcie Hadley had not known the extent of his depravity! "You … '*You're not a man, you're a machine*'!" A comment that provided some immediate and totally satisfying release for her feelings.

"I might have known Will would have to get his say," he quipped.

"Well, you are wrong! It isn't Shakespeare – it's George Bernard Shaw, if you must know."

"Excuse my ignorance."

"You, you Bluebeard! And that is me!" she informed him, articulating her previous thoughts before words failed her completely. The implications of his revelations were too overwhelming, even for William.

Her pacing up and down was making him dizzy, so he grabbed her by the arm as she was passing him for the hundredth time. She stopped and looked down at his hand on her arm, but he didn't release it. Instead he said, "Stop being so holier than thou! What did you expect me to do? Say, 'Yes, you are very nice, but I don't go to bed with nice ladies'?"

She nodded mutely, unable to do anything else, though she wanted to ask, "Why not?"

He must have read her thoughts because his next sentence answered her unasked question. "Sarah, this is the twentieth century, and it is what happens. It's how the world operates, it's reality." She dismissed the fact that he had said her name so nicely and shook her head to show she disagreed. That made him more impatient. "And if you can't see that, then you may as well go and live in a convent," he said in utter exasperation.

"The line is '*get thee to a nunnery*'. *Hamlet,* act three," she said bleakly, believing she had found the perfect put-down for such a hurtful comment. There was but a brief moment between this small elation and other emotions that were more intense, and all that happened in between was that he delivered a withering response without any reservation or hesitation.

"You misheard me," he said quietly. "*I* said you might as well go and live in a convent, and that was Rick Masters, 1986."

Her face flamed with embarrassment. He had exposed her folly so neatly that she felt foolish and a show off to boot. She shifted from one foot to the other and cleared her throat, ready to try to retaliate, but he didn't allow her time to recover.

"Because," he continued firmly, not releasing his grip on her arm, "whether you like it or not, it is what happens. It is reality."

"No, it is not!" she exclaimed passionately, breaking free from his grasp. "You think it is reality because you see it happening, and you encourage it, but that doesn't make it real. It's still an illusion!"

"Why?" he asked patiently. "Why do you persist in calling it an illusion when it's all around you?"

"Because it promises you instant satisfaction and happiness, and what it delivers is something very different."

"Look, reality or illusion, does it matter? I came here to clear the air and apologise. I am sorry about Friday night. You will have to excuse the fact I didn't recognise who you were, either." She wasn't sure whether that was meant as another insult, but he grinned and added, "There aren't as many ladies around these parts as there are movie stars."

"No thanks to you!" He overlooked her insult and nodded slowly as if accepting that it could have some basis in fact, so she was a little sorry she had made the remark so bitterly.

"I accept I should have told you who I was, okay. I am sorry. There was no malice in my not telling you," he pointed out frankly. "And if you really want to know the other reason, I didn't tell you -because I couldn't believe you didn't know who I was. And if that sounds like conceit, then I guess I will have to admit to that as well. What else can I say? I have known you less than forty-eight hours, and I am already apologising for the second or third time today. That's not something I am too good at – in fact I never apologise."

"I thought you said you didn't recognise GBS." It had tripped off her tongue without thought, and by the time she had considered it, it had already been said.

"I am not with you."

"'*I never apologise*' – that's George Bernard Shaw again," she pointed out hesitantly.

"No, it's not, it's Rick Masters," he affirmed convincingly, though it was said a little more kindly this time. "Let's get this straight: I only need other people's lines in movies. In life I make my own, so please accept my apology, and let's stop playing these stupid games. I had Molly save you some dinner. Come in and eat it, or she's going to want to know why you haven't." She must have taken longer to consider this proposition than he thought necessary, because he added meanly, "You are not so desirable that I can't control myself, you know. I'm sorry – I shouldn't have said that. Forget it. But I did mean the bit about burying the hatchet. Come on, truce. Admit it: we have both made some errors of judgement this weekend. Let's forget all of them and be friends for the last few hours, till tomorrow."

Sarah heard his words, though she doubted he really meant them. She could find neither the strength nor motivation to speak, nor even the means to quell her rapidly rising emotions, because suddenly everything seemed too much to handle. She felt tired and drained, and she suspected she was very close to shedding more tears, so she diverted all her energies into preventing that. Crying in private was one thing, crying in front a stranger was something else. As a result she missed the concern in the face of the man in front of her. For someone she had written off as a completely insensitive egomaniac, he was actually doing a fair imitation of that Good Samaritan right at this moment.

Rick took her gently by the shoulders to try and break the morbid, trancelike state into which she had drifted. "Hey, it's not that bad," he said candidly.

She lifted her face to his. "Isn't it?" she asked as the tears wobbled threateningly.

"Go on, have a cry if it will help." He could hardly believe he had said that, but he had.

And his permission on top of everything else was too much, and seconds later she was sobbing as violently as she had done earlier in her room. How she got in his arms was never discovered. He didn't say

418

anything, simply held the heaving shoulders while they sobbed away all the pains self-awareness had caused. She hoped he would not understand, but she had to admit that he was more perceptive than she had given him credit for, so he probably understood at least some part of it.

Sarah sat brooding on the edge of a sofa, staring vacantly into space. Her little outburst in the van had made her feel worse, not better. Her head throbbed, and she felt hot enough to be running a temperature. She wondered if that would be an adequate reason to excuse her tantrum. It had felt strange being shepherded indoors like a hurt child, and it was highly embarrassing to think about it now, so she tried to focus on finding some justification for her performance … except there wasn't any. Maybe she didn't deserve any. Unlike Jodie, there was only one person to blame for all the mess she had got herself into. She had been angry at Rick Masters when her anger would have been better directed at herself. This afternoon's little homily about watching desires so that they don't get one into trouble was desperately ironic; especially when she remembered Friday night's only desire had been to get away from that deserted road – and look what a price she had paid for that!

She resolutely refused a brandy but took the tonic water like she had Friday night. Rick sat down beside her, intent on getting to the bottom of what was causing such anguish. He put a hand on her arm. It was some of that undeserved comfort. Nothing could have hurt quite as much. A solitary tear coursed a lonely path down her cheek as he handed her his hankie to remove it. She accepted that but moved away quickly. "Hey, come on, smile," he said. She managed only the smallest and briefest of smiles before he added, "That's better. I've said I am sorry and there's no real harm done, is there?" Such softly spoken encouragement produced exactly the opposite effect to what he had intended.

"I am sorry, too," she wailed, trying to stem the tears. "Please forgive me. I don't usually make such an exhibition of myself. I don't know what is wrong with me today."

He nodded, unsure of what else to do. He hated tears, and though he had never dealt with female distress very well, this time he didn't say anything to make matters worse, so he was amazing himself as much as her. When her last tear had been wiped away, she handed him back his sodden hankie as he observed, "Okay, panda eyes, how about you telling me what's been going on today? Here, hold still." He used the mangled hankie to wipe away the last wayward streak of mascara.

Sarah didn't answer immediately, but she did question how such concern could equate with her present judgement of him; this was another attribute that didn't figure in her assessment of his real identity. She didn't confess that, but she did reconsider her answer. "Nothing much." It was still contrived and false, though noticeably less defiant.

That provoked him to insist, "Spare me the innocent answers! If you don't want to tell me, say so, though I will still think that just finding out my name could not reduce you to this by itself." Her smile came out crooked. "Only guessing, of course," he continued, "but would it have anything to do with those weird clothes?"

Perhaps she did owe him an explanation. She didn't have time to relate all the drama because as she got to the scene at the excavation they were disturbed by some commotion in the hall. She looked up from the contemplation of her feet.

"Go on, ignore that; Molly will sort it."

Her tale had barely recommenced before they were interrupted again, this time by Molly bursting in unceremoniously. "I am sorry to interrupt." She shot a hasty, sideward glance at the clearly distraught house guest, who had moved quickly away from her employer's side. "I am sorry to interrupt," she repeated, sniffing.

"What is it, Molly?" She didn't answer him quickly enough, so he presumed it was something and nothing. "I am not home, whoever it is. If it's someone from the station, tell them I will be up in the morning."

She shook her head. "It's no one for you, Mr Masters," she confided. "It's two gentlemen for Mrs Chadwick. Two gentlemen from Billington – two police officers." If she had been announcing an unexpected call from the president himself, it could scarcely have been given a better build-up.

Sarah stood up but Rick motioned for her to sit down again. "Okay, show 'em in," he said casually, much as if he had been expecting them all along. While Molly went out to show the two men in, his troublesome guest mumbled yet another apology. "I take it they haven't come to arrest you, have they?"

"No, of course not! Well, I hope not." Today had been such a strange day, full of all sorts of unlikely things, that she could not back her judgement that nothing else strange could or would happen. When she had suggested to Jodie they were following Alice down the rabbit hole, she had not meant it seriously. Now she wasn't so sure.

"Are you up to this? Do you want me to stay?" His voice brought her back to the present, and though she was unable to answer, she did manage a grateful nod and threw him a heartfelt look of thanks as she collected herself to meet these two unexpected visitors. There was barely enough time for him to come and stand back by her side and give her a quick smile of encouragement before they could hear Molly talking through the open door. "Here, you had better have this back," he said, offering the mangled hankie with another encouraging smile. She took it from him but felt duty bound to promise him she would not need it; she had cried her full quota of tears for today and there was no way she intended to add any more.

They were exchanging something very different as the officers were ushered in. She had simply meant it as another expression of the gratitude she could not trust herself to utter. He was simply trying to give her some more of that Good Samaritan support. It may have started out that way. She certainly did not remember that Shakespeare had been credited by some as coining the phrase *the eyes are the windows of your soul*. She realised it when her eyes met his. Each examined slowly what they thought they saw there. Both visitors witnessed it, though neither assessed it correctly. Both did guess they were not meant to be there. One of them coughed discreetly, and the whole thing was over.

Rick crossed the room to greet the two men, leaving a very perplexed woman stood behind him. Whatever it was that had just happened, now was not the time to be thinking about it. She could hear Rick talking to the men, so she tried her best to calm down.

The officer's greeting was pleasant but firm. "Mrs Chadwick?" She nodded. He introduced them both, and they showed their identification and filled her in on the reason for their visit. "We need to speak to you about an incident that happened in Billington this afternoon, ma'am."

He started explaining, but she was hardly listening, being more concerned with wondering what these men must think about her: a married woman for all they knew, alone as a guest in this house. Maybe they didn't know she was alone. Even that excuse was rendered less than acceptable when she remembered what they had recently witnessed. She could hear Rick saying something about not being too long because she was still in shock and very tired. At least they were all in agreement on that.

"We will make it as quick and painless as we can, sir." It was a deferential reply; these two were as polite as any policemen she had heard of anywhere, not in the least like what she expected of gun-toting Americans. Maybe it helped to have influential friends after all, but then, they had hardly come to question her about a crime.

All her protestations that others knew more were dismissed. "With respect, ma'am, you are a material witness and you should have stayed at the scene until we had seen you, if you weren't going to the hospital. It is standard practice."

"I am sorry, I didn't think," she admitted candidly. "I was in a hurry to get cleaned up."

"We know. Daniel Marshall told us Mr Masters was picking you up." The cop grinned, and she blushed. "We realise we are no competition, but perhaps next time you might spare us a thought and hang around long enough for us to get a statement. Mr Marshall could tell us where you would be, but he didn't have an address. It's taken us this long to find you." He turned to Rick, "You are not the easiest person to trace," he said. Rick acknowledged that was how he liked it and as the estate was registered in the name of a company, he wondered how they had done it at all. "We finally persuaded some guy called Wayne Crowther that it was important."

"Well, we threatened to arrest him if he didn't give us an address," the other officer admitted openly. "It usually works."

"Okay, now you know why we are here. Officer Gill is going to take down your statement. We will do it here because we realise you are on holiday and all, so when you are ready ..."

"Can I ask you something before I begin?"

"Sure thing. What do you want to know?"

"Do you know how the little girl is? I haven't had chance to ring and find out."

"Well, right now she ain't so good, but the doctors are pretty positive. She has a great collection of broken bones including multiple fractures of her left leg and some cracked ribs but she has been lucky because there appears to be no serious soft tissue damage so far. The leg seems to be the biggest problem. Let me give you the hospital number, and then you can ring see when the surgery is scheduled for. The kid has been asking about you."

"And Dilys, the stepmother?"

He shook his head, and a cold little fear wrapped itself around her heart. An age of vicarious pain for that small family passed in the second before the other officer explained. "Sorry, we don't have any news about her. Guess you will have to speak with the Marshalls."

She spent the next hour revisiting every detail of the day's action, then telling it all over again, and then answering seemingly endless questions. It was all very wearing, and she had begun to think they would never reach the end when the lieutenant finally said, "Thank you, that's it, Mrs Chadwick." She breathed a sigh of relief.

"There is just one other thing," the other man interposed. "Can you remember what you talked about while you were down there? Over two hours, wasn't it?"

"Is that important?" she asked.

"Could be."

Rick felt her stiffen, and so he said something for the first time. "Is there a point to this? Mrs Chadwick is tired, the kid's out, and there's no irreparable damage. Besides, what does anyone talk about to kids? School, TV, pop music, the usual things. The important thing is that she's okay." Sarah smiled up at him thankfully, but she was never going to get away so easily.

"I appreciate your concern, Mr Masters, but we are just doing our job, and we won't keep the lady one minute longer than we have to. There has been a serious incident, and we have to check out that it was exactly what it seemed to be." Then he added quietly, "We have to be sure that the kid did actually fall."

Sarah looked at him blankly. "Of course she fell. How else?" Her question had been half posed before she realised what he had been hinting at. "You mean, do I think she was pushed?" she asked, aghast.

"No, I mean do you have any evidence that suggests anything other than she fell. That's why I want to know what you talked about. Please think carefully."

She shook her head vigorously. This was distressing, and both the officers and Rick knew that from her manner.

"This is a very troubled family we have here, Mrs Chadwick. The kid had just kicked the stepmother in the stomach. That's not a good thing anytime, but especially not when she is nearly eight months pregnant. There could have been a struggle."

"I don't know anything about that. All I know is what Jodie told me and what Dilys said. Dilys said Jodie had fallen, and Jodie told me the same. I can't believe ..."

"Doesn't matter what we believe – it's evidence that matters. The kid said nothing to make you think otherwise?"

"No."

When they had finished, the officers went off with Rick to get some signed photographs for their wives while Sarah collapsed back against the sofa and closed her eyes, totally exhausted. She was still reviewing all their questions and her answers when Rick returned. He thought she was asleep, so touched her arm gently and whispered her name. When she opened her eyes, she asked, "Have they gone?" but the words and the meaning did not match.

He nodded. "You okay? You look exhausted."

"That's a fair appraisal," she said, recovering her composure and trying to make light of it.

"Quite the heroine aren't you?"

"Don't feel like one," she admitted. "I was scared – correction, I was petrified! I don't think I have ever felt as ill in my entire life as when I looked down that shaft for the first time and saw the bottom was nothing only blackness. Well, maybe when I lost my shoe, and it seemed to fall for ever before it hit the water." She shuddered at the memory. "I nearly blacked out then!"

"So that's why you were wearing the slippers. What happened to your clothes?"

"I used part of the skirt to stop my leg bleeding. The jacket was covered in so much mud and blood by the time I got out that it was beyond redemption."

"You injured your leg? Where? Has it been seen to?"

"The ambulance man cleaned it up," she said, indicating her thigh. "It's fine, just a scratch. Nothing to worry about."

"You sure?"

She assured him by explaining, "It is a bit sore now, but it will pass. I had to promise the paramedic that if it's not better by the time I get to Shelagh's, I will go see a doctor." It seemed to settle the matter.

"Never met a real heroine before," he pointed out as she struggled to her feet.

That made her laugh at last. "And you haven't now," she warned as he rose to steady her. "So stop sending me up," she pleaded, trying to ignore his closeness.

"Know something else? The real sort has more guts than the make-believe ones."

The grateful smile that this compliment earned him was satisfying for both of them, but she excused herself to go to bed before it could trouble her any further. The undeserved support she had received in the last couple of hours might have softened how she felt about him, but she was not about to allow it to turn into permission for making any more mistakes. She stopped halfway across the room and muttered a serious thank you as she struggled to inform her eyes of that decision so that she could drag them away from his. How come she had never noticed before how really nice his eyes were?

By the time she reached the door, other feelings were prompting her to do something even more brave and radical. She wrestled against them too, concluding she had been brave enough for one day, but these feelings would not be denied. "By the way," she said before bravado could evaporate. He looked up from the script he had picked up to stare at her back. She sensed his eyes on her and turned round, but then her courage ran out, and she shook her head. "It doesn't matter," she said, turning back to the door.

"What were you going to say?" he persisted.

"It really doesn't matter," she repeated, turning again and giving him a brief smile as compensation. There it was again – more satisfying warmth. "Good night."

"Good night." A second passed before he called her back. "Sarah?"

It was a long time since anyone had used her name in that manner. She turned back automatically; her entire body now completely disregarding instructions.

"Tell me what doesn't matter."

She smiled briefly at his humour but realised that there was a seriousness behind the question. "Why?" she asked a mite suspiciously.

"Because either it really doesn't matter and is the irrelevant rambling of a traumatised mind ..."

"Thanks!"

"Or it is something that really *does* matter but it's easier to say it doesn't because it saves you from having to expose yourself to whatever consequences come from saying it." She had to think about that for a moment and had almost decided to ignore his bait when he added solemnly, "But then, I don't suppose it's the second because you have already told me you can stand up and be counted, what was it, "take the stick" for your principles? So forget it." Her turning away signified she was

Leah Duncan

about to do that. She even opened the door very deliberately. At the last moment he added, "Although, the only way to be absolutely certain, is to tell me and see."

Her body relaxed as she grinned. After a moment's consideration, she came back into the room, closed the door quietly behind her, and leant back against its handles.

"Well?" he asked at length.

"Well, if you must know I found out something today that really does matter. I am not sure yet how it will affect my life, so maybe that's why I am not rushing to share it. That's all."

Rick was anxious to confirm his theories. Even now. And that she was about to make the declaration he had been waiting for since early yesterday morning? "Check it out," he suggested. "It sometimes helps to test things out on friends."

She looked at him to try to establish if she could – or should. It was difficult to decide which it was when there were factors pulling her in both directions. She wanted to tell him, and that side eventually won. "Remember last night when I said I didn't know if I believed in God?" He nodded to hide his astonishment. "Well, I remembered that today just when I was swinging on the end of this rope over a big gaping hole - asking for his help. Strange thing, to be asking for help from someone who doesn't exist."

"It happens."

"Maybe. Anyway, what I was going to say to you was ..." She took a deep breath and blurted it out. "I found out today I *do* believe in him." That produced a different sort of silence than any they had shared so far. "And I believe in Him so much that He was my very first port of call when I really needed help. Know something else? He didn't let me down. That wasn't me down there being heroic – I am a natural coward. I simply asked for whatever it took for me to be able to do it, and He supplied it. When I think about what I did down there, it makes me feel sick, so I can't take the credit. I just thought I needed to put you straight, that's all." She waited for a moment and watched her companion absorb what she had just said. Their eyes connected briefly, and then she moved away from the door as if she was making to leave, "Know something else? I am ashamed to admit to this. When I was stranded in the van. I was terrified then as well, so I asked for His help then. I didn't recognise that until today."

"Nice to know I'm the answer to some of your prayers."

"I thought you deserved the truth," she confessed, before adding more cheerfully, "So now, good night. I am going to bed." Then she closed the door after her, but a second later she popped her head back round it and smiled. "And don't think I didn't realise you were attempting to manipulate me," she warned, "because I did."

"Didn't stop me being right, though, did it?"

She sighed. "No, I suppose not. So now I have told you. Which one was it?"

"You need me to tell you?

She allowed herself one last smile as she shook her head, then closed the door for the second time.

Rick watched her go without comment. In a day full of weird happenings, this latest revelation really crowned the lot. It took guts to say something like that – but then, he knew the oddball had guts.

Chapter Twenty-Four

Sarah's "Good morning," was breezy but noticeably false. If she had hoped assumed bravado would be an effective way of telling her host that she was back to normal and that the affairs and emotions of the previous day were mere aberrations, she had overdone it so he simply looked up at her with the same puzzled, indulgent look – the one he had used yesterday with such devastating effect; the one that implied, so you are still suffering! In a matter of two days this routine had become something approaching ritual. How could anything become so established in such a short space of time? She did not waste time trying to find a satisfactory answer, but sat down at the breakfast table and smiled as graciously as she could at her bemused companion. Right now other things took precedence over a detailed examination of their strange communications, but at least rehearsal had paid off: she had made it out here!

She had lain awake since seven this morning reviewing the tumultuous events of the previous twenty-four hours, examining each in minute detail now that emotion had subsided and rational thinking had resumed its rightful place. It all looked very different this morning. She was pleased that she had been able to conquer her fear to help Jodie; not so pleased about some of the other events of yesterday and crowning those was the painful recollection of that highly embarrassing scene in the garage. She was determined to apologise for that at the very first opportunity, except every step that had taken her nearer to the breakfast table and the opportunity to carry it out, had depleted her courage until she had stepped onto the terrace and uttered only that very noticeably false greeting.

If Rick was intrigued by such fierce cheerfulness, he hid it well because apart from the puzzled look, he simply returned his guest's greeting and then carried on eating his breakfast and reading his mail while she helped herself to some juice, fruit, and yoghurt and initiated the inevitable in-depth examination of his reply. It had seemed "just normal", but how could she possibly know what "just normal" was, any more than she could establish ritual? This was only her third morning here! She brushed aside the reminder that it was also her last. Deal with what you know, she told herself heroically. Between slicing a banana and pouring yoghurt, she did exactly that. She could see that he wasn't remotely uncomfortable after yesterday's charade, and though she couldn't know what he was thinking or feeling, any more than he could know of her thoughts and feelings, that much was fortunate at least. If he could look so unconcerned, then so could she; that garage scene had not been all her doing, and he had been almost entirely to blame for the scene at the Marshalls'.

"Molly says the man from the van company is here already," she muttered.

He looked up from his mail and scrutinised her over the top of his glasses, "Yeah, I saw him on the way in. He's been around since about seven."

"Oh." Back to eating breakfast. She wanted to ask where he had been so early in the morning, but she stifled her curiosity in the same manner as she had the apology.

He had read several pieces of his mail before he spoke again. "He thinks he has it sorted. Says it should be ready to roll by lunchtime."

"Oh."

"I was right about the points, but I told him to check it out thoroughly in case there was anything else."

She had the grace to blush, recalling the garage conversation in every lurid detail. "Oh." It did occur to her that she was getting a trifle predictable, to say nothing of boring, so she struggled to find something different to say that was safe and that could break her monosyllabic record. "Thank you. I will go down and check with him when I have finished breakfast." It seemed a reasonable place to start.

Despite all her intentions of keeping up the pretence of pleasant normality, they ate breakfast in silence; the fact she did not want to say certain things seemed to inhibit her ability to say anything at all; all the energy focused on prevention meant there was nothing left for creation. He continued to be absorbed in his mail, so neither of them had spoken for ten minutes by the time they had finished. There seemed little point in sitting and staring into the depths of an empty cereal bowl so she rose to leave. Any slight hesitation at this juncture was simply because she was still debating about the apology, but Molly chose that moment to bring out the morning papers so it provided her with an excellent excuse to leave without fulfilling her mission, if she acted quickly. The only trouble with good excuses is one cannot avoid knowing that is exactly what they are. While she was struggling to sort this out, Molly disappeared again, leaving her free to deliver her apology – except that it stuck in her throat, and a croak was all that she could manage. Its intended beneficiary was fully occupied sorting through his papers, so he wasn't tuned in to her struggle.

"You made the headlines," he observed casually, handing her a paper as she walked past him. She stood, stupidly frozen to the spot as she absorbed the screaming headline: "*English Tourist Helps Save Child!*" Memories of the other headlines she had been imagining Friday night made her blush. At least these were more acceptable than those. What was underneath was not: a large photograph of some deranged, wild-haired woman being helped out of a crane's sling by a young medic. It did her no favours! Why did there always have to be a camera around to record what should definitely remain unrecorded?

"What an awful photograph!" she groaned, passing the paper back quickly. "Hopefully no one will ever recognise me from that."

"Why is it that no matter what has happened, women are only ever concerned about what they look like in a photograph?"

"And you are not?" She had said it before she could stop herself, and so she smiled and apologised. "There is something else I need to say," she blurted out, thinking that if she was going to do it at all, this was the time for that other apology. He must have sensed an occasion coming up because he put his papers down and lifted his head in anticipation. That was intimidating to start with. "I just want to say ..." She paused, trying to draw courage, inspiration, or whatever it was that was needed from the floor. "I just want to say, I just want to say I feel really awful when I think about how badly I behaved yesterday, and I would like to say I am very sorry and ..." She lifted her eyes from the floor to meet his. "And thank you," she continued hastily as her brain went blank. "You have been very kind to me, and I have behaved very badly. I may not have seemed grateful, but I am – honestly. Thank you." These last words were little more than a whisper, so she coughed, pushed her hand through her hair, and attempted a grin as she excused herself. She needed to get away from this place fast.

She had got as far as the open window when he called out, "It's been great having you."

It hadn't been said as a joke, so this time she replied happily. "Thank you for saying that, though I doubt it could possibly be true."

He denied that, adding that it had been mentally stimulating and he had enjoyed the games.

"Tennis and chess of course?" she asked.

"What else?"

She laughed and nodded her head. "Me too, even though I lost both times."

"Tennis and chess?"

"What else could I have lost?" Her look said it all.

Sensing his opportunity Rick added persuasively, "So if this guy doesn't get your van going, my invitation is still open: I challenge you to another game of chess and anything else you want to risk. Chance to show me what you can really do."

It was obvious from that he harboured no ill feeling towards her, and that was sufficient to make her feel ridiculously happy, but it also stirred up a whole load of other feelings. She smiled at him, easily convincing herself that he must have said that simply to show her that he had forgiven her. "I don't think there is much chance of that," she pointed out honestly. "I don't think it can be anything really serious."

"But I am. I would like you to stay."

Once again she really did wish that she had more experience in handling these matters, but all the years of self-imposed social isolation had left her more gauche and awkward than she had ever recognised until now, and though she knew she had never been exactly an adept, Elinor was right, she was socially naive – incompetent, even. That was depressing enough on its own, but when Shakespeare deserted her as well, it was serious. And right now William had absolutely nothing to offer except the Escalus quote, and she considered it prudent not to mention that again. This must be one situation he had missed. Further deliberation only produced more confusion, and so in the end she went for the straightforward approach. "Thank you, but I really can't stay – and I wouldn't, even if I could," she added gently. "The circumstances are the only reason I am here. When my van is fixed, I no longer have that excuse."

"Why do you need an excuse?"

"Okay, wrong word to choose. I don't need an excuse, but Shelagh is expecting me, and she will need a reason if I don't show up. More than that, I would need a reason for *me* to stay, and there isn't one – not one that is acceptable to me. You do see that, don't you? No you don't, do you?" This explanation was causing more problems than it was solving. She tried a different way, but it was no more successful.

"Sure thing," he said, the finality evidenced in his voice putting an end to the conversation.

As much as she hated leaving it like this, it had to be done. Further explanation must compound the risk of getting involved in more arguments, so she smiled sadly, realising this was the time to do it. "I had better go and organise my things," she said cheerfully, much as if nothing else had been said. "I will see you before I go, I presume?" There was no answer, but as he hadn't said no, she didn't push her point and left quietly.

Her packing was almost complete when there was a gentle tap at the door. She tried her best to control the spontaneous grin that would spread itself across her face if she let it, though she still rushed to open it, but it was only Molly. She greeted her cheerfully, dampening the smile to an acceptable level.

The lady appeared not to notice any disappointment and merely sniffed, "Doctor Watts is here for you. Shall I send him up?"

"Doctor Watts? I didn't ask for a doctor."

"Mr Masters said to call him. So what do I do with him? He's here!"

There was little Sarah could do except accept. Molly went away down the stairs, tutting and airing her favourite saying, muttering that this girl had only been here three days and already they had needed the police and the medics. As she had not yet seen the morning papers, she didn't know why the medic might be needed. She was followed a minute later by Sarah speculating on how much this doctor would cost.

The half hour spent with Doctor Watts was painful in more ways than one. He put four stitches in her leg and administered an equally stinging reprimand about the folly of leaving gaping wounds untreated. Her excuse that it hadn't been untreated earned her more derision: butterfly stitches were not intended for such injuries. His reluctant patient apologised and promised that she would go to see a doctor to make sure it was healing okay. He had made sure of that because his stitches would need removing.

When she tried to close the whole uncomfortable encounter by paying his bill, he shook his head. "Don't have anything to do with money. Filthy stuff carries germs. Secretary sends out all the bills."

"But how long does that take? You can't send me a bill – I won't be here!" she protested. "And I don't have a permanent address here, I am on holiday. I go home in three weeks. I need to pay you now."

"I was told to bill here, so that's what I intend to do, young lady. Now, seven-day check-up, remember!" All further attempts to change his mind failed.

The leg throbbed with renewed ferocity as Sarah limped back upstairs. That provoked a brief consideration about how she could manage to drive, but she cut that short with an acerbic, "Don't even think about it! It's only a little cut, so stop whingeing and finish packing." It was useful to have something else to fret about to divert her mind from other matters.

"Poor bag, you must be dizzy, too! In and out, in and out." The bag withheld its counsel as she hoisted it onto her shoulder. It was as heavy as lead so comparisons were inevitable. "So why not stay?" she asked the mirror by the foot of the stairs. "One more day. What harm would that do? My leg is really painful, and another day would give it a chance to settle down; nobody knows I am here except the Marshalls and Shelagh. And Chas and Molly are here, too, so why shouldn't I stay?"

The question had hardly passed her lips than she shook her head at her reflection. "For someone who has been rattling on about principles all weekend, you are not doing such a terrific job of living up to them right now. Molly and Chas do not live in this house. They live in the same building, that's all. Stop rationalising! Staying would be as bad as giving in to what he has been saying all along, and that would risk losing …" She stopped short of itemising what it was she thought she would risk losing, but for support she quoted the Escalus line softly to herself, only recognising as she finished it that it was exactly what this was, and that was why the quote kept popping into her head: she was being tempted! She had almost thought herself beyond it! She even managed to feel some sympathy for Elinor right now.

"No need to drive farther than I can manage, but I *do* need to go. Leave on a reasonably friendly basis, and then I can write and thank him for his hospitality. Might even send a Christmas card."

Chas came out of the kitchen at the right moment. "I reckon this is where I came in," he said as he took the heaviest bag from her. She nodded. Fortunately he was not as emotional as she was about the situation and could talk easily. It wasn't long before he commented on her quietness, and then he noticed her other problem. "You're limping real bad! You okay after yesterday?" he asked looking to take the other bag from her as well.

She surrendered it gratefully. "I am fine Chas. I have a small cut, and I am still a bit stiff. I daresay some of it could be down to the effects of riding. How do you know about yesterday?"

"Molly just showed me the paper. You fit to drive?" She nodded but didn't say anything else, so he changed the subject.

The mechanic was finished by eleven thirty even with the owner fussing around irritating him, slowing things down and generally getting in his way. The lady was not top of his popularity chart, but he was still mystified as to why she clapped her hands when he switched on the ignition and the engine purred into life. "Why so happy? You picked a good spot lady!" he observed, looking around the garage at the desirable display of metal and especially taking note of the Ferrari.

When he had gone, she wandered back to the house, intent on saying farewell to everyone, but there was only Molly there. Chas had gone down to the stables, and Rick had disappeared. "You sure you won't stay for lunch?" Molly enquired solicitously. It wasn't clear whether it was the fact that she was now a heroine, or just that she was leaving, that was behind this sudden change in attitude. It didn't matter now either way.

"Thank you for the offer, but I need to get going so that I can make it halfway to my friend's before dark. Is Mr Masters around? I wanted to say good-bye."

Molly had to admit she didn't know where he was, or when he would be back; all she knew was that he had gone out after breakfast and had said nothing about coming back.

"That's okay, I said good-bye at breakfast. I just thought if he was around …" She hugged Molly because it seemed the most obvious diversion, though it quite surprised the lady. Then she picked up the milk she had been given and held it close for comfort as she headed back towards the van. There was no way she was about to let Molly see her disappointment.

It was difficult to avoid considering why he had chosen to ignore her, but she tried hard. Every time he crept into her thoughts, she dismissed him in exactly the same way she used to dismiss Michael Davies. She would not allow him to rent room in her head either. After yesterday she could not condemn him, but she could not allow the luxury of believing in him, either, so it would be better not to think about him at all. Practice sometimes makes perfect, and for once Michael Davies was repaying all the hours she had spent on him.

Then her current problem strolled into the garage, and all struggle was abandoned. He showed no trace of ill feeling about the breakfast discussion and so she was happy to do the same for no other reason than he was there and was still a friend. I am so glad you are the man I thought you were, she thought, though she chose not to delve any deeper into that or pursue why she should be so easily restored to happiness by his arrival.

"Ready to go?" he asked.

"Mm, just about. Thank you for getting Doctor Watts for me," she offered sensibly as she climbed down from the van and rubbed her painful thigh. "You shouldn't have gone to all that trouble, but thank you. I am afraid he wouldn't let me pay him, so will you send me the bill when it comes?"

"Forget it," he said solemnly and then he grinned. "I hear he told you off."

She nodded and blushed. "It's happening a lot these days," she confessed as she tried her best to stay calm and collected despite the opposition. "Would you do one more thing for me?"

"Sure."

"Show me how to get back onto the interstate without getting lost!"

She held out her map to him and he grinned as he took it from her. "My, my, Alice. Risking directions from the Cheshire Cat?"

"Do you know something?"

"What?"

"Even Alice didn't have to contend with anyone that remembered everything all the time. And you twist things!"

It hadn't been meant, or said unkindly, and so he bowed. "Alice, this Cheshire Cat stands corrected, and seeing as how you know exactly where you want to get to, I will tell you exactly how to get there – well, the interstate anyway. The other place you are interested in is beyond me."

"Then I will send *you* directions sometime," she said automatically as she leant forward to watch his finger trace her route.

He paused from his task, looked across at her seriously, and nodded slowly. "You do that. Don't forget, eh?" The look that accompanied this request was a re-run of Sunday night's connection, with exactly the same special effects: triple somersaults with cannon and fireworks. "Yes well, the Interstate is here and we are here," he said, dragging himself back to the task in hand. She tried to listen to the instructions, but all she really wanted to do was repeat the last frame over and over again. When she did look up at him, he was concentrating on the map, but for the first time in more years than she could remember, she felt an overpowering urge to reach out and touch someone. The feeling was scarcely recognised before she squashed it, only to find herself wondering if he might chance kissing her good-bye.

That was destined to be frustrated as well because Chas came into the garage at the very moment she was beginning to think that it might not be unappealing. Her heart sank. "Oh good, you are still here. Molly sent you this," Chas said, puffing as he thrust a small plastic hamper into her hands. He removed his hat and wiped his arm across his sweating brow. "I guess I ran faster than I should at my age in this heat!"

"Oh, that is so kind of her going to all that trouble. Please tell Molly thank you from me." He nodded and shuffled some more. "And a very big thank you to you, too – for everything," she added. "The bag carrying, the conversation, the tour, the ride. Especially the ride. Give Anatu a carrot from me, huh? Good-bye." She reached forward and kissed him briefly. Chas shuffled much faster; whether from embarrassment or delight was difficult to say. His boss stood viewing this strange scene with his usual detachment. He was the guy who usually got the kisses, not his odd-job man! This woman never failed to amaze him, but he need not have worried – his turn was coming.

Sarah had gained courage from kissing Chas, but she knew it would not last long so before it could desert her altogether she turned to Rick and hugged him briefly. It was as much as she could manage. "Good-bye, Rick. Thanks for everything. You take care."

Bemused as he was, he didn't miss his cue, and after returning her hug, he brushed his lips across her cheek briefly. "You take care too, Alice! No more adventures eh!" She forced her mouth to smile when it wanted to do something very different. "No more rabbit holes, anyway!"

"I promise," she said solemnly, turning away quickly before he could see that her face was on fire. She had climbed into the van before she had recovered properly enough to ask, "Can William say farewell?"

"Don't see why not," he sighed. "He's had his say on most other things. What's he got in mind?"

She thought for a moment and then decided. "How about, '*If we do meet again, why we shall smile. If not, why then this parting was well made.*'"

"*Hamlet?*" he asked. She shook her head. "*Julius Caesar,* then?" She clapped enthusiastically because speech was beyond her. "I reckon I must know enough of both of them to do your A-level next year."

"*Julius Caesar* is O-level," she corrected him indulgently. "And sorry, *Hamlet* was this year's A-level."

"Pity. Might have gone mad and done both. Do you do postal tuition?"

She shook her head and laughed again, but she couldn't bring herself to say that she might make an exception for him. She concentrated on getting the engine started instead. When she was ready to move, she dared herself to look up again. "Tell you what," she challenged. "You do O-level by correspondence course, and I will go and see your next film. That's if it is a good one with no bad language!"

"Shakespearian standard?"

"Why not?"

She thought better of adding her usual farewell, "Be good," and so repeated, "Take care!" in its place. He nodded and waved, and then she was off.

It seemed to take an age to reach the gates. She slowed as they swung open to release her, and then she indicated to turn right. She could still see the two tiny figures in her mirror and she leaned out of the window and waved one last frantic farewell before turning onto the road. "San Francisco, here I come," she promised, though it lacked gusto.

"Better get back to work," Chas observed, replacing his hat as he walked away. "Still just another day with the same chores to do."

Rick nodded and watched the older man leave the garage before he looked round for the keys to the Ferrari. "Same chores, just another day," he repeated slowly. "And just another woman," he added as he searched for the music he wanted. He couldn't find the Cosi score anywhere, so he gave up, acknowledging, "Okay, maybe *not* just another woman …!"

Chapter Twenty-Five

The clock on the dash said 12.05. Sarah breathed a long sigh of relief. The weekend was finally over, her disaster was sorted, and more to the point she had survived it and was back on schedule. Shelagh's was maybe eight or nine hours away once she reached the interstate, so she put her foot down, intent on getting there today if her leg would hold up.

She made the decision to stop somewhere around the vicinity she had broken down Friday, supposedly to get some relief from the pain in her thigh; however, as this was less than fifteen minutes travelling time from Box without rain, it should have alerted her to the inconsistencies in her logic. She would be lucky to reach Shelagh's by Christmas, travelling at this rate! She pulled the camper over onto the dirt the same as she had Friday night. This time the bumping motion caused a sudden surge of pain in her leg. She patted it gingerly and climbed out of the cab – the same as she had Friday night, albeit a lot slower. The similarities ended there. This time there was no dark, no breakdown, no torch, no panic, no wild animals, no storm … and no rescuer. It all looked absolutely normal and she knew there was no reason why it shouldn't. It *was* normal. Normal Californian, anyway. It had been her frame of mind that had been abnormal. No wonder he had thought she was strange. She spent several minutes indulging the flood of memories, trying to find a common thread that would lead to some acceptable conclusion, but there didn't seem to be any thread or conclusion to be had, so she dismissed all of it by reminding herself that the purpose of stopping was to relieve the pain in her leg and she proceeded to limp up and down to make it look authentic.

Reason had insisted there would be no marker to show the exact spot where it had happened, and she knew why that was, the only landscape feature for miles was row after row of look-alike orange groves, but it seemed important that she should try to find one, so she limped around some more, hoping to sort of accidentally locate it, then she could mark it. But it was impossible. There was nothing - not even tyre marks; the storm had seen to that. Kicking the earth in utter frustration produced only another acute stab of pain, but at least this pointless exercise forced a different pain out of the shadows. Was it her head or her heart that needed

438

this marker? She pushed that away, too, and returned to the van. "We will have no more tears," she admonished sternly, effortlessly paraphrasing William for her own instruction. She did not understand as yet that this sort of desolation would not be assuaged by mere platitudes or calculating distances and petrol consumption.

She did try lots of things in the next few hours, including whistling, which had been the advice handed out by the old film she had seen in the New York hotel, to tame this perplexing desolation. The film or its advice was out of date, because it didn't work. So much for movies and their advice! Just illusions! Like the people in them, she thought. She was not at all sure whether she was still being deceived by illusions. Rick Masters might have turned her life upside down in three days, and she had the grace to concede that, along with the fact that she had been wrong about many things about him – but that did not mean she was wrong about the important things, or that she had to accept his version of how the world was, any more than she had ever accepted Elinor's. Except, he had made an impact on her that Elinor never had. She smiled at that. Thankfully he didn't know that: it could so damage his modesty. She was the one who *needed* to believe that there had been some sort of connection between them, but for the life or her she couldn't think why, but whatever it was that she had felt back there, it had not been unpleasant, and it was difficult not to want more.

Resolution stayed just beyond her grasp even though it constantly taunted her to pursue it. Late in the afternoon she finally considered the worst-case scenario: was there a faint chance that Elinor could have been right about her needing some different male company? Once posed this question could not be avoided even though it raised all sorts of difficulties concerning her relationship with Len and even whether Shakespeare could cope with competition from a second mentor. Then again, she could hardly acquiesce so easily after so many years resolute stubbornness, so she made a swift decision to try harder with Len when she got back, hoping that would soothe the insanity. It would have to do for a start anyway. This simple resolution triggered all sorts of unwanted repercussions. The memory of that one moment of complete acceptance last night begged to show her things about her relationship with Len that she did not wish to see. It was a cruel world where she could stumble across such truths in the least likely place and through the least likely person imaginable.

Around the time Sarah's dusty camper was rolling into a campsite some miles south of San Francisco, Rick Masters was wandering around his house. He had spent all day wandering around his packing station, checking that the repairs to the storm damage had been properly organised because Perry was away. Perry had been away before, and he had never felt the need to deputise. It did not go unnoticed. It had seemed a legitimate task the first time round. Why it needed doing twice was beyond anyone's understanding, and three visits in three days after five years without any at all only succeeded in generating all manner of speculation. Him staying all afternoon and actually talking to people elevated that speculation to plausible gossip; the favourite theory was that he was preparing to sell.

Since dinner he had tried to settle down to read a recently arrived script, but his mind had different ideas and lacking the necessary concentration, he had abandoned it and sat drinking instead. He was unable to satisfy himself with one or two whiskies and so embarked on a tour of the house as a means of helping himself stay sober, though he had refilled his glass several times before he was completely satisfied that every painting in the place was absolutely straight, and that every room was as tidy as it should be. Inspection complete, he returned to the script, though by now he had drunk too much to have any ability left for studying. He flung it down a second time and picked up the phone. At length a sleepy voice answered.

The call was not one of his brightest ideas. Extricating himself needed more than regrets – it needed invention. When he did manage to get more than one word into the conversation, he generated the necessary excuses: this had to be a quick call because he was busy; he had decided to go away for a couple of weeks and so he would not be able to contact her next week as he had promised. It was amazing how easily the excuses flowed once he had got started, and by the time he finished he half believed them himself.

Paula didn't, and although she heard him offer the sort of solicitudes he usually meant, she pushed for more. He stood his ground in spite of the tearful protests. No, she could not go with him! That was the point of going alone: he needed some space. He needed to think some things through. No, he would not have access to a phone; she could not ring him. Sure, there were plenty of places left on the planet without access to a phone. Finally she managed to wrestle a promise from him that he would call her when he got back, and then he hung up.

He replaced the receiver thoughtfully. Paula had amused him and helped him fill some time, but that was all, and now that she no longer did that, neither the memory of her sexy little pout nor her flashing eyes kindled the smallest spark of interest. He felt only relief that he had been able to get rid of her - mixed with a little disgust that lies had worked. He couldn't even figure out where his solution might have come from until he remembered about Jon and his fishing, and then Laura. Laura had suggested he go there, so why not do it? He had promised Nina he would visit and doing it would sort of exonerate the lies. Well, give them some legitimacy because he did need to do some thinking. He almost felt good about that until an ugly word popped into his head, -manipulator. He dismissed that. He'd had enough problems before this weekend. Damn the woman and her crazy ideas! After a phone call to set up his visit – and three or four more extra-large whiskies to set up his head for sleep – he went to bed still denouncing crazy women. His last words before sleep were kinder, if more ambiguous. "Stay away from trouble."

Sarah switched out the light in her skybunk and lay there for a while, not really thinking about anything in particular but allowing her mind free access to all sorts of traffic as she drifted towards sleep. Life would go on. She would go on. She would go on teaching and Rick Masters would go on being a movie star, and that was exactly how it should be. Their paths had crossed for a brief moment, that's all. She had learned a lot during the last couple of days and she hoped that he could feel the same, -but they were always going to be passing ships. Her mother had an old black-and-white film with a similar sort of plot, but it was too much of an effort to recall how it ended, so she promised herself sleepily, "I must try to stay out of trouble though," as consciousness prepared to stand down for the day.

A mischievous spectre filed a beguiling question for her consideration. What if this pain is the beginning of admiration? It was an audacious question even after some of the earlier revelations, and it had only been allowed now because her guard was down, but she could not ignore it. After all the empty years, if this should turn out to be that now, it was definitely not fair. William had no suggestions to offer so Jonathan Spicer had the last word: no happy endings! "Grow up," she chastised her pillow, thumping it fiercely. "Stop moping and just get on with it!" The adage had served her well this far, and there was no reason to doubt it would continue to serve her equally well from here on in now she had sorted her restlessness. She tried counting her blessings as an act of diversion ending with the most recent ones, realising only as she said them, "So, maybe I am normal after all!" The last ten months of soul searching and striving, reaching for she knew not what, parachuted into one moment of blinding recognition. It had taken her ten years to get here, and she knew she might never have discovered any of it without Rick Masters' help. It had been a difficult weekend, but it had had its compensations. Helping Jodie was one, finding a fledgling faith was another... but this, "I am normal after all," this was something else. "Why did I stop believing that?" Only the wilderness of silent wasted years could answer that, or understand. "I need the same as other human beings." Acceptance cleared the tumult inside her head and left space for peace. This was that new knowledge she had been seeking. "Just like falling down a rabbit hole and then waking up," she mumbled contentedly. Sublimation achieved, she turned over and went to sleep.

Lightning Source UK Ltd.
Milton Keynes UK
UKOW04f1325080715

254786UK00002B/150/P